AFGHANISTAN

ALEX ULLMANN

AFGHANISTAN

A Novel

TICKNOR & FIELDS

NEW YORK

1991

For information about permission to reproduce
selections from this book, write to Permissions,
Ticknor & Fields, Houghton Mifflin Company,
2 Park Street, Boston, Massachusetts 02108.

Library of Congress Cataloging-in-Publication Data

Ullmann, Alex.
Afghanistan / Alex Ullmann.
p.   cm.
ISBN 0-89919-968-2
I. Title.
PS3571.L58A68   1991   91-2382
813'.54 — dc20   CIP

Printed in the United States of America

DOH 10 9 8 7 6 5 4 3 2 1

To Andrea di Robilant

AFGHANISTAN

I

ON THE DAY I left for the war I woke at six, long before the alarm clock was set to ring, and couldn't go back to sleep. My bags were already packed; my apartment (my room, actually — what New Yorkers agree to call a studio, wrapping drab penury in a bohemian cloak) was ready for the subletter, with the more personal of my odds and ends distributed among the highest shelves and deepest recesses of the closet; my traveling clothes, chosen for comfort and abundance of pockets, were laid on a chair, from the back of which hung my old leather jacket. I had debated taking that last article with me, because the cuffs were beginning to fray and the lining was torn. Recently I had come to feel a stab of guilt every time I thought of the thing — it had been expensive to buy and I had had to promise myself I would take good care of it and make it last. Now, staring at it from my bed, scratching my left calf with my right toes, I saw that jacket differently, noting with pleasure that it looked as though it had swaggered about many distant and dangerous corners of the world — a completely fraudulent effect, caused by the humdrum agencies of New York winters and my own carelessness with objects.

The streets were quiet. The sun poured a swath of rich light in from Queens, soaking the pavement and the brick town houses in an orange wash. Blinding rays bounced off the windows and the chrome of the cars. Lurking in the air was a sharp hint of autumn that still awoke in me, at the age of twenty-seven, a ghostly thrill connected with the start of the school year; nowadays less a thrill, actually, than a kind of itch, unscratchable, on a limb amputated years ago. It was a perfect day to embark on something foolish.

I ate breakfast in the coffee shop on the corner of Second Avenue, taking my usual spot by the mirrored wall at the end of the counter, where there was room enough to lay the newspaper flat. It was rare that I arrived so soon after opening time and for a few minutes I was the only customer. The boss, Yannis, normally a nightmare of early morning cheer — he liked to bellow Greek-accented refrains of Beatles songs as he decapitated muffins and juggled cups of coffee and punched the keys of the cash register, inserting into these actions all sorts of exuberant ritual gestures — was asleep in one of the booths, his head on his arms and his bald spot attracting flies. The cook stood behind the counter, a pair of fried eggs goggling him from his plate while he smoked a last prebreakfast cigarette. Out of sight in the kitchen, the simpleton dishwasher was hammering, judging by the sound, on a thick slab of meat. All this was familiar and comforting to me, and the *Times,* too, contained all the articles I had read daily for half a dozen years. I was able to skim through the entire front section without finding a single reference to the fighting in Afghanistan. The last piece I had seen, about a week earlier, was datelined IN A REBEL CAMP. It had made me shiver.

Officially, I was to be away for a month. I was traveling first to Switzerland, to write an article about the ski resort of Giffern ("Winter Wonderland," "Playground of the Stars"; I'd think of something), where I had spent much of my childhood. Then I was going to Provence to do another one on a small market town near Arles. I would spend a week in each place, and then take my yearly two weeks' vacation.

I also had an errand to run for a friend. In Geneva I was to deliver a batch of photographs to a young woman named Hélène, who had recently spent some time in Afghanistan and would soon be going back. She was a doctor with Médecins sans Frontières. My friend hoped that Hélène and I would like each other. I hoped that she would help me get where I wanted to go. Not that I wouldn't like her. I had been shown pictures of Hélène, and on seeing them had asked whether she was single.

I had trouble concentrating on the paper. Apart from the foreign news on the front page I usually paid little attention to the political reporting. Despite surges of good intentions I had never learned to keep the various government agencies straight, even at the federal level, and as I descended toward local squabbles and scandals, wherein city comptrollers accused borough presidents of graft and wearing toupees, I grew increasingly confused. That morning it all seemed more remote than ever. I extracted the Home section from inside the Business section, skipped a great number of articles about unclogging sinks and locating Biedermeier furniture, glanced at the book review, and arrived at the crossword puzzle.

"Chief, may I borrow a pencil?" I asked the cook, after checking my pockets. I had not equipped myself for a normal day. "A pencil," I repeated when he stared at me. I wrote a squiggle in the air above my plate.

"Pancakes?" he said.

"Pencil." I pointed to the crossword puzzle.

Grudgingly he removed a ballpoint pen from behind his further ear and placed it on the counter. It was a nasty object, its thorax and abdomen held together by a lumpy bandage of Scotch tape that was black with ink and grime. My fingers curled in at the idea of handling it, but I couldn't leave it there without offending the cook. Besides, I was going to have to learn to be less fastidious. I wiped it surreptitiously on a paper napkin.

The *Times* crossword puzzle is easy on Monday and more difficult on each successive day. Today was a Thursday, when I was usually unable to complete it until I got to my office, where I could steal the dictionary and thesaurus from the copy editor's desk. Failing to solve the first few riddles, I wandered randomly Across and Down, searching for something easy that would let me into the grid. Then, at 47 Down, I came on an innocent coincidence — "Evening, in Arles," four letters — which caused inside me a convulsion of longing, an upheaval similar to nostalgia but directed toward the future. Soon I would be in that very place, at that very time of day — at a small table under a fig tree, say, in a cobblestone square, with a swarm of swallows above me and a cool glass within reach; somewhere in an alley a woman would call from a window, summoning her children home for dinner; walking toward me on the cobblestones, a bundled sweater hanging from her hand, came a slim blonde beauty who could only be Hélène. She smiled as she floated nearer and then, still smiling, turned her body in profile to slip between the first tables . . . I could tell by that smile that we already knew each other quite well.

"My pen, chief," the cook said. "I need my pen."

He looked horrified. I made an internal check and discovered that I was smiling through him across the sea.

Outside, a gang of Con Edison workers fired up a roaring compressor and attacked the sidewalk with jackhammers. My spoon began to rattle in the saucer.

I had butterflies in my stomach as the taxi hurtled up the East River Drive, airport-bound. Once again I made sure I had all my equipment: suitcase, carry-on bag, plane ticket, traveler's checks, credit card, passport, French visa in passport (the French had recently decided to require visas and abandoned the requirement shortly afterward). I patted all my pockets for security. I patted the envelope I was to deliver to Hélène in Geneva. I reminded myself that the ride to Kennedy, through aching nowheres of graveyards and graffiti, was usually the worst part of any trip. I told myself that the habits I was about to abandon were not comforts but chains. I tried to focus on the fact that right now I was headed not for the Pakistan–Afghanistan border, but for cozy old Europe. I had made no commitment to anyone but myself; I could always back out; no one would ever know. Meanwhile, I swayed every time we swerved to avoid a pothole, and bounced every time we failed, and also rocked back and forth as the driver, an unsubtle man, alternated kicks to the accelerator and the brake. He appeared to have connected the latter with the horn in such a way that one activated the other. Through a gap in the partition (its surface almost opaque with scratches, its upholstered base patched, like the seat, with silver duct tape), I could hear him bellowing curses that may have been meant to break the ice between us, for they were in English, clearly not his first language. I peered at the medallion on the dashboard, trying to determine his nationality, but its metal frame was folded over in such a way as to obscure his last name. His first name was Abdul. No longer a New Yorker intent on protecting myself from my own city, already a reporter and traveler in search of contact with simple people, I thrust my face into the gap, commiserated with him on the state of the traffic, and asked where he came from.

"Very far away," he said, and then he readjusted his position at the wheel and honked three times.

All right, I thought, after waiting for clarification. Sorry I asked, asshole.

"Very far away, my friend," the driver repeated, much louder.

"Really?" I asked. "Where?"

There followed another silence. Serves me right, I thought, mentally rolling my eyes.

"Oh, yes!" he shouted. "Very far away!"

I turned back and contemplated the bristling forest of Manhattan in the distance, determined now to ignore him. We had just left the Triborough Bridge, and the traffic was looser.

"You know Afghanistan?" the driver shouted.

First Arles, then this. It was an omen.

"I've never been," I said, leaning forward eagerly. "It's a brave country."

"Very bad place!" the driver said. "Russians!"

"Yes, the Russians," I said. "But maybe not for long." I thought of adding "*Insh' Allah*," but restrained myself.

"Russians! Russian army!" he shouted, explaining. "Afghans have no food, no weapons, nothing!"

"There's going to be more help from the West, you'll see," I said smugly. "The West has to be told."

"No food, no weapons, no money, no nothing," the driver continued. "No food, no weapons, no money . . ."

"When did you leave Afghanistan?" I asked.

He didn't answer.

"Before the invasion?" I asked.

"Very bad place," he said. "My country, very poor country, and now the Russians."

"Not La Guardia!" I shouted. "Not La Guardia, Kennedy! Kennedy Airport! JFK! Turn around!"

"No turn here, my friend. Plenty of time. What time is your plane?"

"In an hour," I said through my teeth.

"No problem. Where you going? Continental? What terminal? United?"

"Not this airport, dammit! Kennedy Airport!"

"You're excited, my friend," he said. "You said La Guardia."

"I said Kennedy."

"You didn't say Kennedy!"

"All right," I said. "My mistake. Just get me there."

"I say, I get you there, my friend."

"*Insh' Allah,*" I added under my breath. What a relief it was to be leaving New York . . .

As we meandered back to Grand Central Parkway the traffic coagulated again. I arrived at Kennedy a half hour after check-in time and tumbled into the terminal, my bags bumping against my shins, without waiting for my change from Abdul. Luckily it turned out that my flight, a charter, was to be delayed by two hours, and then four, and then seven; in the end, we were stranded in the terminal for nine hours.

Among the first things I did was to buy a James Bond at the newsstand. While conducting this transaction I found myself staring at a stack of October issues of *Glee,* the magazine I worked for. I was surprised to see it already released — boxes of that issue had arrived at the office only a few days earlier, and I had not had time to examine it carefully. The cover consisted mostly of the tropical-lagoon eyes of a model who went by the name of Blue, a six-foot bionic creature with skin that looked like animal gold. The travel

article I had commissioned and edited for that month — on
Seattle and the Olympic Peninsula — was advertised on the
cover, under Blue's right eye (actually her left; our art director always reversed the negative of the cover shot so that
even a face as familiar as Blue's looked somehow different on
our magazine.) After a moment's vacillation I decided, guiltily, not to buy one.

I ate a hamburger. I bought some potato chips and ate them
too. I had a terrible craving for cigarettes. I walked a few
miles around the terminal and stood by the huge tinted windows, watching the planes land and take off. I saw two baggage handlers wearing headphones lie down on the tarmac,
cross their hands behind their heads, cross their feet — pointing into the wind — and go to sleep. I observed my traveling
companions, some of whom were also asleep. They had
seemed at first a picturesque lot — an assortment of students
and retirees flying on the cheap — but they grew tiresome as
the day wore on. After a few hours some students began a
noisy game of touch football at one end of the terminal, using
a roll of toilet paper for the football, but security agents put
a stop to it. Having amassed some change by buying more
potato chips and other cigarette substitutes (I had quit almost
three years earlier and couldn't understand this sudden yearn-
ing), I called my office and several friends. In the last ten days
I had called practically everyone I knew in New York to say
I was leaving. Of course I had not said a word about Afghanistan. I was going on a month-long working vacation to
Switzerland and the south of France. No one knew what I
was preparing. As I spoke to my friends I was unable to re-
press the note of finality that kept creeping into my voice.
They must have thought it strange, even comical, given the
brevity of my trip and the banality of the destinations. But
then they knew me as a quiet man of regular and orderly
habits, and could have thought that even a brief European
jaunt might seem to me a great journey.

There was one person I hadn't called and wasn't going to call: my recent wife-to-be, Irina Albers. In fact, it pleased me that I was about to remove myself from the temptation to call her, which continued, four months after we had parted, to gnaw at me like another old addiction. It was satisfying to imagine how she would continue to think that I was still at my office every day, at my apartment every night, and how she would learn, by chance, that I was gone — or she might not hear about it at all, and then, months later, a year later, happen on one of my dispatches from the front.

"Hello, it's me," I said.

"Yes," she said.

"I'm calling from the airport," I said.

"Yes," she said.

"I'm going away."

"So I hear."

"Who from?"

"Everyone, everyone. Excuse me half a second," Irina said, and I heard her mother's French voice warbling in the background. No one in the Albers family respected telephone privacy.

"It's Patrick," Irina told her mother.

Her mother began to say something but was muffled out. It was Irina's habit, when she didn't want to be overhead, to cover the mouthpiece by pressing it in the soft hollow beneath her collarbone. On such occasions, in happier times, I had thought I could hear the beat of her heart; but it may have been my imagination, and besides, in her case, it was a purely functional organ.

"Okay, okay," Irina said, her voice returning to its normal clarity. "Mama says to give you Michael's number in Paris."

I didn't want her wretched brother's number.

"I'm not going to Paris," I said.

The public address system pinged somewhere near the ceiling of the terminal, and a woman's voice wafted out over

my head. At long last my flight was being called. A few
halfhearted cheers rose from among the students, but even
they were too tired for real enthusiasm.

"What?" I asked Irina.

"I'll give it to you just in case," she said.

"Thanks, really," I said. "Listen, they're calling my flight.
I'm off —"

"Do me a favor," Irina said slowly. "Take the number,
okay?"

The arctic tone, I knew, was meant not for me but for her
mother, who would still be hovering behind her. Once Mrs.
Albers formed a notion, you had no choice but to go along
with it; she had the ability to repeat a request or an opinion
patiently, in the same words, without raising her voice, forever.

"Really, I assure you," I said out of cruelty, "I won't be
going anywhere near Paris. I'll be busy as hell —"

"Forget it," Irina said. "Drop it. Have a great trip. Have a
really great trip," she said, and she hung up.

II

WE LANDED at Geneva in a downpour. After enduring hours of flight with only minimal discomfort I began to suffocate from claustrophobia when, once the plane slowed to taxiing speed, a kind of slow trot, we were told not to leave our seats. For a moment I grew nervous about Hélène's envelope in my breast pocket — among the snapshots inside were some of Mujahedin happily brandishing hideous weapons, and I wondered how a snooping customs official might interpret my possessing them. Spy? Arms dealer? Perhaps another, less obvious pocket . . . but I didn't want to draw attention by transferring things all over my person — although we were all doing exactly that, hunched over in our seats, juggling passports and boarding passes and tickets and immigration and customs forms. In any case there was nowhere to go but forward, inching ahead between the seats, getting bumped from behind, ducking the bags that rained from the racks overhead, and then shuffling by the smiling crew at the cabin door, at last, onto the ramp that connected the plane with the terminal. (Despite its rubber bellows this tunnel was not airtight and allowed some of the stormy morning to seep in, a refreshing twenty-second interval between two climate-controlled deserts.) Besides, I could tell that among the scruffy students who had been my flying companions I was already too old, too ordinary, too staid-looking, to be suspected of carrying drugs, which would have been the only reason to search me; and indeed I trudged uneventfully through customs and passport control, my heart beating at its normal rate against Hélène's envelope. It was nice to hear Swiss accents again. A Swiss voice rises and falls several times on even the briefest statement, as though it were clambering over Alps.

I headed for the change booths, where I converted some dollars, and then tried to call Hélène by telephone. I swallowed several times as I waited for her to pick up. I would have to explain who I was, and then attempt to transform what was supposed to be a mere delivery into a lunch date. I pictured us in a small restaurant in one of the steep cobblestone alleys of the old town, with rain flowing in the gutter. Hell, if lunch went well I could even suggest she come up to Giffern for the weekend . . .

But no one answered, from which I deduced that I was probably calling her home number. I couldn't think of the name of the clinic at which she worked; I couldn't even remember whether I had been given the name. I would have to wait for evening and call her from my hotel.

After spending a few minutes in the taxi line under the overhanging roof of the terminal, among humid passengers burdened with baggage and children, I witnessed, with a small thrill of recognition, the arrival of the bus headed for the train station. I staggered across the lanes to the shelter and rode into town in a stately elevated bus seat beside a gray-tinted window covered in quivering droplets and streaks of rain. This little city had once been an exciting faraway place, only rarely accessible from my boarding school in the mountains. One came down here, usually on forged weekend passes, in order to get into trouble. I recalled how puzzled I had been, as a child, because the airport was named Cointrain, which suggested a train station, while the train station was called Cornavin, a word that seemed to have no relation to the place but invariably brought to mind the image of Gauls drinking wine out of oxen's horns at a feast.

To be a boy in Switzerland is to spend a great deal of time on trains. At least that is how it was with me, and now I looked forward to finding once again the Gauloises-impregnated waiting rooms and railroad cars, and the smell of steel that lingered on one's fingers after even the shortest journey. The Geneva station, however, had been renovated. Moreover some disinfectant or "freshener" had been introduced into the atmosphere, adulterating the evocative stench of railway dirt and old cigar that had once haunted the structure. And I myself had undergone a few changes and was now forced to install myself in a *non fumeur* car — a new car, too, its flanks sprayed a bright orange instead of the former forest green. The back-to-back seats, which in profile had looked like stylized ten-gallon hats, had been redesigned for greater comfort or efficiency and no longer looked like anything but seats. My ticket was not the small rectangle of compact cardboard, the color of milk chocolate, whose possession had automatically meant freedom and adventure, but a flimsy computer-generated chit. My fellow passengers were not ghosts hired from my past to haunt me but solid citizens traveling on errands that had nothing to do with me. They read newspapers or magazines, or dozed, or knitted; one young woman

next to me nodded a chinless head encumbered by large eyeglasses on a red cord, a hairband, long earrings, and a Walk-
man headset that leaked a tinny beat. It continued to rain
intermittently as we raced, with hardly a jolt from the new
silent rails (the wooden ties had all been replaced with concrete), along the northern shore of Lake Léman, through a
landscape of vineyards and small orchards, silos, and deserted
soccer fields at the outskirts of identical small towns —
roughcast walls, black iron grillwork, television aerials,
clotheslines, geraniums. The train had grown so swift in my
absence that I could barely read the names of those towns as
we rushed through the stations, and wouldn't have caught
them at all if I hadn't once known them as a litany, each of
them having had, in the past, secret associations that I now
realized were quite lost to me, unhearable through the static
of years of adult life: Versoix, Coppet, Nyon, Rolle, Au-
bonne-Allaman, Saint Prex, Prangins — that was it; that was
where Hélène worked — Morges, Renens . . . Whenever the
tracks drew close to the lake, I could see the pebbles of the
shore gleaming in the rain and a fifty-yard stretch of pock-
marked water of the same slate color as the stones, beyond
which the lake and the fog and the reflections in the window
all shaded together. Here and there a gull stood guard atop a
half-submerged rock, adjusting the webbed grip of its feet
and drawing its head in to withstand the momentary storm
created by our passage. On a clearer day the white Alps of
France would have loomed across the water, massive and yet
insubstantial, a mirage suspended in the sky.

At Montreux I had the familiar forty-minute wait between
trains, a respite before the assault on the mountains. In childhood I had been accustomed to spending it in the station's
café, if I was alone, smoking cigarettes, reading, and drinking an elongated bottle of Coca-Cola, which I would order
with ice and lemon. The cigarettes would contribute to the

motion sickness that inevitably overwhelmed me as soon as the little mountain train, having climbed through the vineyards in easy loops, and skirted a plateau on the lip of which hung the fortified town of Voringes, found its route carved nimbly through rock and forest. From there on it rattled and whistled along the wooded flanks of steep ravines, dived into tunnels that twisted unpredictably in the dark, re-emerged on a trestle high above a torrent, and then snuck back into the mountain on the opposite side, coming out for good in a steep pasture where cows grazed at difficult angles, separated from the tracks by two strands of electrified wire, indifferent to us and to the pipe-smoking peasant (we get a panoramic view of him as we curve through his meadow: first the creased nape of his neck and the rumpled billow of shirt sticking out beneath his waistcoat, then the stubbly profile above the collarless shirt, the curved pipe clenched in his teeth, and a weathered face with tiny eyes receding in the window, as indifferent as the cows), the peasant, as I was saying, who climbed among them at an even pace, headed for the pines above, using a pitchfork as a staff. I had traveled this famously beautiful route dozens of times, perhaps over a hundred, in an agony of nausea. A grownup now, a nonsmoker, no longer vulnerable to motion sickness, I ordered a beer.

The station café offered far more mnemonic rewards than the preceding train ride, for this place at least remained completely unchanged: I found the same large tables of polished wood, the same tall counter with beer pulls and coffee machines and racks of glasses, the same floor of small octagonal white tiles, and also the same smell, once present in all Swiss cafés (though even during my childhood it had begun to grow rarer, as Formica metastasized throughout the country), of wood saturated with decades of beer, coffee, French tobacco, and a secret ingredient, a kind of meaty element mingled, I think, with soapsuds, the real nature of which I will probably never know. Someday, in my reading, I may come across a more accurate description than the one I have just offered, for other writers have passed through this region and will pass again. Vladimir Nabokov spent the last decades of his life a short walk from here, in the Palace Hotel, whose lakeside esplanade is an amusing toy Riviera with a dozen palm trees; and Ernest Hemingway opened a short story, "Homage to Switzerland," in the very room where I now sat. The scenic poster of the railway bridge spanning a narrow gorge near Giffern (an image you see all over the world — my schoolmate Eric Steyer had found it peeling off the wall of a coffee bar in Kathmandu) still hung over the banquette, facing, at the opposite end of the room, an advertisement for a soft drink named Amiral, which had also been there forever but which I now stared at with astonishment. That black-haired girl beaming at me from the wall, holding out a glass for me, a half-noticed, quite forgotten presence throughout my childhood, was a dead ringer for Irina.

III

I KNOW exactly when it was that things began to go wrong with Irina and me. It was the day I decided to marry her.

On the previous Saturday we had gone to the wedding of a colleague of ours, at a château in New Jersey, and once again I had felt that Irina was waiting for me to say something. Every time I suspected her of wanting to marry me, I was overcome by queasiness because I had, so far, done nothing with my life. I did not know why this was so, I did not know how to change it, and I did not like to discuss it with Irina. I was afraid I might drive her away. You might imagine that if Irina wanted to get married she could have said so; but she had a way of not asking for things and then reproaching you for not giving them. She hid and demanded that you find her.

That day she and I planned to make dinner together at my

apartment. We did not often eat in. My kitchen was the size of a closet, indeed it had once been a closet, and the state of the building and the remoteness of the lease (I was an illegal subtenant) were all too obvious. The cabinet doors sagged on their hinges, the wells of the electric range were rusted, and the edge of the scorched and scored counter turned into Niagara every time I washed a plate. Worst of all was the tenacity of the cockroaches, which made their rounds with cartoonish stealth, pausing every second to wag their antennae, giving me ample time to fetch a weapon, and then fled like sentient quicksilver, with prodigious feats of speed and agility, while Irina or I, a slow-witted giant, battered the counter with a rolled-up issue of *Glee,* always late, always off the mark, and the dishes and cutlery jumped in the drying rack, and I cursed New York and my poverty. And yet to cook here with Irina was a cozy affair, involving her flying wet hands, her frowns of concentration, collisions of blue-jeaned buttock and hip, steamed kisses, Irina reading aloud from the cookbook while unconsciously making chopping or stirring motions with her free hand, consultations about salad dressing and pasta sauce, confusion as to whose glass of wine this was — all those things. At intervals during the afternoon I looked up from my drudgery at the computer and reminded myself of the reward awaiting me. When Eric Steyer, who was back in town, materialized on the phone and tried to invite himself, I put him off. Instead I arranged to have a drink with him after work, at Kiely's, the only quiet bar in my neighborhood. Then I dialed Irina's extension to let her know.

"Why don't you eat with him? I think I'm going to stay home," Irina said.

"It's just a quick drink. I didn't say you'd come. Look, he's only in New York for one night," I explained.

"It's not that. My mother needs an evening off, and someone has to stay with my grandfather. It's better like this, really."

"Oh, no," I said.

"What's wrong?" she asked.

"Oh, hell," I said.

"Really," she said. "I don't see what the problem is."

We had become skilled at talking to each other on the telephone from our respective desks. We used code phrases, and we never said our names or any endearments. But in an argument like this one we had to retreat to the precarious privacy of the fire stairs, where we carried on in whispers and pantomime.

"I simply cancel dinner," Irina said, releasing the banister with disgust and wiping her hand on the seat of her jeans, "because my grandfather is dying and my mother is going out of her mind, and you behave as though I'd done I don't know what."

"I didn't invite Eric to join us," I countered. "I didn't say that you'd come to Kiely's, even though it would make me happy if you did. I've made no change in our plans except to postpone them by half an hour. I'd like half an hour to have a drink with a very old friend. You get so pissed off that you throw everything out the window — dinner, the whole evening . . ."

"Look, I don't even want to talk about it," Irina said.

"Okay," I said. "Let's not talk. Let's just be mad at each other for no reason."

She looked at me through a mask of indifference. It wasn't that Irina disliked Steyer that much. She disliked me when I was around him.

"Whenever the time came for prayers," Steyer said, his mug of beer pausing in mid-ascent, "and that was just about every other hour, I'd throw myself on my face with the lot of them.

I must say, they sometimes had the oddest notion of where Mecca was. Never had the guts to correct them, though."

The mug made it all the way to his lips, stopped, and descended. We were sitting at the bar in the smoky gloom of Kiely's. Because I had told him on the telephone that I could not have dinner, Steyer had called a girl he knew vaguely, a friend of a friend, and I did not want to splice myself into their date. A long evening yawned ahead of me.

"Of course I had no idea what they were saying, I'd just mumble along. The first time, I did it out of politeness. You know, you don't want to say, Look here, you chaps, don't mind me, but I'm not terribly sure about Allah. I just did as the Romans do. Mistake numero uno. Because after that I couldn't very well say, Oh look, dammit, I was only joking. I was convinced that once they spotted me for an infidel, they'd slit my throat or shove an RPG down it. I was much more frightened of them than of the Russians."

Steyer had left his job at a London bank two years before so that he could travel, in a variety of disguises, from Istanbul to Ayatollish Iran, Afghanistan, which was at war with itself, Pakistan, India, Nepal, where he had nearly died of dysentery on a previous visit, and Tibet, which at the time was sealed off by the Chinese. In the last six months he had come to America three times to raise money for a shipment of medical supplies to a Mujahedin group — the Muj, he called them. He usually dressed in odd rags and sandals, wherever he went, and like many compulsive travelers he was forever growing beards and removing them. On this particular visit to New York he had cleaned up his act and resembled his former banking self.

Steyer liked to talk about his travels; to do so freely he had created, in the English manner, a comic stand-in for himself. All his stories portrayed him as a bumbler, often drunk, craven but also lacking any instinct for self-preservation, and therefore constantly entangled in nightmare situations among nightmare people. Irina and I each thought the other was fooled by this routine. Irina believed that the twit act concealed a genuine twit, whereas I had known Steyer since childhood and knew this not to be true. On the other hand, Irina could do a funny and cruel imitation of him; she got his accent just right, and his way of leaning forward as he spoke while his eyebrows followed a program of their own. Imitation was a family skill. Her grandfather was a famous mimic, despite his own Russian accent, and her brother too was good at it.

"And then, after three weeks of this, when I was leaving that particular group . . . well, they made rather a big deal of it, lots of nonsense about international friendship and lots of embracing, you know. By that time I smelled exactly like them, so I didn't mind. I'd gotten to be good friends with one of them, and because we'd smoked some more truth serum again, I went and told him about the prayers. That I'd been shamming. Of course he'd figured it out for himself. Most of them had. They'd decided to go along with it. When I owned up, they thought it was the funniest thing they'd ever heard. They made me do the whole act, over and over again. I'd say '*Hmalahlilallahmniahalilhmnianaha . . .*' "

I too began to laugh, not just because it was a funny story, but because Steyer (leaning forward, eyebrows jumping) was unwittingly giving such a vivid rendition of Irina.

"They were *howling*," this false Irina said, eyebrows rising.

I couldn't stand our being mad at each other. I couldn't stand not seeing her that night.

"Anyway I'm off to Washington tomorrow," Steyer said, himself again. "They actually paid for my ticket. I'm sure they're CIA people."

Under the torn awning outside Kiely's I wished him a good trip. "Call me when you get back," I said. I shook his vast hand, extracting mine in a hurry to flag down a passing taxi.

Then I rode uptown through Central Park, among evening joggers and cyclists, on an artificially winding road overhung with green vaults of branches. I planned to surprise Irina, make up with her, and get her to come back to my apartment for the night.

It was about eight-thirty. Up at Central Park West, Irina and her mother would be in the kitchen, opening and shutting the refrigerator, picking at platters and containers of leftovers set on the table, walking circles around each other on the speckled red linoleum; the radio, tuned to a classical music station, would be spewing advertising for restaurants. In the back of the apartment the night nurse would be spooning dinner into Kuratkin, her left hand holding a paper napkin under his chin, her eyes traveling back and forth from his mouth to the television across the room while Kuratkin's face turned blue, then red, then blue again as more ads flickered on the screen.

A few days earlier a heat wave had descended on the city, and that night the air was heavy and humid, without the promise of a storm. Beyond the snaggled skyline of the West Side, a red glow lingered in a few clouds above New Jersey. As we drove through the park I rolled the window down and placed my head in the wind. I felt supremely contented.

The young doorman on the evening shift, a recent arrival from Poland, consisted mostly of a scrawny neck with an Adam's apple like a yo-yo. He sometimes blushed violently when spoken to. That night he answered my greeting with a strangling noise and omitted to call up to the apartment to announce my arrival. This was strange, but it suited my purposes, increasing as it would the element of surprise.

It was Michael Albers, Irina's brother, who answered the doorbell upstairs. I was startled to find him there, with a cigarette smoldering between thumb and forefinger; and he looked at me with some puzzlement before stepping aside to let me in.

He shut the door softly.

"Irina called you?" he said.

"No," I said, and then I knew, before another word was spoken, why Michael was at the apartment.

"My grandfather died an hour ago," he said.

"Oh, my," I said.

He blew smoke at the ceiling and looked at me. It was part of Michael's charm that he appeared to take a deep interest in one's reactions. I looked back at him, not knowing what to do. I thought I heard Irina coming down the long hall, but it turned out to be her mother. She was wearing sunglasses.

"Oh," she said.

"Mrs. Albers, I'm so sorry," I said.

"Well, yes," she said. "Go make yourself a cup of tea if you want. The water just boiled. Michael, call down to that idiot doorman and tell him he's to use the intercom when people come."

Usually her heels rang out like small hammers on the polished wood. Tonight, as she retreated down the hall, she made a skimming sound, like her daughter. It did not occur to me that she might be walking lightly because Kuratkin lay dead in his room. I only thought that she had shed twenty years all at once.

"To hell with tea," Michael said. "You're going to want a drink. *He* would have had a drink."

He started toward the pantry. I tried to protest, but just then the bell for the back door rang. It was a loud old-fashioned apparatus and in the stillness of the apartment it sounded like an explosion.

"The undertakers," Michael said, stopping in his tracks. "When you rang the doorbell we thought you were them," he whispered, and then he grinned at me wickedly. We heard Mrs. Albers fly down the hall again.

"Irina's in his room," Michael said. "Do you want me to get her?"

"I really liked your grandfather," I said.

I had been trying to say that, but it turned out to be the wrong moment: Michael thought I was asking to see the old man a last time.

"Come," he said, and he led me on a zigzag course through the pantry, the kitchen, and the back hall. At Kuratkin's door he stepped aside and ushered me through.

There was a smell of excrement and talcum powder that had sat there all year and had recently begun to invade the rest of the apartment. The room was almost dark. One small lamp on the night table illuminated a forest of plastic pill bottles and gleamed in the chrome armature of the hospital bed. In the gloom by the curtained window Irina sat in Kuratkin's rocking chair, still in the blue jeans she had worn to the office, her legs crossed and one red sock pointing forward. She was reweaving her braid on her shoulder, her eyes dry and unfocused. It may have been my glimpse of the head on the pillows, or the presence of this new, grieving Irina — my legs weakened briefly. Irina dropped her braid and stood up, still staring at nothing. When I took her in my arms, she was completely stiff. For the first time in months her hair smelled of cigarette smoke. She drew two or three sharp breaths, which was usually how she began to cry; but then she quieted down, and when she released me she turned me away from her, toward her dead grandfather.

A linen hand towel had been tied around his head to keep his jaws together, so that he somewhat resembled an Easter egg. Otherwise, Kuratkin looked like the corpses I had encountered in movies: his nose seemed sharper and thinner than in life, his skin had acquired a waxy polish, and he appeared much younger than I had ever seen him. The difference was that all those corpses had had color; the real thing proved to be entirely gray and white.

A hum of running water was stilled beyond the bedroom

wall, the bathroom door swung open, and the night nurse walked in on a path of light. She was a young Barbudian woman with a soothing singsong voice and a behind like a shelf. After contemplating Kuratkin for a few seconds, she bent over and massaged his cheeks with her fingertips. She smoothed his eyelids, pressed his lips together, and stroked the wings of his nose. Then she stepped back to examine her work.

"Hello, Satyra," I said, afraid she would continue.

"Hello, Patrick," she sang. "He went very peacefully."

There were footsteps behind me. Satyra looked up with an air of interest.

"I think you'll prefer to leave us," a man said from the door, in the kind of voice one uses in a church or a museum.

"Yes," said Mrs. Albers. "Come, children."

Two men stepped over the threshold, carrying a black doctor's bag and a large object which they lowered to the floor and then attacked. It looked as though they were pitching a tent in the middle of Kuratkin's room. They kept doing knee bends and bobbing up again, unfolding metal supports that clanged and snapped as they locked into place. Both men were pudgy, and huffed and sweated in the heat. The younger one, who had acne, wore a stiff blue suit whose sleeves and legs bunched up when he crouched, uncovering a white stretch of calf cinched cruelly by the top of a sock. His middle-aged colleague had an ill-fitting brown wig tilted forward on his head; he wore neither jacket nor tie, and two ballpoint pens stuck out of his shirt pocket. In the time it took us to group together and leave the room — Mrs. Albers, Satyra, Michael, Irina, and I (we were herding one another through the door, everyone touching the others for reassurance) — the men had assembled a gurney. The one with the wig wheeled it toward the bed while the other shut the door behind us, his eyes fixed cautiously on the floor. Immediately we heard their voices through the door, speaking in a normal tone, but I couldn't make out what they were saying.

Mrs. Albers led us across the hall into Kuratkin's study. In his better days it had been a jumbled room littered with stacks of books and magazines, with one cork wall (like those of the art room at *Glee*) covered in photographs and clippings, but in the last year it had gradually been taken over and tamed by Mrs. Albers. She turned on the light over the desk and pushed the curtains apart to open the window. A moth began to flap hysterically across the desktop. Mrs. Albers shut the window. The moth was much too big to kill. We watched until it got control of itself and settled on the lampshade. Mrs. Albers pulled the chair out from the desk and sat down in it sideways and started to rub her temples.

"I was about to make Patrick a drink," Michael said. "Is there any whiskey in the pantry?"

"For God's sake," Irina said.

"Whiskey?" Michael asked me, heading for the door.

"No, thanks," I said. I didn't know whether I should stay or go.

"Satyra, would you like a drink?" Michael said.

Satyra stared at Michael as though he were mad.

Mrs. Albers removed her sunglasses, closed her eyes, and took a deep breath.

Then the door of Kuratkin's bedroom opened and the men wheeled out the gurney, forcing Michael back into the study. Kuratkin was strapped down inside a body bag, his feet sticking up at the end. There was a corner to turn as they came through the door, a difficult maneuver, and twice they had to back up and try again. The wheels clattered back and forth over the marble threshold. The men's faces looked boiled. They scrupulously avoided our eyes, and I began to wonder whether they were trained not to look at the family. When they had completed the turn into the hallway, Satyra went back into the room to strip the bed.

"No," Mrs. Albers said. "Not the back elevator."

"The front elevator's too small, ma'am," said the older man in his church voice.

"He's not going down the back elevator. With the garbage," Mrs. Albers said, her voice rising alarmingly.

"Mama," Irina said, "they can't go down the front."

"*Ils peuvent le mettre debout,*" Mrs. Albers said.

"Mama," Irina said between her teeth.

Mrs. Albers sank back onto her chair.

"Okay," Michael said, taking charge. He motioned toward the back elevator and followed them out. Irina went with him. I remained alone with Mrs. Albers, who began to massage her calves. Then she kicked her shoes off under the desk. To give myself something to do, I walked over to the window and pushed aside the curtains and looked down over the park. Spherical streetlamps shone among the trees; there was a ring of them I couldn't quite figure out, with strange elastic shadows — the reservoir and its joggers. Judging by the sound, the men were trying to wheel the gurney into the elevator, another bumpy and complicated turn.

Across the hall Satyra finished stripping the bed. A terrible smell wafted into the study. Without asking Mrs. Albers, I opened the window again. Another moth swooped in, brushing past my face, and repeated its fellow's performance on the desktop. Mrs. Albers switched off the light, leaving us in darkness.

Irina returned with a wild look in her eyes that I had never seen before. It vanished as soon as she saw me staring at her.

"Michael had to go down with them to give them a hand," she said. "It's the night shift, there's no one on the back elevator. Did you *see* those guys? Why is it dark in here?"

"I left the sheets in the bathtub," Satyra said, a silhouette in the doorway. "I think I should be going home now, if you don't further require me. Please accept my sympathies," she added after a silence.

"I'll see you out," Mrs. Albers said, and she leaned on the desk and raised herself to her feet.

"Should I stay?" I asked Irina once we were alone.

"Yes, a while," she said. "Why did you come? Did you feel something?"

"No. I thought I'd come and kidnap you back to my place."

"Not tonight," Irina said.

"Well, of course not."

Michael returned with a glass of whiskey and ice.

"The Stimsons were coming in just as we went through the lobby," he said, "with old Stimson in his wheelchair. There was a near collision. Why is it dark in here?"

Kuratkin, Mrs. Albers, Satyra, the corpse squad — all the grownups were absent. "I think I'll have a drink after all," I said.

"I'll just smoke your cigarettes," Irina said.

"Okay," Michael said, and he left the room.

"Did you have your drink with Eric?" Irina asked.

"Yes."

"And he bored you so much you escaped to come up here," she said.

"He doesn't bore me," I said.

"You envy that life of his," she said.

"I don't envy anyone who doesn't have you," I said.

"That's a nice thing to say," she said.

She climbed onto my toes.

"I kept thinking," Michael said, entering with another glass and his cigarettes, "that if Papa" — the children had always called their grandfather Papa — "had been able to see the scene, he would have turned it into one of his sagas, imitating the clanking of the two vehicles as they got wheeled through the lobby, the necrophiliac leer on those people's faces as they sized up old Stimson for their next coffin, the doorman losing his head . . ."

"Where's Mama?" Irina asked.

"In her bedroom."

Their eyes met briefly. I didn't know what they were telling each other.

"She's calling Leningrad. She just needs something to do. We have a sort of distant cousin there," Michael said for my benefit. "I think he's the son of a cousin of our grandfather's. He came here once. Asked if we could open a bank account for him. You didn't want water with this, did you?"

The doorbell rang. It was Mrs. Stimson, down from the tenth floor, with a ham. She went straight back up again. We took our glasses to the kitchen and started on the ham; no one had eaten dinner. It was almost ten o'clock. There seemed to be a rule: we could say funny things, but we weren't allowed to laugh. Mrs. Albers, waiting for the call to Leningrad to come through, came to sit with us. The ham was huge, glazed and checkered, with cloves stuck in the fat like nails. Michael kept carving more of it.

"She must have cooked this for something we weren't invited to," Irina said through a mouthful. "I think there's some more cold rice in the fridge. I'm going to fry it up."

"I should have called the *Times* first," Mrs. Albers said. "If it's in the paper tomorrow or Friday, we can have the service on Sunday or Monday."

"A service?" Irina said, rummaging inside the refrigerator.

"Well. Isaac will read something, he promised to, and Harrison will talk a bit. I have to figure it out."

"It was Papa's hunch," Michael said as he opened and shut each of the cabinets above the gas range, "after living through two world wars, a revolution, and a civil war, that God probably exists and is probably off on a bat."

"You know, I think I heard him say that once too often," Mrs. Albers said.

"He said it to the Pope."

"What Pope? He never met any Pope."

"It was the Russian Orthodox priest, Father Halitosis," Irina said.

"Or Cardinal O'Connor. Mayor Koch." Michael slammed the last cabinet shut. "Roosevelt. Trotsky. Dammit," he said, "I'm all out of cigarettes."

Tears appeared in his eyes.

"He used to keep an emergency pack under his shirts after we made him quit," Irina said. "Even changed them once in a while, so they'd be fresh if disaster struck."

"I threw them out ages ago. Michael, can you wear his clothes?"

"Not immediately," Michael said.

The tears welled over.

"Excuse me, excuse me," Michael said, and he rushed from the room, his sister in pursuit.

When the elevator arrived it was cool from the air-conditioned lobby. Kuratkin was probably in a refrigerator by now, drained of his blood. I experienced a moment of claustrophobia as the door rattled shut and the floor sank beneath my feet. Downstairs, the doorman stiffened and clenched his jaws when I came out. He had started the job only two weeks before and hadn't been ready for a death in the building.

Above me the night sky was a dull orange. The leafy darkness of Central Park looked cool and inviting, but it was too dangerous to enter on foot. Along the avenue some of the doormen had left their lobbies to stand outside under the awnings. One of them, who had already removed the jacket of his uniform, lifted his cap and scratched his head, apparently in wonder, as he contemplated a pretty prep school girl waiting on the curb for her spaniel to finish dealing with a parking meter. I hadn't realized that I too was staring, and when she smiled at me, just as the dog towed her away with a jerk of the leash, I was too startled to respond. Her smile cast a glow over the next few blocks of my walk.

Then my memory mugged me as I crossed Columbus Circle. My own father had died ten years earlier, in a gleaming lakeside clinic near Geneva, just a few hours away from my school. I had awakened from a nap that afternoon, from a gummy afternoon dream of my mother, to find her entering my room with a teacher I detested and feared. Half awake, with my blood pounding in my head and my dream still swirling about me, I had thought, He's dead, *and they've come to tell me they're getting married*.

Up at Central Park West they had spent two years waiting for this, and now they were all going to change their lives. If I didn't ask Irina to marry me soon, she might shed me, along with her job and her bedroom at her mother's. But I couldn't ask her now, just after Kuratkin had died.

IV

KURATKIN was still sharp and spry when Irina first took me
to meet him, nudging me into the darkened library one Sunday afternoon while he watched a baseball game on television, at head-splitting volume. Despite the vast difference
in our ages, he insisted on getting up from the sofa, after
carefully zapping down the sound with the remote control.
He was only slightly stooped, still a tall man; as I walked
over to shake his hand he dropped his speckled head forward
and peered at me over the top of his glasses.

"Yes, how are you, how are you," he said slowly, rolling
his r's. He peered into my eyes. "Are you by any chance a
Mets fan?" he asked.

I know nothing about baseball, and am sometimes shy with
old people, and his question paralyzed me. He started to turn
back toward the mute television and pointed helpfully at the

screen, at which moment I recognized him. Since my arrival in New York I had seen him several times; I would come on him sailing down Madison Avenue or across Central Park with a slightly wobbly but still commanding step, long-limbed and supremely elegant — once with a great loden cape about him, and another time swinging a cane upward at every third step. (I have to mention that the latter object, which was made of thick bamboo, and which Kuratkin wielded as though he were deep in the country somewhere, as though it were normally used to beat paths to felled animals, or to point out that lightning-struck beech at the boundary of his land, seemed purely ornamental in Manhattan, an Old World prop, like a monocle or a pair of spats. A few months later, however, I happened to arrive at the apartment just as Kuratkin was leaving for his afternoon stroll. While he stood by the open front door, rummaging in a pocket, I teased him about not needing that cane, trying to flatter him — and immediately he picked it off his forearm and slid the handle away from the shaft, baring twenty inches of triangular steel blade. Then he snapped it shut and gave me a satisfied grin. "Yeah. I know. I know," Irina said later, bringing her hand to her head.)

As I was saying, Kuratkin, at eighty-two, was sharp of mind and sword, if slightly deaf, and still cut a notable figure in the streets; but then he lost everything, all at once, after a fall in his bathroom one lonely Saturday evening, minutes after Mrs. Albers had phoned to check on him.

She had been away at their country house in Fincham that weekend; Irina and I were at a friend's in East Hampton. Kuratkin slipped or lost his balance while trying to climb into or out of the bath. He hit his head, probably on the sink, and broke two ribs on the edge of the tub. It is possible that he suffered a brain hemorrhage. Unable even to crawl, he lay naked on the checkered tile, in terror, pain, and shame, for more than twenty-four hours. When Mrs. Albers found him on Sunday night, he was conscious but incoherent. An ambulance took him uptown to Columbia Presbyterian, where, as a result of the broken ribs, he developed pneumonia. His ordeal also caused a further series of small strokes that robbed him of his balance, the use of his legs, and, worst of all, his sense. "Multi-infarct dementia," Irina said, articulating the syllables carefully. For the first time in her life, Irina went alone to a church — the Orthodox church on the Upper East Side, to which Kuratkin nominally belonged — and prayed for him to die. Up at the hospital, Kuratkin shouted, "I will not die! I will not die! I will not die!"

He didn't, despite the doctors' predictions. There was some talk of a nursing home, but not much; three months after his accident, half paralyzed, quite mad, he was returned to his room at Central Park West, which had been equipped with a rented hospital bed and a nurse. He lasted another two years, gradually subsiding into silence, his eyes clouding over, his flesh withering on his bones. In the last year he never once left that chrome bed.

On infrequent trips down from Boston, Irina's brother, who, unlike the rest of us, saw not the steady deterioration in Kuratkin but only shocking turns for the worse, begged that he be taken back to the hospital and that something be done to save him. Michael refused to accept that Kuratkin could not be restored to an acceptable existence. He wept and shouted, ignoring threats that if he continued to carry on like that he wouldn't be allowed to come at all. Mrs. Albers, Irina, and the doctors were all determined to keep Kuratkin at home and let him die at his own pace, though at one point Mrs. Albers grew fearful of being blackmailed by one of the nurses, a woman who spent much of her shift reading the Bible and once called an ambulance when she was alone in the apartment and thought that Kuratkin was about to die. Mrs. Albers had returned just in time to convince the paramedics not to take him, which she accomplished by calling Kuratkin's doctor in their presence and having him tell them he was on his way over. What happened between Mrs. Albers and the nurse afterward left both women sullen and muttering, and eventually the nurse was sent away — nurses came and went at a great rate in those first months — with thanks and rather a large tip.

Michael had long been barred from Central Park West and was allowed there only to see Kuratkin. He found these visits agonizing and could not face them sober. He was never left alone with Kuratkin, who was also easily upset. After Michael's first and last unsupervised visit, during which he tried to talk to his grandfather about money, which was in any case the subject of many of his delusions, Kuratkin banged at the bars of his bed, knocked all his pills off the nightstand, dirtied himself, and howled obscenities in four languages.

For two years life in the apartment was suspended. Mrs. Albers had been planning to sell the house in Fincham, which had become somewhat neglected since Michael and Irina's schooldays, but she now declared the whole matter shelved "until Papa goes," a phrase that became so crucial to all Albers affairs that even I used it almost comfortably. Irina, who had moved back to her childhood room at Central Park West temporarily, after separating from her previous boyfriend, felt that she had to stay and prop up her mother. Kuratkin's few surviving friends stopped coming when he was no longer able to recognize them, but he remained sensitive to foreign presences in the apartment and became terrified if he heard any unusual sounds outside his door.

Kuratkin's slow loss of consciousness, although distressing, was also a relief to everyone. In the first few months, when he was still alert, he lived in constant fear of the nursing home — expressed often, at the top of his lungs — and of having all his money stolen from him. He could not adjust to the presence of the nurses. Sometimes he mistook them for servants, and demanded that his daughter or Irina do something about their appalling bossiness and familiarity; at other times he had no idea who they were. "Come here," he said to Irina one afternoon when I was with her. "Come closer"; then, gazing up at her with his marbled eyes, he asked, in a stage whisper, "Why is my house filled with Negroes?" The day nurse uttered a long wail of laughter, which caused Kuratkin to shout with fear and thrash about in his sheets. "Papa, please, please," Irina begged, reaching out to touch his forehead while the chuckling nurse bustled over to tuck his legs back in. "You just take it easy, Mr. K.," she said soothingly. "I'm not so ugly, am I? I'm not so ugly now, am I?"

His most persistent hallucination was of chickens in his room. "And your grandfather?" I'd ask Irina. "Chickens. Everywhere," she'd answer.

I hadn't known Kuratkin for long before his accident, but like everyone else I had been charmed by him. All his life he had been a famously entertaining man, a sought-after dinner guest. Unlike most storytellers, he listened well, and until his accident he lacked entirely the mental impermeability that often comes over old people. He even knew, approximately, the names of the current nightclubs: opening the door for me one night when I came to see Irina, he declared, "You have come to take my granddaughter to the Pandemonium," meaning to say Palladium. He had a way of looking you in the eye, with just the beginning of a smile, as though encouraging you to continue, that made you feel interesting — an ability that had bypassed severe Mrs. Albers as well as her fidgety and volatile daughter, but which Michael had either learned or inherited from him. I believed, moreover, that Kuratkin liked me. For one thing, I suspected that he took some prurient pleasure in the idea of his granddaughter's love life. For another, I was a new audience, a rare commodity, and I worked at being a good one.

Finally, it must have pleased him that I was an editor at *Glee,* the magazine he had founded thirty years earlier.

His family was surprised that I continued to call on him every time I came to the apartment, long after all conversation had become impossible. I was mistaken successively for a brother who had stayed in Russia and died in the terror of 1938; for a son, though Kuratkin had never had one; for Michael. And one day he looked at me angrily the moment I walked in, and demanded that I increase his allowance. The truth was that during my own father's death of cancer, a decade earlier, I had often fled him, in body as well as in spirit. Sitting at Kuratkin's bedside — never for more than a minute or two, because Satyra or the other nurses would eject me when the time came to feed him or turn him over to dress his sores or fetch the bedpan (which he demanded very loudly, with a note of rage in his voice, as a kind of insult to any healthy person there) — I felt that I was both acquitting myself of a debt and exercising the mastery of adulthood.

Another benefit of those visits was that they disarmed Mrs. Albers, who had hoped to see Irina cleave to a man richer than I. Besides, the wanderings of Kuratkin's mind were not all frightening or unpleasant. More and more he seemed to embark on loony journeys that took him, in no particular order, through Saint Petersburg and Paris, Berlin and San Francisco, Baden-Baden, Biarritz, and many places in between. He imagined himself flying through the air in jets or crossing oceans on big liners. "How did you find me here?" he would ask, in a quavering voice that mingled French and Russian intonations, as I — or whoever I was — reached for his claw. When he was enjoying his phantasms, his face would wrinkle into a grin and remain that way for several minutes, his sunken eyes hardly blinking. I liked to try to imagine what he saw and who he was at such moments — a small boy with a crew cut and a bicycle, who had just heard his first motorcar and was waiting for it to turn the corner and putter into view, or a uniformed adolescent who thought he had glimpsed, in the crowd on some Petersburg avenue, the red cheeks of his fur-clad love, and the plume of her breath in the winter glimmer.

More factual details of his life appeared on Friday under a two-column headline in the *New York Times:* NICHOLAS KU-RATKIN, 84, FOUNDER OF GLEE. They were accompanied by a photographic portrait made during Kuratkin's and the century's mid-fifties by John Stewart, a photographer whose work and person had come to be identified with the magazine. Kuratkin had owned, at the time, a full head of white hair. The picture showed him resting his cheek on his fist and gazing into the camera, a pair of tortoiseshell glasses pushed up on his forehead. Except for the white hair and a softness under the jaw, it might have been a tired, sour Michael — a hung-over Michael.

Before reading the obituary I glanced at its last lines, searching for Irina's name, but I saw only that Kuratkin was survived by an anonymous daughter and two anonymous grandchildren. (Perhaps Mrs. Albers had been unpleasant to the writer or the reporter on the telephone. I knew for certain that she would not be satisfied with the length of the piece, nor with its position on the page, under an obscure dead public servant.) Kuratkin's late wife, however, proved to be "the former Françoise Rubinstein," whom he had married in Paris in 1927. Kuratkin's mother had been "a society portrait painter" in Saint Petersburg; his father appeared as a more prosaic "successful businessman." The mother's genes had prevailed, at least in the professional sphere, for Kuratkin, having studied painting as an adolescent, had "worked as an illustrator in émigré publishing, and also designed sets for ballet and theater, collaborating on separate occasions with Picasso, Matisse, and Jean Cocteau on the sets for productions by Sergei Diaghilev's Ballets Russes."

Having moved to New York in 1939 (a further westward flight prompted, presumably, by fear for his Jewish wife and daughter), Kuratkin had continued to illustrate books, producing, "most notably, the woodcuts for *Wise Vassilissa,* a collection of Russian fairy tales written by Ivan Fedorov, which was published by St. Edgerton Press in 1941 and has never been out of print. During World War II," the obituary continued, "he served in the Office of Strategic Services under Colonel William Donovan. Parachuted into occupied France in early 1944, he was instrumental in the escape into neutral Switzerland of Resistance leader Alain Jouly-Maranon, later Minister of Finance during de Gaulle's second term as President. For a decade after the war Mr. Kuratkin was a highly innovative art director at several publications within the Condé Nast group, which he left in 1955 to launch *Glee,* the fashion magazine . . . In his later years Mr. Kuratkin resumed his painting career. Reviewing his first one-man show in the United States, a critic for *The Times* described his work . . ."

I hadn't known about Kuratkin's sky diving, and at first I was disturbed by the image of the frail old man hurling himself from an airplane into the night, until I remembered to subtract forty years. No mention was made of his earlier battles: too young to enlist during the First World War, Kuratkin had given his parents the slip after the revolution and fought briefly on the side of the Whites; he was wounded almost immediately, in both legs. Perhaps the omission was due simply to lack of space, a problem I could well understand, since my own job caused me to struggle every day with the problem of shoehorning human lives into short paragraphs. Probably the writer had faced a choice between mentioning the Russian civil war and the Picasso-Cocteau episodes and had decided that there were already enough of Kuratkin's wartime heroics . . .

I too had articles to edit. I folded the newspaper, replaced it in my officemate's IN box, and switched on my computer terminal. Clicking at the keyboard, I called up from an electronic hinterland a piece about a twenty-one-year-old television actress who had been giving me trouble precisely because there wasn't anything to say about her past. "At an age where most little girls are preoccupied with dates and proms," I read on the luminous screen, "Nora Scranson was fantasizing about . . ." There was a glossy picture of the actress clipped to the press releases, and I stared at it for a moment, seeking inspiration. I had seen her on television, and this photograph was remarkably unlike her. By association I remembered that Mrs. Albers had told me once that her grandmother, the "society portrait painter" of the obit, had at some point done a likeness of the wife of Prince Yussupov, one of the men who murdered Rasputin. She was said to be the most beautiful woman in Russia, and her name, come to think of it, may well have been Irina . . . I had heard that phrase in Michael's mouth: "the most beautiful woman in Russia" . . . yes, but he had been speaking about Pushkin's wife. For years Michael had been writing his thesis about Pushkin . . .

Clearly it was going to be one of those days when *Glee* paid me a salary to daydream and drink coffee.

I had an appointment to see the editor in chief that morning to discuss the urgent matter of a profile of a clothes designer that contained a potentially libelous paragraph hinting at cocaine binges in the discothèques of the seventies. The editor in chief, Nancy Eberstadt, was an angular creature with a permanent tan. She looked as though she applied several coats of lacquer to her face and hair every morning before leaving for the office.

"To hell with it, I say," she said, opening her eyes after a second of contemplation. "Why don't you lose that paragraph? He's a sweetheart, that man. If you really want to keep it you'll have to schlep it to the lawyers upstairs."

"Okay," I said. "Did you see Kuratkin's obituary in the paper this morning?"

"Who?"

"Nicholas Kuratkin."

"Oh."

She looked at me expectantly.

"God!" she said. "Not *Glee* Kuratkin!"

"Yes."

"What — today? I thought he'd died years ago!"

"Well, he didn't get around much. He was Irina Albers' grandfather, you know."

I had planned not to say that.

"Yes, I did know," Nancy said thoughtfully. "I sent her a note yesterday, but I thought it was some other grandfather." She laughed and shook her head. "I must have put my brain in storage with the furs," she said.

We both started talking at the same time.

"You first," Nancy said.

"Maybe we should jam something into September," I suggested. "A short tribute by someone who was in on the start, some shots of the first covers . . ."

Nancy thought for a second. She always closed her eyes when she thought. It was suspected that she consulted a spirit.

"Nah," she said. "We want to be young, we want to look ahead, not backward."

I called Irina as soon as I got back to my desk, before my officemate arrived.

"I'm all right," she said.

"And Michael?"

"He's on his best behavior."

"And your mother?"

"My mother's been in training for this for ten years."

"Shall I come by after work?"

"No," she said. "A bunch of creaky Russians are coming over. They're all clucking and scraping their feet over the cremation. They don't like it one bit . . ."

It was I who needed her presence that day, not the other way around. She was all absorbed in this great new thing, her grandfather's death.

In order to put off my work a little longer I went to get another cup of coffee. This led me past Irina's desk, which seemed to be glowing with her absence. Apart from two or three personal objects (including a small glass box I had given her, my first and ill-chosen present, which had remained empty for a long time and now contained two stamps and the beads of a broken necklace), it was cluttered with the same paraphernalia as every other desk — a jar of pens and yellow pencils, a tray with paper clips and rubber bands and small pieces of office flotsam, the telephone, the open engagement book, the bristling Rolodex. But these objects seemed arranged in a cunning pattern that could have been created only by her own hands, an expression of her as personal as her smell. It was the same occult order that reigned, with greater freedom and authority, over her bedroom and bathroom at her mother's, and it warmed me whenever I saw it. Pinned to the bulletin board above her desk, among layouts clipped from *Glee* and other magazines, postcards of palm trees and beaches, and a patchwork of receipts, invitations, schedules, and ticket stubs, there was a black-and-white photograph of a Tuscan landscape, with a stone farmhouse among cypress trees, which Irina claimed was a cryptogrammic portrait of me. Although everyone knew all about us, our seeing each other outside the office was supposed to be a secret.

It was at that desk — almost bare at the time, beneath a
virgin bulletin board — that I first saw her, on the day of my
twenty-fifth birthday. She had sprouted there overnight, replacing a nameless plump girl who had lasted less than a month
and departed in tears, I don't know why, leaving, as Irina
later told me, two sealed condoms among the coffee stirrers
and pennies in the middle drawer. I was struck by Irina's
looks, in part because her black hair and black eyes and the
narrowness of her face all reminded me of another girl who
had ruined my life a few years earlier. She looked unhappy
that first day, her clothes were wrong (down at her end of
the offices, the Fashion end, most of the girls dressed as though
it were a rainy weekend), and no doubt she was dependent
on others to give her work. She smiled, miserably, at everyone who walked past her desk.

In the next weeks she settled in and began to acquire all the
mannerisms of her colleagues in the Fashion department, sitting cross-legged on the blue carpet as she sorted through
Polaroid snapshots of clothes and models, tripping down the
corridors at high speed while talking to herself, and shrieking
as loud as everyone else when things went wrong. Having
discovered long ago that I was more intelligent on my feet
than sitting down, I had developed a habit of wandering about
the offices while I thought, ostensibly fetching supplies or
refilling a polystyrene cup from the stained coffee pots in the
mailroom. Most of the girls had learned to ignore me, but
Irina, at least when she was in a good mood, smiled generously every time our eyes met. It is difficult to isolate these
things, but I think it was her slightly snaggled lower teeth
that began to haunt me, and also the brave bad French, un-
grammatical but surprisingly idiomatic, that she poured into
the telephone while haggling with contacts in Paris. At any
rate, it wasn't long before she began the metamorphosis by
which someone who seems at first an ordinary human (nice,

perhaps, amusing, a pleasure to look at) gradually separates from the rest of the species, revealing a superior vividness, a reality richer and brighter than anyone else's. She came to look as though she carried with her a private source of light — candlelight, firelight, something like that — while the rest of us shared the neon tubes overhead.

After a collision in the doorway to the mailroom one morning, she steadied herself by grabbing my arm.

"Sorry! Sorry!" she said. "You've got to honk on this corner. It's —"

"Are you free for lunch?" I asked.

She let go as if I had burned her.

"My boyfriend's coming to take me out," she said.

We repeated variations of that scene several times. A year later we still hardly knew each other. We exchanged jokey comments when we met around the office. She appeared to be pleased when I complimented her on a new haircut. When we chatted at birthday parties or parties honoring departing staffers, I found that I could make her laugh, and at the big Christmas party, in a club downtown, I even got her to stammer by flattering her, in French, about her French, and then adding — liberated from office protocol not just by the occasion but also by the foreign language, which functioned as a joke mask — that she was, that evening, *très belle*. But she had a way of preventing these exchanges from becoming conversations, and she always managed to thrust some mention of the boyfriend, Bob, between us. I met the man once, in the elevator, and craned my neck, and shook his hand — or rather his fingers, because I eagerly tightened my grip a second too soon. There was a long stretch of pinstriped lapel and a lofty pair of yellow eyes examining me through tortoiseshell glasses.

I had cast about her the usual innocent questions fitted with hooks and lines, and retrieved several coincidences (in descending order of importance: I had known her brother slightly at school, in Switzerland; she and I had a common acquaintance, another old schoolmate of mine whom she knew through that same brother; we each had one American and one foreign parent; we were both in awe of my officemate, Mary Donoghue, the foul-mouthed Food and Wine editor), which I tried, unsuccessfully, to exploit. I used to ask her how her brother was and tell her to say hello, if he remembered me, but it seemed that she didn't see him much. I also learned that those tortoiseshell glasses had been sleeping on her night table since her junior year in college.

I had given up when, late one Friday in June, we were the last two people to leave the office. All afternoon there had been a slow attrition around me, as the telephones grew silent and my colleagues left for Long Island or the New Jersey shore. For the last half hour the sun had projected a slanting beam through my office window, filling the room with swirling motes and an air of abandonment. I was editing a travel piece about a town in Brittany and its environs, written by a moderately well-known gourmet and bon vivant, as he himself would have put it. There were grammatical errors so deeply embedded they couldn't be corrected without altering the meaning of the sentences, and a large number of these had been constructed, for purposes of cuteness and local color, to fit French phrases that, unfortunately, did not mean what the writer thought they meant. Finally, shying before a particularly thorny paragraph, I stood up and switched off my terminal and the office lights and headed down the deserted hall to the elevators, my hand jangling the keys in my pocket, thinking that I would first check the messages on my answering machine at home and then, if they yielded no invitations — and I knew they wouldn't, not on a summer weekend — search the movie listings in the newspaper. I found Irina on her feet, bent over her desk, stuffing a sweater into a hefty *Glee* bag. (The air conditioning in her part of the offices was especially fierce, but it had been shut off an hour earlier.)

"Hang on, hang on," she said. "Let me get my raincoat."

I had the distinct feeling that she had been waiting for me, and this unexpected development, at first, snatched from my mind all the brilliant and hysterically funny things I might have said. We rode the elevator down in silence, except for the sound of her rummaging inside her bag, which she propped up with a bare knee. The revolving door rolled us out into a breezy evening that smelled of the river. She paused to readjust the strap of her bag, making a small grimace of discomfort.

"Let me have that, it looks heavy," I said.

"No," she said. "But you can keep me company for a few blocks. Which way are you going?" she added.

She was already tilting away toward Fifth Avenue. I had assumed she would be headed in the opposite direction, toward Grand Central, where we would each take our subway. The spontaneous change in my plans gave me a cheering sense of leisure. I had no appointments, no chores that couldn't wait, no one to answer to until Monday morning. I could stroll with pretty girls to the end of the world and back.

"My brother's coming down from Boston for the weekend," she said as we skirted a Senegalese jewelry vendor at the corner of the avenue.

"Give him my best," I said. "I'm not really sure he'd remember me, he was several classes ahead of me."

We had already been through all that, but a few months before.

"We're both going to a party tomorrow night, downtown, for a friend's birthday. It's a big, vague thing. I think it'll be fun," she said.

I was so accustomed to her ducking my own invitations

that I didn't catch on. There was, however, a sudden fluttering inside me.

"Would you like to come?" she said.

"Me?" I said.

Eventually we got it sorted out, though not without effort — I think both of us were displeased with ourselves by the end. We returned to the uninteresting topic of her brother. What I felt like saying (apart from asking about the status of the tortoiseshelled fellow, which I wanted to do so badly that I almost had to bite my tongue), as we continued to stroll up Fifth Avenue, was that the light around us reminded me of those schooldays in the mountains. It was a phenomenon I had often noticed. Like the valleys in the evening, the streets were dark with shadows, while above us the towers still glowed in soft sunlight, against a deep daytime blue, their steel and glass standing in for granite and snow. But I couldn't say any of that yet; that sort of thing would have to wait until later. In the meantime Irina seemed to be in no hurry at all. She even stopped to peer into shop windows, and to give a handful of change to a beggar who was leering at her; whereas I had to restrain my feet, even though I had nowhere to go and nothing to do.

V

IN THE DAYS after her grandfather's death Irina claimed to miss me; she was generous with endearments and expressions of love, but she also kept me out of her life. We spoke only by telephone. She wouldn't let me come to the apartment or meet me outside for a meal.

Finally, I asked: "Is there a problem?"

Perhaps I had misbehaved in some way on the night of Kuratkin's death; perhaps I had failed to comfort her . . .

"Is there a problem?" Irina answered. "Is there a problem? Papa died!"

"Yes, but that doesn't mean we can't see each other," I said.

"I know, I know. I'm crazy," Irina said. "I'm crazy. Things are hard enough, but the thing is, I can't stand having my brother around. I look at him and I want to kill him. Then I feel guilty. He keeps trying to be helpful . . . and I want to put my hands around his throat and . . . God! What am I saying!"

"Look, you've got to get out of that apartment," I said. "Come and have dinner with me. Your mother and Michael will survive."

"I can't. I'm sorry, I'm really sorry, I just can't."

The next day, the steamy day before the "gathering," which is what the family, with some self-consciousness, had come to call the memorial ceremony for Kuratkin, she asked me at last to join them for dinner at an Indian restaurant on East Sixth Street.

"East Sixth Street?" I said. It was an unlikely place to take Mrs. Albers.

"It's Michael's idea. He says he's inviting us, so we have to go cheap. Mama's never tasted Indian food, except for some curry a friend of Papa's made once, or something like that, but she's in this strange mood, she keeps wanting to try anything new. It's wild."

"I haven't seen you in so long," I said.

"I'm the same, only fat," she said. "I don't know how this gathering thing is going to work. Michael's sulking because he wanted to speak at it and we won't let him."

"Why won't you let him?"

"You know how he is," Irina said.

"Are you going to speak?"

"No. If I won't let Michael, then I shouldn't either. Not that I want to."

I had arranged to meet them all at the restaurant, so I was surprised when Michael appeared at my office, without warning, in midafternoon. I was on the telephone at the time, as was my officemate, Mary Donoghue. It was one of those days at work when you have a single important task to accomplish but there are so many interruptions that you never manage to get started. Michael leaned through the doorway and waved, and then, having made his presence known, teased our secretary in the hallway until I finished my call. Michael had come to *Glee* once before, around Christmas, to try to borrow money from Irina. He claimed it was like sneaking into a girls' locker room. Because of his grandfather, he enjoyed a kind of proprietary illusion about the magazine.

"Can you slip out for a cup of coffee?" he asked.

"I'm too busy, we're all going nuts here," I answered.

Michael inserted a cigarette between his lips and gazed around the office as he fished for matches. After lighting the cigarette he looked for an ashtray, and, failing to find one, blew carefully on the spent match and dropped it into my trash basket. I followed all this with only a corner of my mind, as I was busy writing down some information I had just gotten on the phone.

"Excuse me, would you mind not smoking in here?" Mary Donoghue said, hanging up and replacing her earring. Once, long ago, I had thought Mary had a beautiful voice.

"I'm sorry. Sorry," Michael said, freezing in the middle of the room. He looked very surprised.

There was still no ashtray. He stepped over to the window and yanked it up. A blast of damp heat flipped open the magazines stacked on the windowsill and rattled their pages. Papers sailed off my desk. Michael slammed the window shut, the cigarette still in his lips, and began to straighten out the magazines.

"Sorry. Sorry. Sorry," he said, exactly as his sister would. He pulled the cigarette out of his mouth, looked at Mary, and uttered a laugh of helplessness.

For a horrible moment I thought he might be drunk, but his eyes were sharp and clear. For all I heard about Michael's habits, I had seen him drunk only once, at that first party Irina had invited me to, that spring evening a year earlier — an occasion on which he had been merely expansive, loud, and affectionate, even though we had not seen each other since boarding school and had not been friends even then.

Yet that troubled decade was visible in his features. While other schoolmates encountered in adult life were invariably sleeker and stronger than the adolescents they replaced, Michael, who had been famous at school — handsome, bright, and always in trouble — looked as though he had suffered some mysterious fall from grace. Most of him was as thin as always, but his face had grown broader and coarser, and the buttons of his shirt — a silk shirt of European cut, possibly Kuratkin's — were straining over the beginnings of a small belly. His hair was retreating messily from his forehead. One could barely discern the lines of his real nose in this fleshy and pitted new one, which had grown a pair of wire-rimmed glasses whose branches bit into his temples, and which, moreover, looked as though they had been sat on several times. He was smiling through them at Mary Donoghue, apparently savoring some private joke.

"Here, give me that," she said, swiveling out of her chair. She took the cigarette from him and carried it out of the room to the secretary's ashtray.

"Really, I'm sorry," she said as she returned. "I'm allergic."

"No, no," Michael said. "Don't apologize. You're in the right. I'm Irina Albers' brother, Michael," he said suddenly, holding out his hand.

"Really? Why has Irina been hiding you?" Mary said.

Her telephone rang. She resumed her usual scowl, punched the flashing button with her thumb (the nails on the other fingers were too long), and unclipped her earring.

"One of the reasons I came," Michael said to me, "is that I wondered whether you guys had an archive here, with all the old issues. I'm kind of curious about what they looked like when it started. You know, my grandfather started it the year I was born."

The request made me uncomfortable, but I couldn't immediately think of a reason that Michael shouldn't be allowed to look at past issues of *Glee*. They contained no secrets; presumably he wouldn't steal them or set fire to the furniture; and I wanted to get rid of him and return to work.

The library, as it was known, was located on the floor above, along with the magazine's business offices. We found the door locked, but after a moment of reflection I tried, successfully, my key to the men's room. With the feeling of having done something that, although not expressly forbidden, was not quite allowed either, I returned downstairs to my desk. First I had to run the gauntlet of the main hall, a vast low-ceilinged room that in summer was always freezing. Along its walls the white Formica desks of the secretaries and assistants alternated with humming Xerox machines, scruffy drunk bookshelves, and the open doors of editors' offices.

"Was that really Irina's brother?" one of the stylists' assistants asked me. You could never bring a man to *Glee* without having to explain him.

"Yes. We were in school together," I said, circumventing the connection through Irina.

"He's real cute," she said.

"I think he might be a bit wild for you."

"That's my type. Trouble," she said.

"Boy, isn't he a charmer, that one," Mary said when I made it home to my desk. "Does he have a girlfriend?"

"Several," I said.

"Typical. Wish he didn't smoke, though," Mary said. "I find it a sexual turnoff. Well," she said with a sigh. She was arranging her hair in a promotional *Glee* mirror. "I'm off to the shrink. See you tomorrow, hon."

Actually I didn't know much about Michael's love life, except what Irina had said: "Anything. Anything. He's like an animal." But Irina thought that of most men. My predecessor had been the second man to cheat on her. Irina's opinions about men were very close to Mary Donoghue's, but that was the only thing they had in common.

Michael came down from the library an hour later, looking pleased.

"Listen," he said, "do you think I could drop in on the editor in chief? What's her name?"

"Nancy Eberstadt," I said. "Probably not. What for?"

"I think I ought to ask her to come to the thing tomorrow. As the current editor of the magazine."

"Did your mother . . . Well, why wouldn't Irina do that," I said.

"Nobody thought of it. It's been total chaos up there. But there should be someone from *Glee*. I mean officially, apart from Iri and you. Where's her office?"

"Wait a minute," I said.

I picked up my phone and called Nancy's secretary.

"It's Patrick," I said. "Nancy's in a meeting, isn't she?"

"No, she's right here. Just a second, I'll transfer —"

"Oh, well, I'll catch her some other time then, thanks," I said and hung up. "She's in a meeting," I told Michael. "You should tell Irina to give her a call."

I didn't think it safe to collaborate with Michael on anything, let alone Albers internal affairs.

My phone rang. It was Nancy's secretary.

"Patrick, you just did something like really weird," she said. "You asked if Nancy —"

"I know, I know, I can't talk about it," I said. "Sorry."

"Okay, sweetie," the secretary said.

"Pity," Michael said. "I have to speak to her, too, and you can't really do that at funerals."

"What do you have to speak to her about?" I asked.

"Can you keep a secret from Iri?"

"No."

"Well, then," he said.

At the Indian restaurant we ate out of doors in a humid lamp-lit night, in what was called the garden but was in fact a large airshaft behind the kitchen. It was planted with a few young trees and tented with an outspread parachute that concealed the iron-laddered tenements above and protected us from the spittle and missiles of their occupants. Under his family's anxious eyes, Michael restricted his drinking to Coca-Cola. He also took it on himself to keep everyone both fed and entertained. He ordered every dish himself, displaying an uncanny knowledge of all the different Indian breads and condiments. He did a sly imitation of our waiter's accent while giving Irina a recipe for marinating lamb, a recipe that started innocently enough and then gradually — though you couldn't have said exactly how or why — turned into something extremely lewd. He teased his mother for eating so suspiciously, timing his comments in such a way that her efforts to bring one particular forkful to her mouth were thwarted again and again; finally she had to put it back on her plate when a sudden quake of laughter — I had never seen her laugh like that; it created a terrible jiggling effect in her wattles — made her too weak to hold the fork. Then, to collective astonishment and some discomfort, for none of us believed he would actually go through with it, he slid the bill away from her outstretched hand and refused to hear her protests.

As we said good night to Michael outside the restaurant, everyone turned solemn, because of the circumstances under which we were to meet the following day. Michael walked west toward Second Avenue. He was staying in Chelsea, on a mattress in a loft belonging to a former drinking pal of his, a printmaker. (This man, I can't remember his name, it was a German name, had reformed a few months earlier; he went to Alcoholics Anonymous meetings and allowed Michael to sleep among the presses only on the condition that he not bring so much as aspirin or a beer into the loft.) As for the Alberses' edict barring Michael from Central Park West, it seemed to have been lifted, temporarily at least, since the night of Kuratkin's death, but he was being so cautious with his mother and sister that he hadn't tried to assert a right to sleep there. The rest of us hijacked a taxi that had just deposited a fresh group of diners. As we rode uptown, Mrs. Albers, with her handbag in her lap, asked, "Where does he get that money, to take people out like that?"

"He must have borrowed it from someone, against what he expects to be getting from Papa," Irina said.

"Well, that's not going to get any of us very far," Mrs. Albers said in French. "I wish you children weren't getting anything," she added a moment later. "Because of him, not because of you. I've been meaning to ask you, Patrick," she said, placing her fingers on my forearm, "if you would come up to Fincham this weekend to help us go through some of my father's things. There may be some heavy lifting to do, large canvases and such, and I was hoping you might be able to give us *un coup de main*."

Mrs. Albers liked to speak French to me. She always said *vous*, which I found disconcerting. Having left Switzerland at seventeen, I had almost never heard adults address me formally.

"Patrick has other things to do, Mama," Irina said.

"No, no, I'd love to help," I said.

We had spoken about accepting an invitation to Long Island for the weekend, but that had been before Kuratkin's death.

"Well, in any case, Michael's not to know about it," Irina told me. "It's hard enough having him around here."

Leaning across me, Mrs. Albers said to Irina, "There's no need for you to come home tonight, you know. I'll be perfectly —"

"No, I want to," Irina interrupted, just as the taxi swerved onto my block.

I had to clamber over Irina to get out, an annoying and

somewhat humiliating exercise. In her mother's presence I couldn't take issue with her over this refusal, for the fourth night in a row, to stay at my apartment. I also made note that today was a Monday, shrink day, as Irina sometimes called it. We seldom discussed what went on in Dr. Scheinbaum's office, but I had figured out some time ago that to Dr. Scheinbaum I was a purely incidental character, with none of Irina's vivid hundred-dollars-an-hour presence. I liked to blame Dr. Scheinbaum when I was angry at Irina. That way I could be angry at her not only for what she had done but also because she lived her life in thrall to a quack.

At the last minute I changed my mind and turned away from the entrance to my building. The sweating night porter had already pushed the door open for me and made an Italian gesture of protest, palms outward, as it swung back uncaught, a pantomime which, at that point, accurately expressed my own feelings. At the corner of Second Avenue I overtook the taxi while it waited for the light, but I did not peer inside or wave or give any indication that I had seen it. Had it been winter I would have turned up the collar of my coat and thrust my hands deep in my pockets, assuming that Irina was looking at me, but as it happened I had to content myself with shamming nonchalance as I stepped out into the avenue. I paused in the middle to let another taxi shoot by, made it safely to the other side, and then walked downhill on a dark block, past shuttered loading docks and a fragrant mountain of garbage bags whose oily black folds gleamed softly under a streetlamp. I turned under the old green awning of Kiely's and stepped through its swinging door into a long room that smelled of smoke and food, with a scuffed linoleum floor and a wooden bar along its entire length.

The light, both dim and raw, seemed left over from a vanished decade when men had worn hats and smoked cigars. A huge electric fan in a wire cage vibrated in a corner, and a television set emitted a modulated hiss of cheers from its perch above the wooden telephone booth. Several newspapermen from the nearby *Daily News* building watched a baseball game with craned necks, one hand on their drinks, one foot on the railing. Farther along the bar was a loud kinetic knot of young executive types in shirtsleeves and loosened ties, with identical haircuts, gesturing with their bottles of beer as they interrupted one another. At the far end, near the final curve of the bar, two women in their thirties talked intently over sinking glasses of white wine. Sidling in next to them, I ordered a beer and put some money next to it and then threaded my way back to the telephone booth to call Eric Steyer, who had returned from Washington and was camping on a friend's couch in a new high-rise just a few blocks away.

After inviting Steyer down to the bar I went back to my stool, trying to remember the subject of the quarrel I had had with Irina the day that Kuratkin died, but I was distracted by a young man with a dirty suede jacket and thick eyeglasses who had taken the spot I was saving for Steyer. This person looked sane, if a little eager, but he immediately explained to me, while chewing on a plastic stirrer, that he had just been discharged from the Navy, where for four years, he said, he had spent his days and nights flying fighter jets from the deck of an aircraft carrier. He made whooshing sounds with his cheeks as he landed his open hand on the surface of the bar, and then stared at me through his glasses.

Steyer came with the friend at whose apartment he was staying. While sipping at my beer and examining the curled and smoke-stained photographs taped to the mirror above the bar — a haphazard quilt of newspaper clippings and book jackets and fading snapshots where the people's eyes were red dots reflecting the flash — I had managed to freeze out my neighbor; it had become evident, besides, that his loud lies were designed not for my benefit but for the two oblivious

women seated beyond me. The liar politely made room for
Steyer and his friend, distancing himself farther from his intended audience, but watched for a chance to enter the conversation. Both the new arrivals were tall (Steyer could do a
funny demonstration of himself on a recalcitrant Afghan
donkey, lent to him because he couldn't keep up, with his
ankles trailing in the desert), and Steyer's friend had, in ad-
dition, a massive torso and a neck the same width as his head.
A reporter stationed in Beirut, he was at work on a series of
articles on the warring militias' drug trade. Once we had been
introduced, he and Steyer resumed in midstream a conversation about the complicated provenance of weapons in the
Middle East. Steyer was expounding on the relative virtues
of the old AK-47 and the newer version, the latter being, according to him, a sign of great status among the Mujahedin.
At several points during his recent journey he had been made
to tote one or the other, as part of his Afghan disguise. Leaning over the bar and pumping his elbows, he described what
it felt like to run in a crouch with it banging on his back, an
exercise, he said, that had given him a spectacular set of bruises.

"And now let me tell you about the time I peed in my
pants," he said.

"Don't," his friend said.

"It's a good story," Steyer said.

"I know — you already told it to me."

"Those people you went to see in Washington," I said.
"Did they turn out to be from the CIA?"

"Ah, I couldn't tell you that, could I," he said happily.
"But let me get you another beer."

The liar, intimidated, had turned away. He was pretending
to watch the television at the other end of the room, though
it was too far away for him to see anything.

Suddenly I remembered Steyer as a child, squatting in a
forest at night, shining a flashlight on a map while I and several others crowded around him. Our headmaster, a colonel

in the Swiss army, had liked to send us, several times a year, on strange paramilitary excursions — usually in the form of treasure hunts — that could last anywhere from a weekend to a week, and sometimes took us all over Switzerland, by train, boat, bus, or on foot. It seemed to have stuck to Steyer. I wanted to ask him about it.

"Well, it's harder to sell M-16s," Steyer's friend said, finishing a thought. His voice was as big as the rest of him. "With an M-16 you're lucky if you can get half a clip off before it jams. Another problem is the way the bullet tumbles as soon as it hits anything," he added, demonstrating with a basketball referee's "traveling" sign. "The theory behind it is that it'll make a bigger hole, but what it really means is that even a leaf can deflect a bullet."

Like the liar, I too was becoming embarrassed. I wasn't sure why. It may have been connected with Irina; I had just remembered the reason for our quarrel. It had been because of Steyer. Conversations like this one made her climb the walls. But then I became aware that we were being stared at, by a haggard man seated beyond the curve of the bar, behind a long-necked bottle of beer and a full ashtray. There was an air about him — his mustache, his undefinable age, the length of his hair, the way his eyes looked washed out — that reminded me of something I couldn't at first identify.

"If you have a clear field of fire, you're all right," the reporter boomed, "but in the jungle you're going to have a problem. In Vietnam," he continued, and then I recalled where I had seen other faces like the one staring at us: in all those documentaries that open with rotor blades beating a tropical sky and end twenty years later, in drizzling rain, in tears, at a black granite wall in Washington. I fled the conversation and tried, as an excuse, to get the bartender's attention.

"And what do you do?" the reporter asked me.

"I'm an editor at *Glee*. The fashion magazine," I said.

"Yes," he said. "Yes. There's a good piece to be done on

how the militias dress in Beirut. They're terribly elegant. It's terribly important to them."

The veteran — but now I experienced a twinge of doubt, because the bartender, while pulling back one of his draft levers, had begun to develop some of the same traits — placed a few bills and some coins beside his empty bottle and stood up.

"In restaurants, for instance, they have to leave their weapons with the hat-check girl, and it makes them feel positively naked. So they have these . . . symbols, I guess you'd call them. Like the top of a Marlboro box sticking out of a breast pocket —"

"Accessories," I said. "It's a question of accessories."

"Accessories," Steyer said. "I can just see it. Guerrilla chic," he said. "Actually, there are great accessories in Afghanistan, too. Downed helicopters, and burned-out troop transports."

"We could do a big story," I said. "Good backdrop, the desert. Shows off the clothes. We'll use local talent. Are there any female Mujahedin?" I asked.

"You're in trouble there," Steyer said. "I came across only one woman in the whole country, a Swiss doctor with Médecins sans Frontières."

"Well, I could do an article on her," I said. "A good role model for our young readers. Is she pretty? Is she young? We have only young pretty people in the magazine."

"Are you serious?" the journalist asked.

"Yes. Literally. There are no unattractive people in *Glee*. And every story has to be upbeat."

"How on earth did you end up at a fashion magazine, anyway?" Steyer asked.

On his way out, the veteran picked up a black umbrella that stood in a corner by the door. He examined its clasp, gave us a last glance, and pushed the door open onto the night.

VI

AT LEAST twice a year there appears in the Sunday *New York Times Magazine* an article that used to make me envious. It is entitled "Return to X," wherein X is a distant city from which the author covered crisis Y or war Z. It is Saigon, Pnom Penh, Managua, or Beirut. The article is meant to bring us up to date on the situation, but in reality that is not the point at all. In reality our correspondent has a secret agenda, and he almost always betrays it in the very first paragraph — when, as the airliner banks on its final approach, he turns to his curved little window and peers down along the wing to the exotic but familiar city below. He is traveling back to a place where he once was younger, and where, he suspects, he was more alive than he will ever be again. In the course of this trip he hopes to recapture a taste of that existence, even if it is only in memory. There were episodes of terror, to which he gladly admitted, and of exhilaration, which he tried to conceal. Everywhere there were stories: stories heard, overheard, told, and invented, stories that were other people's property but later became his own, stories about guns and cameras and rolls of film, stories about damp wads of dollars, about cartons of Marlboros and fifths of Johnnie Walker like those on the table here in the hotel bar, where stories are told, in English, by Dutchmen, Frenchmen, Germans, South Africans, Australians, Spaniards, Italians, and Portuguese; stories written or not written, or written and not filed, or filed and not printed.

As we climb down to the tarmac in the suffocating heat (despite the kerosene fumes and the concrete underfoot, we can feel the proximity of the jungle), a whole tsunami of recollection overwhelms us, first in the heat itself, then in the smell of those fritters we never quite trusted, and in the sinuous local pop music lacing through the airport lounge. A slight young man in an impeccable uniform hides his thoughts — his whole country, really — behind mirrored sunglasses, a delicate golden hand resting on the barrel of the machine gun that hangs from his right shoulder. Already flies have begun to dart about our neck. The fans that knead the heavy air overhead bring to mind adventure movies of another time, as well as the rotors of the helicopters on which we used to hitch rides upcountry, and which still throb in our dreams in the rainy neon nights back home.

I always wanted to be a certain kind of journalist, because of the stories, because of the travel and the secrets, because of Tintin (who introduces himself thus: *"Je me présente: Tintin, reporter"*), because of John Reed, and Bob Woodward and Carl Bernstein — whom I kept running into on Madison Avenue, by the way; for some reason he always thought he knew me, too.

On the day of the memorial gathering for Kuratkin, I spent

the entire morning attempting to arrange a meeting, which seemed as complicated as an outer-space linkup, between an interviewer and a movie star who was on the third comeback of her career. The movie star's publicist was making absurd demands: her client would grant the interview only if the pictures were taken by a specific photographer, and she also wanted to read the text of the article before it was published; the magazine's travel agent was unable to find an airplane seat for the journalist on the necessary date; the art director happened to be feuding with the photographer on whom the movie star insisted; *und so weiter, und so weiter,* as Kuratkin had been fond of saying. My ear began to ache from the pressure of the telephone; it became difficult to ignore Mary Donoghue, who was popping her chewing gum and saying extraordinarily cruel things into the telephone; and by the time I found it necessary to drop the whole matter in order to go to a business lunch — I had been ordered, as the only male editor, to participate in a campaign to seduce a big-name astrologer away from another magazine — I had reached that state of frustration, already familiar to me, in which I could not understand why I had kept this temporary job for so long. Just a few years earlier it would have seemed inconceivable that I might soon find myself, while still so young, riding the subway every morning, working at an office in a big city, and preparing to marry a girl I had met there, behind a desk (not on a tropical beach, not at a masked ball, not in a panicked flood of refugees swarming the gate of an embassy somewhere); that I should find myself chained to a computer that I operated, in my modest way, for the further enrichment of the megalomaniacal developer who now owned *Glee,* and whose colossal towers were gradually robbing the city of sunlight and clogging its streets with more people like me, scurrying to and from other computers each morning and evening.

"Carl Bernstein?" Mary Donoghue said into the phone. "The one who cheats on his wife? He should be hung by his own prick."

The ceremony was to begin at four, but I had promised to come early. Having plied the astrologer with wine, listened to conjecture about my past lives (she said "Tibetian"), hinted at sums of money that I myself could only dream of making, and phoned in a detailed report to Nancy Eberstadt, I strolled up Central Park West, under the trees on the park side of the avenue. I carried my jacket over my shoulder and walked slowly, not wanting to arrive drenched. Despite all the food I had just eaten, despite the wine and the nervous exhaustion caused by the insane babble I had endured, I had the same hollowness in my stomach that I used to feel, as a child, on trips down to Lausanne to visit the dentist.

I had never seen the apartment prepared for guests. During Kuratkin's illness Mrs. Albers had once in a while had a friend over for tea, and nothing more. With the help of a Chinese butler and maid on loan from a friend who lived across the park, she had distributed all the flowers about the long-unused living room and covered the tables with white cloths and trays of food. The newly tuned piano had been moved out from against the wall. It was an intimidating arrangement, and we chose to wait next door in the library, drinking tea, until enough people arrived. The front door was open, the doorman downstairs had been instructed not to call up when people arrived (though he tried to at first, until Irina barked at him through the intercom), and the guests were allowed to wander in on their own, pick glasses of wine off the trays, and greet each other in low voices. Nobody wanted to sit, except Satyra, the only one of the nurses to have come. She and her five-year-old daughter were in fact the first people to arrive and therefore waited with us in the library, where Satyra remained throughout the proceedings, glued to the only hard chair in the room, with a handbag in her lap, while her silent daughter parked herself in the doorway to the living room and between bouts of fidgeting observed everyone with fierce concentration, as though she intended to stampede the guests and eat one of the slower ones.

I tried to keep out of the way. Neither of the children had invited any friends, not wanting to have to take care of them, so I knew almost nobody. It was one of those affairs where no one introduces himself or anyone else unless it becomes absolutely necessary to do so, and acknowledges one another with nods, and indicates that under different circumstances he would smile. I did meet one old lady who thought I was Michael, until the real Michael arrived to untangle us. Hours later I remembered why there was something familiar about her name, and realized that she may have been related to people who had known my father — but by then she was long gone and I knew I would never see her again. I recognized a face or two from a party I had been to somewhere, or perhaps from the newspapers or television, and heard names I had heard many times before; there were at least two women obviously connected with Kuratkin's years in fashion, who in spite of their age and the nature of the occasion displayed a liveliness of manner and a slight eccentricity of dress typical of fashion people. They looked as though they breathed a different kind of air, something that made them a bit giddy.

Nancy Eberstadt was not there.

"Michael wanted to ask her," I told Irina when she paused at my windowsill on one of her rounds.

"She and Papa never met, and it's such ancient history anyway," she said.

"I think maybe he was right," I said.

"It's just his usual nonsense," she said. "Meddling," she added. Her eyes were traveling about the room, checking on things.

Every few minutes I found an excuse to wander away and

take refuge elsewhere in the apartment. I was sitting on the edge of Irina's bed with my hands between my knees, killing time, when Michael pushed the door open and flew by me into the bathroom.

"All the performing bears are here. I think we're going to start pretty soon," he said, his voice echoing on the tile. A faucet groaned and gushed, and a second later he appeared in the doorway, holding a glass of water.

"Want one?" he asked, holding his hand out palm upward. In it were two of Dr. Scheinbaum's Valium, which he had just filched from the medicine cabinet.

"Do those things have any effect on you?" I asked. At Harvard and afterward Michael had had several bouts with heroin.

"Oh, yes," he said cheerfully. "God, it's come to this," he said, stepping over to Irina's desk.

For several years Irina had painted, in gouache and India ink, reproductions of official documents of all kinds. She liked to duplicate the ink stamps askew on the page, and the shadow of the embossed seal on the photograph that gave the bearer a harelip, and, most of all, the scars of age and wear and travel on the paper — foxing around the edges, water stains, and delicate trompe l'oeil folds. For my most recent birthday she had reproduced the opening pages of my last, and now expired, Swiss passport (framed by the protruding edge of the red cardboard cover), having spirited the original from a desk drawer where I hadn't known that her fingers ever wandered. In rendering the photograph she had taken the further liberty of crowning my plump fourteen-year-old head with a Swiss skullcap embroidered with edelweiss and heraldic badges. Now, neatly placed on a blotter in the center of her leather-topped desk, next to a glass containing a rounded fan of paintbrushes, was a yellow-and-black copy of Kuratkin's death certificate.

"That's morbid, not to mention a lot of boring work," Michael said, reading the information as he tapped the pockets of his jacket. "Look at that, and she's never even gotten a stain on that desk."

He gulped down both pills and put the glass on the blotter. He pulled his cigarettes from his pocket, lit one, sucked on it three times, and stepped through a billowing blue cloud to drop it in the toilet.

"You know, they wouldn't let me speak, those bitches," he said. "My own grandfather. I might just get up and —"

"For God's sake," I said. "Don't."

A minute after we returned to the living room, Mrs. Albers walked to the mantelpiece with an elderly man in a business suit, exchanged a few words with him, and then left him there, under a muddy abstract canvas of Kuratkin's, while she took up a position facing him at the edge of the crowd.

"Please," this man said, holding a hand out before his chest. "Please, everyone.

"We have all gathered together," he began, and then he stopped and cleared his throat. "We have all gathered here," he said, "to honor the memory of Nicholas Kuratkin, an extraordinary man." He cleared his throat again, violently. "An extraordinary man, a wonderful man. In the course of his long life, he was a friend to many who are not with us here in person, but whose spirit fills this room, this beautiful room, where Kuratkin — no one but his beloved family ever called him anything else . . ."

Irina and Michael had gone to stand at their mother's side. It gradually dawned on me that the man delivering this eulogy — nobody had introduced him — was the owner of the gallery that had handled Kuratkin's paintings. For a few moments he praised Kuratkin's work, assuring the company that it would long outlive "his mortal coil." He spoke of the hardships Kuratkin had endured as a young man, his heroism during the revolution, the poverty of his years in France, and the triumph of *Glee*. He was doing all this without notes; the only flaw in his preparation was his hands, which quickly became a problem. They ended up hovering at chest level in front of him, as though ready to ward off a blow. He mentioned Kuratkin's generosity, in both time and money, to several foundations that took care of émigrés and refugees, and announced that there was among the assembly a poet, a great Russian poet, who had asked to say a few words. Might he introduce Isaac Behr.

He stepped away from the fireplace, gesturing toward a man with narrow shoulders and thin curtains of red hair on the sides of his head. He wore a tweed jacket with sagging pockets, blue jeans that were too short and gray at the knees, and scuffed ankle-high boots. The man sidled up to the fireplace, unfolded a piece of paper, and bared a row of gleaming dentures. With a heavy accent and a slight hiss, he said: "This is first poem I write in America. I write it in this house. In English, title would be 'Sunrise in the West.' More or less."

He closed his eyes and began to recite in Russian, in an alternately lilting and rolling voice. Suddenly, across the room, Irina made a squeaking noise that might have been a stifled sneeze, or even a stifled sob, but which I recognized as the murder of a giggle. I looked down at my feet and bit the inside of my cheek. After briefy regaining control of herself, Irina squeaked again and then flew from the room. Isaac Behr had spent three years in a labor camp. He had been tortured with drugs in a mental institution. He had been exiled to a Siberian settlement where he could not find work. Because he was well known to Amnesty International and to poets everywhere, the authorities eventually emigrated him to the West, where he arrived without any possessions, manuscripts, or teeth. While awaiting a position teaching Russian literature (he had ended up, in an informal capacity, at Yale), he had lived, between fittings at the dentist, in the guest room at Kuratkin's. During the poet's stay there the apartment had filled, day after day, with the recent émigrés whose accents and manners caused pre-Soviet Kuratkin sorrowful amazement. Irina called him the "grant wizard."

Several times we all thought he had finished his poem, but then, without any visible intake of breath, he would start up again like a badly extinguished fire. When at last he was through, he stood still for a moment, his eyes closed, as though awaiting an echo, until Mrs. Albers dislodged him with a gentle "*spasibo,*" one of the two or three dozen Russian words she had.

Irina snuck back in while another émigré, a student at Juilliard, played a Rachmaninoff prelude at the piano. Mrs. Albers took over again at the mantelpiece, thanked everyone, and enjoined us to eat and drink. A few minutes later people began to drift discreetly toward the elevator. Irina looked as tired as I had ever seen her.

"You should go now; there's no reason for you to stay," she told me when almost everyone else had left. "I'll call you later. I may come to the office tomorrow if I feel up to it." We were standing in the tiny entry by the elevator. She was loosening my tie.

"Hold the elevator!" Mrs. Albers said, and Isaac Behr rushed in, the tails of his tweed jacket spread out behind him like wings. Irina gave us a small wave as the door rattled shut. We nodded at each other and rode down several floors in silence, not having been introduced. Then he turned to me and, with his thick accent, said, "You know, with Kuratkin, it is the end of something." He shook his head. "The end of something," he repeated, speaking to his shoes.

Outside the lobby it was like a forge. At the entrance to the park I joined a line waiting by an ice cream truck. It was a Tuesday evening in May, but it felt like midsummer.

Grownups in ragged shorts and T-shirts waited patiently among the children and their skateboards. The diesel motor of the truck's refrigerator throbbed loudly and evenly, giving off a smell of fuel. I was reminded of waiting in a crowd on a dock to get on a ferry, and a great longing to travel came over me.

VII

MRS. ALBERS and her children began to disperse Kuratkin's belongings and reorganize the apartment on the day after the ceremony. Irina seemed unable to leave Central Park West for more than a half hour at a time. She announced that she would not return to the office for another week. Every evening I rode the subway up the West Side and took her out for a walk, in the park or along Columbus Avenue, where we would go into an air-conditioned coffee shop or a bar. Pale, her clothes dirty, her hair piled up off her neck and lashed to her head, Irina would drink iced cappuccino and give me a progress report: her mother was planning to convert Kuratkin's bedroom into a second guest room and adapt his study for her use; the whole apartment was going to be repainted and contractors were coming to give estimates; this had been taken to the thrift shop; that had been given to a

Russian charity; the lawyer had said one thing but the accountant predicted that the insurance company would say another . . .

One night Mrs. Albers cooked a leg of lamb and I stayed for dinner. I think this was the first actual meal there in a long time: Irina tended to starve herself, Michael forgot to eat when he was drunk and gobbled candy bars when he was not, and Mrs. Albers claimed that after you reached the age of fifty food was just another thing you could go without. That day, however, it got into her head to roast a leg of lamb (it was over ninety degrees outside), and we all sat down in the dining room together, Mrs. Albers, Irina, Michael — those two just out of the shower, their identical black hair identically wet — and me, before a white tablecloth set with silver and crystal that had not been used in years.

Michael had just stabbed the joint with the carving fork and was sliding the knife in, his jaw tensed in a way he had learned from his grandfather, when the intercom rang to announce the arrival of two men from the medical supply company who were coming up in the freight elevator to remove Kuratkin's rented hospital bed. They had been expected since ten o'clock that morning. One of these men proved to be a huge and voluble fellow wearing a baseball cap back to front. He had a big double chin like a goiter and a tiny mouth with fat lips, from which there issued a steady stream of inanities, each of them repeated at least once. His abdomen, only partly covered by a stained undershirt, was a vast barrel lacking a waist or hips for his belt to grip, and his blue jeans had sunk a considerable distance since the morning, freeing the upper half of his buttocks. Apparently oblivious of this, he maintained a steady monologue about the heat, the humidity, and the difficult nature of his work, while he joined his partner in dismantling the bed, inadvertently mooning us every time he bent over.

All four of us, having gathered in Kuratkin's doorway for the spectacle, started to make horrible grimaces to contain our laughter. We stepped back to allow the men to carry out the bed, the nude giant still going on about cool swimming pools and frosty beers, but they encountered exactly the same problem as the undertakers had with the gurney and Kuratkin's body a week before, so that in their hefting and staggering and advancing and backing up they came to seem a slapstick takeoff on their predecessors. I thought I was alone in seeing this, but then I realized that the others were seeing it too, and at that moment each of the Alberses recognized that we were noticing the same thing and wondering whether it was funny or not; and all of a sudden we were having hysterics. The baffled men continued to struggle in the doorway with a hundred-pound bed and an invisible cadaver in their arms. Irina screamed with laughter. Tears fell from her face onto the floor. Mrs. Albers hugged her elbows to her chest and turned away, her wattles shaking. Michael clutched his forehead with one hand and held on to his sister with the other.

Finally the handyman stepped out of the elevator and took charge, and got the men and the bed out for us while we staggered away down the hall.

Michael stayed on in New York, day after day, sober but in the way. He would appear at the door (he didn't have a key) around eleven in the morning, by which time Irina and their mother would already be exhausted and irritated. From what I saw at the end of the day there must have been a lot of desultory wandering from room to room with objects (Kuratkin's custom-made shoetrees, his dozen pairs of glasses) that had led innocent and useful lives but had now become problems. The women tried to send Michael back to Boston, but like Irina he seemed tethered to the apartment. At first I thought he was waiting for Kuratkin's money to be released, or trying to get his mother to lend him some in the meantime, but in the end it turned out that he kept hanging around partly out of mistrust. One day, in the course of a routine argument, something about removing a painting from its frame, he became enraged and yelled at his mother that she was doing all she could to erase every trace of Kuratkin's passage on earth. After that it became even more important to keep him from finding out that we planned to continue this work without him in Fincham over the weekend. His mother told him she was going to stay with a friend in Summit, New Jersey, and Irina said that she was going to Shelter Island with me.

Neither Irina nor her mother seemed to share my discomfort at this deception. They were used to it. Friday morning I took my bag to the office and after lunch I walked over to meet Irina in the bedlam of Penn Station. I could always find her in a crowd, without even looking.

Having driven up the day before, Mrs. Albers met us on the platform in Fincham, wearing a faded print dress and old navy blue sneakers, a pair of sunglasses pressed down on top of her tinted hair. I had never seen her in the country — I'd been up to Fincham only once before, alone with Irina, the previous autumn — and she seemed older and smaller and less formidable than her New York incarnation. It was just before dusk, and when we got off the train the air was so soft and welcoming that I wanted to close my eyes, stand still, and breathe.

Mrs. Albers was an energetic driver. When we swung off the asphalt onto the dirt road in the woods, the station wagon bounced over the ruts and I almost banged my head on the roof. The branches of young birches whipped the windshield on Irina's side. Small stones kept popping out from under the tires and hitting the tree trunks with a crack, sometimes pinging back against the side of the car. Driving with one hand — the other groped along the top of the dashboard for a set of keys that was trying to slide off — Irina's mother gave us updates about various neighbors, whose houses could be guessed at from the occasional tin mailbox listing at the entrance of a narrower graveled track. Her own place, a gray clapboard farmhouse that Kuratkin had bought and restored in the fifties (for a sum so small it had become a family legend), stood atop a long wild meadow that tumbled down in ridges toward the valley and the river, bordered on one side by the birches along the track and by a pine forest on all others. Mrs. Albers had made separate beds for Irina and me in the same room on the second floor, a gesture I found touching in its confusion, although it occurred to me later that she may simply have thought one bed too narrow for two. She herself occupied the master bedroom downstairs, directly underneath a squeaky floorboard that had been a snitch throughout Michael and Irina's childhood.

As on my first visit, three seasons earlier, I found an air of desolation about the place. Its life had been ebbing for twenty years, leached by the death of Kuratkin's wife, Mrs. Albers' divorce, Kuratkin's age and his reluctance to travel, and Michael and Irina's growing up. As small children they had spent three months of every year here with their mother, an ever-changing au pair, and a black Labrador named Doctor, now buried in the woods. The adults and their guests would arrive on Fridays in cars packed with groceries, fishing tackle, a new badminton net, and sometimes other children, whose annoying presence destroyed the routine of the solitary weeks; but in the last years only Mrs. Albers had stayed there for more than a long weekend, unless you counted Isaac Behr, who claimed there were small pockets in the area, a forest clearing here and a brookside meadow there, that gave him the illusion of having stepped over the Pole into northern Russia. He had kept the key that Kuratkin lent him years earlier and sometimes drove up from New Haven with a female graduate student. It was a practice Mrs. Albers now intended to stop. The house was cared for by a carpenter who lived out of sight on another flank of the hill. The structures were well maintained, but the lawns and the garden had long ago reverted to countryside, and mildew and human absence had darkened the rooms, where closets held the lost Scrabble letters and unmatched sneakers that had last been missed a decade before and would never be missed again.

Once Irina and I had left our bags upstairs, Mrs. Albers suggested that we put on some water to boil, which, here as well as in the city, was her way of coping with any loose moments that might arise in her day. I wanted a drink — my own way of coping with unfamiliar places if I happened to arrive at a propitious hour — but I thought it would be rude to ask for liquor five minutes after walking into the house. Mrs. Albers abruptly took Irina by the elbow and led her outside, saying that she wanted to show her something. I was left in the kitchen with only the kettle, which began to quiver, and a local newspaper, the *Binghampton Thistle,* for company. Sitting down at the flaking white table, I made an effort to find something quaint in the *Thistle,* but I couldn't concentrate enough to read more than the headlines and the captions under the murky photographs: a bridge had collapsed somewhere in the wilderness around me, a child who had vanished a year ago was still missing.

When the kettle began to rattle in earnest I rose from the table to turn off the gas, located three mugs, one of which wasn't chipped, and set about searching the other cabinets for some tea, keeping an eye out for any booze that might be put to use once a decent interval had elapsed. Failing on both counts, I decided to start off by having a cup of hot water — *de l'eau chaude nature,* as my Swiss aunts, who deplored caffeine, had called it — because I was getting cold. I could have gone upstairs to fetch a sweater from my bag, or, better still, have built a fire, so after reinstating a modest flame under the kettle I took the box of kitchen matches to the living room, where I crouched before the fireplace and began to stack kindling around crumpled sheets of last week's *Thistle* — I was surprised to see that Mrs. Albers' handwriting had filled not only the crossword puzzle but also the word games for children.

When Irina and I were here last fall I had built just such a fire the first evening; it was the first time I had seen her features transformed by firelight; a bramble had scratched her cheek as I pulled her sweater over her head. The couch had sagged uncomfortably beneath us but released a delicious smell of summer house, a mixture of dust, humidity, wicker, dried flowers, that obliterated the smell of the forest in Irina's hair. "Wait," she whispered, "wait, wait," and when I released her, imagining some mysterious diaphragm problem, she twisted her arm beneath her body and groped between the cushions, extracting the Mont Blanc pen I am using at this very moment — no doubt a gift from a female admirer to Isaac Behr, may all his pens run dry.

I struck a match and held it to the paper, which curled in with a hiss and sent a sheet of flame up through the kindling.

I turned at the sound of footsteps on the porch. Mrs. Albers pulled the screen door open and came in while Irina paused to scrape her shoes on the mat. Irina had been crying; shocked, I found the same signs of recent tears on her mother's face.

"Thank you. What a good idea," Mrs. Albers said cheerfully, though her voice was thick.

"The water's boiling, but I couldn't find any tea," I said.

Irina knelt on the floor and held her hands out to the flames.

"What's the matter?" I asked, once her mother was away in the kitchen.

"She scattered his ashes yesterday without waiting for me," she said.

"The reason she did that," I said — uneasy at being in Fincham in Michael's stead, I had already thought about the problem — "is that on one hand she didn't want Michael here this weekend, and on the other she didn't want to scatter the ashes with only one of her children and exclude the other. So she did it alone. But she can't tell you things like that, so she pretends everything is normal."

Irina blushed suddenly. It may have been just the heat of the fire. I didn't want her to start crying again; I crouched down and took her in my arms. Experimentally, I conjured up a vision of this room filled with people, with two children, with Kuratkin's ashes in the forest and Michael falling down in the garden, the fireside crowded with laughing friends, and more people arriving that evening, though no one knew where to put them.

"I bought the most marvelous cookies," Mrs. Albers called from the kitchen.

"Oh, goody," Irina said, and, steadying herself on my shoulder, she rose to her feet.

That night she brought up the subject of Michael again. She was lying in my arms under the quilt in the dark. We hadn't said anything for a while.

"It was a terrible thing, not telling Michael we were coming here," she said. "Even drunk and making scenes, he should be here."

"Tomorrow, if you want," I said, "I'll get drunk and make a scene, just for you."

"You never get drunk and make scenes," she said.

"Don't you find me dull?"

"Terribly dull."

"Don't you wish I were an adventurer all burned by the sun, who'd fly into town between two expeditions and hang diamonds from your ears and take you dancing?"

"Yes," she whispered.

"Well, you have me, anyway."

"Yes."

I awoke the following morning with the pleasant feeling of not being in my usual berth. At first I was suspicious, because the moment of my waking could sometimes be treacherous. Sometimes I blundered into consciousness without even knowing who I was. Various possibilities would present themselves, each one crowding out the others: I was an eight-year-old boy on holiday in the mountains, an undergraduate in a scruffy house on a hill in Providence, an adolescent in a sun-filled room surrounded by melting snow . . . but each of these mirages vanished as quickly as it formed, and within seconds I would be back on the dry sands of the present, my eyes irrevocably open. Yet this morning I was indeed away in the country, and my happiness, when I tested it, gave a solid ring. The air I breathed was warm and slightly dusty, and the sheets still smelled of cleanliness. A single blade of sunlight had slipped between the shutters and split the room diagonally, folding over a chair occupied by Irina's traveling bag, a battered and stained leather sack stamped with the initials NK. She was already gone, having made the other bed (to which she had transferred herself in the middle of the night) and having, moreover, placed a flower in a glass on the night table next to mine. I could hear voices and footsteps in the attic above me, as well as an occasional loud sneeze.

I was examining the contents of the refrigerator when mother and daughter came into the kitchen. Irina carried under her arm two yellowed shoe boxes filled with letters. When it became clear that I meant to cook the eggs rather than just hold the carton, Mrs. Albers pulled off her work gloves and rushed to my rescue. "You sit down and take your time waking up," she said. "There'll be more than enough for you to do."

She cracked two eggs on the edge of a spitting frying pan and stood by as they cooked, with a fist on her hip and a spatula at the ready.

"What are you doing with all those letters?" she asked.

"I'm sorting out the ones in Russian," Irina said. "We can take them back with us and have Michael or Isaac tell us what they are."

"We're going to find many more boxes of them. He never threw anything away. All painters are terrible pack rats."

"All these Russian ones are from a P. Karazin in Yonkers," Irina said. "Are we going to discover terrible secrets, do you think? And what about his memoirs? Do you think they're here?"

"Well, they're not in New York. They weren't in the bank vault, which is where I expected to find them. I think he never got very far with that project and just destroyed it. But Karazin, that rings a bell," Mrs. Albers said. "Karazin. Wait a minute. No, that was someone else."

"So what's the plan?" I asked.

"You just bring your plate here and I'll slip the eggs on it. Do you want them runny or hard?"

"No, I meant what are we going to do this morning," I said, obeying nonetheless. "Thank you."

"There are two trunks of old clothes in the attic that I want to take back to New York," Mrs. Albers said. There followed a detailed list of small chores. "Then I want to dust the canvases in the studio and stack them all properly and clean the place up. They'll have to be inventoried at some point. That barn would be perfectly livable if it were clean, and I could rent the house for a lot more."

"Why rent it? You should sell it. No one comes up here anymore," Irina said.

"Oh, no, don't do that," I said.

"And where are all his old documents? Passports and marriage certificates and things like that," Irina asked.

After my breakfast we trooped upstairs to the attic to remove the trunks. There were stacks of children's books along the walls, including many volumes of Tintin's adventures, whose magnetic pull I had to fight. There were also a number of paintings of landscapes that were not by Kuratkin — some rolled and some stretched, some of them partly eaten — which resembled the dismal unframed canvas that hung in Irina's bedroom in New York. They had an unfinished air about them that may have been a deliberate form of abstraction but that looked to me like the result of an amateur's impatience. "My father's," Irina said when I asked, and she made a curt gesture with her left hand, drawing a line across the whole topic, while Mrs. Albers' back seemed to bristle. For reasons that even Irina claimed not to know, Jack Albers, who had at some point been a colleague of Kuratkin's in New York (another art director), had been banished and declared a nonperson more than two decades earlier. Irina said that she had only a very dim memory of him, and had somehow come to decide that she wasn't the least bit interested in finding out who he was or what crime he had committed. When I asked her why she wasn't curious, she simply said, "He probably cheated on her, that's all," as though infidelity on the part of men was something to be dismissed as normal and yet neither tolerated nor forgiven.

We manhandled the two trunks down the ladder, Irina guiding them from above while I acted as the brake. Mrs. Albers stood behind me on the landing with her hands held out before her, recommending caution. Once I had carried them downstairs to the ground floor, it became evident that despite her apparently detailed plans Irina's mother had summoned us to Fincham without any real idea of what she wanted to accomplish. The barn, which contained two small bedrooms as well as Kuratkin's studio, was so messy and cluttered it would have taken a week's work to make a difference. There had been a time when Kuratkin planned to make sculptures from dismantled farm machinery, and heaps of rusting metal scraps grew in two corners of the studio; no arrangements had been made to have them collected, and there was no question of taking them to the dump in the station wagon. Dozens of paint-stained jars and coffee cans, some still filled with dusty brushes, littered every surface. Several raccoons had danced a jig all over the floor after stepping in blue paint. No sooner had we begun to work than both Irina and I started to sneeze and weep and scratch ourselves wildly, and we had to drive fifteen miles to a hardware store to buy dust masks.

"I'm sorry you got dragged all the way up here for nothing," Irina said, wiping her nose as I inched the car down the track toward the main road. "I knew it was going to be like this."

"Why? It's so nice here. We should bring some friends up before the summer is out," I said, glancing over to see her reaction.

"Do you want to stop at the supermarket and get yourself some beer?" she asked.

"What about making banana daiquiris this evening? Do you think we could get your mother interested in a banana daiquiri?"

"You might get me interested, given a little . . . left, left, make a left here," she said.

Back in the studio we humored Mrs. Albers for the rest of the afternoon, having decided that if the weather was still good on Sunday we would go on strike and head for the swimming hole and then insist on leaving early for New York.

Mostly we just lifted objects and shifted them so that Mrs. Albers could determine what was behind or underneath them. The carpenter who took care of the house came by to examine the roof; we had found a large stain on the attic floor that suggested a leak. A neighbor also came sniffing around; she was the local eccentric, a female Humpty Dumpty with a battered wig and eyeglasses an inch thick, who, Irina whispered, kept a barrel filled with used toothbrushes on her front porch. Aided by a beer or two, I actually came to enjoy our senseless labor, and by evening, when I was showered and scrubbed and manipulating bananas and a blender by myself in the kitchen, hearing through the open window a creak and a snap from the wicker chair that held Irina, who in turn held a crumbling paperback *Anna Karenina,* I was having chills of happiness. My arms ached from the day's exertions and felt as though they had recently belonged to someone else. The light was growing softer, and in the window above the sinks the wooded hills gradually faded from green to a smoky blue. Leaning on the porch rail a minute later, my hand around a cold plastic glass printed with brightly colored elves, I filled my chest with the cooling air, in which a hint of wood smoke mingled with limpid, greener smells. Two swallows swooped acrobatically across the meadow. A page of *Anna Karenina* rustled behind me, and then everything was still again except for the murmur of the river, which, I now realized, I had heard all day without noticing it.

Twenty-four hours after leaving New York, I invariably came to feel that I rushed through my days with dark glasses over my eyes and cotton in my ears.

"Do you know," Irina said, "that my grandfather used to claim that the first three women he fell in love with were named, in that order, Anna, Karen, Nina?"

"Good story," I said. "Look, visitors."

A car was struggling up the dirt track. The driver ground

the gears as he tried to find one that was comfortable. Through the gaps in the birches I could see the car rocking as it lurched in and out of the ruts. It was a blue Toyota jeep, tall on its wheels, with a white roof. For a moment I imagined it was going to pull up on the grass before me and surrender a man who had been looking for me for years — to offer me a fascinating job, or to give me the vast fortune that was rightfully mine, to reveal at last that I was really the son of the king. It proved to contain only a family of lost tourists, but I found solace and joy in the swing of Irina's hips as she crossed the lawn toward the idling machine, already smiling, eager to give the lost souls whatever help they needed.

VIII

ON SUNDAY it poured. Irina had no license, and it was apparently Mrs. Albers' old-fashioned theory that men should be asked to drive, if only to avoid hurting their feelings. The windshield wipers on the station wagon were singularly ineffective, and my normal tendency, even on dry roads, was to drive at thirty miles an hour. Peering through a cascade, my left sneaker poised on the brake pedal, I tried to match my speed to that of the other cars. Irina held on to the back of my seat and argued, six inches from my ear, with her mother. Both women were prey to passenger's jitters, and fearing that I would miss the road signs in the downpour, they had issued contradictory directions for the past ten miles. I knew exactly where I was.

The rain let up just as we cruised onto the George Washington Bridge. Realizing we had made it home, Irina stopped in midsentence and fell back in her seat. It was one of those dark Sunday afternoons when New Yorkers return to a city that seems to have been evacuated during their absence, and the deserted streets among the warehouses near the Hudson River touched me with a familiar dread. After unloading the station wagon at the curb at Central Park West, Irina and I went up to the apartment, and Mrs. Albers took the car to the parking garage. Exhausted by the drive, I fell asleep on the couch in the library while Irina took a shower, and was awakened by her voice in the entrance, speaking angry words again to her mother. "Why don't you just leave the trunks there and stop fussing about things for just five minutes," she was saying, to which Mrs. Albers replied, "All right, all right, all right, sorry, sorry, sorry," and retreated toward the kitchen with her hands raised in surrender.

Irina and I took a taxi down to my neighborhood and ate there in a dim and almost empty restaurant where we often went.

"What does 'probate' mean, exactly?" Irina asked me.

"I don't know," I said.

A waiter handed her a menu.

"Hello," he said. He was grinning madly.

"They've made you a waiter!" Irina said.

"Just on the weekends," he said. "As a tryout."

"Congratulations," Irina said.

Until now he had been a busboy and we had kept him working late several times, somewhat guiltily, because he studied accounting all day before starting his eight-hour shift at the restaurant. He came from El Salvador. He had waded across the Rio Grande two years before. Now he was trying to get political refugee status and bring his wife and two children over. He was twenty-two years old and half in love with Irina.

"For the specials, we have snapper," he said, carefully. "It is cooked . . ."

"It won't be fresh, on a Sunday," Irina said.

He peered around.

"Not really," he said.

"I'll have the usual salad," she said. "I wish we'd gone to a new place," she told me once he had left. "He makes me feel guilty."

"Don't worry about him, he'll do better than both of us in the end. Is that a new blouse?"

"I bought it Friday. It cost a fortune. I also bought three pairs of shoes."

"Are you a rich woman?" I asked.

"No, this is all credit. It's still going to be a while. There wasn't much left, you know. There hasn't been for a long time. He spent it all on the magazine. Let's say that I can afford a few pairs of expensive shoes. Michael got his share, too. We thought he'd been cut out."

"Good for Michael," I said.

She raised her eyebrows skeptically.

"I give him six months to spend it all, every penny," she said. "Why did we come here, anyway?"

We went there because even on drizzling evenings like this one it was an easy walk from my apartment. In the last years I had become reluctant to travel about Manhattan, to brave the misery of the subway or waste my salary on taxis or suffer the roaring and stuttering progress of the buses. After just two days in the country, I found it depressing to be back in New York.

"I'm tired of this whole town," I said. "I'm tired of my job. I have to do a new résumé tomorrow."

"You've been saying that for a year," Irina said.

Second Avenue was dark when we emerged. I felt somewhat better. The wet asphalt reflected the headlights of the few cars that sailed by, each one wreathed in a portable mist. It was so quiet we could hear the windshield wipers clacking at red lights and the clicks of the DON'T WALK signs. We passed an anxious semaphore attempting to hail off-duty taxis, and a woman in a plastic raincoat and kerchief walking a moplike dog, a rain-streaked newspaper under her arm. On one corner a drenched and barefoot madman, a newcomer to the neighborhood, hugged a bundle to his chest as he paced a small section of pavement, jerking his head violently, as if he were plagued by flies. I took Irina's arm and drew her under the umbrella, remembering my loneliness on similar evenings before I had found her.

The newsstand on my corner shut early on Sundays, but we found some damp leftover copies of the *Times* on a crate under the dripping awning of the Korean greengrocer's. Two miniature Latino adolescents sat on other crates and cleaned carrots in silence, while inside the store their Korean bosses ate noodles with chopsticks to the wail of a country-western ballad on the radio. It was a cheerful little oasis, well lit and bright with fruit and flowers. I bought a plastic basket of raspberries and some heavy cream, simply as an excuse to linger. While the Korean set his noodles aside and tapped the keys of his cash register, I propped the massive newspaper on the counter and began to remove the advertising inserts and the sections we wouldn't read.

"Don't throw away the Real Estate," Irina said.

I had known this was going to happen. She was going to leave her mother's apartment; she had been waiting for Kuratkin to die.

"Are you looking for a place in the Olympic Tower or at River House?" I asked.

"Bowery's more like it," she said, and for the moment we left it at that.

In the lobby of my building Irina and the night porter kidded each other about the weather as we waited for the elevator and rain dripped from the tip of my umbrella into a puddle on the tile. Upstairs, we read the newspaper and ate the raspberries, exchanging sections. I sat in my one comfortable chair; Irina had the couch — actually a fold-out bed, lumpy and sonorous, that had often been opened for overnight guests in former years, when friends had been poorer and less settled. I noted that *Doctor Zhivago* was playing at a revival house in Greenwich Village; it was a movie I had seen as a small child, and wanted to see again, and kept missing.

Irina scraped her spoon on her plate as she read, gathering up the last traces of cream. As usual, she leafed quickly through the Magazine and the Book Review and then extracted from the pile the second news section, which contained what she called the "women's sports," the wedding and engagement announcements. Having spent all her life in New York, she always knew some of the pearl-collared maidens, if only by name and reputation. She stuck her spoon in her mouth in order to turn a page and then left it there, humming through it quietly as she scanned the columns. I prepared to put down the Travel section, walk around the coffee table, pull the spoon from her mouth like a doctor about to consult a thermometer — and then take her hands in mine and fall to one knee. Or I could ask her to humor me, to put her shoes back on, to follow me downstairs and out into the street, where I would get us a taxi. Beneath the shining windows of the Plaza I would transfer us to a horse-drawn carriage and ride with her into the shadows of the park (all at once it was a warm dry night, with silver highlights on the leaves, crickets imported from Fincham, moths swirling about the globes of the street-lamps), and as I went down on my knees the coachman's ears would redden and grow to twice their normal size and the horse would snort softly with approval. I tried to superimpose on her present look of concentration (*Miss Albers, who attended the Chapin School and Wheaton College, is currently a fashion editor at* Glee) the lunatic bliss I had, on several occasions, seen in her features, but the experiment failed. I just watched her, my heart out of control in my chest.

She had removed the spoon herself. "Sleepy time," she

said, on her feet now, reaching for my plate. "Do you have
a clean T-shirt?" she asked.

"Yes," I said. I was thinking, Wednesday; I'll propose on
Wednesday. Still stuck to my chair, I asked, "Are you free
Wednesday night?"

She stopped on the threshold of the bathroom and looked
at me with amusement.

"Let me consult with my secretary," she said. "What's
Wednesday night?"

"I don't know," I lied. "Dinner. A movie. We can go see
Doctor Zhivago."

I called my mother twice a month, late in the evening, when
the rates were low. She had never met Irina, not even on the
telephone, and it had taken me a year to teach her not to say
"Irene-a." I had sent her a windblown photograph snapped
by a helpful stranger, with Irina's camera, on the Nantucket
ferry the previous summer. It was a good excuse to write my
mother a letter, something I hadn't done in several years, but
it proved to be quite a task. Everything I wrote sounded stupid and artificially cheerful, and there had been an astonishing few seconds when, my pen poised over the envelope,
having just written, along with my address in the upper left
corner, the family name we had once shared, I couldn't find
her new married name anywhere in my brain. She herself
sent me newspaper clippings once in a while, which came
unaccompanied by any explanation. These were items whose
random nature puzzled and even alarmed me — an article describing community opposition to a development scheme near
her house, another one debunking a Mexican cure for cancer
(this must have been connected with my father's death). I
would read the first half of each one and then throw it out,
depressed.

On the telephone we spoke about our health, about money,
about the earthquakes at her end and the hurricane watches

at mine, and about our jobs; she worked for the Chamber of Commerce in Asuncion, California. Once a year she had a lot to say, when she returned from visiting her younger sister in Wisconsin. For some reason we both relished her accounts of these visits, catalogues of horrors that included a drunk husband or two, a daughter incapable of managing birth control, air-guitar-playing sons who took drugs I had never even heard of and crashed cars they borrowed from unaware acquaintances, all this amidst assiduous churchgoing and constant invocations of the Lord.

This time I called her from my office. I wanted to tell her about my plans. It was a change, to have something to say. My mother had just gotten up and I could hear her moving about a kitchen I had never seen, rattling cups and slamming the refrigerator door.

"I still have the ring your father gave me when we got engaged," she said. "Would you like to have that?"

"I'll fly out this weekend to get it," I said. "We haven't seen each other in over a year."

"Calm down," my mother said. "I'll insure it and send it UPS. Come out with her for a few days later on."

"You come to the wedding," I said. "It'll probably be here, or in a little town upstate called Fincham."

"I wouldn't miss that," my mother said.

"Let's invite the cousins," I said, imagining with pleasure the effect they would have on Mrs. Albers.

Then Mary Donoghue charged in with her daily bran muffin in a paper bag and her face like a steel shutter. I had to cut the conversation short just as my mother was beginning to warm up. Mary was the Food and Wine editor, however, and that gave me an idea.

"Mary, I need some advice," I said.

"What, hon," she said, her eyes bulging as she read the headline of the *New York Post*.

"My mother's coming to town," I lied. "I haven't seen her

in a year, I'd like to take her out Wednesday night. Some-
place romantic and cozy. Where should we go?"

"Ocean Four," Mary said.

"That's a thought. What about that Tourterelle place I keep
hearing about?"

"Real fancy," Mary said.

"I guess I couldn't get a table on short notice," I said.

"Yeah, yeah," Mary said. She bit into the muffin and then
wiped a crumb off her chin with her finger. "I'll give them a
call," she said through the muffin.

"Thanks a million," I said.

"Nothin', hon," Mary said. "Wednesday? Nine o'clock?
Two people? Your mother, I'll bet it's your mother," she
said. "Her tits," she added, chewing as she turned a page of
the paper. "I mean, look at these tits."

The ring was delivered to my office Wednesday morning,
but Irina had canceled dinner and gone home fifteen minutes
before, with menstrual cramps. I went to the men's room
with the package and opened it in one of the stalls, like a
mugger. Inside was a kitchen-sized Blue Star matchbox filled
with cotton. The ring was a disappointing object, a narrow
white-gold or platinum band with a small diamond clamped
in prongs. A Swiss's extravagance, I thought. I couldn't remember seeing it before. I was both moved and upset. I wished
there were someone I could show it to beforehand, to ask if
it was suitable; but the only people who occurred to me were
Irina, Mrs. Albers, and Nancy Eberstadt.

Since Irina and I weren't going to get engaged that evening, I had to come up with another plan. At noon, when
Mary left for her exercise class, I closed the door to our office
and made two phone calls. The first was to Tourterelle, where
I canceled our reservation. I was going to have to tell Mary;
in fact, I was going to have to buy her some flowers. Then
I called Jamie Schwartz. He was a friend of ours, a Wall

Streeter conveniently endowed with a house in East Hampton. Irina and I used to go there a couple of weekends each summer.

"Sorry about last weekend," I said. "I had to go up to Fincham and be Mrs. Albers' slave. But I was wondering if I could collect on the raincheck this Friday."

"I'm staying in town this weekend; I've lent the house to a colleague," Jamie said. "There may be a free bedroom. I can ask."

"Damn," I said. "I was going to propose to Irina."

Jamie laughed. He whooped into the telephone. He banged his fist on his desk. He said he'd retract the loan of the house. It was all mine.

"What's your plan? Is it the full nine yards? Are you going to kneel?" he asked.

"I'm going to tell her there's a black tie dinner on Friday night," I said. "When we're all dressed up I'll say that I want to go there on foot, by the beach — that it's just a few houses away. So we'll take off our shoes and go down to the ocean, and that's where I'm going to do it."

"You'd better say that they're short of champagne and they asked you to bring a bottle," Jamie said. "And you'll have to hide two glasses somewhere under your clothes. I'll tell you where to find them."

"Good idea," I said, thinking I would substitute a bottle of wine for the champagne, because Irina didn't like anything with bubbles. "The thing that worries me is, then what? We're all dressed up with nowhere to go."

"Don't worry about it," said Jamie, who had been married once, for a year, a long time ago. "At that point things take care of themselves, you'll see."

I got so excited about having the house that I couldn't work at all. This was much better than the original plan. I was staring at the green characters on my screen a few hours later when I heard Mary utter a cheerful "Hello, there!" and looked up to find Michael in my office.

While the rest of us were away in Fincham, Michael had allowed his host, the dry printmaker, to take him to an AA meeting. Apparently he had gotten hooked immediately. We knew about it because one of the tenets of the program held that he had to apologize to his mother and Irina for all the grief his drinking and drug taking had caused them. But Irina refused to rejoice in this development; she had seen him reform many times before.

A co-conspirator in the Fincham affair, which remained a guilty secret, I started at the sight of him.

"I wanted to go back to the archive," he said, "if it's all right. I'm interested in those old mags."

"Look, Michael," I said.

"Oh, come on," Michael said. "I'm not tearing pictures of girls in bathing suits out of old issues."

"Up to the library? Of course he can go," Mary said.

"Okay," I said. I fumbled inside my trouser pocket for my key ring. I pried the office key out and handed it across the desk.

"Do you remember where it is?" I asked.

"First door on the right. Thanks. Can I have this too?" he said, picking a yellow legal pad off my desk.

"Come back and visit when you're through," Mary said. Once he was gone, she asked, "Doesn't he have a job, or is he just wealthy?"

"He's very, very rich," I said, making mischief.

I still couldn't work. I began to wander about the offices. In the mailroom I poured myself a cup of tepid coffee and chatted with the two men who worked there. They had long ago given up trying to talk to me about sports — I had never fixated on American sports in the proper manner — and instead used me as the main repository for their complaints about the office manager. We also liked to argue over which of the girls were improving in looks and which had gained weight. Once these matters had been settled, I strolled down the back corridor to the art room, the most pleasant area of the magazine, where over the course of each month the next issue was gradually laid out, in black-and-white photostats, on the cork walls. The designers, Ginny, Frances, and Ann, who worked impossible hours and had the appealing black humor of the beleaguered, sat on stools at inclined drafting surfaces around the main work table, a wide field of carved-up photostats, drafting tools, and containers of congealing Chinese food. It was the only department where people didn't work on the telephone and a radio was allowed to play in the background. Ann, a sly, mobile girl, had a weakness for me that she expressed through constant teasing. She didn't look up from her work and continued to wield her metal ruler and razor knife without interruption. She wouldn't look at me even when she got up and brushed past me to go feed a sheet of type through the waxer. I followed her and watched this operation over her shoulder.

"Go away," she said. "You're bothering us. Don't you ever work? Don't you ever do anything but hang around the art department? Are you some sort of inspection officer at this magazine?"

At six o'clock, wanting to go home, I took the elevator upstairs to dislodge Michael from the library.

He had built three stacks of bound issues of *Glee* on the library table. Additional volumes lay open around him, under a rolling cloud of smoke. At his elbow stood a blue cardboard cup printed with images of the Acropolis and containing lees of coffee and ashes. Several sheets of my yellow legal pad were flipped over and curling with ink. Bent over like a schoolboy at an exam, Michael scribbled diligently with a ballpoint pen.

"They didn't have a masthead when they started," he said,

looking up. "Where do you think I could get my hands on one?"

"I wish you'd tell me what you're up to," I said. "It's making me nervous."

"Just snooping. I'm curious."

We replaced the books on the shelves and rode the elevator back down to my floor, Michael holding his evil-smelling cup and the pad. He had folded his notes in four and put them in the hip pocket of his khakis.

"Amazing thing, fashion," he said.

"Are you thinking of starting a magazine, or what?" I asked.

Michael found this funny. "Perhaps I should," he said. "Or a modeling agency. God."

When we got to my office he placed the cup atop the papers bulging out of my trash basket and picked up the telephone. He dialed two numbers but got no answer. I untangled the wilted newspaper and went through the movie listings. Many of them were missing, because Mary, before leaving early to go see her psychic, had cut out several articles. It was Wednesday, when the *Times* is bloated with food and wine.

"Michael," I said, "do you feel like sitting through four hours of *Doctor Zhivago* in the Village? We can just make it if we hurry."

I thought I was joking.

"Yes," he said brightly, putting the phone down after a third attempt. "I tried to see it once, but I was hung over and slept through most of it. Let's go. Come on," he said when he saw me hesitate. "Russia, love, and war. What more do you want?"

He placed one hand on his heart, tilted his head to the side, and hummed the opening bars of the theme song. He closed his eyes in bliss and put his arm around an imaginary feminine waist.

When I was ten years old, that waltz, distorted by the static of an old loudspeaker, had swirled almost continuously over the skating rink of my village in Switzerland. "Lara's Theme," it was called. I came close to laughing, half at Michael, half at my own nostalgia.

The theater smelled of popcorn and mildew, the soles of my loafers stuck to the floor, and all the seats tilted forward. Michael made sucking noises through a straw. As soon as the music started, launching the flashback, and there appeared before my eyes the movie-commonplace of a funeral in a storm, I knew that a tender nest of childhood memories was about to be overrun and crushed by Hollywood. I had been taken to see *Doctor Zhivago* on a class outing. I was much too small to follow the story, I hadn't even understood the identity of the orphaned boy at the funeral with the adult Zhivago, but in the darkness of that stuffy theater, where I was so rarely allowed to go and where everything was mysterious and important, certain images had bored into my mind: the icicles in Zhivago's beard, a convict chained to a bunk in a cattle wagon, a pair of lost eyeglasses on the ground, an enormous red patch of blood in the snow. I had had nightmares about them. Then the passing weeks softened these memories, gradually blending the fierce snows of Russia with those among which I walked every day to the village, my skates tied together by their laces and hanging from my left shoulder, my hockey stick balanced in my other hand, already hearing, more often than not, that haunting waltz in the distance. As I grew up, *Doctor Zhivago* had become, in my memory, an infinitely truer and more beautiful movie that was secretly about my childhood.

For a moment I considered getting up and leaving, but soon my present self became absorbed in the story, in that same old music, in the luxury of the Moscow sets and the wonderful villainy of Komarovsky, the heavy. I had no recollection at all of Lara herself from my boyhood viewing, but now I was moved by the actress's beauty and her youth. The last reel was even more scratched than the previous ones, the sound more muffled, Zhivago had already turned white with pain and clutched his chest on a snowbound street, and though my trousers itched and one of my feet was completely asleep, I didn't want any of this to end. When we stepped out of the theater it was night and I was in love. I was humming. I wanted to skate. I had to fight the urge to abandon Michael and go home to call Irina. Michael was rolling Russian names around his mouth as we walked.

"Strrrelnikov. Yuriatin. Outrageous movie," he said. "But a completely unreadable novel. It's weird, his poetry . . . Hell, apart from Blok, and Mandelstam, who had the same birthday as I do, by the way . . . Listen," he said, putting his hand on my shoulder and stopping me on the pavement. He pursed the fingers of his right hand and held them before my chest. " 'I was born on the night between the second and the third of January in the uncertain year of eighteen-ninety something or other, and the centuries surround me with their fire.' God!" he said. "Strrrelnikov. And now what we need is a glass of vuodka," he continued, pronouncing it with Isaac Behr's accent. "Where can we drink vodka and hear Gypsies?"

"In Brighton Beach, but I'm not at all sure about the Gypsies. I could have a bite to eat," I said. I didn't like this talk about vodka.

"Let's go to Brighton Beach," Michael said.

"It takes an hour to get there. But we can go some other night, with Irina, and we can take some old crony of your grandfather's as a scout."

"My grandfather knew Pasternak when they were kids," Michael said. "Or actually my great-grandparents were friends with Pasternak's father, who was a painter, like my great-grandmother." He paused to light a cigarette. "He did the illustrations for *War and Peace,* and when Tolstoy saw them they matched his own imagination so perfectly he claimed there had been some sort of ESP."

He tossed the match into the street. All the stores were still open, and the sidewalk was crowded with slow summer pedestrians in a chaotic diversity of types — people of every imaginable ethnic combination, adolescents whose clothes and manner denoted allegiance to various rock 'n' roll subcultures, white heavy-metal kids from the boroughs, hip-hop black kids, downtown punk-rock kids, arty NYU students, black leather homosexuals and lavender cotton homosexuals, grizzled old winos and jittery crackheads, bony bearded academics with astonishing shoes, local Italian workers popping around the corner on errands, towering Scandinavian tourists looking for a place to sit down. Michael and I had just fast-forwarded through Kuratkin's entire life, from the coziness of aristocratic life in turn-of-the-century Russia to the wild bazaar of Manhattan in 1984, a time that seemed to me ahead of itself, or at least it did that night, because the strange fauna on Bleecker Street had a kind of postapocalyptic look to them, as though we were all survivors of the Third World War we had been brought up to expect.

"The problem is," Michael said, "I've got about ten dollars."

"Don't worry about it."

"I know where we should go," he said. "We'll go to Big Tam's. It's just around the corner."

"Never been there."

"It's a person, not a place. Though she weighs about four hundred pounds," he added. "You've got to meet her. She gets up at six in the evening and never goes out before eleven. Until then she's at home," he said, implying quotation marks around the last two words. "Once in a while she gives the wildest parties."

"This place looks all right," I said as we passed an Italian café. I didn't want to start with strangers. "What about this place?"

"I'm taking you to Tam's," Michael said. "Live a little. Store up some experience before you don the marital shackles." He looked at me sideways. "Are you going to get hitched with Irina, or what?"

"I was going to propose tonight," I said.

"Hah!" Michael said.

"I had everything organized, starting with dinner at Tourterelle," I complained, "but she said she wasn't feeling well and bagged out on me. She's having her period."

Michael grabbed my shoulder again and laughed.

"That's the way it's going to be," he said, shaking his head. He thought it was hilarious. "You're signing up for a lifetime of it!"

He grabbed my other shoulder with his cigarette hand and slammed me on the back.

"Okay. Celebration," he said. "Big Tam's."

We had some trouble getting in. Michael had to identify himself twice over the intercom, and there was a long delay before the door buzzed open. Something about the house seemed familiar as we entered, but then I decided that all the brownstones in this part of town were probably laid out according to the same plan. A short man in black tie and cowboy boots came out of a kitchen at the end of a hallway to shake our hands.

"I'm Ernie," he said. "Tam's getting dressed to go out to dinner, but she asked me to welcome you. Make yourself at home upstairs; help yourself to the bar."

"This is purely a social visit," Michael told him.

Ernie smiled and displayed the staircase, as though introducing it. A small dog yapped somewhere behind a closed door.

Again I experienced a feeling of familiarity as we ap-

proached the bend at the top of the stairs, and when we walked
into a room that stretched the whole length and breadth of
the house, one of its walls painted a bright Chinese red, I
remembered coming to a party here, at least two years before, with my previous girlfriend and some college pals
of hers. We had come from a nightclub, very late, our ears
bruised by loud music, and this room had been so packed
with night-crawling New Yorkers that I had had to hold
my glass above my head and walk sideways. I also remembered Tam, a female Buddha painfully ascending the stairs,
holding the folds of a black dress out of the way of delicate patent leather pumps. I had been told she was a cocaine
dealer.

At one end of the room, behind translucent white curtains
that billowed inward as we passed, two sets of French doors
gave onto a narrow stone balcony. The windows at the other
side, above the street, were shuttered. Seated on one of the
couches, with a man beside her, was a young girl of extrav-
agant beauty, a very long creature all in black, her hair and
skin an almost uniform shade of gold, her eyes so green that
I saw their color from the other end of the room. She had her
elbow on the back of the couch and her golden head resting
on her fist. She and the man wore identical boots of creamy
black leather that bunched up at the ankles. I thought that I
had also seen her before; this was an illusion I often had when
meeting a very beautiful girl, but in this case there was a
reason: it was the model called Blue, who often appeared in
the pages and sometimes on the cover of *Glee*. That very
afternoon I had seen a whole series of pictures of her, almost
naked, on the cork walls of the art room, and I had wondered, while staring at them, how I was going to remain
faithful to Irina for the rest of my life — what it would take
in the way of discipline and resignation, ten, twenty years
down the road. I had come up with no answer except that

many people had been faithful before me and therefore I could be so too. Besides, other fancies — my wanderings around the world, my exploits in exploration and war, my career as a foreign correspondent — all these had faded without my having to fight them, overshadowed by the task of living in the world, leaving behind only the occasional twitch and pang. So it would be with Blue, though that did not mean I couldn't bask in her beauty this evening. The green eyes were like a lock.

Her companion declined to tell us his name but greeted Michael and me with what I thought were Spanish grunts while looking at a coffee stain on my shirt; then he stared away vaguely, stroking his neck with his fingertips. Blue had a thin little voice, a Southern accent, and a kind of earnest friendliness where I had expected ice. When I explained about *Glee,* she expressed a degree of delight that would have seemed sarcastic — "Well, isn't that . . ." — if it hadn't been for the doll voice. "Would you like a nut?" she asked, pushing the bowl across the table. "Let me show you where Tam hides the hootch." The Spaniard looked down at his glass, saw that it was still full, and stared off into his boredom again as Blue unfolded from the couch. With Michael, I followed her to the row of cabinets along the wall. Each of her legs was like a whole other girl.

"It's all here," she said in her tiny voice, opening two of the cabinets. The one on the right was a refrigerator.

"What are you having?" I asked Michael.

"Vodka, vodka. Are you kidding? We just saw *Doctor Zhivago,*" he told Blue.

"Doctor who?" Blue said, a mischievous light coming on in her eyes. She thought the doctor had something to do with drugs.

Just being in Blue's presence made me feel guilty about Irina. With Michael drinking, it felt much worse.

For some time already the staircase had been creaking and

thumping, and now the enormous Tam surfaced in the room, a snuffling pug tucked under her arm like a football.

"Oh, look," she said. *"Everybody's here!"*

Then it was four in the morning. Blue, the Spaniard, and Tam had not returned from dinner. Others had come and gone, cared for by Ernie, but now I was all alone with Michael. The inside of my skull was fizzing with alcohol and cocaine, and my heart was beating much too fast. I had smoked a great number of Michael's cigarettes. I couldn't drink whiskey anymore and had switched to beer, but it tasted impossibly bitter.

Michael was telling me what he was going to do with his grandfather's money. He was going to take a year off (though he didn't say from what — perhaps from his dissertation on Pushkin) to travel and research his grandfather's life. He was going to write his grandfather's memoirs, he said, in the first person, using his grandfather's voice. Now he was describing various high points to me — Kuratkin sneaking out of his parents' house in Petrograd and running off to join Denikin's army; Kuratkin struggling on crutches to the Odessa docks to board the very last boat to Constantinople — while stubbing out another cigarette in the smoldering ashtray. Earlier in the evening there had been an unpleasant moment for me; it had become evident, in the course of a previous monologue of Michael's (about the effect of Kuratkin's death on Mrs. Albers' psyche) that Irina had left the office that morning not because she was feeling sick, as she had claimed, but because she had an appointment to see a real estate agent. I was aware that all the Alberses liked to operate in secrecy, but I had already known that she was looking for an apartment and couldn't understand why she would now try to hide it from me. At any rate, everything was going to be settled on Saturday. We were going to take a walk on a beach, barefoot, in evening clothes; we were going to toast each other as the sun went down behind the dunes, and throw the glasses in the surf, and then a whole new life would begin.

I was waiting for a chance to tell Michael all about it.

Even Michael was going to pull himself together now and write this thing he was describing with such passion. As soon as he paused for breath I was going to tell him how important and wonderful this whole evening had been: what the movie meant to me, and how it tied in, in such intricate and mysterious ways, with his plan to invent his grandfather's memories, versions of which we had just seen on that scratchy screen on Bleecker Street. I would tell him something I had never told even Irina: how thrilling it was to think that I had probably seen her several times when we were children — on another continent, when Mrs. Albers would come to watch Michael compete in a track meet, or pick up his prizes at the ceremony that marked the end of the school year, or on less festive occasions: noon on Saturdays, the hour of approaching liberation, when one's attention would begin to exclude the droning teacher and latch instead onto the parents' cars coasting up the last curve of the driveway, the popping and crunching noise their tires made on the gravel of the courtyard, which spread outward from underneath a giant maple, its vast trunk encircled by a wooden bench. I had no memory of seeing Irina, but I loved to imagine her there, at thirteen or fourteen, standing beside her mother's rented car, excited at the prospect of seeing her brother but doing her best to keep from looking toward the row of classroom windows, because they were filled with boys' eyes.

Michael, however, would not stop talking. As he talked he stared at my hands, which were unwrapping a little waxed-paper envelope of cocaine. Michael was flipping a ring between his fingers. I was surprised to recognize it as my mother's engagement ring, but at the cost of a small effort I remembered that I had taken it out of my pocket to show it to him a long, long time ago.

IX

I woke very late, sick and in pain. My whole head hurt, especially in the front. I could breathe only through my mouth. It felt as though I had been punched in the face repeatedly. Worse than that was the feeling of humiliation; worse still was the agitation, the inability to lie still and go back to sleep, the cacophony of disconnected thoughts and phrases leaping about my mind; but the real torture was the nausea. Already an hour late for work, I blundered across my room to call the office. At first there was no dial tone, and it took me some time to figure out that I had unplugged the telephone on coming home. Neutralizing the phone was part of a drill I had elaborated in college, where my companions and I had brought astonishing hangovers on ourselves. Hangover prevention and cure had been, in those days, important topics of conversation. Remembering this, and finding nothing changed, deepened my misery.

It was Mary Donoghue who answered. I could tell that she had just arrived, because in the pause before she said hello — she had an infuriating habit of holding the receiver in limbo if something else needed her attention — I heard our secretary relaying the morning's messages.

"You sound terrible," Mary said immediately.

"Food poisoning," I explained.

"You got food poisoning at Tourterelle?" she asked.

"What?"

"At Tourterelle? Food poisoning?"

"Oh," I said. "Mary, I forgot to tell you, I had to cancel."

"I didn't go to any trouble to get you a table, so don't think twice about it," she said.

"Mary, I've got to go," I said. I could feel a new surge of nausea coming on. "I'm going to pull the phone out and try to sleep, so I'll be unreachable."

"Okay, you feel better, hon," she said, relenting. "You really sound like a mess."

Immediately after throwing up, when I knew I would have a few minutes of respite, I took the two Valium I had cadged from Michael some hours earlier and waited under a cool shower for them to take effect. Then, in rubber-legged relief, I went back to bed.

When I woke again at four in the afternoon I was groggy and ashamed but no longer quite so sick. I drank almost a quart of water from a glass orange juice bottle I kept in the refrigerator. Though I still wanted to hide under my eiderdown, behind drawn blinds, with the air conditioning on and the phone unplugged, I knew that I had to act. For one thing, a meal would accelerate my recovery (I had a sudden mouthwatering craving for something spicy, perhaps some chili, or some Hot and Sour soup from the nearby Chinese restaurant); for another, Irina would by now have tried to reach me several times. There was a chance that, unable to raise me on the phone, she might show up after work with a plastic pot of chicken soup from my favorite delicatessen, or, if she had heard at the office that I had food poisoning, simply a bunch of irises; this was standard procedure between us. I longed for her warmth and her arms, but I didn't want to tell her about the night I'd had. I didn't even want to be tempted to tell her. I called her to make sure she wouldn't come.

"Darling, I feel wretched," I said.

"Really?" she asked.

"I've got food poisoning," I said.

"Really?"

"I was sick all night, didn't get any sleep."

She did not comment or offer comfort.

"Is everything all right?" I asked.

"I had a difficult morning," Irina said.

"I'm sorry," I said with an effort. "What happened?"

After a silence — it may have been a sigh — Irina said: "The editor in chief of this magazine was the first person to arrive here this morning, as usual. Well — actually I think I'll make it short. I don't particularly feel like talking to you."

"Hey, wait a minute," I said.

"You wait a minute," she said. "Just let me tell you what happened. When Nancy got to the office she found a strange man asleep on her couch. She rushed back to the elevator and went down to get a security guard. When they brought the guy down, his nose was bleeding and everyone thought they'd roughed him up, but in the end it turned out they hadn't. By that time Frances and Ginny had arrived and everyone was waiting downstairs in the lobby. They were going to take him into that little office they have there and call the police, but then Ginny realized the guy was Michael."

"Oh, God," I said.

"He said you'd given him the key to the office," Irina said.

"Oh, God," I said.

"He threw up in the lobby. It must have been nerves, he used to do that as a child. It may be true that you really are sick," Irina said before hanging up. "If it is, I hope you die of it."

Next morning I was completely recovered. As I rode the subway to the office I decided it would be safest for my job as well as my soul if I acted conciliatory but firm, if I showed Nancy an awareness of the gravity of my crime but only minimal contrition. It amused me, somewhat grimly, to realize that in adopting this stance I was modeling myself on Michael, for it had been a long time since I had had to answer for bad behavior to anyone but a girlfriend, and now that I was trying to settle in advance on an attitude to wear before my inquisitor, the image that came to my aid was of an adolescent Michael facing our giant headmaster one evening in the yellow hall outside the school dining room, with the dinner bell ringing insistently in the background and several other boys, myself among them, loitering shamelessly. Even at the time I hadn't known what infraction Michael had committed, but I had been impressed by the polite and utterly unrepentant attention with which he had heard out that large and angry man, who happened, that day, to be wearing his military uniform, and ever since then I remembered it whenever I found myself in similar circumstances.

I knocked on Nancy's door, which was open. Her back was turned; her desk stood diagonally at the center of the office, so that when sitting at the wing that supported her computer she faced the sky over the West Side and New Jersey. She was scrolling a luminous green story upward on her screen, and as she swiveled around in her chair I tried to read her lacquered face, but it was opaque. Irrationally I felt that she too must have known that the illness that had kept me at home the previous day had been self-induced. I was even convinced that she knew about every terrible thing I had done at Big Tam's, not just the drug taking and drinking but also the disgraceful cocaine confidences Michael and I had exchanged until dawn.

"Are you feeling better?"

"I feel fine," I said.

"Good. Good," she said, without irony.

"I wanted to apologize about Irina's brother," I said. "It's partly my fault, I'm the one who lent him the key."

"I know," she said. She was looking at her hands, which were struggling on the desk with a matching paper knife and scissors and their red leather scabbard. Behind her back, abandoned, possibly being erased, the green characters continued their jerky ascent on the computer screen. "I don't know quite what to say to you, though," she said, looking up. "I'm not really sure I want to know why you would give Irina's brother a key to the office, but I guess I ought to ask."

So I tried to explain about Michael's visits to the library upstairs, his curiosity about his late grandfather, and how I had forgotten to retrieve the key. I had rehearsed this tale before coming; I had planned to tell it in a casual, uncomplicated manner that would make it seem no big deal, but now it sounded faintly ridiculous to my own ears.

"Somehow he got locked out of the place where he was staying. He's very upset about his grandfather," I added. (That was how Mrs. Albers habitually tried to account for Michael's misdeeds — by attributing them to some recent tragedy, named or merely hinted at. Irina, on the other hand, had some time ago taken to explaining them with uncharacteristic terseness: "My brother is an alcoholic," she would say.)

"Well, I would have thought you had better judgment than that," she said.

"Uh," I said. If she wasn't going to fire me, I was prepared to let her have the last word and slink out.

"I'm aware that because of Irina he's more than just a friend to you," she said, "but to tell you the truth I've never been very happy about this in-house romance."

"Nancy," I said in an indulgent tone of voice, "you're the one who ran not one but two articles on the subject in the last eighteen months, and if I recall, your position on these matters was —"

"Be that as it may," she interrupted. "Be that as it may," she repeated more slowly, "I want that key on my desk by tomorrow morning."

"Actually, I need that key to get into the men's room," I said.

Then we stared at each other for a moment.

The telephone was ringing in my office when I walked in. It was Irina, getting ready to come down from her mother's.

"I just called to warn you," she said. "I don't want you to try to talk to me. For the moment you're just a guy who works in the same office as me."

"Look, you can't blame me entirely for what Michael —"

"Yeah, but did you have to tell him about Papa's ashes? Do you really think it was any of your business?" she asked.

"What? What about your grandfather's ashes?"

"Why did you tell him about Fincham? Why did you —"

"I didn't say a word about Fincham," I said.

"How can you try to deny it? What kind of idiot do you think I am?"

"I swear —"

"Oh, don't lie," she said, with despair.

"How can you possibly think," I began, and then I remembered. Or at least I thought I remembered. It was like trying to catch a slippery dream by the tail. A great wave of heat swam up through my body. A lump appeared in my throat. Maybe I had. I thought I might have.

"Are you still there?"

"I'm here," I said. "Irina —"

"Well, goodbye, then," she said.

I hadn't noticed Mary Donoghue's arrival. She was seated at her desk, carefully unwrapping aluminum foil from around two hot dogs covered in steaming sauerkraut.

"Mary," I said, "it's nine-thirty in the morning."

"Don't ask," she said. "Don't say another word."

She slid the first one toward her mouth, pinching the bun between her thumb and middle finger.

"You've got problems too, eh," I said, suddenly fond of her.

"Today I'm going to eat myself to death," Mary said, and with her free hand she waved away the dragon's breath rising from her mouth.

Irina didn't look at me all day. Whenever I had to visit her end of the offices I bypassed her desk by using the art department as a corridor. It was a hectic day; we were preparing to close the September issue, the fattest of the year. At home after work I tried to write a note to Irina, wanting to send it up to Central Park West with some flowers. I used up all my best paper, and then several sheets of *Glee* letterhead, filched from the office. Nothing sounded right. I couldn't find any middle ground between abjectness and self-justification. Finally I settled on telling her that I loved her and that I was sorry, counting on the flowers to make up for the poverty of the message. I thought of delivering them myself, but leaving them with the doorman might look cowardly, while taking them up to the apartment in person would not only make the note stupidly redundant but would also entail facing a still angry Irina, in whose eyes, besides, I didn't want to appear desperate. It was now getting late and the idea of venturing out into New York had become distasteful. I put it off until the next day and had them delivered to the office.

"Please don't send me flowers. Please," she said. I had just walked by her desk, having tired of making detours, and she stood up in my wake and followed me to the water cooler. "I'll get over this, one way or another, but for the moment I don't know what to do with you. I just don't know." The irises, however, were standing by her telephone, in a green vase that had been used until that morning to hold address tags in the mailroom.

"Look, you can't just go on pretending that I don't exist," I said, but she was already walking away and I was left with my thumb on the button of the water cooler, no longer thirsty. I had meant to tell her that she was making me pay for Michael's delinquency, and not just its most recent manifestation but a full ten years of it. One of the stylists dashed across the corridor and into a colleague's office, grasping in her right hand a sheaf of pink message slips.

"It's me," I heard the stylist say, "in a darling new blouse. Do you love me in it? Do you still love me?"

So that week I settled into the doghouse usually inhabited by Michael. The hours at the office were awkward, but I found it not unpleasant to have my evenings to myself. I saw movies: it was the time when the big summer blockbusters are released, and although they were all old news to me, because the production companies' propaganda flowed into *Glee*'s offices months in advance, I liked the standing in line on warm nights among uncharacteristically cheerful New Yorkers, the promise of spectacle, the previews of forthcoming movies. I tried to read several novels I had bought and neglected. Unexpected difficulties arose in that regard, however: I kept examining the characters' relationships for similarities to my troubles with Irina, which ruined all those books for me; I never got past the initial chapters.

I found myself keeping my apartment much neater than

usual. At first I thought it was because I was spending more time there, but then I realized that I half expected Irina to show up unannounced, in tears, unable to be without me for another minute.

I was vacuuming the floor one evening — using an old dachshundlike Electrolux of Mrs. Albers' that I had borrowed six months earlier and failed to return — when I thought I heard the phone ringing over the roar of the machine. I was at that moment in the midst of upending my bed, which stood too low for me to slide the aluminum pipe underneath, and I left it balanced precariously on its side while I dashed across the room, lifting my feet high so as not to trip over anything. I paused on the way to yank the plug out of the wall, but because the whine of the turbine was still subsiding, because I had expected to hear Irina's voice, because, moreover, my attention remained fixed on the bed, which I feared would topple over and crush the coffee table, Michael had to identify himself no less than three times, at last losing patience and yelling his name, which, in turn, angered me.

"Look, pal," I said, keeping an eye on the bed, "you've gotten me in a whole lot of trouble."

"At work?" Michael asked, concerned.

"Well, that too. I meant with you sister."

"Oh, that," he said. "I know all about that. She was trying to bawl me out yesterday, but all she could do was complain about you. Well, not complain, exactly. She seems to be amazed that you could be so foolish as to have me for a friend. At least that's the way I interpret it. I thought you might let me buy you dinner tomorrow to make up for it. I'm going back to Boston on Sunday, and then I'm off to Europe."

"I can't have dinner," I lied. Then, catching myself, I said, "I can manage a drink. Can you bring me that key?"

"What key? Oh, yes, the key," he said.

Twenty-four hours later, after acquiring a sunburn from reading the afternoon away, or attempting to, on a bench in Central Park, I stepped into a restaurant off Third Avenue that was paneled entirely in well-polished oak. In fall or winter the effect would have been reminiscent of a men's club; now, on a warm July evening, it had a bogus nautical feel, heightened by the brass fixtures of the bar. It was called Cuthbert's, and it was famous for the snobbery of its owner, who bore unself-consciously the name of Eichmann, and the indifference of the food he served. There was something typical and annoying about Michael's insistence that we meet there, though I couldn't have said exactly what. Perhaps I worried about feeling out of place there, among expensive East Siders, in his somewhat squalid company. He was late, of course.

Above the twinned tiers of glinting bottles in the mirror was a ship's clock that allowed me to keep track of Michael's tardiness. It was surprising to see how many of the other patrons I knew by sight, by reputation, or even personally, especially because I would have expected their kind, at that particular moment, to be drinking wine on perfect lawns overlooking the ocean. Here was a superb couple I thought I recognized from the photographs in the back pages of some magazine, the woman golden, the man all silver; two or three others — a long effeminate fellow with a drinker's ruined nose, a stiff frosted woman wearing sunglasses even in this burnished gloom — I had seen in Madison Avenue bookstores or on the Hampton jitney the summer before. The man presiding at one of the better tables in the front was not, as I had first suspected, the gallery owner who had delivered Kuratkin's eulogy but a famous theatrical agent; there at the bar, whispering into the ear of a disturbingly attractive blonde, looking very prosperous, was a former classmate of mine from college whom I had last known as a total nerd — whom I remembered chiefly, in fact, for his habit of wearing galoshes to class when it rained. And now, coming in off the warm asphalt of Third Avenue, was Isaac Behr — funny that he too should go in for this kind of place — followed, more surprisingly still, astonishingly, by Irina, who smiled as she spoke over her shoulder to someone bringing up the rear: the solution to the puzzle, Michael Albers, in the jacket of the suit he had worn to Kuratkin's funeral. He was bobbing up and down and swaying from side to side as he looked for me over Isaac Behr's stooped shoulders.

It was Irina who spotted me first. I saw immediately, by the way her face hardened, that Michael had sprung the same trap on both of us. He beamed at me innocently, taking Isaac's elbow to lead him over.

"I don't know if you've met," he said. "This is my friend —"

"Yes," Isaac answered unexpectedly. He gave me an enormous limp hand. "We met in the elevator but did not introduce each other," he added, injecting a ghostly third party, perhaps Kuratkin himself, into the proceedings.

"Hello, darling," I said to Irina. "Here, have my seat."

"We need a table," Isaac said. "I don't like stools. After two whiskies I fall off." He bent at the knees and hooded his eyes in demonstration. Then, abruptly, he thrust his bald head at me, his face burst into a radiant smile, and he uttered a high-pitched whinny.

"Michael," a voice quavered lower down. A small otter-like man had joined us. "Where have you been?" he said, drawing the words out through his nose. He clearly meant to be cordial but sounded querulous instead.

"Eichmann," Michael told us after pumping the otter's paw. Then he designated each of us in turn: "My sister Irina, my brother-in-law Patrick," he said, "Isaac Behr . . . I know you're busy and it's a lot to ask, but could we have a table just for drinks? We can't decide whether we're hungry."

"Of course," Eichmann said a number of times. "But it'll

have to be upstairs." He led us briskly through the tables to the foot of the staircase, questioning Michael about his health and activities but clearly not hearing the answers. Then he waved us upward to the less crowded and less elegant of his two dining rooms.

"What's this brother-in-law gig?" Irina asked Michael as we climbed.

"Just a term of endearment," I interjected. I meant to ask Michael how he'd gotten to be such a regular here, but before I could start, he addressed Isaac in Russian. The only word I recognized was "Siberia," pronounced with a short *i*.

"Eh," Isaac answered in English. "Looks better than Siberia. More food," he explained. "Even champagne. I think that's what we need, no? Champagne?"

"Just a Perrier for me," Michael said as we sat down.

"I still have this," I said, having brought my drink from the bar.

"Then just for Irosha and me," Isaac said. "Do you have adequate slippers for me to drink from?" he asked Irina, repeating the performance of the butting head and the whinny before hiking up the tablecloth to look at her feet. She withdrew them demurely under her chair.

"Irina doesn't like champagne," I said.

"I could have told him that myself, thanks," Irina said.

"Okay, red wine," Isaac said, breezily.

So we sat at a table in a restaurant and chatted like normal people. I began to feel tremendous admiration for Michael. How was it that somebody like him, whose life was in all respects a disaster, could find the peace of mind and self-assurance to bring a quarreling couple together in public? Where could I acquire the same virtues? And it was working, too. Compelled by circumstance — mostly the presence of Isaac, who, having decided that he was hungry and ordered a steak, had half turned from the table, hitched one knee over the other, and was rocking a foot back and forth, its loafer hang-

ing from his toes — Irina was being civil to me. As a matter
of fact a spirit of peace and cordiality seemed to have descended upon our table, for Michael was now coolly discussing the possible sale of the house in Fincham, a measure that
would increase his mother's capital — it was time, he was
saying, to reorganize her finances, time for her to start living
solely on income — whereas I had imagined that Fincham
still couldn't be mentioned in his presence without igniting
some fearful outburst. It occurred to me that now was the
right time to ask Irina out on a date, in the presence of Michael and Isaac, but I made the mistake of putting it off, waiting for a suitable moment. Halfway into his New York sir-
loin, some of which was hanging over the edge of his plate
and dripping grease onto the tablecloth, Isaac had just declared that, having secured a small grant, he was treating us
"young people" to dinner (though only he was eating) when
Irina overtook me.

"Do you want to play hooky on Monday?" she asked.

That was something we had done several times — three
times, to be precise — in our first months together. One perfect day we had gone to Jones Beach; another day, in the fall,
we had spent at the Metropolitan Museum, out of the rain;
and on the third, after a midweek party at which we had
stayed very late, we simply never got out of bed. It had pleased
me, then, that Irina should be relaxed enough about her job
to do that; but we'd had to stop when it became known among
our colleagues that we were having an affair, because our
coincident absences would have been noticed. Her suggestion that we do it again, rather than just have dinner, for
instance, on Sunday night, seemed a generous gesture of rec-
onciliation.

"We can't both call in sick on the same day," I said.

"One of us calls in sick — you do it, say, and then I claim
that I have a business lunch and a doctor's appointment and
a couple of appointments in the market."

"What about tomorrow? Why don't we do something to-morrow?"

"I'm seeing apartments all day," she said.

"I already called in sick one day last week, if you remember," I said.

"Philip," Isaac said.

"No, Patrick," I said.

"No, flip a coin," he said, "to see who gets sick on Monday."

He leaned to one side and scooped from his trouser pocket a handful of change, along with the corkscrewed remains of a paper napkin and some lint that stuck to his huge blunt fingers. He selected a quarter, placed it on the tablecloth, and dropped the rest into his jacket pocket.

"Okay, heads," Irina said. "If it's heads, Patrick is sick."

"Heads it will be," Isaac said. He picked up the quarter again, wedged it between his wide thumbnail and middle finger, and flicked it upward. It soared over our plates, evaded the hand that grasped for it, and dived into Michael's glass. A spray of spots appeared on the front of Irina's dress, from inside which there issued a loud gasp. The patrons at the nearest tables turned to look. Michael leaned over and peered into the bottom of his glass.

"Yes, heads," he said.

Ignoring her victory, Irina continued to dab at the spots with her napkin. In trying to see what she was doing she forced out a small double chin whose rare appearances had always inspired a special tenderness in me.

"It's lucky you're drinking only water," Isaac said to Michael. "You couldn't have seen the coin through this sea-dark wine." He raised the bottle and poured into Irina's glass, and then mine, and then his own.

We met in the rock 'n' roll section of Tower Records at twelve-thirty and headed down to SoHo. We were going to be rec-

onciled, cautiously at first, while wandering around art galleries and clothing stores, among tourists and honeymoon-
ers. Once the apologies had been made and accepted, once
they had come to seem, in retrospect, not just excessive but
unnecessary, we would return to my apartment on some pre-
text or another; and late afternoon would find me lying face
down in a cool pillow, in the breeze that swelled and swung
the blinds, while my future wife, her hair wet and her moist
body wrapped in a towel, called the office to say she wouldn't
be able to make it back after all.

Upstairs at the Barston Gallery there were large installa-
tions that replicated the neglected corners and surfaces of
imaginary dwellings: a stretch of linoleum floor on which
rested a television, a pack of cigarettes next to a butt-filled
ashtray, a dog-eared *TV Guide,* and, I think, a pair of nail
clippers (it may have been a large cockroach), a paint-spat-
tered kitchen sink in which empty apple juice bottles con-
sorted with soiled dishes and paintbrushes, a pile of sneakers.
All these objects, including the linoleum and the sink, were
made of wood, stone, or wax, carelessly painted and scored
with random pencil marks. Some were unidentifiable. Irina
stalked around these displays intently, her eyes traveling from
one to the other, her lips always on the verge of speaking.
There was something in this work that appealed to her coun-
terfeiter's soul. I had forgotten that she got this way around
exhibits that intrigued her and tended to make a spectacle of
herself. My own interest was already exhausted, and while
she stood before an open closet, empty except for a tangle of
wooden hangers and wooden shoes, I experienced a moment
of satisfaction as I pictured my own room, which I had vac-
uumed and dusted again that morning.

"If you see anything you think is really good," I told a
silent Irina as we climbed down the steep stairs to the street,
"you should say something. We never get good young artists
into the magazine. Ginny's supposedly in charge of art, but

it always looks as though she's five years behind whatever's going on."

"Why do I never have time to do my own work?" she asked.

"Because you wouldn't have met me if you hadn't taken a job," I said. "But now that we've met, you can leave *Glee* and do anything you want."

"Starve, you mean."

We were outside, squinting. A cruel midday sun shone on everything. There was no shadow anywhere. The block was deserted except for a moving van on the corner, from which two men were unloading filing cabinets on a dolly. Earlier, in the record store, we had made plans to visit several galleries, and now I didn't remember where we were going next. Irina didn't seem inclined to discuss the matter.

"But I have to earn *money*," she was saying.

"Relax, will you?" I said. "You've got some money, you don't pay rent, you don't have to buy food —"

"I'm moving out. I can't live with my mother at my age."

"You know, I love it that you live with your mother," I said. "It makes me feel that I'm comin' a-courtin' when I go up there. But listen," I said. "Let's move in together. Not into my hellhole, we'll find a bigger place."

As we walked, Irina had climbed onto a steel loading dock in front of a building, and now she stopped there, perched above me. She banged her heel on it, twice, just to hear the clang. I had to shield my eyes to see her.

"No," she said. "Oh, God," she said in a helpless voice, "I think I've got to do this now. I've got to tell you this just isn't going to work out. You know it; we're bad for each other."

"Do you get this way every time you come across another artist whose work you like?" I asked.

I was trying out something new. The argument she wanted

to provoke was a normal if unpleasant stage in our reconcil-
iations. In the past I had always suffered it stoically; I had
never tried to kid her out of it.

"You like me for all the wrong reasons," she said.

"Come on down from there. It's an unfair advantage; you're
giving me a stiff neck," I said. "You're absolutely right, it's
obvious we're completely incompatible." I opened the issue
of *The New Yorker* I'd been carrying under my arm and started
walking again.

"I want to have an affair," she said when she caught up.

"You are having an affair, with me. Come on, we have to
decide what to see next."

"I think I'm going to sleep with Isaac Behr," she said.

We both stopped walking in order to laugh.

"I forgot to tell you," she said. "Before dinner on Saturday
he came over to the apartment to help us go through some
of Papa's letters that were in Russian, because Michael can't
manage the handwriting. There was a whole pile of letters
that I'd brought down from Fincham that were all from the
same person. They were spaced exactly one month apart and
they all began exactly the same way: 'Dear Nikolai Vassiliev-
ich, thank you for the fish.' After opening the third one Isaac
was laughing so hard, there were tears streaming down his
face."

"Here," I said. "Small papier-mâché constructions, some
of them representing mutilated bodies. Sounds great. Are you
hungry yet? Listen, think of them up at the office, stabbing
each other in the back under the neons. Aren't we clever to
have come down here?"

"No, wait," Irina said, and she stopped again. "Wait a
minute. I have to tell you this now, I have to do it now."

"Oh, no," I said.

"Okay. I have to tell you I don't want you to come to the
office tomorrow," she said.

"What, again?" I said.

"We have to break up. I can't go on like this anymore."

"Well, neither can I," I said. I said it calmly, although I was beginning to lose patience. I was about to tell her, still calmly, not to start on this topic again. But she had misunderstood me: a look of hesitant relief had floated into her face. It made me feel sick.

"I was going to ask you to marry me," I said.

"I know I'm a monster,"'she said because of the way I was staring at her. "It's not even worth saying I'm sorry —"

"I want you to marry me," I said.

It was amazing, how easy it was after all.

"Stop saying that," she said.

"I'm tired of all this!" I shouted.

"Don't shout," she said. "I know it's my fault. I'm the one who's breaking us up, so I'm the one who's going to leave. I gave notice last week. Tomorrow's my last day. There's going to be this silly party for me."

"Wait a minute," I said. "You gave notice last week?"

"Yes."

"Why didn't I find out?"

"I said not to tell anyone yet."

"You mean you said not to tell me."

"I wanted to tell you myself," she said.

"You told Nancy not to mention it in front of me."

"I didn't put it like that," Irina said.

"And you told Eliza and Susan and Harriet and Beth —"

"It wasn't like that at all," she said.

"Stay!" I shouted. "Stay at the fucking magazine! I'm the one who's quitting! I quit!" I shouted.

X

I HAD no money, so I kept my job, but every day was like a
rainy Monday.

After an initial bout of oblivion, I began to discover interesting facts about the magazine. To begin with, the layout of
its offices was not what I had imagined. The blue-carpeted
alcove where Irina had worked, its bulletin board now bare
and mute, revealed itself to be not the glowing heart of *Glee*
but a backwater; and because her replacement was not hired
for several weeks, the head of Fashion being difficult to please,
Irina's desk was used by everyone but never neatened or
cleaned, so that it grew mountains of discarded newspapers
and magazines that gave it a seedy, somewhat sullen appearance. At first I had to fight absurd tender impulses to tidy it
up. Even after I grew accustomed to Irina's absence, it happened more than once that as I wandered by that abandoned

desk, chasing after some elusive punning headline or caption in my head, I noticed its dishevelment as though for the first time, and vaguely wondered about it — and then immediately wanted to hurl myself on the thing and smash and tear at it with huge suffering hands.

I dreamed of Irina every night. Whenever I ventured into the streets I came on countless doubles of her that she had let loose upon the city.

Another discovery involved the amount of time I needed to devote to my work. It became clear to me, soon after Irina left, that what had once seemed an inhuman daily workload could actually be dismissed in an afternoon of moderate exertion. There was ample time in the morning to repair the damage of the night before — I went out every evening, having renewed a number of friendships that had lapsed while I was with Irina — by lingering under the shower and eating a breakfast of eggs and rubbery sausages at the coffee shop across Second Avenue, with the newspaper at my elbow; time to tramp, on arriving at the office, through the mulch of gossip and crime in the *Post* and the *Daily News,* which I spirited from Mary Donoghue's IN box. (In those weeks the feud between the mayor and the owner of *Glee,* who had just offered to buy several of the city's bridges and restore them, was becoming increasingly vulgar and entertaining.) On several occasions, when the previous evening had flown particularly high, I even found the leisure to return home to sleep for an hour at midday. The work almost always got done in the end, and if by chance I did miss a deadline, the next issue of the magazine closed anyway, and the subway ran neither more nor less reliably, and the sun could be counted on to rise over Long Island the next day — though that was not an event I ever witnessed.

The monthly travel article was my main responsibility, and in that area I was still able to coast on a healthy backlog. A piece on Bangkok and the Thai islands was already in the computer and partly edited; a hateful but prolific hack, a fake Englishman whose paeans to the British Royals appeared every month in a different women's magazine, had been lent to me by another editor to write something on Scotland (he lived in London and his travel expenses would therefore be small, but most of it would have to be rewritten); I had recently bought a witty account of a sojourn in the Seychelles, sent to me by an unknown woman who had four apparently brilliant children, all of them snorkeling fanatics; I was hunting, and had almost bagged, the right person to do a foot safari in Tanzania; and I was trying to convince Nancy Eberstadt to let me commission something about a cluster of villages near Arles, centering on the market town of Caziers, an idea I had stolen from a French magazine.

The week after Labor Day all the staffers had their salaries reviewed. Nobody liked to talk about it, but everyone knew what was afoot and waited to be summoned — or not — to Nancy's office. Several women resigned or were fired. It was like that every September. Every September Mary Dono-ghue got a huge raise, threw a tantrum, and got even more. I did not expect much for myself, but when my turn came I was awarded a raise that was not insulting; I hadn't yet exhausted Nancy's reserves of good will, though since the Michael Albers incident she could rarely spare a moment to see me and thereby forced me to communicate with her by memoranda — which often went unanswered. It became clear to everyone, and sometimes even to me, that I would soon be leaving the magazine. Nobody told me that I was no longer welcome; no one was told by me that I had finally lost all interest in my work; but some of my responsibilities began to drift toward other editors' desks. The monthly group meetings around muffins and coffee in Nancy Eberstadt's office found me doodling and stifling yawns and spasms of an-

noyance; no new assignments came my way; few new suggestions issued from me; and neither I nor anyone else seemed
the least bit surprised or concerned.

The women of *Glee,* however, were very kind to me after
Irina's desertion. They appeared to have, all of them, some
acquaintance with heartbreak, and unlike my male friends they
did not fear that commiseration would encourage me to go
to pieces. They even demonstrated their solidarity by saying
appalling things about Irina. In the space of one month I heard
condemnations of her clothes, her intelligence, her character
and industry. Within this criticism lurked the twin assumptions, both of them false, that Irina did not need to work and
that Nancy had been forced to hire her because of her family's connection with the magazine.

I sometimes went out for meals with my colleagues, singly
or in groups (which had been awkward in Irina's day), and
twice I even attempted to take Ann, the designer in the art
department who liked me, to bed. I thought it would do me
good, and as for the all-too-familiar problems of entangle-
ments with officemates, they were more than outweighed by
the potential satisfaction of having Irina find out that I had
simply replaced her with another item from the same shelf —
although it is true that when I thought of this I felt I was
about to weep again, and then I cracked my telephone at home
one evening by clubbing it with its own receiver after dialing
the first digits of her number four times in as many minutes.
My first date with Ann, which involved a Japanese dinner, a
Brazilian movie, and Mexican drinks, all on a ten-block stretch
of Broadway and Columbus Avenue, was not a hit. The
wisecracking rhythm we achieved effortlessly in the bright
fluorescence of the art room failed us under the pressure of
candlelight and piped-in mariachi music; and on a darker
stretch of Broadway Ann grew stiff and unwilling when, on
a now-or-never impulse, I steered her to a doorway and took

her in my arms — and in the middle of that clumsy kiss (our mouths seemed somehow not to fit), I became acutely aware of being in Irina's neighborhood, and from behind closed eyelids I saw her stroll by, for some reason walking a tremendous dog, and glare at us with scorn.

I had in fact spoken to Irina twice, after successfully dialing her number through to the end. Or rather I had spoken to Mrs. Albers, who then put her nervous and uncommunicative daughter on the line. The principal note in Irina's voice, when she came to the phone, was one of pain, and she grew additional bristles when I, unable to help myself, became jovial and jokey. Irina had decided to be ruthless. She wasn't going to let me believe for a second in the possibility of a reunion. I already knew about these methods of hers, because when she and I first joined forces I had witnessed several calls from the previous boyfriend, the one of the tortoiseshell glasses, who had had the same trouble getting it through his skull that it was all over — although unlike me, he was clearly at fault, having messed up by falling into bed with someone else during Irina's tenure. Even now that I was the banished one, there were times when I admired her firmness. There were times when I was almost grateful for it. But that did not prevent my forlorn feet from leading me, on weekend afternoons, through the big meadow in Central Park that lay beneath her windows, and lingering there longer than was necessary, ducking Frisbees and kites and dodging the barefoot teenagers who pursued them, their long hair flying and lighted cigarettes clutched in their fingers.

She was not looking for another job. She might try to freelance at other magazines, she said, but when I asked where, and even offered a suggestion or two, she clammed up. It was not a positive sign. In my experience vague statements about free-lancing were the standard smoke screen floated by the recently fired, especially those who were too dazed and depressed to replace the ribbon cartridge in their home type-writers and begin fussing with the margins for a new résumé. It pleased and distressed me in almost equal measure to think that she might have sabotaged her career by her quixotic sacrifice of her position at *Glee* — though of course that had as much to do with her inheritance as with me. I learned from Michael that she had for the moment set aside her apartment search and was thinking of spending much of the fall in Fincham. Michael called me from Boston almost every other week, not always sober. It did not occur to him that I might not be thrilled by his attentions. I got tired of hearing about his plans for his book. He was about to leave for Paris to start research on the European years of his grandfather's life, and wanted to know whether there was a chance that Nancy Eberstadt and *Glee* might be interested in excerpting — and funding — portions of this work. Typically, he seemed blind to the impression he had made at the magazine, unless he had forgotten that hangover morning altogether.

One night, not sober myself, I called the house in Fincham and hung up as soon as Irina answered. I hadn't really expected her to be there; I think I just wanted to let the phone ring for a minute or two in an empty house where we had been happy. I didn't envy her the long and ever-colder evenings alone in that strangely soulless place. On the other hand, each one of them might make her more vulnerable to me — unless, of course, some silent, sinewy young farmer, who happened to keep two riding horses . . . It was better not to think about such things. I asked Ann out to dinner again, and she accepted.

Perhaps she blamed herself for our first dud date. During the second dinner she drank a great deal of wine, with determination, and developed over the Sambuca a haggard stare; then, up at her apartment, which was unexpectedly untidy and smelled of her cats, she sank suddenly into unconsciousness, her eyes toppling shut like a doll's, just at the moment when, having collaborated on the removal of much of her clothes, I was lowering her backward onto the pillows. She lay there in disarray, her lips swollen and her breasts flattened by their own weight, her left arm draped over her belly, which rose and fell with oceanic smoothness. For a time I sat on the edge of the bed — actually a Japanese mattress laid on the bare floor, an object I had once heard Mrs. Albers call a "tofu" — holding my ankles and wondering what to do next. Ann would sleep more comfortably if I pulled her jeans off, but I feared she would wake and imagine I was trying to seize for myself a solitary and vaguely necrophiliac thrill. I bent over her and lifted her hips to yank the sheet out and cover her. She breached out of sleep for a second and whispered, with a long sibilance, that she was sorry. It sounded as though she were in terrible pain, and the apology may have been directed at a dream creature that had nothing to do with me. "It's okay, here's a pillow," I said, nudging her with it, but she was gone again.

I took my shoes off and lay down beside her, bunching the second pillow under the nape of my neck. I was already telling this story in my head, only the person I was telling it to was Irina. I reached over Ann's body to switch off the dim lamp that stood on a cinder block by the mattress, and after a second of pitch darkness the room reconstituted itself in furry shadows. Lit from a lower apartment across the air-shaft, the blinds projected a limbless zebra into the far corner of the ceiling. Ann was breathing evenly. Carefully I turned onto my side and inched over to her back, draping an arm over her blanketed waist and dislodging a cat that had managed to install itself between us unnoticed. I tried to pretend that this warm body against mine was Irina's, but it felt completely foreign; then I tried to think of it as Blue, and then another model, a raven Chilean girl whose beauty caused me moments of disbelief. Through these serial substitutions I was even able to create the pleasant illusion that I myself was someone else, a stranger turning over onto his back again, sleepless in his clothes on an unfamiliar bed, beside an unfamiliar girl, a man who had never trod the blue carpets of *Glee,* who had never met any Alberses, who was merely pausing in this darkened room on his way to some other place . . .

I slept awhile and woke sneezing. A headache, temporarily magnified by the sneezes, was returning to an acceptable intensity. My mouth was caked and dry. I sneezed again and yet again, and rubbed my itching eyes and then my whole face. There was a slight rasp to my breathing. It couldn't be just the dust; my allergy to cats, which I had outgrown in adolescence, had just crept back in the night. Two of the beasts were staring at me from the foot of the mattress. Ann stirred, turned over, opened her eyes, and turned back again, wrapping the sheet tighter around herself.

The cats followed me into the bathroom, perhaps to make sure I didn't interfere with their litter, and spread their poison scent on my ankles while I examined the medicine chest behind the mirror. It was a hypochondriac's dreamland, a four-tiered Manhattan of bottles and tubes, but I found nothing that looked like an antihistamine. One white-capped column of amber plastic contained a poetically named tranquilizer I had recently read about in a terrifying *Glee* article on the dangers of psychopharmacology: Ms. Ann Plez, 1–2 tablets as needed for anxiety . . . prescribed by Dr. J. Scheinbaum, my old pal, Irina's psychiatrist, who had also obliged with a nearby stash of sleeping pills. Perhaps all *Glee* girls, maybe even my officemate, Mary, went to the same shrink. Odd to think that I led a second existence, a stranger to myself, in the files of an Upper West Side psychiatrist. I ought to track down all his other patients and seduce them one by one.

Here was yet another sedative, indicating that Ann rarely fell asleep as easily as she had tonight, unless she had snuck a couple of these during her retreat to the bathroom when we first entered the apartment. The bottle was half filled with little oval pellets of a delicate blue, like the eggs of some diminutive magical bird. In imitation of Michael Albers I shook two of them into the palm of my hand and dropped them in my shirt pocket, having decided — after another burst of sneezing had doubled me over — that I would abandon Ann and her animals and go home to treat myself to a good night's sleep. These two pills were the first objects I had ever stolen in adult life (except, of course, *Glee* office supplies), and the act awoke in me once again a pleasant feeling of being not quite myself, abroad in the dead of night, and somewhat dangerous to know.

Back in the bedroom I stuffed my shirttail into my pants, stepped into my shoes, and knelt on the futon to shake Ann's hot shoulder.

"I've got to go. I'm allergic to your cats," I said.

"I'm sorry," she whispered again, without opening her eyes.

"I'll see you at the office," I said.

She didn't answer, but I knew she was shamming — she just didn't want to deal with me. I checked my pockets before leaving to make sure my keys or my money hadn't fallen out on the bed. One of the cats tried to follow me onto the landing, but I forced it back with the toe of my shoe. I was only halfway down the first flight of steps when I thought I heard Ann throw the bolt stealthily, just at the moment when I remembered that my wristwatch lay curled on the floor beside the bed.

Ann lived on the edge of Spanish Harlem, and it occurred to me as I approached the ground floor that I might be in some danger once I left the building. As a precaution I transferred some money to a second pocket, and worked out in my head the route I would take if I didn't find a taxi immediately: down the avenue to 110th Street, which at least was wide and well lit, and then toward Broadway. I stood up straight, squared my shoulders, and installed on my face an expression of self-confidence in preparation for my walk in the dark. I sneezed violently as I unlocked the door, and failed to remember that it stood atop a step, but I was able to grab the iron banister as I clattered down the stoop on my heels.

All around me the night was hopping. There were multicolored lights everywhere, in storefronts, on the tails of cruising cars, flashing above the intersection. A bright bodega across the street throbbed with music. Entire families were out taking the air, spilling off the stoops among giant radios and giant bottles of soda, the children screaming in a mixture of English and Spanish and clapping their sandals on the pavement as they ran. In my rapid descent I had narrowly missed upending an ovoid young mother in gym shorts, topped by a tall bun, who was rocking a baby carriage by applying a thonged foot to its suspension. The young man she was chatting with, a piratical chap hanging out the window of a high-tailed hotrod, suggested cheerfully that I take it slow, man. By the neon Pepsi-Cola clock in the window of the booming bodega I saw that I had completely misjudged the time. It wasn't yet midnight. It was like waking from a dream in which one had been, without warning, terribly old.

Over on Broadway the urban Caribbean gave way to a quieter but equally thriving mixture. The occasional darkened stretch of corrugated steel shutter was barely noticeable among the candlelit restaurant windows and the white neon of expensive delicatessens. Well-excercised young couples, dressed in their weekend worst, were sharing the burdens of grocery bags and ice cream cones and obese newspapers on slow homeward strolls. Spotting the awnings and the pointillist sidewalk bins of two adjacent greengrocers across the avenue, I discovered in myself a craving for a peach.

In one of the stalls outside the nearest one I found several that were ideally ripe. After six years in New York I still wondered at the year-round bounty of the stores. It was almost autumn, but in the warm night, among the slow-moving crowd, weighing a peach in the palm of my hand, I might have thought myself back in June. I returned the fruit to its plastic bed, because the summer was over, because there had been no summer that year, only a long hot season of loneliness, frittered away night by night. And why was I constantly engulfed by longing for someone who had been only cruel and deceitful? Why was I still at my hated job? Why was I still in New York?

At 110th Street a chain was strung between the dwarf lampposts at the entrance to the subway; suspended from it was a stenciled sign announcing that the station was closed for repairs. I could still take a taxi home, but I was no longer in a mood to indulge myself. I strolled on toward the next stop, at 103rd Street. A few blocks above that station, Broadway veers to the left, deflecting off the northernmost point of West End Avenue and flowing past a triangular traffic island lined with benches where neighborhood street people hang out with their bundles and their fortified wine. In order to avoid it I continued straight down West End, planning to cut back to Broadway along a cross street. There were no shops here, and little traffic, and I felt better for having left Saturday night behind.

A few moments after I crossed West End and turned onto a block of tenements that sloped eastward to Broadway — I would remember exactly, afterward, what I had been thinking of: I had been contemplating, for unknown reasons, a pair of red high-heeled shoes that had lain askew the day before in the doorway of the fashion closet at *Glee* — a thick arm embraced me, quite tenderly at first, from behind. It cut off my breath, but I suffered only a split second of confusion. By the time I was half shoved, half dragged across the sidewalk to a wall of dark bricks and powdery mortar, I knew exactly what was happening to me. I had been expecting it for years. What came over me then, instead of fear, was an immense annoyance, a rage directed not specifically at my attacker but at the whole horrible world I lived in. I swung my right elbow back as hard as I could, digging into an elastic mass that produced a gratifying sound halfway between a cough and a grunt. Then, realizing that I had begun to defend myself (an awareness tinged with surprise, and, at last, panic) and would have to follow through, I stamped my heel down, searching blindly for a sneakered instep. But I never knew whether I hit my target, or indeed whether my foot landed at all, because at that moment my head was rammed from behind and cracked smartly against the bricks, causing a blue flash bulb to explode before my eyes and an incongruous taste of hard-boiled egg to appear in my mouth.

The second time this happened I tried to scream, but was unable to get my breath organized to do so; after the third impact (its particular luminosity was just a slow blush, and the horrifying thing was that even though I knew it had taken place I neither heard nor felt it, as though my skull had gone soft), I attempted to fall to the pavement, feigning unconsciousness more for my benefit than anyone else's, but I was brutally yanked up by my belt. Two fists kept me pressed against the wall while an additional pair of hands sprouted from the night, startling me — I hadn't realized there were two — to grope inside the pockets of my trousers. A black man's voice was insulting me in soft explosions of fricatives. It was interesting, given the extent of my other problems, that these hackneyed accusations of maternal incest and homosexuality could be so wounding, that they should make

me feel so miserable and alone. The hands retracted. Antici-
pating a parting blow, my whole body went into a cringe —
but now the hands were back, mining my pockets for dimes
and pennies; a muscle underneath my scrotum cramped up in
its deluded efforts to escape their proximity; my calves had
begun to shake; the fists pressing on my back were interfer-
ing with my breathing; the stream of oaths and insults and
hot breath continued to pour into my ear; it was taking so
long . . .

An enormous foot slid over mine, mashing my toes, and I
was pulled off balance again and thrown to the ground. Immediately I dragged myself on my elbows to the wall and
curled up, but the expected kicks didn't come. I heard footsteps running down to Broadway, and a woman's high-pitched
laughter; it seemed I had been attacked by a mixed-gender
team, but I couldn't bring myself to open my eyes and try to
see them. A coin fell far away and rolled in a long arc before
toppling on its side with a click.

I moaned experimentally — it was really a question of
testing my voice; I wasn't sure how long it had been since I
had last drawn breath — and opened my eyes. I found myself lying on the ground by the wall, curled up like an arma-
dillo, shaking. Nothing around me had changed, the same
cars were still parked nose to tail along the curb, the same
iron-railed stoops sloped down from the tenements across
the street, but it felt as though I had been absent for hours.
Sensing that something was wrong, I closed my eyes again
and wiped a finger carefully across them; it came away dripping like a paint stirrer and spattered black droplets on the
pavement. A small shower of them fell as I shifted to one
knee and unfolded upward on trembling legs to lean against
the wall. There was no one around, but I knew I would find
an open store, a restaurant, a taxi, something alive on Broadway. I set off down the hill, gingerly, because my brain had

come loose inside my skull. My legs were trembling more and more violently. I felt a cockroach walking on my neck and grabbed at it, but it turned out to be a rivulet of blood. Under the first streetlamp I left the support of the wall and went to look at my reflection in the window of a parked car. The whole right side of my face wore a dripping black mask, some of which I was able to dab off with my shirtsleeve. Above my right eyebrow a two-inch gash was bleeding with amazing generosity. I propped my elbows on the roof of the car; it was essential not to faint.

XI

"GOODNESS!" Nancy Eberstadt said on the telephone.

I wasn't tired of telling the story yet but I felt that I ought to be, so I acted reticent about the details.

"Fifteen stitches," I told her. "I'm supposed to spend a couple of days in bed in the dark, in case I have an undetected concussion. But I need to talk to you when I come back to the office. I want to take my vacation soon. I've got to get out of New York for a while."

"We can discuss it," Nancy said.

"I really need to get out of here for a couple of weeks at least," I said.

"We'll arrange something," she said. She was not enthusiastic.

I kept the telephone next to my bed. Mary Donoghue was smoothing out the last problems in an article that belonged to me and had to go to type that evening. She called every ten minutes. I'd answer the question, I'd hang up, and she'd call again.

"Okay, hon," she said, "I'll take that out, but it'll probably leave us with a widow. Where did you find this asshole, anyway?"

"I don't know. He sent in some clips. They weren't bad."

"Jesus H.," Mary said. "Listen, some Limey called for you."

"Eric Steyer?" I said.

"He didn't leave his name. I didn't tell him you were at home; I thought you might not want to be disturbed."

I called Steyer.

"Not bad, thanks," I said, "except I got mugged on Saturday."

I told him the whole story.

"Irina taking care of you?" he asked.

I told him that whole story.

"I've decided to take a vacation. I'm going to go to Europe for a few weeks, if I can scrape some money together. I've had a hell of a summer," I said.

"That sounds like a good idea," he said. "Are you going to Geneva?"

"Maybe. I ought to go visit my aunts."

"You could do me a favor if you're passing through Geneva."

"Sure," I said. "What?"

"I'll tell you when I'll see you. A delivery," he said.

"A delivery," I repeated.

"A small package. It's nothing, really. Let's meet for a drink when you're up and about."

At the emergency room at St. Luke's Hospital they had not bound my head in one of those picturesque bandages, with a rust-colored stain on one side, that had looked so dashing on the Napoleonic officers among whom I had spent my boyhood. The intern, who I guessed was younger than I, had merely stitched the gash tensely, muttering to himself as he guided the thread through my skin with a surgical clamp and a needle that resembled a fish hook. "You're grunting again," said the white-haired nurse who was assisting him. "Sorry, I have to stop grunting," he said. "That's all right, grunt away," I told him, because I found his manipulations disgusting and wanted him to get on with it. A minute later I caught him humming "Eleanor Rigby," and the song festered in my brain for a week afterward. Over the stitches he spread thin little strips of white tape, so that when we were through I looked as though I had a white picket fence above my right eyebrow. Harried as he was, the intern did not let me go without telling me all about his own mugging, which had taken place a year earlier in the lobby of his apartment building. Since we were fellow victims, I got him to prescribe a stronger painkiller than he had intended to.

Behind the white picket fence was a large bruise that underwent several interesting changes of color during the first few days, in which mauve and black competed with an obscene green. I liked to tap it with my fingertips. This caused a small, not unpleasant ache that disappeared almost immediately. Only the first day was painful; even the special painkillers couldn't quite dull my headache, and as I lay in bed behind drawn blinds, fielding Mary Donoghue's calls through an opiate haze, I kept remembering the details of the attack with a peculiar feeling of shame. I dreamed about it all the time. The strangest people clubbed me while I dozed, including a fellow whose features I couldn't recognize but whom I knew to be one of the undertakers who had come to collect Kuratkin's body at Central Park West some months earlier. Each time I woke I knew there was something new in my life — yes, I had been mugged, but I had lived through it and now I was going to be fine.

I shuffled about my room, putting clothes on myself as I

prepared to go meet Steyer at Kiely's and see what he wanted of me. I did this slowly, because my head didn't like to be jolted, and also because of the vagueness that had come over me after two days of bed and painkillers. I had to pick my way carefully between abandoned sneakers, empty plastic bottles of mineral water that toppled and rolled if I looked at them too sharply, and the smudged corpses of half-read newspapers. Steyer, I imagined, was going to involve me in some wild Afghan scheme of his. A delivery, he had said. I could already see him peer at me through the smoky gloom at Kiely's, examining my wound with interest and appreciation, and off-handedly suggesting that I carry packets of drug or gun money to a shady contact in Geneva. Oddly, I pictured this spylike creature as Dr. Halik, our old mathematics teacher — a face served up by my imagination almost, but not quite, at random. Dr. Halik was an ageless and melancholy Pakistani about whom his students had known little. He lived not on the campus but in rented rooms, I presume, in a nearby village, commuting in an antiquated but immaculate Panhard, which he took ten minutes to park each morning, with a maddening combination of meticulousness and incompetence, in the teachers' parking lot behind the uppermost chalet of the school. He usually managed to evade the supervisory duties that brought the other teachers into informal contact with the students, and there was about him a deep sadness and dignity that kept him apart from his colleagues — we never saw him attend, for instance, the faculty's ritual afternoon tea on the headmaster's balcony — through whom we might have come to know some details of his life and his personality.

It was not just Dr. Halik's Eastern origins and his enigmatic quality that spliced him, that evening, in the peaceful disorder of my thoughts, to Steyer's endeavors on behalf of the Mujahedin. Once, at age twelve, during one of those

weeklong treasure hunts that used to take us all over Switzerland, following absurd clues devised by our headmaster,
whose imagination combined the military and the fantastic in
equal proportions, I had had precisely such a meeting with
Dr. Halik, though not in a café. It was in front of the bear pit
in Bern. (The clue that had led my team there, handed to us
by another teacher atop a mountain near Lucerne, was "In
the Capital I pace on four paws.") Dr. Halik had given me a
sheet of paper on which were instructions in a language no
one on my five-man team had ever seen; the only recogniz-
able word was the name of our English teacher, Moriarty.
Someone thought the language might be Polish, so we walked
across Bern to the Polish embassy, where, after some trouble
and delay, we had it translated. It read: "Here I lost my pipe,
my magnifying glass, and my life, along with Professor
Moriarty" — which led us, the next day, to the Reichenbach
Falls near Basel to pick up the next clue.

In the dull world of adulthood, Dr. Halik was no more a
likely candidate for a liaison man to Afghan rebels than I was.
Probably he persisted, and persists to this day, in his unvary-
ing and unadventurous routine, perhaps at this very moment
scribbling $\dfrac{ax+b}{2ab}$ on a blackboard — there is a sudden snap
and a tooth-shattering screech as he attempts to draw the di-
viding line, for Dr. Halik has never mastered the use of
chalk — for the edification of my successors, under the eaves
in that same uppermost chalet of my school, where, if you
look closely, you will still find, on the inside of the closet
door, a faint graffito hailing Stalin and cursing Mussolini,
inscribed there in the winter of 1941, when that chalet, I believe, housed a small group of Italian refugees. But had Eric
Steyer really asked me to go search for Dr. Halik in a café in
Geneva to collect information, let us say, about a certain man
to contact in Peshawar, my astonishment would have been

caused not by the unlikeliness of the errand, but instead by its secret beauty and plausibility. I always knew, as a child, that my adult life, like my boyhood, would be rich with great and meaningful coincidences, with frequent changes of place, activity, and companions, with danger that was the necessary consequence of my missions and interests, and with knowledge about certain friends and certain locations that could never be divulged.

Kiely's was closed. Though I had been going there for two years, I was still puzzled by its erratic schedule. More than once I had been forced to loiter outside while waiting for a friend I had planned to meet there. It was a grim block, particularly at night, because its buildings had no stores at street level. The only life was provided by a lighted ramp leading down into the bowels of a parking garage, from which there issued at intervals an echoing clang, the muffled roar of an engine, or the ringing of an electric bell. Next to it, across from the bar, was an empty lot, a hole in the row of buildings, piled high with rubble and inhabited by nimble rats. Right next to Kiely's, the steel loading ramp of an office-furniture outlet provided shelter every night for a crazed and ragged creature, the furthest gone of the dozen or so street men who had adopted the neighborhood. He was a babbler, particularly at night, but the language he babbled in was completely unintelligible, except for a few words that returned often to his toothless mouth: Jesus, United Nations, and Good Evening. I had never seen him violent, I had never even seen him address his gibbering to any particular passerby, but I would have been uncomfortable standing next to him for any length of time, which was exactly what Steyer was doing when I found him. Not only that; leaning his long frame against Kiely's locked door, Steyer was attempting to speak to him, in polite British tones. My skin had begun to crawl the minute I set foot on that dark block — a result of the mugging, despite my having sworn that I wouldn't let the experience spook me — and on top of that I felt a stab of annoyance at Steyer when I realized what he was doing, as though he ought to have known better than to try to get some sense out of that wretch. I didn't walk all the way down to them but instead hailed Steyer from up the block. He gave the man a cordial goodbye, still unnoticed, and strode up to join me at the intersection, where I stood nervously, hating myself and everything else.

"Interesting chat?" I asked. When we reached the comparative bustle of Second Avenue, I steered him northward. There was another bar nearby where one could eat good hamburgers.

"I was trying to find out what language he was speaking," Steyer said. "There was a moment when it sounded like Farsi; then I thought it might be an Italian dialect of some kind . . ."

Maureen, the waitress, took a great shine to Steyer. Like Michael Albers, he was good at kidding strangers and charming service out of people. It had something to do with his height; looking down at you, leaning forward, he spoke with the care and politeness with which one addresses a child one has just met, with the same incipient smile hovering somewhere behind his features. I could imagine that this manner of his, this mixture of courtesy and self-assurance, would make friends for him in his wanderings. Maureen, a small pneumatic red-haired girl, immediately began to thrive under this treatment as she bustled about the preparation of our table, while Steyer bothered her with all sorts of questions about where he should sit, on the chair or the banquette, what kind of hamburger, cheeseburger, California burger, or chili burger he should eat, and with what kind of "garnishes." Maureen's word appeared to please Steyer, and he repeated it several times with a thoughtful air, as though he had never heard it before and were trying it out for the first time.

Settled in at last, with Maureen galloping off to fetch the

beers, he did a brief imitation of the babbling derelict, in which "U-ni-ted Na-tions" sounded quite clearly.

"Couldn't understand a word of it. Thought it was Pushtu or something. It was like a hallucination."

"Well," I said, "he was hallucinating, and you were hallucinating too, so the both of you were just cozily hallucinating away at each other — a nice little New York scene."

"He doesn't seem unhappy, actually," Steyer said. "Perhaps he has pleasant hallucinations. Perhaps he thinks he's a sultan with a large harem."

"When it gets to me," I said, "I hope that's what I'll think."

"There you are," Steyer said when Maureen arrived with a hamburger. "This is it? What did you call it? Guacamole?" he asked, amazed.

"Put some meat on those bones of yours," Maureen said.

"That's a lost cause," Steyer said.

"Speaking of lost causes," I said. I was about to mention Afghanistan, but Maureen interrupted.

"Enjoy your meal," she said.

"Weren't you bringing one of these for me?" I asked.

She slapped her forehead and uttered an incredulous giggle. "I plum forgot," she said. She dashed off toward the kitchen.

"I've never had a real hallucination," Steyer said.

"Not that you know of," I said.

"Right," he said, after thinking it over.

"Start on that thing; don't wait for me," I said. "I wanted to talk to you. I'm off to Europe. You said there was something I might —"

"Did you ever take LSD?" Steyer asked, cutting into his burger with a knife and fork.

"No," I said, discouraged. "Lots of people used to take it in college. I never tried heroin, either, though I was curious about that."

"Ugh," Steyer said. "Makes you vomit, and strangely, you don't mind vomiting."

"Michael Albers got badly addicted," I said. "At Harvard. He went through detox at least twice. Do you know that he's got it into his head that he's going to write a book about his grandfather?"

"Wasn't he writing one about Pushkin?"

"That was last week," I said.

"And what did he do, the grandfather?"

"He had an interesting life," I said. "But his descendants have made a kind of cult of him."

"So what about you and Irina?" Steyer asked.

I drew a finger across my throat.

"When he was dying," I said, returning to my subject, "he was in an almost constant state of hallucination — speaking of hallucinations." For once I didn't want to talk about Irina. "Sometimes it was as if he were inhabiting all the different periods of his life simultaneously. You know, how sometimes when you wake up in the morning you don't know where you are, or how old you are, and there's a moment of slight panic when you sort of palpate yourself to find out. He was like that for days at a time. It seemed sort of cozy to me, to tell you the truth."

Steyer was chewing.

"Anyway," he said at long last, "I wanted to ask if you could run an errand for me in Geneva."

"Yes."

"You'll enjoy it."

"Good."

"It's just a question of delivering a small package to a friend of mine."

"All right."

He put down his knife and fork, reached into the inner pocket of his jacket, and pulled out an envelope.

"Take a look inside,"he said.

It contained photographs of Afghanistan. Or rather the rocky backdrop was Afghan. In the foreground of the pictures was a smiling sunburned girl, her hair almost white. In some pictures, where the frame was oddly angled, she was with Steyer, their arms about each other's shoulders; Steyer had a turban and a thick beard and a desert-colored robe, and she wore a mixture of fatigues and blue jeans. In others, she was with a scrawny Afghan with ruined teeth, who was grinning madly and holding a rocket against his hip. You could tell that he was trying to get both in and out of the photograph simultaneously, closer to and farther from the blonde.

"That's my friend Hélène," Steyer said. "She's with Médecins sans Frontières. She was one of the first medical people to get in, two years ago. She's in Geneva now. I promised I'd send her some pics."

"She's the one I was going to profile for the magazine," I said.

"What?"

"You remember — when we were at Kiely's with your friend from Beirut. We were talking about guerrilla chic."

"Ah, yes," Steyer said. "You never suggested doing a profile of me."

"You don't look like that," I said. "Is she single?"

"Yes. You might get along."

There were still wisps of the Dr. Halik fantasy clinging to me like cobwebs. "So what's so important about these photographs?" I asked.

"Nothing," Steyer said. "Is there anything wrong with them?"

"No. Why don't you send them through the mail?"

"So that you can meet her," Steyer said, patiently. "Do you need any more help? Should I tell you about the birds and the bees?"

"Oh," I said. "You see, I imagined you were going to send

me to Peshawar with thousands of dollars to buy guns, or to trade guns for opium, or something like that."

"Well, for that I'd send someone else," Steyer said.

"Thank you," I said.

"You can get Hélène to take you. She'll be going back at some point. If you start writing articles about her you'll have to see her in action — amputating limbs and so on. Good photographs for your magazine."

"Well, that's very kind of you," I said.

He beamed mildly at Maureen as she deposited my plate on top of my fork, beaming back at him. I pocketed the photographs, a neat little package, looking forward to going through them again when I got home.

He'd given me an idea. The problem with taking a vacation in Europe — let alone sneaking off to Afghanistan — was that I couldn't afford it. I spent almost all my salary trying to make New York livable, and the little money I had set aside was accessible only at the cost of monstrous penalties. I had to work out a deal with Nancy. When I returned to the office, the morning after my conversation with Steyer (I had planned to take advantage of my injury and stay home for a week, but my priorities had now shifted), I suggested to her that I take a working vacation, from which I would bring back two travel pieces. Nancy had already approved the article on Caziers, in a part of Provence that was beginning to grow popular, but I hadn't yet assigned it to a writer, and I now proposed to do it myself. I would, in addition, be visiting my aunts in Switzerland, and while there I could do something on the resort of Giffern. The village had already been featured in every magazine in the world because of its beauty and its winter population of millionaires, movie stars, and doddering relatives of deposed kings. But I had spent many years there, in boarding school, and I was able to convince Nancy that I had special knowledge of the place that would allow me to take a different angle: Giffern off season, when the kings and stars go there for seclusion and rest, a far more glamorous business than the Christmas or February madness.

"And while I'm at it," I said, "there's another possibility I want to look into for the front of the book. Have you ever heard of Médecins sans Frontières?"

I told her about Hélène.

"We're always talking about role models," I said. "She's under thirty, stunning, and best of all she has nothing to do with entertainment, media, or business."

"You're very pale," Nancy said. "And that's a nasty-looking cut."

"I feel fine, fine," I said. "Let me do this. I need some time off."

"I know you need some time off," she said. "But you've been sort of absent anyway, the last couple of months. Maybe you want to think this over. You could take just a week off and go rest somewhere, and then we'd see. We have an ideas meeting in three weeks."

"Oh, come on," I pleaded. "I'll write you a memo."

"Okay," she said. "I'll read your memo. Forget the beautiful doctor for the moment. The travel stuff sounds good."

Three days later we had a deal. I would pay for the plane ticket to Europe out of my own pocket; the magazine would take care of my expenses in Provence and in Giffern, provided I kept them to a minimum. My fee for each article would be half the going rate for free-lancers, which was the standard arrangement for editors' extracurricular work.

Nancy said: "I'm pleased that you seem to have found something that interests you, I was getting worried."

As for me, I felt that I had broken free. I had three people to thank for it: Irina, for firing me; my two muggers, for their salutary blows to my head.

XII

MY CHILDHOOD was in some ways a makeshift affair, patched together out of temporary arrangements that kept stretching into near permanence.

My father, a round Swiss with hair cut like the bristles of a brush, came to America in slim youth as a fitness instructor, collected, along with some antique furniture and a painting or two, by a Fifth Avenue, Greenwich, and Adirondacks couple who toured Europe every spring. Although they bear some responsibility for my existence, I never met these people, who exited the picture some years before I was born; but at the ceremony for Kuratkin Michael Albers introduced me to a woman who bore their name, a brisk Yankee dowager, as wrinkled as Saran Wrap but otherwise intact. The name only faintly rang a bell at the time, in the midst of the solemn and somewhat intimidating proceedings; when I questioned

Mrs. Albers afterward she told me that the woman and her late husband had been friends of Kuratkin's in the fifties and early sixties, and yes, Greenwich, but only maybe the Adirondacks; she could have been a cousin, or merely a homonym. The coincidence raised the interesting possibility that Kuratkin and my father may have met, introduced in the woman's vestibule, perhaps, one man departing via the elevator in which the other had just arrived, or in the locker room of some club, both of them juggling towels and racquets in order to shake each other's hand. At any rate, my father, three years after his arrival in New York, while working as a coach at a West Side prep school, married my mother, who taught English, and settled down to stay. Eventually he gave up his work as a trainer, and grew fatter and slightly wealthier as the commercial representative in the United States of a company that crafted precision instruments in the clipped countryside near Neuchâtel. I still have, somewhere, an altimeter that was a favorite posession throughout my boyhood, and that I kept on my desk while in college, the object of no end of hilarious comments and readjustments when my friends and I happened to be high.

For two weeks each Christmas and two weeks every summer we went to stay in my father's native village, which lies folded into a valley near the border between the French-speaking canton of Vaud and the German canton of Bern, in a region that is called Le Pays d'en haut or the Oberland. My grandmother and my two aunts still lived together there in a house whose inner walls, floors, and low ceilings were made of pale knotted pine. In addition to these vacations, my father returned alone to Switzerland every year to put in his three weeks of military training, which all Swiss males do until the age of forty-five. In my father's desk in New York I had a stiff red Swiss passport as well as my soft green American one, but in all other respects, omitting the embarrassment I sometimes suffered after my discovery that my father talked funny (it was pointed out to me by a little girl I often played with; I remember exactly where she told me this, by the swings in the playground at Seventy-ninth Street on the east side of Central Park), I must have been indistinguishable from the other kids at school or in our Lexington Avenue apartment building.

It was during our seventh summer together in Switzerland that my father's round belly proved to contain a tumor the size of a grapefruit. *"Gros comme un pamplemousse"* was a phrase I heard over and over in the following week, and to this day I can seldom see a grapefruit without hearing, in my mind, its French name spoken with my aunts' nasal Vaudois distortion of the first syllable, and setting my teeth. Having examined the rest of my father's abdominal cavity and sewn him up, the doctors told him that he shouldn't expect to live out the year. He resigned from his business, installed my mother and me in an apartment in a chalet above the village (there wasn't really room enough at my grandmother's, and the three ladies, besides, disapproved of my anarchic American upbringing), moved in with us, and prepared to die in the shadow of the mountains he had tramped as a student and a soldier, among the familiar smells of cow dung and damp hay.

It took him six years, most of which I spent in boarding school in nearby Giffern. Like my father's agony, and equally ruinous in financial terms, this arrangement was meant to last only a matter of months; the headmaster, a high-ranking officer in the army, had at some point commanded my father, and must have thought highly of him if he accepted me as a temporary boarder on short notice. Although I never questioned my mother on this matter, I think it likely that, as my father lingered on and on, the two men reached some sort of compromise about the school's fees, which were astronomical. I sensed this even at the time, and worked very hard, and participated in the school's activities more than most students. I liked the school immediately, and liked it more as the years went by; it was a refuge from the grimness of home, half an hour away in Valsins; I was constantly torn between my guilty wish that my father would die soon, for his was not an easy death, and the fear that, as soon as he did, my mother would take me back to New York.

From the moment we found ourselves trapped, so to speak, in Switzerland, my mother began to reveal an intense and irrational hatred of everything Swiss: the dullness and insularity of the country, the smugness of the national character, its worship of rules and order, the petty distrust of the foreigners who fund both ends of its economy. After a quarrel with the village butcher or the harelipped girl at the post office or her own sisters-in-law, my mother would declare, spitefully, and within earshot of my father, who lay supine and blanketed on the living room couch, dazed with pain from the pressure of a new tumor on his spine, that she had no business living and raising me in that fussy, stupid, old-maidish country.

She also disapproved, in her American puritanical way, of my classmates, and the manners and turn of mind I acquired in their company. My school was a Babel of the children of the rich, many of whom had no other real home. It was housed in eight large chalets just outside Giffern, and though only a half-hour train ride from my father's town, and much less as the crow (and now the hang glider) flies, was completely different in character. Giffern had been a resort since before the First World War. Every year at the approach of Christmas it began to bubble and seethe with exotic fur-clad fauna that spoke, in twenty different languages, a single simple idiom of money and sex. We too — most of the boys were the sons of that migratory race, and some parents kept chalets in the village — came from many different countries, and prepared for American, French, or Swiss universities. As a compromise between my parents, I was placed in the French section, where we were taught mostly by Frenchmen, and followed the curriculum of the French lycées; and as I stayed on, year after year, I developed a ghostly third nationality, in the scheme of which my ancestors were Gauls, Paris the glittering source of all civilization, and my heroes such men as Charles the Bold and Napoleon — for the virtues we aspired to were cunning, *audace,* and brilliance. From that perspective, my American self belonged, still — this was the mid-nineteen-sixties — to a race of kindly, slouching giants who twice in the last half century had alit on the continent, casually it seemed, with bright grins chewing away and their helmets askew, to make everything all right; while my Swiss half, less pleasingly, was associated with a dim nation of trolls obsessed with money and cleanliness, useful mainly as providers of comic relief.

Gradually I became my mother's accomplice in her contempt for everything Swiss, though that alliance was one I could not remember without pain after my father's death. Besides, the landscape of the Alps is not an invention of calendar printers. If you happened to be a child in it, and went to bed each night in one of the huddled wooden villages, which spend half of every day in the shadow of granite peaks; where the slopes around you are warm, green, and sweet smelling, but you need only raise your eyes to see storm clouds tearing themselves to shreds on a wilderness of rock and ice; where the earth is so folded and gnarled, and so alive with woods, water, and men, that a boy and a pair of walking boots can traverse whole countries in a day, hearing French in the morning and several German dialects in the afternoon, and still be home before dark — it will always seem that you once lived within a story, and although you're convinced that you know better, you will never quite cure yourself of the illusion that the routine exile of adulthood is, in your case, at least partly a matter of geography.

Only once since leaving boarding school had I gone back to Europe: also for one month, the summer after graduating from Brown. It had been a disappointing trip, an attempt at revisitation, undertaken either too early or too late, assuming that such things should be undertaken at all. At no moment during that month — the rainiest August in a century, all the newspapers said — did my memory speak to me. I had very little money and traveled in discomfort and sleeplessness on crowded summer trains, from friends' couches to friends' floors, seeking no new sights or experiences but wanting instead, for a brief holiday, to re-enter old ones. I seemed to imagine that the life I had left behind might still be waiting for me there, like a suit of clothes hanging in a closet. Of course it no longer existed, my band of friends having disbanded, and it soon became clear that the most important activities of my adolescence — trekking to certain cafés, haylofts, and forest trails where you could smoke and drink with your friends or bring a book without them — were rituals that had thrived on repetition. Doing them again once, four years later, without the risk of discovery and punishment, was a meaningless exercise in nostalgia. I spent only a brief week in Switzerland, preferring to visit friends, most of whom, students still, were passing the holidays at their parents' summer houses in the country or by the sea, or working at beginners' jobs in big cities — London, Paris, and Geneva — where I stopped for a few days at a time. The fact that they were rich and I was not had become a problem, because I had trouble keeping up with the round of restaurants and nightclubs that filled their evenings. And when I finally left the plains and boarded, by the shore of Lake Léman, the familiar blue-and-white train that would carry me up its winding tracks to the haunts of my childhood, it was not to my father's village that I went, but to a schoolmate's chalet in Giffern. He had not been a close friend. It rained incessantly. We had only a motorcycle for transportation, and we spent the better part of my three days there eating, smoking marijuana, and then eating some more. One evening, in desperation, we braved the downpour to ride over to the village movie house, where we saw a Burt Reynolds cop movie that had already depressed me six months before, in its original language, in Providence, and through which I sat miserably in my clammy clothes, feeling sick as I sobered up.

The records at the chalet were the usual rejects and hand-me-downs that get abandoned at country houses, on which the scratches and skips become an integral part of the songs. There was, however, an interesting collection of comic books, Astérix and Tintin and the French Air Force aces Tanguy and Laverdure (the latter a buffoonish sidekick who looked like my host, a resemblance enhanced to side-splitting effect, on one occasion, by the marijuana, of which there was so little left that we were contemplating a trip down to Geneva to buy more), and the Belgian Formula One driver Michel Vaillant and his big American pal Steve Warson, formerly a rival and now a teammate and ally. For these familiar companions I forsook Hans Castorp and *The Magic Mountain,* which I never picked up again, and which probably remains unread in that chalet, in yellow paperback, between the two books on shelves otherwise populated by gewgaws: the autobiography of David Niven, who lived nearby, and the collected stories of Natacha Stewart, a writer who was also a local, whose sons had been at school with me, and who must have been an acquaintance of my host's parents. At the last minute I shirked a visit to my father's grave. True, there was a violent storm that morning, and it continued to pour all day, and for some reason Bernard, the stationmaster at my father's village, wasn't answering his telephone, so I couldn't make sure that a taxi would be waiting to take me to the graveyard: I could have stayed one day more, even with the drugs all consumed and the comic books all reread, but I didn't. I didn't even call my aunts and my grandmother, who was then within a year of her death, and fed my conscience with the assumptions that, on one hand, the old lady, who had grown senile, would not recognize me (this information came from my mother, who I knew was not a reliable source) and on the other that my aunts had not answered my letter of two months before, announcing my impending visit.

Half a dozen years had elapsed since that trip, and I had never been tempted to repeat it.

Yet here I was again, in the unchanged café of the Montreux train station, with my bags at my feet and a beer before me, under the unsettling poster of Irina's double peddling soft drinks. I pulled my notebook from one pocket of my leather jacket and a *Glee* ballpoint pen from another, and began to write down ideas for my article on Giffern, listing the hotels, restaurants, ski trails and hiking trails, nightclubs, tennis courts, and so forth, that I planned to mention — provided they were still around, of course. I have often wondered why it is so difficult to scribble notes in public. There is the fear of being mistaken for a police informant or an anthropologist. Apart from the young waitress, who was leaning back against the counter and sifting dreamily through the coins in her kangaroo pouch, my only company in the café was a dough-faced man in a brown suit who had entered a few minutes after me, heaved a massive briefcase onto a chair, and called for *un ballon d'rouge* in a thick Vaudois accent, which had also been my father's. While I examined him, wondering briefly whether he came from my father's valley or another one nearby (he could have been a distant cousin of mine), he took a sip of wine, smacked his lips, and replaced the glass meticulously in the wet ring on the table. Then he removed his eyeglasses, pinched the bridge of his nose, cleaned the corners of his eyes, and finally rubbed his whole face with both hands, in a growing frenzy, moaning softly behind them.

Despite the American passport in my pocket and the suitcase at my feet, I had probably known this café longer than either of these people, a realization that afforded me a moment of self-satisfaction — a Swiss feeling, in fact. I could remember sitting here one afternoon at the age of eleven or twelve, while returning to Giffern from a session at the orthodontist's in Lausanne, on a day when the snow was piled high outside and still swirling down silently in the windows. Someone's gloves were drying on the radiator. My mouth was a mysterious throbbing city filled with aluminum bands and rings that I would soon show off to my classmates. My numbed toes, imprisoned in wet city shoes instead of the usual snowboots, just reached the floor. I was reading, for at least the second time, Jules Verne's *Michel Strogoff*. (This was shortly after I saw *Doctor Zhivago,* when I had developed an obsession with Russia.) The clock above the counter indicated that I had twenty-two minutes until departure, and that up in Giffern the torture of German class was proceeding without me. The radio was on, and as I accompanied Strogoff on his secret mission from Moscow to Irkutsk, I kept an ear tuned in case my favorite song was played. It was an overwrought French hit called "Les Neiges du Kilimandjaro," and sure enough it did come along — but by then my train was about to leave and I had to settle the tab and go, though I took the risk of waiting until the end of the first chorus, which I then carried out into the snow like a treasure. Sixteen years later, in that same café, I realized for the very first time that the title of that song was lifted from the Hemingway story. Simultaneously it occurred to me that Hemingway may have sat at this table for a few minutes in the nineteen-twenties, waiting between trains, and perhaps even pulled a notebook from a leather jacket and begun to write something down . . . The last chapters of *A Farewell to Arms* unfold in a town a few stops up the line on the train I was about to board, and the short story "Homage to Switzerland" opens in the very room where I now sat. I made a note to mention in my article that Hemingway had skied — or ski-ed, as he would have spelled it — in Giffern. In several biographies and memoirs I had seen a photograph of him smiling jauntily on a Giffern slope (according to the caption; I had pored over this picture carefully, examining the configuration of the pines and the steepness of the hill, but I was unable to recognize the location), with a pair of old-fashioned mountaineering goggles pushed up on his hat. I couldn't think of any such use for Nabokov, however, because he would probably have shunned the glitter of Giffern — though he too, in his later books, made use of the towns above Montreux. It was possible that Kuratkin may have known Nabokov, in Paris or Berlin or New York, or maybe even when they were children in Saint Petersburg. I wondered whether Michael had thought of contacting Nabokov's widow, who as far as I knew still lived in the pastry-cake hotel down by the lake. Even if she and Kuratkin had never crossed paths, she would be a good source on the period Michael was researching. As always when struck with a good idea involving a friend, I had an urge to call him immediately and make the suggestion, and also to find out how he was doing — which was odd, considering how annoying I usually found him. But then I found within that urge, coiled inside it like a snake, the need to call Irina to get his number, which I had refused to take on the phone at Kennedy Airport.

On second thought, recommending that Michael start importuning Nabokov's elderly widow might not be such a hot idea after all.

I heard a familiar whistle; my train was rounding the last bend between the villas and orchards above the town; soon it would come to a stop, with a long loud sigh and a final clank, on the siding right outside the café, wait for twenty minutes, and then start back on its ascent toward the Bernese Oberland. I paid, pocketed my notebook, picked up my bag, and went out to greet it.

Most of it was still my old friend, except for the first car behind the locomotive: a fancy new thing as long as a streetcar, with a rubber bellows in the middle and windows in the roof to offer the tourist a better view. I was examining it with mingled disappointment and admiration when the rear door of the next car opened slowly, pushed by a frail form holding a red shopping net that was empty except for a leather change purse. It was Mme. Marthe, the always sad, always silent mother of the baker in Valsins. She climbed down to the platform in several stages, rested, and then started toward me. She was in a miraculous state of preservation. Her bow-legged gait hadn't slowed, not a wrinkle in her face had lengthened or deepened, her gray chignon hadn't whitened or thinned. She wheezed past me without a glance, rolling like a sailor as she made for the stairs that led down to the underground tunnel. Her free hand reached for the banister when she was still five steps away.

Halfway down, she paused to await the passage of two boys who were clattering up at a run. Both of them toted shoulder bags of a color and shape that were extremely familiar to me, because by the time I reached their age I had already lost or worn out several. The taller boy was wearing the school blazer, which he had outgrown, and although he was shouting at his companion in French — *"Grouille-toi, grouille-toi,"* he was saying — I could tell, by the Brooks Brothers shirttail hanging out from under the blazer, and by the way he was treading on the backs of his loafers, that he was American. At the top of the stairs the other one consulted a giant diver's watch, far larger than his wrist, compared the results with the clock suspended from the roof of the platform, swore, and dashed back down after handing his bag to the American. A few seconds later he emerged on the other platform, where one caught the Geneva-bound trains, and started to pour coins into a cigarette machine, scattering some on the concrete and allowing them to roll off onto the tracks.

I might have spoken to the American kid, who was now hurling both bags up into the car that Mme. Marthe had just departed, but several things held me back. For one, it was a smoking car, and ever since arriving at Kennedy Airport the day before, I had been battling my old addiction and didn't want to put myself in the way of temptation. For another, I hadn't liked the child's face, which had that swollen, ferrety look that boys get in adolescence, possibly exaggerated, I thought, by a few recent tokes on a joint. I was torn between the desire to eavesdrop on their conversation and the knowledge that it would soon bore and annoy me. Finally, putting myself in his battered loafers, I pictured a middle-aged stranger accosting me on a train to tell me that he had been to my school, that his teachers had been So-and-so, and that Dr. Halik had had this way of breaking chalk on the blackboard, and decided it was too depressing a role to play. I climbed aboard another one of the four cars, installed myself, and pulled the *Herald Tribune* from my bag. This being Switzerland, it was out of the question that I put my feet up on the seat opposite me. In the minutes that followed, a few other passengers came to join me — peasants who farmed near the towns up the line, nondescript storekeepers, a mechanic or plumber in blue overalls on his way up to fix a generator or a water pump somewhere. Delayed by a mysterious further errand, the second schoolboy made it back only at the last minute, dashing by under my window with his hands full of candy bars and cigarette packs just as the conductor leaned out the door of the last car, his blood-red leather case hanging from his shoulder, and brought the whistle to his lips. Remembering protocol, I pushed the window shut before any of my fellow passengers could begin to protest; one of them, a lady who bore an amazing resemblance to a hedgehog, was already staring at me with hostility.

Twenty minutes later, at Les Avants, we waited on a siding to allow our sister train, coming from the opposite direction, to pass us on its way down and leave us the use of the track. Then we entered a long winding tunnel filled with echoes and shrieks, like a giant scare ride at a fair; and when at last we emerged into light again, after several minutes of artificial night, we found ourselves, as I knew we would, high within the mountains, out of sight of the lake and the plain, with tall arêtes and peaks all around us. It often happened that the weather at one end of the tunnel was different from that at the other — one entered in fog and came out in blinding sunshine, or vice versa — but today there was no change in the misty dampness that had followed me all the way from Geneva. Here the train halted again, at a tiny station, a small rust-colored shack and a siding. Six soldiers in full battle dress clambered into my car, making a lot of noise as they clomped about the cramped passage, distributing their guns and packs on the seats and the overhead racks. They were in a bad mood, apparently having lost the rest of their unit in the course of some exercise, and annoyed at having to make their way back by train. They were clean and clean-shaven, but their eyes looked as though they hadn't been getting much sleep. One of them in particular was in a foul temper, and I could tell, by the way he handled his gear, though he did it carefully, that he really wanted to bang it around. With a few sharp words he denounced the stupidity of a certain individual, presumably an officer, whom he didn't name but referred to as a testicle. While his comrades settled in, unbuckling their belts and rubbing their heads to loosen the hair matted by their helmets, he sat down without removing his, propped his elbows on his knees, and placed his face in his hands.

"You really don't have the morale, *mon vieux*," one of the others said, at which point he raised his steel head and declared that rather than face another week of that testicle he was going to have himself put behind bars, "so I don't have to look at his *tronche de merde* anymore," a course of action none of the others seemed to have an opinion about.

As a reporter in search of local color I was far more inclined to strike up a conversation with these men than with the students of my alma mater, but I was even more self-conscious about doing so. Whereas in one case I would have been burdened by a surfeit of knowledge, a dammed-up lake of garrulous memory, in the other it was my ignorance that troubled me. I wouldn't have known what to say to these people, even though my own father had been in this army all his adult life, flying over from America each year for his stint in uniform. (He kept this uniform and his assault rifle not on Lexington Avenue, of course, but in the family house in Valsins. The gun lived at the back of the broom closet on the ground floor, behind my aunts' jungle of mops and vacuum-cleaner tubes. My rare inspections of this object required tremendous stealth. And on a summer evening, once, I was able to nag my father into putting on his uniform, because I had never seen him in it, and he came into my room like that to put me to bed, smelling of naphthalene, still my father but also something different in those thick gray-green clothes, exactly the color of a fir tree dusted with snow. His feet were clad in carpet slippers. He pulled the curtains shut the moment he entered — the neighbors might have wondered what was going on — and my aunts, who had followed him in, teased him from the doorway. It was one of the rare occasions on which I saw them display humor of any kind. "Feel how itchy it is, it's very uncomfortable on long marches," my father said — he was right; it was a kind of rough felt — while he, perhaps for contrast, placed the palm of his hand, large, warm, and dry, on the side of my face; and then it was back to business, the fluffing of pillows, the click of the light switch, the adults' voices receding behind the closed door, and the lingering naphthalene.) As I said, my father served in the army for twenty years, but when he died — I was seventeen, allergic to orders and regimentation, and, as an American, an occasional protester of the Vietnam War — I renounced my Swiss citizenship precisely in order to avoid military service. As it turned out this was an unnecessary gesture, because I could have shirked it by the simple expedient of living abroad, which I planned to do anyway. But it is not uncommon to make silly gestures at that age, not that one doesn't continue to do so afterward, and my mother, encouraging me in this decision, read to me some alarming phrases from the back page of her own passport: "You may lose your nationality, blah blah blah, or by serving in the armed forces, blah blah blah, of a foreign state." They were all approximately my age, these men, and had I chosen differently ten years earlier I might have found myself riding on their side of the aisle that afternoon; I might have known them all; I might have had the right words of encouragement for the fed-up soldier, who was claiming once again that he would rather be *"dans l'trou"*; he seemed hypnotized by the horror of the idea. There was a promising moment (we had shed the other passengers at recent stops and I was the only civilian left in the car) when one of them began to pull bottles of beer from his pack and hand them around, and I thought I was about to get involved. But suddenly we realized, as the train embarked on a long banked curve through a meadow, that the next stop was Valsins, which turned out to be their destination. Back went the bottles, unopened, and the Swiss Army knives that had begun to appear (they're black, not red), accompanied by curses. They all rose to their feet on the swaying floor and began to buckle and snap their gear back on, like horses getting into their own harnesses.

I grasped the handles atop the window to pull it down as they detrained, and leaned out into the cool mountain air. On the windowsill of the waiting room were some boxed flowers that I didn't remember, but otherwise everything was unchanged. An unhitched wooden cart stood at the end of the platform, laden with aluminum milk canisters; an obese retiree, his face blue from drink, sat expressionless on the bench outside, his paws folded atop a cane, not even bothering to look at the soldiers as they wedged themselves sideways out the door and down to the tracks. They stopped to consult with Bernard, the stationmaster, who was at his post with his dark blue uniform, his képi, and his hand-held signal. I could not see our house from the train — it was on lower ground, hidden from me by the station — but my eyes followed the white road up the hill across the river, where, half concealed behind the larches atop another fold in the land, rose the shingled steeple of the church in whose yard my father lay. I would go there tomorrow. As the train lurched forward, the soldiers, having extracted the information they needed from Bernard, trooped away toward the village. If these were large maneuvers, one or more of them — or more likely their officer, the testicle — might be billeted, that night, in my aunts' house, perhaps in my old room.

XIII

I TRIED to call Hélène several times in the next two days, but I never got an answer. I even called Steyer in New York to make sure I had the right number, but I was unable to reach him either.

I had looked forward to putting a few thousand miles between the Alberses and myself, but I found I was unable to get away from Irina. It wasn't, as in the songs, that everything reminded me of her. On the contrary: I had indeed left behind in New York all the places and activities that bore associations with her. Moreover, by traveling to Giffern and Valsins to research my article, I had stepped into a realm where the memories I encountered were bound to be more prodigal than any connected with adult life, even life with Irina. The problem was this: as I went about my business, renting the smallest room in Giffern's cheapest inn (Hemingway's old haunt), the Gasthaus Oehrli, visiting the tourist bureau to collect a sheaf of brochures and statistics, exploring the new hotels, tasting the new restaurants, or taking the afternoon off to wander along a familiar old trail, I felt a need for someone to talk to. Not that I was alone; off season the colony of foreigners in Giffern dwindles almost to nothing, but there were two elderly couples I could claim as acquaintances through their sons, and did. I went up to the school, saw some of my old teachers, and had lunch with one of them, the bearded old M. Crauste, who had taught me history, and who seemed delighted that I should have chosen his subject for my major in college. (I also wanted to see the headmaster, but he was on maneuvers.) In a restaurant one evening I found a contemporary of mine and accepted his invitation to his table, but he had taken to booze very seriously, living idle in Giffern all year round, and after asking for news of other old classmates he immediately cut me short, giving me to understand that his had been a miserable childhood and he didn't want to be reminded. And finally, over in Valsins, where I went for a day, there were my aunts, and even the storekeepers — or at least the tobacconist and the stationmaster — remembered me cordially after minimal prodding. It was Irina whom I wanted to talk to; and what I wanted was not so much to talk as to lead her around these places, to have her see them with her own limpid eyes. When I had climbed through this particular copse of trees one morning, oh, twenty years earlier, with a plump rucksack on my back and stiff new walking shoes on my smarting feet, surrounded by the shouts and babbles of my companions, none of whom was over nine years of age, an illumination had come to me like a state of grace. I had been thinking about something entirely unrelated, if I had been thinking at all, when at last, after weeks of classroom struggle, I grasped suddenly and effortlessly the key to long division, the way the numbers transubstantiate as they leap the inky barrier between the part and the whole. Years later, while doing words-per-column calculations at *Glee,* or while trying to work out, yet again, how it was possible that my semimonthly paycheck should be so diminished by the depredation of the government, I would sometimes glimpse in the corner of my mind a particular pinebranch, wide and flat and bent by its own weight, nodding after the passage of the boy in front of me, who was carrying his rucksack by only one of its straps, and who had a clump of hair, stiffened by sweat, sticking up on top of his head, and who, while I worked at *Glee* in boredom and comfort, was in prison in Ecuador, already nearing the end of an eight-year sentence earned while trying to smuggle an amount of cocaine out of the country, in the company of another boy who may also have been in that column of climbing children, on that day of excursion, probably a Thursday, probably in October, in 1966. Time and again, in the course of that week in Giffern, I ached with a surfeit of knowledge and memory as I passed, with my faithless love suddenly at my side, the hedge where the grass snake had lived, or the plane tree that still — still! — bore the mark of its inopportune encounter with my bicycle, a scar that had a brother, born at the same moment and similar in shape, on my ankle, a Y-shaped welt of shiny rippled skin, which she herself had asked me about, and along which she had run her fingertips and her lips.

In that other autumn, when I had first fallen in love with Irina, at a time when I had had to rise from my desk at least once in the course of each morning to peer out the door and make sure that she was sitting at hers in that alcove at the end of the blue-carpeted passage, she and I had driven up to Fincham together for a weekend, through the incandescent woods of New England. It was a cold, calm morning — sweater weather, college weather. In those days we did not yet know each other well, and I had been driven to small frenzies of tenderness by the gradual revelation of the details of her childhood, by the knowledge that she'd had a dog named Doctor and also a rabbit, Tobias, and that when very small she had been bitten by a horse. (I could see it all: the animal's huge head canting from its neck, the hairy lips drawn in, the long, foolish teeth, and Irina, tiny Irina, squalling.) When, driving up through the Berkshires that crisp Friday, we came to a bend in the road and saw beneath us a shallow valley half in sunlight, with a white clapboard village and a narrow steeple, and Irina said, very matter-of-factly, "This is where I spent all my summers" — confirming what I had guessed just a second before, the moment that new landscape had slid into the windshield — something had tightened in my chest and my eyes had begun to sting. And now, as I trudged up the white road to the Valsins church, on a similar autumn day, aiming for another steeple, the memory of that moment of unrequited emotion so disturbed me that I wanted to take it all back, to have it never have happened, and to hell with the dog, the rabbit, and the horse, and little girls.

I thought I remembered the location of my father's grave in the churchyard, but in the ten years since his burial my image of the place had become both schematized and distorted, so that I had to wander the gravel paths for some time before finding his cross. At one point I was even threatened by the panicky suspicion that I may have substituted in my memory this particular graveyard for another. It was a simple Protestant place, an approximate square on a fairly steep slope, closed on the lowest side by the rough-cast white wall of the church and on the other three by the inevitable pine hedge. I was alone there except for a family of Germans — on my way up I had had to step off the road and straddle the ditch to make room for their wide Mercedes-Benz, with the oval German rear license plate — who had come to visit the church out of touristic habit, as though they were in Italy; as far as I knew it contained nothing of any interest whatsoever. At last I found what I was looking for. By coincidence, the stretched and flattened cross at the tip of the steeple's shadow lay draped at that moment over the limestone twin engraved with my father's name; by the time I left, it had crawled through the grass and the gravel to lie across my grand-mother, three feet away. My thoughts, as I watched its slow progress, simultaneously defending myself against a persis-tent bee, were those which are often reported by men of my age when they return from contemplating the mounds of earth and the markers under which lie the supine skeletons of their fathers — ghoulish objects whose connection with the for-merly smiling, fleshy parent seems trivial and far more ten-uous than that of the things he once handled: his shoes, his pen, his hairbrush. I wondered what was expected of me, what I was meant to feel, whether I was betraying my father by not weeping, and how much, how often, and how long I had betrayed him when he was alive, by wishing and waiting for his death. I thought of Irina and her mother, and how they too had waited for Kuratkin to die: only Michael had fought alongside his grandfather, only Michael had raged and refused, while the rest of us cringed and looked away, find-ing his behavior both childish and slightly shameful. In ad-dition, I thought of my miscarried ambitions — relieved, for once, not to be a journalist, for as I palpated my soul and poked at my emotions, I knew that I would otherwise have been tempted to write, for money, a few thousand words for the "About Men" column in the Sunday *Times Magazine,* on my visit to my father's grave, in quiet and reticent tone, mentioning such things as betrayal, my father's uniform, my father's cancer, and my chances of making peace with his ghost and with myself, all of which would indeed have been a betrayal of that reserved man, who had stiffened at displays of emotion and shunned self-analysis.

And now I see that I have done it anyway, and may as well continue. I wondered what sudden wanderlust or hopes of enrichment had led him to pack a suitcase one day and head for America, for he was a methodical man not given to brainstorms or whims. It occurs to me now that — for these things have a way of happening — he may have had his heart broken, or had some other kind of trouble, and wanted to get away for a while. Maybe it was disappointment: he had been a promising skier and soccer player and came close to playing on the national team one year, but had settled for coaching tennis in summer and and being a ski guide in winter in Giffern. I regretted not questioning, at Kuratkin's funeral, that old WASP woman, who, I now thought, may even have been the surviving half of the couple who had hired him to return with them to New York. They must have brought him back with them as a curio, and lent him to their friends. And being still very young, he may have been taken in by their sweet American ways, their immediate expectation that he call them by their Christian names, their assumption that nothing could be simpler for him than to drop everything and sail with them across the Atlantic; by that breezy self-assurance of theirs, which, unlike its European counterpart, can be so contagious in its cheerfulness, and so happy of that contagion, that to a middle-class Swiss it would have seemed to be unrelated to money, or to the narrowness of bloodlines, or to tiered depths of ancestors buried in the same soil. I am making all this up, of course; I do not really know who these people were, but that is how I happen to imagine them. And I assume, because of his insistence on remaining in Switzerland when he first fell ill, and then remaining steadfast in that decision through six years of my mother's sniping, that the previous decade in America and his marriage to an American must have caused him a lot of homesickness. The Swiss have a rare aptitude for it (the term the French use, *mal du pays,* is in fact a Swiss expression), which they no doubt developed during the centuries when the men used to leave the country, generation after generation, to fight as mercenaries, on every side, in every European war. They were known to their paymasters and their victims alike for ferocity and courage, traits they sometimes exhibited to an unnecessary and self-destructive degree, and their leavetakings from their high-perched villages must very often have been final. Swiss songs of nostalgia are even more childish and naïve than those of other countries. They tend to be not about a girl left behind, but simply about the mountains and valleys and lakes, the land whose poverty drove you away in the first place.

And now my aunts. I was late in getting to their house, having taken the long way from the church to the village, starting along a track consisting of two bald lines worn in the meadow by tractor tires. It soon died out in the middle of a cow pasture, where one animal caught my eye and followed me like a dog all the way down to the electric fence, licking her shiny pink nose in an eager way. I had once known an easy technique for slipping between the two electrified wires of such fences, a sort of forward limbo movement combined with a breaststroke and a final sideways hop to regain my balance on the other side. As I approached the fence, with the inexplicably bonded beast still at my heels — she had rather long horns — I was happy of the chance to repeat this athletic feat, but being out of practice I forgot to check for cowflops, and at the very last moment had to grab the lower wire to avoid stepping in one, zapping myself mildly for my pains. At the bottom of the hill I crossed the footbridge over the river, passed the sawmill whose whines and shrieks had awakened me every morning during holidays, and strolled up through the village, thinking I should have picked some flowers for the aunts — I hadn't brought them anything from New York. On the balcony of their house a fat stranger was reading a newspaper in the sunshine. (It may not be fair to call him fat, because all I could see from below was a bald pate and the top of a newspaper protruding above the parapet, but the distance between the two suggested a large intervening belly — then again, it may have been merely a concession to far-sightedness.) Perhaps one of my aunts had taken on a man, a surprising and exciting possibility, or else another relative, some distant cousin of mine, may have moved in or come to stay for a few days.

Corinne, the younger sister, opened the door for me. "*Te voilà donc,*" she said, as though I were late for a meal, which I had often been in the past. Like Mme. Marthe, the baker's mother whom I had seen at the train station in Montreux, neither Corinne nor her sister, Valérie, had aged a day. It was as though these women reached a plateau at fifty from which they didn't budge for several decades — but then none of them smoked, drank, had affairs or financial troubles, and they walked everywhere and went to bed every night at nine o'clock. I had grown accustomed to the phenomenon that causes one's childhood surroundings to have shrunk to half their size by the time one sees them again, but the vestibule at my aunts' (to dignify it with a name it didn't deserve) had undergone this transformation to an unsettling degree. Moreover, none of the doors was where it was supposed to be. Most disturbing of all was the disappearance of the staircase leading to the upper floor.

"But everything's changed," I said, observantly, struggling for balance. (I had forgotten that Swiss kisses, like Russian ones, are given in threes.)

"We moved down here after your grandmother passed away," Corinne explained, "and we rent out the top floor and the attic, which we converted. We live modestly," she added, initiating a theme that began to be developed as soon as she led me into her sister's presence, in the tiny, tiny living room, where Valérie was seated, or rather posed, on a hard chair by the window, through which I saw the friendly branches of a cherry tree I had liked to climb and gorge on after dinner on long June evenings. I knew my aunts well enough to be certain that Corinne, who had always run the show, had, after consulting the cuckoo clock that told them I would soon be arriving, installed Valérie in that rustic chair (of the type whose back is a single piece of carved wood, with a heart-shaped hole in the center) as part of some scenario, but I had forgotten too much to know what that scenario might be.

We moved to a narrow table in a narrow nook at the far end of the room, which connected to the kitchen. I am not a large man, but in that apartment I felt like a Kodiak bear. Valérie had not changed any more than Corinne, but in childhood I had been unaware of her remarkable resemblance to my father, especially in profile — mostly a question of noses. The table was newly made, of unstained varnished pine, with a surface of pink Formica embedded in its center. Following some plan, Valérie fetched from the sideboard a pint bottle of kirsch and one miniature stemmed flute. It was 11:02 A.M., according to the cuckoo clock (whose mechanism I had once deranged while removing the counterweights, for no reason at all; they were made of brass and shaped like pine cones), and I would have much preferred a cup of tea. Indeed, I had expected one, for this was the hour at which the aunts normally had their hot water with lemon and their piece of zwieback toast.

"How nicely you've redone all this," I said.

"It was an expense," Corinne said, "but we had to do it if we were going to rent out the upstairs, which had become a necessity. As I'm sure you realize, your poor father's illness, and of course that expensive school of yours, were costly matters."

Then, at 11:05, I understood that the old ladies had feared I might claim a stake in their financial affairs; that they had fretted over my visit, and worked out between them what to say, probably including several contingency plans, and had perhaps even paid a visit to Maître Favre, the lawyer in Château d'Oex, to take stock of their rights against me. They had worried about this for ten years. I drained the kirsch. "It does one good," I said, in imitation of my father. "*Ta maman is remarried,*" Valérie said. My eyes smarted from the kirsch, and my throat was tight, and it seemed possible for a moment that through some sympathetic reaction this might set off the real thing, perhaps stored up while I stood, dry-eyed, at my father's grave an hour before. At the same time I was thinking that as far as I knew I was indeed these women's closest living relative, and that after all it would be nice to have this house after they died, and why hadn't I thought of it before? To bring my future family here to ski . . . I hadn't thought of it because of Fincham; that was why. When I had thought of family life in the country, I pictured it in Fincham. Surely the aunts had not prepared for themselves for my bursting into tears and laying my head on the pink Formica.

"Yes, remarried," I said. "She married a retired building contractor in California. She lives there, and every winter she goes to Florida. And of course she still has an apartment in New York."

Only the first two of these statements were true, but I could think of no other way to tell the old ladies, whose eyes, behind their magnifying lenses, looked even more worried than they probably were, that they were safe from my mother and me, that we wanted nothing. And although I was successful in this, it did not make the remaining half hour of my visit any easier. I declined a second shot of kirsch and departed at 11:45, wearing on my wrist my father's beautiful gold watch, which I had thought lost; my mother had forgotten to collect

it from the hospital after he died, and it had been delivered to
my aunts. Before putting it on I had removed the brightly
colored Swatch I wore, an object of neopsychedelic design
that Irina had given me, and tied it to Corinne's birdlike wrist,
so that once, at least, the three of us laughed, but not very
hard and not very long.

I walked all the way back to Giffern along the river, a three-
hour walk, with that comforting new weight on my wrist,
pausing at the riding school outside Giffern to watch a small
boy on a huge horse circling the ring on a lead held by a
booted riding master, who bore a striking resemblance to
someone I had once known, somewhere, whom I had seen
often . . . It tortured me for a while, and then at last, with
great relief, I remembered who it was — Edgar, the man who
brought the coffee cart up to *Glee* every day.

The thought of Edgar made me hungry, and when I got
back to Giffern I stopped to eat in a tearoom that overlooked
the tennis courts, whose upkeep had been abandoned a week
earlier and whose clay was already pitted and matted by rain.
In two months they would be iced over, and "Lara's Theme"
and "The Godfather Theme" and Strauss waltzes would begin to pour from the loudspeakers in the wooden stands. I
lingered over this meal, which, since it was past four o'clock,
I pieced together from croissants au jambon and pastries and
tea. Then, full-bellied and tired from my walk, I returned to
the Gasthaus Oehrli. Frau Oehrli intercepted me on my way
up to my room, with a message that a Mademoiselle Irina
had called from New York.

"At what time did she call?" I asked.

"It was while I was trying to serve lunch," Frau Oehrli
said.

Now it was almost midnight in New York, and having
been trained not to call too late, so as not to wake Mrs. Albers, I put off returning the call until morning. I needed to

take a nap before going out to dinner — at a chalet just outside the village, belonging to the parents of an old schoolmate, people I hardly knew — and as I stood in the shower
and then made for my narrow bed, I tried not to wonder
what Irina wanted from me, and discovered with some satisfaction that it didn't seem to matter. Perhaps fatigue, or
some unconsciously cathartic moment in the graveyard . . .
It had been a good thing, anyway, to see the aunts . . . Still
damp from the shower, I inserted myself between Frau Oehrli's
rough linen sheets, under the massive weight of the eiderdown, crawled to the very bottom of the bed, bunched a
pillow under my head — one of those ideal pre-foam pillows, which, once you've found the proper fit, stop struggling to regain their original shape. I set my alarm clock for
an hour later, and decided that when I woke I would try to
reach Hélène again and make a date for next week. Just before falling asleep I heard beneath my window the character-
istic noise of a 50cc moped from whose carburetor its teenage
owner had removed the air filter, simply in order to make it
louder, just as I had done with mine . . .

Somewhere in Geneva, at long last, someone answered the
telephone.
    "Yes, I am Hélène," the woman said. "Who's speaking?"
    "I'm a friend of Eric Steyer's," I said.
    "Ah!" she said. "Ah! How is he?"
    "I just had dinner with him in New York," I said. "He
asked me to give you a call. I have some photographs for
you."
    "So he's not coming?"
    "He's really very busy," I said. "I'm in Giffern right now,
but I'll be in Geneva in a few days, and I thought we could
meet and I could give you the pictures."
    "Did he say whether he was coming later?" she asked.

"I don't know what his plans are," I said. "I —"

"I have a telephone number for him in New York. Could you tell me if it's the right one? Could you wait a moment while I get it?" she said.

When she came back to the phone, she asked whether I had her address so that I could send her the pictures.

"Well, I'll be passing through Geneva in a few days, as I said. I hoped I could invite you to lunch."

"That's very nice of you," she said. "The problem is that I'm very busy myself."

I tried another tack.

"It's a little complicated to explain over the telephone," I said, "but Eric told me you'd been in Afghanistan with Médecins sans Frontières."

"Yes?" she said.

"You see, I'm a journalist; I'm interested in what's going on over there."

"You should speak to Eric," she said.

"I did. It's specifically Médecins sans Frontières that interests me."

"They're based in Paris. I can tell you how to reach them," she said.

"If you could just spare me fifteen minutes," I said.

"Now?"

"No, when I come to Geneva. It's quite important to me."

"Well, all right," she said, after a silence. Clearly I was a pain in the neck.

But when we met it would be quite different. I took the photographs out of my jacket and looked at them again. She really was very pretty. Yes, it would be quite different. Steyer had neglected to tell me that she was in love with him, but I could work around that. A pity — I had said nothing of what I had meant to say: that I was here working on a couple of reportages . . . I had even imagined telling her how beautiful

Giffern was at this time of the year, and how she ought to see it . . . I began to get depressed.

My hosts at dinner that night, the parents of my former class-mate, were a French couple in their seventies. They had shed all their property in France and made Giffern their main residence immediately after Mitterrand became president. Once it had been established that their son was now a banker in Brussels and I an editor in New York, it became difficult to find anything to talk about. "Do you play golf? Bridge?" the old man roared. "I distinctly remember," he shouted, "that an American once told me he rode to hounds in Central Park. Can that be true? Mind you, it was a long time ago."

I so impressed myself with my descriptions of the difficulty and danger of life in New York — the noise, the filth, the countless madmen raving in the streets, the drug-crazed killers on the subway — that I wondered why I wanted to look for adventure elsewhere. We were waited on by a Spanish maid who was just being broken in, as the wife put it, and my attempts at conversation were constantly interrupted by the necessity of correcting her mistakes. I was about to tell them that I was here to write an article about Giffern when they began to complain bitterly about the arrival in these last years (they meant the last three decades) of "all these people," movie people, tourists, *ces Arabes pétrolifères et je ne sais quoi encore,* who, they claimed, had destroyed the last vestiges of village life. So I remained silent, a smug traitor.

XIV

I ATE AN early breakfast in the dining room downstairs, at a small table by the window. The checkered tablecloth was held in place by the springed clamps I had liked to play with, to the annoyance of my parents. I ordered what the menu called a "continental breakfast," a description held over from the days when all tourists had been British: a croissant and a type of bisected bun that children called *fesses*, though the resemblance is small, and some special rhubarb jam that Frau Oehrli brought to my table, explaining that it had been made by her sister-in-law and was normally reserved for family. I had with me the previous day's *Herald Tribune,* which still arrived every afternoon on the 4:12 train, having left Paris at dawn.

The *Tribune* offered one a pleasant, somewhat distant view of the United States, as a country among others, where Washington outweighed New York in influence. Through the filter of its pages my country and my city's life appeared less chaotic, even pleasantly picturesque. In that particular edition, for instance, there was a color piece about some goings-on within Condé Nast Publications, describing the replacement of the head of one magazine by another, with the fired woman being given another post at the company, a move that was interpreted by various unnamed insiders as a demotion, a promotion, or a kick upstairs. It was gratifying to see this story presented with an edge of irony, the implication being that all this was a tempest in a teapot (my own was growing cold by now, but still I lingered over the comics, over Art Buchwald's column, over the people column), just some entertaining back-stabbing in the corridors of a company supposedly staffed by elegant and slightly eccentric ladies. At home I would have read such an article as closely as goat entrails, not only because the comings and goings at Condé Nast always had repercussions on *Glee,* but also because I would have had to discuss it and exchange opinions and conjectures with my colleagues and any anxious freelance hack I might speak to on the phone that morning.

I was, of course, postponing a climb up to my room to call Irina, proving to myself that I was in no hurry. Besides, I couldn't imagine any emergency in Irina's life — Mrs. Albers falling under a bus, the house in Fincham burning down, Michael stealing the silver again — that might need my attention. I was traveling, I was unreachable, and that was how it should be. I would call Irina, if there was still time, when I returned to the inn that afternoon.

That day I planned, for exercise, for fun, and for my article, to take a small excursion that had been one of my favorites as a child, when I had repeated it, I think, four times in all, though never alone. It involved riding a cable car to the top of a mountain, the Hüttligrat, which looked from the village like a green plum pudding, its lower flanks covered in pine woods that grew scarcer and thinner as you climbed. Behind the pudding, invisible from Giffern, was a saddle connecting it with the taller, rockier Wildengrat, from whose summit — a long, sloping arête well above the tree line — one could see, on a clear day, over a tumultuous blue-and-gold expanse of Alps (rather like a floor of clouds gazed at through the window of an airliner, and with something of the same anxiety) all the way to the Matterhorn and Monte Rosa on the Italian border, to the Dent du Midi near France, and to the Jungfrau in the high heart of Switzerland. Continuing westward on the lower part of the arête — for you couldn't stay too long at the top, leaning into the wind that came all the way from Africa to rush in your ears and make you walk in a crouch, worried about loose rocks — and listening for the sound of falling water, you eventually arrived at what appeared to be an impassable precipice separating you from a massive and much taller rock face. It was actually the edge of a concave slope shaped like the lumpy seat of a giant's chair, made mostly of lichen-covered rock. Near its lower edge was an underground spring, where I had once seen three chamois — though of course they saw me first, and were looking at me from a distance with the same expression you see on the face of a stranger you have just hailed on a city street to ask for directions. From the spring a narrow and loud waterfall dropped straight down into a perfect little bowl of a valley (sometimes suspending over it, if the conditions were right, a ghostly rainbow) that cradled a small pine wood. You reached it by climbing down, carefully, over the boulders of an old rockslide.

Down there, sheltered on all sides, was a perfect place to stop and eat your sandwich, on the spongy bank of the stream, which gurgled away to your left into a marsh overgrown with man-high yellow reeds. On either side, the pine wood's brown elastic floor was veined and wrinkled with roots and littered with pine cones and small stones, ranging in size from a fist to a head, that had bounced and rolled off the tongue of the rock slide above and come to rest in the hollow, gradually sprouting a hard moss in hues of red, green, and purple.

The trick was to arrive there around noon, because the place got no more than two hours of sunlight a day. You felt very safe there, as if held in the hand of the mountain, though you had traveled far from everything and reached the most distant point of your journey. You felt that you had earned the food you were eating, and deserved the pleasant easy walk to come: a five-minute climb up the western side of the bowl, and then, at a spot where there was a hayrack for deer to feed on in winter, a left turn onto the flank of yet another mountain, this one called Mésagine, where eventually you met a proper forest trail that zigzagged down through the trees, and along which you tripped freely and carelessly, propelled by your own weight, which by now had been pleasantly doubled by fatigue, your calves at once aching and relieved; emerging at last into the pasture above the Valsins church, while below you the cows and then the village clustered on the floor of the valley. Beyond the village, just visible in the distance to your left, the tiny blue-and-white train would flash one of it windows as it wound its way over from Château d'Oex, disappearing now into a tunnel and then into a wood, whistling before it crossed the road, and pulling to a stop at the station with a screech that reached you seconds afterward and seemed somehow unconnected with machinery and steel — almost a sound of nature, having the same status, say, as the peaceful clanking of the cowbells in the stillness of late afternoon. Linking as it did my two home villages, Giffern and Valsins, in a difficult and circuitous manner, this route had always held for me a certain symbolic, secret, and slightly haunted value. As a boy I had been proud of my knowledge of the region, of the various ways of getting from one place to another while avoiding the roads and the better-traveled trails, information unknown to my schoolmates, who rarely had the opportunity to wander away from Giffern unsupervised, and who preferred, on their days off (as I came to, when I entered adolescence), to loiter their afternoons away in the village's cafés and tearooms, in groups that grew and split up and re-formed in different combinations, discussing in depressed and cynical tones the topics of the day, all of which, at the time, seemed crucial, but which I cannot reconstruct from memory. Most of my imaginary heroics, the rescues and midnight rides and defenses against superior forces, unfolded in the immediate region, whose terrain I considered, at the age of ten, with an old general's eye. I knew where to place the machine-gun nests, which ravine to sneak along with my bayonet between my teeth, and exactly where to ford the river, just as I knew all these things about the garden of the house in Valsins, where my toy soldiers fought in weirdly hypertrophied country, a rosebush being an entire forest and a footpath between the azaleas a murderously wide field of fire that often cost me my bravest and even my luckiest men.

In adolescence I turned bookish and grew glasses on my nose and forgot this way of looking at things, and took to hanging out; my knowledge of secret places became useful only for rule breaking; but my memory of that earlier time survived far more vividly in my adult memory, and when I set out from the Gasthaus Oehrli that morning, with a picnic lunch prepared by Frau Oehrli in a small rucksack she had lent me, trusting my feet to a pair of modern athletic shoes (which performed very well, though they aged a lot that day), I was thinking much the same way I had thought as a small boy: I was thinking that the country through which I was about to travel was in some ways similar to what I might have to manage in Afghanistan.

As it turned out, I wasn't the only one thinking such things. When I left the center of the village and set off for the cable car of the Hüttligrat, about a mile away, I was passed by a convoy of army trucks rumbling along on knobby tires, the troops facing each other under the camouflage canvas. There were also fighter jets on the wing that day, gradually weaving a cat's cradle of white condensation trails in the otherwise pristine sky. In Switzerland you grow accustomed to seeing military activity wherever you go, and the roads are clogged almost as often by army vehicles as by cattle; but in the few days since my arrival there had been so much of it that I knew I had happened onto a period of large-scale maneuvers, the full-fledged war games that take place every few years, pitting two teams, the red attackers and the blue defenders, against each other. These had been important events during my childhood, not because they disrupted civilian life very much (you might find a road blocked for an hour or two, or a cable car commandeered by troops, or a sentry at a bridge telling you politely but firmly, and without a trace of humor, that the concrete span on which you both stood no longer existed, having been, as the case might be, obliterated by bombs from above or shattered by sappers from below), but because they required the participation of our colonel-headmaster as well as that of two or three other teachers who happened to be male and Swiss. During those infrequent periods of war the life of the school tended to be more relaxed than usual, and greater mischief could be made at lesser risk. The Col de Périllon, which gave access to the Giffern valley, would probably be blocked that day — which didn't mean that civilians couldn't get through, only that the roadblock would cause a traffic jam if there were more than four cars on the road — but I would be bypassing it altogether, on foot, and high above.

In the ticket booth at the base station of the Hüttligrat,

among racks of postcards and candy bars, a young woman
was counting stitches in a pink baby sweater, with an extra
knitting needle stuck through her bun. She informed me that
I was an early riser, and also that tomorrow the cable cars
would shut down for the fall, not to open again until Decem-
ber — a hiatus I had forgotten but now made a note to mention in my article for those readers who might want to come
to Giffern off season. It was pure coincidence that I had
scheduled my excursion for that day and not the next, and
this made me feel lucky and happy that I would probably be
alone on the mountain. I must have been if not the only, at
least the first customer of the day, for as I approached the
station I had not seen a single gondola drifting up the mountainside. The gnome in green overalls who shunted them
around the barnlike structure, where the huge engine spun
with a well-oiled hum, was more stooped than the last time
I had seen him, but he still hadn't shaved his stubble or changed
his cigar butt. After punching my ticket and handing it back
to me, he tramped away to a line of gondolas hanging from
an overhead siding and steered the first one, by means of a
long hooked lever with a black knob, onto the main track,
where it came to rest with a loud, satisfying clack. He unlocked its doors with the socket key that hung from his belt
by a leather shoelace. At the age of five I had wanted to be
neither a fireman nor a policeman but a cable car gnome,
mainly because the operation he now went on to perform,
once I was seated on the bench inside, with the door locked
shut, had a mysterious hold on my imagination: grabbing the
door handle, he began to pull the gondola along the track,
walking faster and faster in his heavy boots, the rumbling of
the wheels growing louder over my head, until at last they
rolled off the end of the track and bit the cable (whose mo-
mentum made the whole gondola swing backward) just as
the man reached the lip of the platform and stopped before a

twenty-foot drop, letting go of the handle and sending me off on my journey, the gondola swaying back and forth like a slow pendulum — until, a few seconds later, its superstructure went rattling through the wheels of the first pylon, which shook everything inside you, and, if it were winter, made your ski poles slide from their propped position against the bench and fall to the wooden slats of the floor.

Atop the not very tall Hüttligrat I already felt the altitude, the thinner air, the hint of ice somewhere closer than before. The smells of autumn, of damp earth and decaying leaves, which had already invaded the Giffern valley, were not to be found up here, as if the air were already too weak to carry them, but its freshness and dryness were another kind of wealth, and equally rewarding. I shouldered my pack, waved goodbye to the identical gnome (literally a twin) who manned the top station alone, and after passing beneath the shuttered windows of the mountaintop *stübli,* now closed for the season, set off toward the saddle that would carry me up to the higher crest of the Wildengrat. The mountain sloped down to my right, with the forest beginning fifty yards below me. On the Alp opposite mine the same forest grew to the same height, its lower hem winding around the belly of the hill, above a diminutive farmhouse, a few isolated barns, and clusters of cows. A hawk drifted by below me, turning, adjusting its wings nervously, searching the trees for movement. At the bottom of the gorge the road to the Périllon pass curved along the river, whose color it matched so exactly they would have been indistinguishable if not for the cars. Another military convoy was thundering by down there, though from where I walked it was completely silent, a brown-banded green snake, small enough to be a good prey for the hawk, who had found an upward drift and was circling inside it blissfully, resting and postponing his hunt.

Steyer had told me, once, of an interesting way in which

the Afghan guerrillas had learned to shoot down Russian helicopters. Lacking rockets that could penetrate the armored
underside of the machines, they had taken to placing bait for
them: a single man would hide in a canyon and fire upward
at the gunship, teasing it with the harmless pinging of bullets
under its chin, and luring it lower into the gorge until it became vulnerable to the men lying in ambush on the heights,
who then machine-gunned it from above. Steyer had told me
about this in Irina's presence, on one of the rare occasions
when the three of us had been together. He had dropped by
my cramped little room for a drink that night, Kiely's being
closed again, and he was still there when Irina returned from
having dinner with some girlfriends. Steyer politely tried to
leave as soon as he had finished his drink, thinking we might
want to be alone, but I insisted that he stay and have another
one, so that he wouldn't be dashing off the moment she arrived. He had been in the middle of telling me about the hel-
icopter business when she rang my doorbell, and he resumed
the story as soon as the greetings were over, and that familiar
frown and slightly disgusted look had appeared in Irina's features. She retreated to my kitchen and took off her rings and
began to wash the dishes I had left in the sink, something she
wouldn't ordinarily have done. Irina loved to laugh, and did
it often, but there were some topics — money, her painting,
the suffering we inflict on animals — that froze her and made
conversation impossible. Any mention of them could ruin
her day and yours. Steyer's months in Afghanistan had become another one of these topics. It seemed to her an outrage
that other people's pain and mutilation and death could become, at a dinner table, or in this case at a coffee table, over
two glasses of brandy, material for anecdotes — anecdotes
told, she suspected, entirely for effect. Of course she was right,
but it was also true that she would have listened to them with
considerably less annoyance had they issued from anyone but

a friend of mine. She particularly disliked my admiration for Steyer's courage and his sense of adventure. That Steyer had run exactly the same risks as the Mujahedin did not excuse him in her eyes, because to her way of thinking he'd had no business being there in the first place. He had gone there to gawk and had returned with stories with which to impress people more gullible than herself. Once he had left my apartment, kissing her in the doorway — she held her dripping hands away from him and presented her cheek stiffly, because her steamed hair was falling in her face — she started in on me immediately, banging the dishes in the rack.

"Look, darling," I had answered, "Eric is trying to help these people. Can't you understand that? Their country's been invaded and they're trying to defend it. They've always been independent. They don't want to be ruled by potato-nosed bureaucrats in Moscow. It's not even weapons, for God's sake; it's penicillin and plasma and blankets, for children —"

"It's their country, not Eric's or yours, and let them defend it themselves. And look, anyway," Irina said, "would you rather be a woman in the Soviet Union or in Afghanistan? Okay, okay," she said when I failed to get the point, "how would you like me to be a woman in Afghanistan, walking ten paces behind some murderous goatherd, not allowed to talk to anyone or show my face? And I missed you all through dinner," she continued, banging the faucet shut, "and I couldn't wait to get away from the chatter about clothes and hair and boys, and then I come here and find this. And that brandy," she went on, "which cost me a fortune, that was for us, it was romantic brandy, not stupid macho brandy," and at that point she began to gulp for air, which meant she was about to cry. "And now this!" she wailed again, but by then she had gone on to some other offense of mine, or of the world's, and I could no longer follow her.

And now this. As I walked alone along the crest of the

Wildengrat, bothered by memories and only half aware of the view I had come for, I had the most frightening experience I had ever been through — far worse than the mugging the month before, because at first it was utterly incomprehensible. The Wildengrat ridge was completely exposed, and you always felt uneasy there, so high above the world, but there was nothing very dangerous about the place. The rock was solid, there was an almost uninterrupted natural shelf along which to walk, and on this side of the ridge a fall would have been no worse, and no more likely, than tumbling down a short flight of stairs; below the rock the scree wasn't steep and you would have stopped sliding after a few yards. The other side of the ridge, just three yards away, was also negotiable, but over there you would have wanted to know what you were doing, because a slip would have killed you. Still, if I mapped out this excursion in my article I would have to suggest the hiring of a professional guide lest the magazine be sued if any mishap, however improbable, occurred. We'd had that kind of trouble before. There was, concealed within the whistling of the wind, a different kind of noise that could have been any number of things — an airplane passing above me, or the sound of the river or the army convoy drifting up from below — and to which I paid no attention until suddenly it grew much louder. What was so startling was the speed and the magnitude of the transformation, the almost instantaneous progression from rumble to roar to skull-splitting shriek, which caused both terror and physical pain. It was the kind of noise one would expect the devil to make before revealing himself. Then it grew louder, again and again, beyond each new limit of possibility, so that "deafening" suddenly proved an irrelevant concept. The mountain had begun to tremble under my feet, and now it felt as though the sky were going to shatter like glass. My last thought, before I went blank with fear, was to wonder what it was going to be like, to fall from so high and have the sky fall on top of me. Then, just ahead of me, a hundred feet above the ridge, there was a great flash of white light, which revealed itself, a second later, as it rocketed down the mountainside, to be a Mirage jetfighter with fire shooting from its tailpipe. As its scream receded — I was wrapped in billows of warm air that smelled of Kennedy Airport, four thousand miles away — I could already feel another one coming. I scrambled up to the top of the ridge and peered over and spotted the second jet when it was still just a toy below me, veering up from the valley and starting to climb the mountainside at an angle. The whole ascent, which had taken me half an hour by cable car, must have lasted no more than fifteen seconds, during the first of which I waved half-heartedly, propping myself against the ridge, until I had to cover my ears, and, despite the greatest effort of will, duck behind the rock. He flipped over the ridge at exactly the same spot as the leader, huge, silver, impossibly heavy, and I saw — probably because I knew they were there — the buglike head under the canopy and the red badges with the Swiss cross on the triangular wings. And I think that he had spotted me waving a moment before, because as he shot down the other side toward the bottom of the gorge, he took the time to execute a slow barrel roll, like a lazy seal turning over in a pool, before flattening out above the river and disappearing around a bend.

I had to sit in the lee of the ridge for several minutes before I stopped trembling. It was as though an alarm clock or a fire bell were ringing inside my chest. It took me a lot longer than I had expected to climb down the rock slide, because I heard every sound as though I were deep under water, and this seemed to make the descent more difficult. I was also a decade older than the last time I had been here, and alone, and more cautious on both accounts. The little wooded hollow, where I had planned to eat by the stream, was already deep in shadow by the time I got there, and the dampness of the earth and the proximity of the marsh gave the place a dank atmosphere that encouraged a mild claustrophobia. Not hungry, I took off my pack and sat down in the woods, where it was drier, and leaned my back against a trunk of coarse and resiny bark, trying to rest while at the same time fighting the pull of sleep — to which I finally succumbed in a corner of the café across the street from the Valsins train station, not waking until the owner shook me and told me the Giffern-bound train would soon be there.

Frau Oehrli scolded me for not having called; she had begun to worry about me, because I had told her I would be back long before dinner; and Mlle. Irina had called again, and insisted that Frau Oehrli have me call her back even if it was late. But surely even "late" could not mean four o'clock in the morning. And there was another reason I was reluctant to call her. I would want to tell her what had happened to me that day on the mountain, and she wouldn't understand. I wouldn't have been able to explain it. She would have thought that I had gone for a walk and been frightened by an airplane, and it depressed me to think about it. I wanted to tell the story to a friend, in a bar, waving my hands as I told it; but there was no one around. As I went up to my room it occurred to me that Eric Steyer was the only person who knew where I was; I had told him, over the guacamole burgers in New York, that I would be staying at the Gasthaus Oehrli. Irina would have had to get in touch with him in order to find out how to reach me, which meant it was probably urgent after all. I would call her first thing in the morning.

I wanted to work on my notes after breakfast. Although I had edited dozens of travel articles during my years at *Glee,* I had never written one from scratch and I was nervous about it. My plan was to organize the notes I had collected in the last few days and write a rough draft of the piece. Having done that, I could then look at it with my editor's eye, determine whether anything important was missing, and if so go out and collect the information while I was still in Giffern. It was for this reason that I had chosen to come to Giffern first, rather than Caziers. Knowing the village and the region as I did, I could cut my writing teeth on it more easily than on a place I had never seen before.

First, however, I made the call I had delayed for two days. I allowed the telephone to ring a long time at Central Park West. Neither Mrs. Albers nor Irina had yet entered the age of the answering machine. There were two lines in the apartment, one of which had been exclusively Kuratkin's but which Irina had taken over after his death. Of the Russian cronies of Kuratkin who remained in touch with Mrs. Albers, a fair number — these were people in their late seventies and eighties — had been unable to adapt to the change in telephone numbers and continued to call on what was now Irina's line. These elderly exiles tended to live in a permanent state of crisis, further enlivened by Russian dramatics. They broke hips, they failed to receive Social Security checks, or suddenly, as they returned with their groceries from the supermarket, forgot where they lived. (This had really happened once; the poor lost man, Prince Sherbatov, had been forced to ask a passerby to read out the number of the payphone so that Irina could call him back, his glasses being somewhere out of reach in one of his many pockets; and then he had used such complicated stratagems to pry his own address out of Irina without admitting that he had forgotten it that she had been unable to get off the phone for half an hour, during which time someone made off with Sherbatov's groceries, which he had rested on the pavement beside him.) Because there was always an emergency of some kind, Mrs.

Albers never let Irina's line go unanswered. If she happened to be on her own telephone in the living room or the kitchen when it rang, she would apologize, always with the same words (also used by Michael and Irina: "Just half a second, please," adding "We're expecting an important call"), and then you would hear her little heels hammering down the corridor to the rear of the apartment.

After the eighth ring Mrs. Albers picked up the receiver and uttered her usual drawn out-greeting. "I'm on the other line with Irina — she's at the airport," she said urgently as soon as I told her it was I. "I'll be right back. Can you wait?"

"Yes," I said. I would find a way to bill the call to the magazine.

"Half a second," Mrs. Albers said. "I'll be right back."

I waited. There were half-audible snatches of other people's conversations on the line, and lots of transatlantic static and clicks. Mrs. Albers returned some time later, out of breath.

"Irina is at the airport," she said. "She wouldn't let me go with her, so I'm here, as you see," she said. "She's at a telephone booth at the airport; I've written down the number. Can you call her there?"

"What's going on?" I asked.

"Irina will tell you. It's my son Michael. Let me give you the number at the airport. Will you call me back if you can't reach her?"

I wrote down the number on the back of a restaurant receipt, hung up, and then dialed it immediately. Twice my call was rerouted to a recorded operator, the first time for unknown reasons, the second because I had forgotten that Kennedy was technically in Queens and I was using the Manhattan area code. On the third attempt Irina picked up before I heard any ringing.

"Hello!" she shouted.

"Hello!" I shouted back. "It's Patrick."

"Patrick," Irina said after an interval of seconds, just as I was beginning to ask her what was happening. Whereas the connection to Central Park West had been relatively clear, this one had strange echoes and delays that destroyed the rhythm of normal conversation. I felt that I was forcing the words through the wires.

"Look," Irina said, her voice suddenly muffled, ". . . other phone, emergency. Where have you been, for Christ's sake?" she said, speaking into the receiver once again.

"I was up in the mountains." I thought this would sound good, but I was drowned out by a series of pips.

"Never mind," Irina said after I began to repeat it, and then she paused to listen to the rest.

"Listen," Irina said. "Listen, Michael is in terrible shape. He's been calling here in the middle of the night and threatening to kill himself. What?" she asked, having heard something I hadn't. "Are you there?"

Then I too started hearing unintelligible voices on the wire.

". . . south of France," Irina said.

"What?"

"In our father's house in the south of France," she said. "He's been drinking and drugging and calling us in the middle . . ."

"Thirty-five thousand francs," someone said, in English, with a thick Swiss-German accent.

". . . before; sometimes it's just threats," Irina said, while the Swiss-German said, ". . . lower rate of exchange."

"So you're going there," I said.

"I don't know what else to do," she said, her voice suddenly amplified and clear. "But I'm having a hard time getting a seat. I'm going to have to take first class or something. I tried to reach you, I thought you were going somewhere near there and perhaps you could look in on him or even just talk to him on the phone, because he'd be different with you."

"Where's your father?"

"I don't know. Could you call Michael? Could you just call him?"

In the background I heard a voice on a loudspeaker calling all passengers for a flight to Lisbon.

"Yes."

"It's this police thing; he keeps going on about the police. He's never had that kind of paranoia."

"Do you have a moment to discuss this, or are you fighting for the phone?" I asked.

"No, it's okay, I'm just worried that a seat is going to free up on some plane and I'll miss it."

"Never mind that; we have to discuss things," I said.

It was still a struggle to hear and to keep from interrupting each other. We could never tell when the other person had stopped and was waiting for an answer. Every few seconds there were a few clicks and bleeps and stretches of white noise. There was in Irina's voice a curiously childlike mixture of frustration and fear, as though she were stamping her feet. It was something I didn't remember hearing before. Normally, anything connected with Michael's intemperance and idleness, what she called his "Russian behavior," brought out in her an anger so ugly that it stifled any sympathy I might have felt.

"I don't know what to *do*," she said.

"Are there any friends of your father's nearby?" I asked.

"I don't know," she said impatiently. "Until three days ago I didn't even know the name of the town. I haven't seen him in twenty years."

"Give me the phone number," I said. "What's the town called, and tell me where it is. I've got a map."

It took us some time to locate the place. The village was called Augères; it was in the Lubéron region of upper Provence. The house, Irina said, was not in the village but up in the hills somewhere. There was something both lucky and baleful about the town's position on my map — about a quarter of an inch from its northern edge, trying to slide off the map but not quite succeeding. It looked to be about a two-hour drive from Caziers, where I was supposed to go for my article.

"The thing is," Irina said, "I was trying to reach you to ask you just to call and talk to him, because it's true he sounds terrible, but when he's talking to Mama or me you don't know how much is real and how much is a put-on. But I couldn't find you, dammit; you weren't returning my calls. That's why I finally decided to get on a plane."

"Okay, you stay put and I'll call him. But it's not as if I'm Michael's best friend, you know. Isn't there someone else? There's that printmaker in New York he used to stay with, the reformed drinker. He's probably more qualified . . ."

"Oh, come on," Irina said, her normal impatience returning. "You know what his friends are like. He's probably got them all convinced that Mama and I are monsters who are trying to cheat him out of some enormous inheritance."

"What about Jamie Schwartz?"

"Oh, stop it," she said.

She was right; I was doing this on purpose.

"I'm not asking you to go there," she said. "I'm at the airport. I can be there in twelve hours if I have to, but if you could just speak to him I'd have a better idea of what's going on, and it might also help him."

"All right," I said. "I'll try to reach him. Call me back in half an hour. If I don't hear from you I'll assume you've found a seat and you're on your way. Try to call me from the airport in Paris and let me know."

"I'm trying to get a ticket either there or to Marseille."

"Whatever," I said.

"Okay."

"I'll talk to you later."

"Yes."

The exchange went on a while longer. Neither of us seemed to know how to sign off. Both of us had things to add, at least I did, but there was a logjam of them, and none was appropriate to the circumstances. I pictured Irina in one of the rows of phone booths at Kennedy Airport. Her grandfather's leather traveling bag would be wedged between her ankles, her address book would be open in her hand, she would have the receiver nestled between her cheek and her shoulder, and when she raised the other hand to hook her hair away, her face would be pale and puffy from anxiety and lack of sleep.

"Okay," I said.

"Okay," she answered, and I hung up.

I didn't try to call Michael immediately, because as soon as I got off the phone I realized I had forgotten to ask an important question: Had she told him she was trying to fly over? If Michael was indeed behaving as he was in order to impress her and his mother with the misery of his existence, then the knowledge that his sister was literally flying to the rescue might encourage him to go through with his threat for any number of reasons. He might decide that he couldn't face her; he might calculate that if he timed things properly and got rescued at the last minute, he would create the maximum level of drama. There might be all sorts of other combinations and alternatives that didn't occur to me.

I also put off calling him because I dreaded doing it. I sat for a moment on the edge of my bed, next to the unfolded Michelin map, in the upper margin of which I had scrawled his number in drunk handwriting. Already I couldn't tell whether that was a 5 or an 8, or whether those first digits were necessary if you weren't calling from the States. I stepped into the corridor, deciding that I wanted another cup of coffee. It would take Frau Oehrli a minute or two to make it, already an important respite. I got as far as the head of the stairs when I noticed that my shirt was hanging out of my pants, that I had no shoes on, and that I was still holding my pen. I returned to my room to make myself presentable for Frau Oehrli, grateful for the extra few seconds in which to concentrate on necessary tasks that had nothing to do with Michael Albers.

"I hope you haven't had bad news," Frau Oehrli said when I entered the café and stepped to the counter.

"A bit," I said. "It would be nice if I could have a cup of coffee to take up to my room. I'm afraid I'm going to have to make several calls abroad, to France and America."

"It doesn't matter," Frau Oehrli said. "It goes directly on your bill." She banged the spent coffee grains from the espresso machine into a garbage pail behind the counter.

"I may have to leave sooner than I thought."

"That would be a pity, but in any case the weather is spoiling now; you've been very lucky. And your article, will you be able to finish it?"

"Oh, yes," I said. "I have all the information I need."

"Don't forget to take one of the brochures from the front desk. And we may be adding some more rooms next year, if this winter is a good season."

I tried the number in France several times without getting through. A recorded operator's voice kept interrupting my dialing to tell me with mechanical severity that all the international lines were occupied and that I was requested to complete my call at some future moment. On the fourth or fifth try, after a long journey through a hissing desert, I came at last to what sounded like a telephone ringing, very faint and far away, but it was drowned out by loud bleeps. This happened twice more.

Then, on about the tenth attempt, there was immediate action. After two rings I heard a clatter, followed by a distant

but identifiable English oath, then some more muffled clatter, and finally a weak "Hello?"

"Michael?"

"Yes," he stated, without enthusiasm. His tone implied that
this had better be good.

"It's Patrick. I'm up in Giffern," I said.

He didn't answer. I just heard him breathing.

"I'm supposedly writing a travel piece," I began jovially,
"but I feel more like a murderer returning to the scene of the
crime. I had lunch with Monsieur Crauste, the history teacher
. . . Are you there?"

Michael grunted. "What time is it? Jesus," he said.

A number of avenues were now open to me, and without
consciously making a decision I blundered onto the first one
my mental feet headed for. "I'm coming down to your part
of the world," I said. "I spoke with Irina, who gave me your
phone number."

I still hadn't decided whether to let him know that Irina
might be on her way. I had been counting on inspiration to
tell me what to do. It did. My long experience with the Albers family led me to behave as an Albers would: to proceed
by half truths and omissions.

"She told me you were feeling kind of low," I said. "I
thought I'd give you a ring and let you know that I was coming down in a couple of days. I'm going to a little town called
Caziers, it's somewhere near Arles, I'm not sure where that
is in relation to you, but I thought we might be able to get
together. You must know the region by now . . ." Then the
line went dead, and all my efforts to reach him again led to
nothing.

More than an hour had gone by since I first spoke to Mrs.
Albers. I went downstairs to ask Frau Oehrli if anyone had
called while I was on the phone. No one had. When I called
Mrs. Albers again she said she hadn't heard from Irina; per-

haps she had found a seat on a plane and hadn't had time to call. Then something horrible happened. Mrs. Albers' voice started to skid into higher registers, the way it had on the night of Kuratkin's death. "I'm just as worried about her as about Michael," she was saying. "She shouldn't have to do this, but she wouldn't let me . . . ." At that point she had to stop.

Mrs. Albers and I had never, through the more than two years of our acquaintance, through Kuratkin's slow death, Michael's reforms and relapses, and several of Irina's minor illnesses, had a serious conversation of any kind. We behaved toward each other as though we had just met, liked each other, but were still exchanging comments about the weather and the traffic. Now I said, "Mrs. Albers, it might just complicate things, but if you think I should go down there and lend a hand, I will."

"Please," she said. "Please."

I had to wait a second before saying yes. I had a hard time getting it out.

"If you'll let me pay for your plane ticket," Mrs. Albers said.

"I'll be going down by train, it's faster," I said. "Don't worry about it. It's not a problem. You mustn't worry," I said.

I imagined Irina on the plane, winging over the ocean.

So I packed my bag and donned my suit of armor, settled my accounts with Frau Oehrli, and rode my charger to the Giffern train station.

XV

IT WAS a swift, easy journey south, with prompt but unhurried connections at Montreux, Geneva, and Lyon; I shook Frau Oehrli's red hand at noon, in midautumn, and stepped off the bullet train at Avignon about three weeks earlier, in terms of weather, at eleven o'clock at night.

In Geneva my car was boarded at the very last moment by a thudding and clattering pile of bags and suitcases, behind which came a panicked Midwestern couple, who had lost the ability to cope at some earlier time in the day and whose limbs and luggage, in the cramped aisle between the seats, turned into dangerous projectiles. From the female half's conversation, carried on loudly and distinctly, in the hopes of rousing a kindly English-speaking stranger, it soon became clear that they had just completed a mad dash from their hotel, were not sure this was the right train — they were headed for Nice — and worried that their last-minute tickets and visas would prove ineffective. I was about to offer some encouragement, reluctantly, when the young Swiss woman who was seated opposite me took them under a hirsute arm and got them sorted out, revealing along the way that she had studied biology in San Francisco. The couple had nearly calmed down when the irruption into the carriage of two uniformed officials, one of whom barked, *"Frontière Suisse, vos passeports, s'il vous plaît!"* almost made them jump out of the clothes they had been smoothing and tucking back in.

"It's like being in a World War Two movie," the wife said, with awe and alarm.

The customs men were paired in an ingenious way: one was short and fat, the other tall and thin. They made smooth progress down the aisle, working back to back, flipping passports open, glancing at their bearers, and sometimes staring up at the luggage rack for a second or two before shutting and returning the document. Then, one row of seats before mine, they reached an obstacle: a small dark-skinned laborer, from Southern Europe or the Middle East, who was sitting mildly by the window with his hands in his lap and his cardboard suitcase, tied with string, on the seat beside him. They examined his papers closely, together, and the tall one put his long fingers on the suitcase and rocked it on the seat, though I couldn't tell what he meant to accomplish by this. They asked him where he was going, for how long, and why, and challenged his answers repeatedly and rudely, with increasing loudness, because he couldn't quite follow them. He was a Yugoslav who worked in Lausanne, I think — it was difficult to understand him, too — and he was on his way to Lyon to visit his wife for three days. He was able, mostly by default, to convince the officials of his right to do so, and they grudgingly left him alone, after instructing him to put his suitcase up in the rack. They reassumed their earlier, cursory mode of inspection as they separated once again, the taller of the uniforms heading my way while the fatter one made for the American lady, who proffered her passport and her husband's with a big smile and a hopeful *"Bonjour!"* that made the husband set his jaw.

Five minutes later the Swiss border guards were followed by their French colleagues, also in a pair. They started from the opposite end of the car and didn't get to the Yugoslav until after checking the American couple's visas and mine, and waving away the Swiss girl's passport without even looking at it. The papers the Yugoslav retrieved from the inner pocket of his jacket, however — he had the thick hands of a mechanic, with fingers like carrots and black-edged nails — failed to satisfy these officials. They had a brief exchange in low voices, during which its object's eyes traveled back and forth from the window to the customs men's black shoes, betraying no anxiety or even interest. Then one of them got his attention by saying "Hep! Hep!" Their tone was not brutal, like that of the Swiss, but quiet and slightly acid. He was told he would have to leave the train at the next station and wait there, presumably while inquiries were made and decisions reached. He gave no indication of having expected anything else. He was a small man, in his late forties, his clothes shabby but neatly put together. The guards made him take his suitcase from the rack again and one of them escorted him down the aisle. It was very depressing to watch. The American wife kept glancing at her husband, who gazed out the window, following the swooping passage of the power lines above the tracks.

Among Irina's grandfather's considerable store of anecdotes, those wide-ranging tales which spanned most of the century and included many famous people, usually presented in a humorous light, some had revolved around the agony of statelessness, the ghastly torments he and his fellow refugees had suffered while trying to secure residence permits, work permits, and travel permits in the years between the two world wars. It was a recurrent nightmare in their lives: the repeated returns to dingy offices where they would wait, day after day, for some lever or gear to shift somewhere within the giant jammed machine; the horror of having to deal with, plead with, and, once in a while, desperately, shout at the dim indifferent functionary who held in his paw their fate and that of their families; the torture of anxiety over which of those paws might or might not take to grease.

After Kuratkin's death Irina had searched diligently through his belongings, both in New York and Fincham, for these hard-earned scraps of paper, wanting to paint them. But he appeared to have destroyed them, or discarded them serially as he went through life, or perhaps even made a bonfire of them all after acquiring his American Certificate of Naturalization (No. 7012387, delivered on November 24, 1952, by William V. Connell, Clerk of the U.S. District Court — a large rectangular sheet printed in a dozen different type faces, framed by a border rather like that of dollar bills; Jamie Schwartz eventually bought Irina's rendition of it). Or else they were stored in some hiding place the Alberses had not yet found, along with the missing manuscript of his memoirs.

One of Kuratkin's stories that I remembered had to do with a Nansen passport, an almost but not quite useless document issued by the League of Nations to stateless people. It was a coveted object, difficult to obtain; once you had it you still needed a visa to go anywhere, but at least it provided a surface on which to put the said visa, which was more than most refugees had. Once — it must have been in the early thirties — Kuratkin had found himself in a train compartment, by coincidence, with another Russian émigré, a pianist named Ania Dorfmann, who was on her way to London to give a recital with Chaliapin. (I remember her name because Kuratkin put down his glass and pushed himself free of the sofa at that point in his story — I was waiting for Irina as she got dressed to go to a dinner — and crossed the library in small steps, and with a triumphant *Aha!* pulled one of her records from his shelves and handed it to me, apologizing because the gramophone, as he called it, didn't work.) Because she was constantly on tour, her own Nansen ("really a Nonsense passport," Kuratkin said) was so thickly covered with ink and stamps, and so padded and swollen with folded extensions, that the visa necessary for that particular border crossing had proved unfindable in the chaos, so everyone had had to leave the compartment and stand swaying in the corridor of the carriage under the yellow light, where there was room enough for Kuratkin to grasp one end of the accordionlike document while the pianist's maid held the other, and the pianist and the official wandered up and down the paper serpent in a peering duet, searching among the hieroglyphs. Laughing at the memory, Kuratkin had gone on to tell me of the night when Chaliapin, drunk, had insisted on carrying the writer Ivan Bunin up five flights of stairs on his back, insisting that Bunin was himself too drunk to make it to his room . . . or something of that order. It was because of these stories that everyone had kept urging Kuratkin to write his memoirs. Of course there had also been an element of flattery in these urgings, a desire to indulge an old man. On the two or three occasions when I had attempted to repeat one of his stories, it had sounded flat and pointless. You needed Kuratkin himself, his bony hands conjuring up characters and waving the narrative along, his yellowed grin, his accent (he had a strange wet way of rolling his *r*'s, which Irina claimed was typical of prerevolutionary Petersburg), the pleasure he took in his memory, in having lived, in living still. Michael, not surprisingly, had something of the same manner, and could on occasion be entertaining in a similar way, and perhaps, just perhaps, might have been able to do Kuratkin justice in his book. But then, given what I had learned that morning, it seemed unlikely that Michael's book existed any more than it had the last time I had heard him speak of it, two months earlier, just before his departure from New York.

A different anxiety came over me then, as I contemplated having to deal with Michael if he really were suicidal. To counteract it, I rose from my seat and took the long walk back to the buffet car, deciding that it was time, at six o'clock, to have a drink and try to think out a plan. The train was so swift and smooth — much more so than the ones I had already marveled at in Switzerland — that it was like strolling down the aisle of a jet liner. There was no rattle from the wheels on the rails, only a muted rush from outside and the hum of the air conditioning. It had already grown dark. A few strings of light trembled in the windows on my right, probably villages in the foothills of the Alps. On the other side, beyond the canal, there stretched a narrow plain, partly industrial, partly cultivated, that vanished nearby in misty darkness. We rushed through towns and villages with majestic indifference; there would be slight variation in the otherwise constant ambient noise, and on either side, a sad deserted stretch of concrete would flash by, fixed in the harsh light of streetlamps, and then it would be gone again, and still I was only halfway down the carriage, four steps closer to the plastic cup of whiskey I had promised myself.

What I feared most was finding Michael not depressed or merely drunk, but demented. I had had just enough experience of incoherent people — my dying father, dying Kuratkin — to know what they did to me: I tended to lose my own bearings as I tried to follow their delirium, and as the conversation grew more absurd, I would begin to feel that I too was going mad. In Michael's case I would be dealing not with a bedridden invalid but with a young man larger and stronger than I; furthermore, if he was threatening to kill himself, what I might or might not say could have terrible consequences.

What if Irina didn't show up? What if she had failed, despite all her efforts, to find a seat on a plane? And how, talking of visas, had she managed to get one on such short notice? Had she even remembered that she would need one? The most horrible possibility that came to mind (by now I was standing in the corner of the buffet car with my whiskey, examining a long horizontal map of the train's route framed above the counter) was that Irina, having learned from her mother that I was on my way, had decided to leave it to me to take care of her brother. Speaking to me from Kennedy Airport that morning she had betrayed none of the rage I knew she felt against Michael, but that had been merely because of the circumstances, the bad telephone connection, the urgency of her errand. She wanted something from me and had therefore controlled her anger, knowing how I usually reacted to it, how I always felt, no matter what she was raging about, that it was somehow directed at me. I could just see her throwing up her ringed hands in the middle of the airport and picking up Kuratkin's old bag and heading for the taxi stand, having decided once and for all, as she had so often before, that Michael was on his own, and that this time, for all she cared, he could die.

But she wouldn't do that. I resolved to call Central Park West as soon as I reached Avignon, even if it meant waking Mrs. Albers at two in the morning.

"Monsieur?" the buffet man asked.

"*Un autre whiskey, s'il vous plaît,*" I said. Then I asked him if he happened to know whether there was a place in Avignon where I could rent a car.

"Ah, that, monsieur, I wouldn't be able to tell you," he said. "I've never been there; I only pass through."

In Geneva I had taken the time, between trains, to go down

to the *bureau de change* and buy a crackling wad of French francs, which had come accompanied by a few coins I would be able to make phone calls with once I arrived. I asked the buffet man for some extra change to make sure I would have enough. I was getting more and more worried.

Of the half-dozen passengers who got off with me in the night at Avignon, two were greeted happily on the platform by friends or relatives; the others seemed to know exactly where they were going.

The station was mostly closed down, and I had no hope of finding an operating information booth. Within seconds my destination had undergone a nasty transformation. It was no longer the beautiful walled city I had expected; it was one of those grim places we had flown through so many times in the last few hours, which jump out of the dark for a few seconds and then slide back in, leaving me grateful that I was headed elsewhere. It was a very long time since I had last arrived alone in an unfamiliar town, without anyone waiting for me or precise instructions for proceeding to a further point; since my last wandering summer after college, in fact. In those days I had gladly slept anywhere, in the waiting rooms of train stations, on park benches — and once a kindly policeman in a Belgian town, when I asked for directions to a youth hostel that was no longer open, lent me a comfortable and clean cell in his empty jail. Had I followed the path I had once chosen for myself, had I become a journalist, this sort of arrival would by now have been second nature to me.

On the heels of the other travelers I walked down a flight of stairs into an echoing tunnel whose tiled walls were hung with framed advertisements — the faces of giants in ecstasy over sundry helpful products. The people who had been met were chatting in self-sufficient little groups as they walked, having been embraced and relieved of part of their luggage.

I followed a lone young woman trailing behind her a wheeled suitcase on a leash, but I had seen her face furrowed with fatigue and misery, and it seemed useless to approach her with questions about hotels or rental cars; I was certain she would misinterpret my intentions. There was also a middle-aged couple of loathsome smugness and ugliness; I had stood near them in the buffet car for a few minutes and listened to their conversation (about a man whom a relative of theirs had been very stupid, they agreed, to marry); and I had improvidently allowed myself to hate them, and to hate the fussy precision with which the husband had halved a croque-monsieur with a plastic knife and bitten into it daintily, with his fat pinkie raised. It would have been abject to ask for their help.

On the main platform, while these people dispersed, I found a row of free-standing pay phones encased in little plastic helmets. I no longer wanted to call Central Park West immediately; the problem of where to spend the night was more urgent. The first thing to do was to call Michael, who had presumably gotten to Augères via Avignon. If I caught him in a moment of coherence he might be able to tell me where I could sleep or find a car and get to him, unless it was too far — but that also seemed daunting, between my bad driving and Michael's lack of practical sense. I didn't want to get lost in the countryside in the dark. Besides, the telephones, which I now stared at helplessly, were of a type I had never encountered before, requiring some type of credit card instead of coins. I read the instructions carefully, several times, hoping they would provide me with a way of calling Michael collect, or of reaching an operator who could help me, but all they did was explain the use of the card I didn't have.

I had become aware, in the meantime, of two separate elements outside the station. One was a red neon sign in the night sky, not far away, peeking above the wall of the city,

that spelled the top half of the word HOTEL. The other was
the sound of voices rising from the parking lot — not the
cheerful southern chatter of the people who had just left the
station but male voices that harbored a disquieting sneer and
boastfulness, with a single explosive syllable rising occasionally above the rest. If you are looking for unpleasant people
in any town in the world, head for the train station after dark,
where you will find them leaning against cars or motorbikes
in the parking lot, drumming their fingers on their blue jeans,
passing the time as they wait for you. The memory of my
recent mugging was still all too fresh in my mind, and I didn't
want to linger too long within sight of these people, displaying disorientation and confusion.

I picked up my bag and crossed the lot with a determined
step, ignoring and ignored by the loitering youths. After all,
what did they know of urban violence compared with me,
an American, a New Yorker? Still, I felt I had left my home
behind on that comfortable train. There was a cold wind
blowing, which I thought must be the famous mistral. I forded
the avenue without waiting for the light, pausing in midstream to let a few cars go by, and entered the city through a
gate flanked by twin towers. I hung a right toward the hotel.

I had imagined a dreadful place that found its trade among
people like me, stranded nighttime travelers, and therefore
had no need to make itself attractive. I was ready to spend a
difficult night dozing intermittently in my clothes on top of
stained covers, with a chair propped against the door handle.
Instead, the entrance was bright, not dingy, and modern
without appearing flimsy. Rather than the unshaven, under-
shirted. Gauloise-smoking night clerk I had expected, there
was a moonlighting student reading St. Augustine through
bright eyeglasses, who seemed even happier at our meeting
than I. My room was so pleasant, the blinds so effective, and
the bed so comfortable that I didn't wake until nine-thirty
the next morning.

The day was bright but cold and windy. I took a shower and put on clean clothes, discussed the hour of my departure with the woman at the front desk, clearly a blood relative of last night's student but too young to be his mother. (She informed me, without my asking, that this was indeed a day of mistral, and did this with pride, as though the notoriously nasty north wind were one of the city's main tourist attractions; it had been blowing for two days, she said, and would be followed, tomorrow at the latest, by rain.) Then I strolled into the streets of the city and ate breakfast at a red-surfaced metal table at a café in a square planted with plane trees. Their bark looked as though it were molting; their leaves were mostly gone now, and odd twigs grew vertically out of the gnarled stumps of amputated limbs. Some of the leaves swirled about the cobblestones in the far corner of the square, where the wind snaked in from a side street, but my map lay unruffled on the table, its eastern half, which dangled over the side, swaying only at the passage of the waitress.

I placed the saucer of my coffee cup to the northwest, near Montélimar, and the plate that had come with the croissant I slid beyond Mont Ventoux, whose white cap I could see from my chair. (Like all newcomers to the region I thought it was a freak early snowfall, but an hour later, when I had bought a guidebook, I learned that it is limestone and remains white all summer.) At Avignon I was somewhat to the north of where I was supposed to go for my article — Caziers lay nearer Arles — but it looked like an easy drive down the banks of the Durance. In fact, if I stretched things a bit, I could have said that the village where Michael was staying lay on my way there.

Once Irina and I had disposed of Michael — sobered him up, got some food into him, seen him onto the Paris-bound train (for I felt rested and optimistic that morning) — we would drive together over the Lubéron range, which looked, from the map, to be rather wild, and then down to Aix, of which I had some theoretical guidebook knowledge, gathered haphazardly in preparation for my article, that would impress her. There were wonderful-sounding towns on the way: Ménerbes, which had a comical phonetic association with annoyance; Bonnieux, which, on the contrary, had a jovial ring to it; Lacoste, which I knew to be the home both of the Marquis de Sade and of Petrarch's Laura, the name of the town having stuck in my mind because of the tennis champion and the crocodile shirts. Irina and I would pause in these places and casually have a drink of water at the fountain and look around . . . Of course it would have been wiser not to think of such things. I was learning that it is better not to try to picture what you want but simply to decide on it and pursue it with as little imagination as possible, because it is a law of nature that whatever you imagine will not come to pass. Bent over the table, my finger on the town of Caziers, I knew all at once that if I looked up now I would see Irina leaning against one of the molting plane trees, her arms crossed on her chest, contemplating me. I knew this with certainty, and kept my eyes blindly on the map while I tore another piece from my croissant and, with meditative slowness, placed it in my mouth, chewed, and swallowed, though that last part was difficult. When I did look up, a young woman was entering the square from the street at its opposite end, pushing a bicycle by the handlebars. She wore a flowing dark skirt that whipped around her legs in the eddy of the wind, and the leaves fallen from the trees swirled about her ankles, one of them floating up to pause for a moment on the shoulder of her sweater and another becoming lodged in the spokes of her front wheel. It was not Irina, I could not have confused her with Irina for a second, and if Irina were here she would not be wheeling a bicycle before her but carrying a bag. Still, I stared at this young woman with such intensity that she finally looked my way, and met my eyes, and kept them with regal unconcern as she strolled on through the square and back into her own life.

Irina had no driver's license. Unless we happened to meet here, she would have to get to her father's house by public transport. There had to be a bus service that went at least as far as Apt. It probably left from the train station. A good idea would be to go back there this morning and snoop around and meet the trains arriving from Paris. In the meantime the best thing was to call New York, which I had delayed doing from minute to minute because I still feared that Irina may have turned back.

After paying the waitress, I asked her for directions to the post office and then got lost on my way there, though she had assured me it was *très simple.* It was my own fault, because I was tempted off the route by a steep lane that seemed to promise a shortcut, but that led me into other steep lanes that branched off at confusing angles and then curved back, taking me away from my goal in cobblestone spirals. The buildings looked tall in the narrow alleys and even appeared to lean toward each other. Washing was strung overhead in the courtyards. Now that the sun was up, the cats were leaving the shelter of the cars, under which they had installed themselves in the cold dawn for a posthunt doze, and stretching themselves on the hoods and roofs of the machines with a possessive manner that reminded me curiously of the New York homeless.

I asked for further directions at the entrance to a building I think was the headquarters of the local Communist Party, where I was told cheerfully once again that it was *très simple;* but this time I toed the party line and indeed found the PTT office five minutes later. I immediately acquired two of those cards necessary for the use of pay phones, allowing myself a hundred units of telephone time, surely enough to cope with any emergency. Then I sat down on the bench in one of the booths and had the operator call New York.

I fingered the two cards while I waited to get through. They were pleasant objects to handle, more substantial than credit cards and loaded with electronic manna. I wondered whether they would be suitable subjects for Irina's paintings, but I thought not, for they had nothing to do with the owner's identity; they were as impersonal as money. As usual I let the phone ring a good long time across the ocean. It wasn't just the problem of the two lines at Central Park West. Since the last time I had been there the configuration of the apartment might have changed completely as Mrs. Albers reorganized her life on a Kuratkinless basis, and she might now be flying from room to room, patting her hair and calling, out, "*J'arrive! J'arrive!*" to the blind and deaf telephone. At least that was what she did when there were other people present, making Irina roll her eyes. But in the end, with the operator's encouragement, I had to accept that the apartment was empty. An image came to me of old Kuratkin lying naked on the cold bathroom floor, unable to move, as the telephone rang and rang next door in his bedroom. If he had been lucky, he was already hallucinating by then, imagining himself somewhere else — perhaps even imagining himself somewhere near here, during the war; as an OSS agent he had operated with the Maquis in some part of the south of France. That might actually be the reason Michael had come here from Paris; until now I had assumed he was looking not only for his dead grandfather but for the live father who had abandoned him years before. Another image came to me, of Michael, also unconscious, perhaps even dead, in his father's house. I should have called him immediately on waking up that morning.

I dialed the number. It was busy.

I called Frau Oehrli in Giffern. Yes, *une dame* had called, not Mlle. Irina. Mlle. Irina had an accent, whereas this lady was French. It may have been Mme. Albers, but no name had been given. The weather had changed: there were torrential rains. I assured Frau Oehrli that it was colder down here in the south than it had been in the mountains the day before, and that although it was sunny, there was a mistral going, and soon there would be rain too. As I signed off, Frau Oehrli said, "*À l'année prochaine*," and it actually startled me to think that there would be another year, and probably others beyond it; that no matter what happened in the next few days I would come out on the other side, still myself, still worrying about jobs and apartments.

Michael's number was still busy.

I was directed to a car rental agency, where I picked up a small blue Renault that had a disturbingly toylike quality. Some years before, while I had been in college, an earlier version of the same model had enjoyed a vogue in the United States, where it had been marketed as Le Car, with those words painted on the door of each auto. I found it difficult to take seriously as a means of transportation and felt almost humiliated as I signed the papers. But it was brand new, and it behaved in a gentle and accommodating manner when I parked it at the train station.

I retraced my steps of the night before, into the terminal and onto the platform, where I met the first TGV arriving from Paris. The station was a friendly place that morning, bustling and noisy, with helpful announcements from the loudspeakers; if I were ever to do more travel articles, I would remember to schedule trips so as not to arrive after dark. When the slope-nosed train drifted into the station, quite a few people alit on the platform and flowed past me, but none of them was Irina. I loitered another minute or two in the terminal, searching the faces, decided it wasn't worthwhile trying to find a message board, and then returned to the car and set off toward Augères, locating the highway without difficulty and then turning east, following the signs for Apt. I drove uncomfortably at a slow American speed while everything from motorbikes to large trucks sped by on my left.

Half an hour after leaving Avignon, I found myself once again among mountains, mere swells compared with the Alps I had left yesterday, but in other ways wilder — less admired, less photographed, their oak forests patrolled by grunting boar. After Apt, the road narrowed and began to twist on the valley floor, presenting me with blind rises and curves that slowed none of the other drivers. On the northern side, sheltered from the mistral, ocher hill villages nestled in the slope, while on the opposite flank only a few stone farmhouses stood on small hillocks rising out of the wooded slope. Their blind walls made them look fortified, but the defenses were only against the wind. Long stretches of the road were lined by close ramparts of poplars that sheltered the orchards in the valley, further limiting the visibility of curves and side roads.

Every once in a while I checked my progress against the meandering red band on the map I had laid open on the passenger seat. After two hours I began to look at the road signs more carefully, searching for the turnoff to Augères; then, finding it, I swung off the main road onto a smaller one that climbed up a fold in the northern slope, wound upward for a minute or two, with all four of my limbs busy at the controls, and climbed into the town I sought, my eyes catching the signpost stuck to the wall of the first house just as I crawled around a curve, trying to make way for a *deux-chevaux* van with corrugated flanks that rattled past me at full tilt. I parked by the fountain in the sloping square, got out, stretched my legs one at a time, and stepped over to the phone booth. Inserting my new card, I tried to call Michael. He was still, or again, on the phone, unless there was something wrong with the line. I tried several more times before giving up. Then I made for the café, my map in hand.

It was just past noon, but because of the chill there was only one couple outside on the cement terrace, Scandinavians seated under a vast Dubonnet parasol that lent their fair skins a jaundiced tint. On the chipped enamel surface of their table were two plain glasses half filled with a grayish liquid I took to be Pastis, the regional drink, which I had never tried, and as I stepped inside I debated ordering one, because I was tense from the driving, but decided I might need my wits about me to deal with Michael.

Behind the counter, polishing glasses and placing them on the shelves, was a huge man with a scarred and battered face, probably from boxing or rugby. I ordered a coffee, which he prepared and set before me, next to my map, without really acknowledging my presence.

"I'm looking for the house of Monsieur Albers," I said. "An American. Would you know where I could find it?"

After a decent interval had elapsed he looked up from his work and examined me for a brief second, his soft eyes traveling on to the only other person there — a toadish adolescent loafing at one of the indoor tables, with nothing to do except pick at his acne with tobacco-stained fingers. The man lifted another glass, and while polishing it stepped to the end of the counter, leaned into an open doorway, and spoke a few words I didn't catch.

"The house of Monsieur Albers," he stated when he returned, still avoiding my eyes and keeping busy. "Well, I couldn't tell you exactly which one it is. It's up there," he said, motioning with his huge head toward the entrance of the café, "but as I say, I'm not sure." His southern accent, more pronounced than any I had heard in Avignon, interjected extra syllables into every other word. I had to repeat his statements in my head before I understood them.

At this point the adolescent volunteered the information

that it was the big one below the spring, next to Vaucher's farm. His voice broke in the middle and he tried to disguise it by feigning a cough.

"As for you," the *patron* said, "you've just missed another good opportunity to shut up. How would monsieur know where Vaucher's farm is? He's not from here."

"It's all right; I have the phone number," I said. "How much do I owe you?"

"You have time for another one," he said. "I've sent for the *gardien* of the house; he'll show you the way."

"I thank you," I said. "I'd prefer a glass of mineral water."

"Go do something useful," he said, addressing the adolescent.

"Me, I'm not bothering anyone."

"I'll be bothering you in a moment."

We were joined after some minutes by a squat man in blue overalls and an incongruous shooting jacket with elbow patches, who limped up the step into the café, rotating his left leg in an arc every time he moved it forward.

" 'Jour, André," he said to the *patron*.

" 'Jour," the *patron* answered. "Here's the monsieur."

"I'm the *gardien*," the gimp said, shaking the hand I offered him. "You're looking for Monsieur Albers."

"For his son."

"Yes, his son is at the house," he quickly agreed. Then, like the *patron* a minute before, he examined me briefly. "You're a friend of his," he said.

"Yes, I've just arrived from America," I said, keeping it simple. "Monsieur Albers isn't there?"

"Monsieur Albers, at this time of year, is in Tangier," the caretaker answered. "In Morocco," he explained. "In fact, I tried to call him on the telephone recently, but he had absented himself from his house there. Are you finished with your drink?"

"May I offer you something?" I said.

"No, thank you," he said.

I paid and left a few coins in the saucer. While this was being taken care of I asked the caretaker if he knew, by any chance, whether M. Albers' daughter had arrived.

"His daughter," he said.

At this point I caught the adolescent staring at the boxer with an expression of idiotic amusement on his pimples, as though I had said something extremely witty. The boxer ignored him.

At the risk of seeming garrulous, I said, "She's coming to look after her brother, to cook for him and so forth. He's a bit of an artist." I had a feeling Michael may have been a problem for this man.

"She's expected soon?" the caretaker asked hopefully.

"Yes, soon," I answered hopefully.

"I'll take you up there," he said. "Do you have a car? Then you just follow me, but you'll have to wait a moment while I get the *moto*. If you'll just wait for me in the square I'll be around in a little moment."

I tried to call Michael from the phone booth one last time. Then I waited inside the car, holding the door open with my foot. The caretaker came puttering and backfiring into the square, enthroned on the front saddle of an ancient BMW motorcycle, an ancestor of the type used by the French highway police. I slammed my door shut and started the engine, rolled out of the square onto the street, and set off behind him.

His driving had the same dignity as his carriage atop the machine, and I had no difficulty following him up the winding road. A hundred yards above the village, as we entered a small forest of oak trees, the paved road forked into two dirt ones, of which we took the higher. Here my guide had to slow the pace to let me keep up. He rode on the hump between the ruts, flattening horse-droppings and sending up a fine mist of dust that settled on my windshield as I bumped along behind him, hearing occasionally an ominous thump and scrape under my seat. When we came out of the trees, the road turned abruptly downhill, pouring us down between two rows of cypresses into the courtyard of a U-shaped farmhouse. Here the caretaker stopped his bike beside an empty stone fountain, with a long squeak of the brakes. After settling the weight of the machine against the fountain, he leaned back and peeled himself off the saddle by grabbing his game leg with both hands and swinging it over the gas tank.

The first thing I noticed was that a pane of glass in the window by the front door was broken.

"*Bon, voilà,* here we are," the caretaker said. "Excuse me, but I have to see to something while I'm here." He limped away toward the barn, extracting an enormous rusted key from his overalls.

I banged the knocker several times without result. Then I tried the handle. It was locked. I reached in through the broken pane, unlatched the window, and clambered inside.

XVI

THE ROOM into which I dropped was a revelation. Most of the wall on my left was covered by a giant white-on-white painting of a naked boy prone in a tangle of sheets. Right next to me, in the corner, staring at me eye to eye from atop an alabaster column, was the turbaned head of a marble Moor. On either side of the doorway stood a pair of stone male figures, all four of them decapitated, their sixteen limbs smashed off at various lengths, and three of them castrated, like the remnants of some doomed patrol from Antiquity. I wasn't, as I thought for a moment, in the wrong house. Propped on the mantel, against the fourth wall, was a muddy unframed landscape I recognized as a brother to the one in Irina's bedroom, and to those I had seen, their edges gnawed by rats, in the Fincham attic; in these surroundings it looked even more innocent and amateurish. Here were both the cause and the place of Jack Albers' banishment.

The room was immense, clearly a converted barn, as tall as it was long, with a wide loft above the area near the fireplace, where two couches faced each other across a chrome-and-glass coffee table. Thirty feet above my head was a roof of weathered oak beams. Underfoot were rope carpets on a floor of milky stone. There was little furniture, most of it covered with white sheets. A rhythmic popping and scratching issued from loudspeakers somewhere, and inside an old raw wood sideboard a record spun on a turntable, whose arm rocked back and forth at the edge of the label. Nearby on the floor stood a half-empty bottle of red wine, uncorked, an empty glass, and a white china plate that had been used as an ashtray. On the coffee table was another wine-stained glass containing a half-consumed cigarette that had been extinguished by dunking, amidst a mass of papers covered in handwriting. I was about to glance at these papers when my attention was diverted by the telephone at my feet. The receiver had been knocked from the cradle and lay on the straw matting. I picked it up and put it to my ear and heard nothing. I jiggled the nubs in the cradle like a telegrapher until I got a gurgle and a dial tone, and hung up. Then I noticed a number of whitish trails on the glass on a corner of the table; I rubbed my finger in them and licked it and tasted cocaine.

"Michael?" I called.

I climbed the wooden staircase up to the loft. There was another couch here, also covered with a white sheet, flanked by two doors. The open one gave onto a small sitting room or library that would have resembled the space downstairs had it not been completely destroyed. There were cane chairs knocked over among hundreds of books yanked from the shelves, along with a large number of framed photographs and knicknacks. On the far wall was a pair of ornate Venetian sconces, one of them smashed, probably by the green bronze Priapus that lay among the shards beneath it. A bottle of red wine had been hurled at the surviving one but had missed, leaving a dripping sunburst stain on the white wall. The curtains had been torn from the window, which was barred by the dangling rod. Another chair had been used on the glass-covered rattan chest that served as a table, crushing it in the middle.

"Michael?" I called.

There was an open door at the other end of this room, but I preferred not to pick my way through the devastation, so I crossed the length of the loft and pushed open the other door. The room was dark and smelled of bitter breath. Much of it was taken up by an enormous bed in which a figure lay huddled on its side, wearing airline eyeshades, with one naked foot protruding from under the blankets. I walked over and made sure it was Michael, and then I shook his shoulder.

"Michael?" I said.

I shook him again, harder. The foot jerked in and a hand appeared instead; it tried to push me away but only waved in the void. Then there was an eruption under the covers, as Michael sat up violently and clawed the mask off his face. He stared at me. His eyes were tiny slits in swollen lids. His whole face was puffy and red, except for his chin, which had an unusually pointy appearance and seemed added on. His hair stuck out wildly, displaying porous patches of pale scalp.

"What are . . ." he tried to say. The first time, nothing came from his throat but a dry rumble. The second time, the words began to turn into a moan and he had to stop.

"What are you doing," he managed. "Here," he added.

"I was in the neighborhood, I thought I'd drop by. We spoke on the phone yesterday, remember?"

Michael swung his legs out of the bed, placed his feet on the floor, and pushed the rest of himself into balance on top of them. Except for his feet, he was fully dressed. Over his shirt he was wearing a green velvet jacket with gold epaulettes, gold frogging, and tails. His lower half was in blue jeans. He swayed and then dropped back onto the bed. He clutched his forehead. He was breathing very hard, his mouth open.

"Get back in bed," I said.

"No, no, I'm fine," he said between breaths. "I haven't been sleeping well. I'll make you some coffee."

"Get back into bed," I said.

He rose again and made his way out to the loft, pausing to steady himself in the doorway. He walked across the loft and shut the door to the ruined room. He walked slowly down the steps, his hand against the wall for support. One of the green velvet tails had been folded underneath him while he slept, and now its bottom half stuck out almost horizontally behind him. The first thing he did when he reached the ground floor was to gather all the papers from the coffee table into his arms, knocking the empty wineglass with its cigarette onto the carpet. He went back to the staircase and started to climb. The tailcoat looked like something out of Pushkin's era. Perhaps he had abandoned his Kuratkin book and gone back to Pushkin. Whatever those papers were, he didn't want me to see them.

"Go to the kitchen and make yourself some coffee," he said. "I'll be down in a minute." Halfway up he had to stop and lean against the wall to catch his breath.

Through the window I saw the caretaker limp across the courtyard, carrying a length of pipe. I unlocked the front door from inside and went out to thank him for leading me here. I would have asked him in for a glass of wine, but I didn't want him to see Michael.

"The young man is all right?" the caretaker asked.

"I think he has the grippe," I said.

"May I ask you how long you plan on staying?" he asked.

"Not long. I'll see when his sister arrives to take care of him."

"Because this is a lot of coming and going," the caretaker said, suddenly growing animated. "Monsieur Albers left me no instructions about his son. To be honest with you, I have known Monsieur Albers for twenty years, I take care of everything around here when he is away, and until the arrival of this young man I didn't know anything about any son nor any daughter. This young man broke into the house, and I came here with the police. He says he is Monsieur Albers' son, his passport says he is a Monsieur Albers, and I'll grant you that he looks like Monsieur Albers."

Having gotten this off his chest — it all came out at once; I think he had planned to be cagey and failed — the caretaker must have felt some relief, because he decided there and then that I must be worthy of his confidence. "*Écoutez,*" he said, "let me tell you something."

Ahead of me he limped around the western wing of the house, away from the windows. We stood next to a wood-pile neatly stacked under a corrugated tin roof that slanted out from the wall at the height of our shoulders. To our right, sloping down toward the valley, was a bristling orchard of bare cherry trees, their bark a deep shade of copper. With his lead pipe, the caretaker poked at the ends of the logs, realigning them as he spoke.

"Monsieur, I am not a curate," he began. "Monsieur Albers has lived here, *dans le pays,* for twenty years. I take care of the house for him while he's away. In twenty years this is not the first time a young man has come here looking for Monsieur Albers, if you understand me. As I say, I am not a curate or an abbot. If Monsieur Albers is not here, I send them away. If Monsieur Albers has left me no instructions to give the keys to anyone, I give the keys to no one. Now this young man comes and breaks into the house, and the police come and he turns out to be the son. I have tried to reach Monsieur Albers in Morocco to make sure that this is all right with him, and all I get on the telephone is an Arab who can

only *baragouiner* a few words of French. There has been damage to the house. There has been damage to the car. There
has been loud music played at night, all night. The police
have come to talk to him about that. Beyond those trees there
is the Vaucher farm; they have a sick child, and they could
hear the music all night. I come here every day to look around
and I have been down to the wine cellar. I have been known
to drink a shot or two among friends, but this young man,
well, sir, we are not talking here about an *apéro* before dinner. Now, if you are a friend of Monsieur Albers' son, do
you know how long he is going to stay? Would you know
by any chance where Monsieur Albers is?"

I nodded grimly throughout his lament. "Yes, yes," I said.
"Yes, I understand perfectly well," I said.

He placed the lead pipe in one of the furrows of the tin
roof and wiped his hands on his overalls.

"I must tell you that things being the way they are, with
Vaucher complaining about the noise and with the young man
drinking like this, I have allowed myself to remove Monsieur
Albers' firearm from the house."

"You did exactly the right thing," I said, genuinely impressed. "*Écoutez, monsieur,*" I said, adopting his own confid-
ing tone. "I'm an old friend of Monsieur Albers' son, since
childhood, and the reason I've come is that I knew things
were not right. His sister, *une personne très responsable,* is also
on her way. I think she'll probably arrive in the village today,
and we're going to drive him back to Paris."

"In that case I am extremely glad to make your acquaintance," the caretaker said, "and you must forgive me for not
welcoming you more warmly *tout à l'heure.* My name is Mar-
cel Laugier and my wife and I have the hardware store in
Augères, and I take care of the houses of several American or
English monsieurs in the *pays,* and I have been worried over
this."

I introduced myself again. We shook hands again. I asked

him to bring Mlle. Albers up to the house when she arrived. We returned to the courtyard, Laugier having retrieved his lead pipe and slipped it into a long pocket of his overalls.

Michael was in the kitchen, visible through the open window. He had removed the Pushkin tailcoat, and he had also done a line or two, because although he still looked awful, he was standing upright and even washing dishes in the sink.

"I'm making you some coffee," he said through the window. I didn't want any coffee, but it was an Albers family habit that a new arrival anywhere should be given something hot to drink, a rule so deeply ingrained that even Michael's miserable state could not suppress it. "I see you've met Quasimodo," he said. "Great friend of mine. *Bonjour,* Monsieur Laugier," he called.

"*Bonjour, monsieur,*" Laugier said stiffly.

"Good, so I'm counting on you to bring the young lady," I said, shaking his hand yet again.

Laugier sidled up to his motorcycle, grabbed his game leg with both hands, and swung it over the gas tank. Once he was astride the machine, he kicked the engine on. It backfired and died. The sound caused Michael such pain that he reeled away from the window. Then the engine got started, Laugier leaned the bike away from the fountain, flicked it into gear with his good foot, and turned it around in a slow semicircle, the gravel popping under his tires. He gave me a last nod and puttered up toward the woods.

"He was talking about the police again, I'll bet," Michael said as I entered the kitchen. There was a kettle heating on the stove. Michael had washed a cup and a saucer and placed them next to the sink. He was seated at the table, which was covered with an oilcloth printed with eighteenth-century pastoral scenes. In front of him was a glass of milk. He stared at it as though trying to decide whether he'd be able to stomach it. The kitchen was a large and complicated affair, hung with a huge number of copper pots and pans. It combined highly modern equipment, including a massive black restaurant stove, with the most primitive, a stone oven that swelled out of the stone wall like a great hollow teardrop.

"Did he tell you he was going to bring the police?" Michael said.

"No. God, no," I said.

"They've already been here twice, they're suspicious, but luckily out here in the sticks these things take a while. It's just a matter of time, though."

"Well," I said, "he told me the police had come because you were playing loud music at night and disturbing the neighbors, and also because they just didn't know who you were."

"Right," Michael said sarcastically. Then he drained the glass of milk at one go, grimaced, and got up and went to the sink, where he rinsed the glass and refilled it with water.

"As though there's never loud music around here. Today is a no-hunting day, but you should hear it normally; it sounds like Verdun from dawn to dusk. The nearest neighbors are half a mile away; they can't hear my music. Besides, can you imagine what goes on normally in this fag palace? Did you know about this? Did Irina ever tell you?"

"About what?"

"That our father was as queer as a tree full of fish."

"No."

"I wouldn't bother to tell her if I were you. So far, she's lived perfectly well without knowing it."

"I think she's on her way here," I said.

"Oh, no," Michael said. "Why? Are you two back together?"

"No. She said you were threatening to kill yourself," I said.

"Oh, shit," Michael said. "That's all I need. Excuse me, I have to pee," he said, and he went off to the bathroom to do another line, in secret, having already understood I was the enemy.

Meanwhile, the water had come to a boil. The coffee machine was of a type I had never encountered before. In one of the rows of glass jars on the shelves — the largest spice rack I had ever seen — were some tea bags, so I put one in the cup and got some milk from the refrigerator. Obviously Michael was functional for at least a portion of the day, because apart from the sacked room upstairs and the slight mess in the living room, which appeared to be the remains of a single late night, everything was orderly and clean. Inside the refrigerator was a half-eaten chicken in a dish, neatly covered in plastic wrap. There were also some bottles of beer, and I decided to have one along with my tea. The ivory handle of the bottle opener chained to the side of the refrigerator was shaped like a phallus.

"Good. Make yourself at home," Michael said when he reappeared. "I'll have one of those beers too. Wait, I have to get some cigarettes," he said, and he made his way up the steps to the loft.

"So," I said a minute later, placing another phallus-opened beer in front of him. "You gave them quite a scare in New York, you know. But that was just a moment when you were feeling low, right?"

He was sitting perfectly still, with both hands on his bottle of beer. In the hour since I had awakened him his face had lost its swelling and its redness, and now he looked gaunt. All the flesh he had acquired as a boozing adult had been eaten away, and he was thinner than he'd been as a child.

"You've been working. I saw all those papers in the living room," I said.

"I'm just keeping busy," he said in a flat voice. "Just killing a little time before it kills me." He took a swig and cleared his throat. He lit a cigarette.

"Objectively," he said, "you're just sitting on the edge of

your cot in your cell, waiting to be taken out and shot. To be tortured to death with bone cancer. You end up a senile piece of meat manhandled by idiot nurses, with everyone around you trying to hurry you out of the picture. I don't see why I should stick around much longer."

He got up and fetched a glass from the cupboard.

"But I'm beginning to feel this is going to be too slow. The government is after me; it's just a matter of time before they get me, and I don't want to start with all that," he said. He poured the beer into the glass, stopping just as the head climbed up to the rim, and then waited for it to settle.

The moment Irina arrived we would have to get him into a hospital, probably in Apt or Avignon. Irina never traveled, I knew, without a little *Glee* promotional makeup bag containing Dr. Scheinbaum's pharmaceuticals, all the nice tranquilizers and sleeping pills he distributed so liberally to *Glee* girls. We would medicate Michael into docility, check him into a hospital, and when he was transportable we would get him back to New York.

Laugier had left only a few minutes ago, but already I was waiting to hear his motorcycle come backfiring down the road again, with Irina riding pillion and her bag wedged between them. As I had so often, for so long, I begged her to hurry. Across the table from me, her brother was shredding the label of the tea bag into the ashtray. He and Irina had the same small hands, with a hint of something simian about the nails. They had put me off in the beginning, and then I had grown to love them. On Michael's bony arms, sticking out of the unbuttoned cuffs of his shirt, they looked obscene.

"Are you working on the Pushkin book or on your grandfather's thing?" I asked.

"Christ," Michael said. "Did you say Irina was coming, or did I imagine that?"

XVII

MICHAEL had come to France to begin the research on the middle years of his grandfather's exile, the two decades Kuratkin had spent in Europe. For a biographer this would have been the richest period of Kuratkin's life. He had arrived from Russia penniless, still recovering from the wounds he had suffered fighting in the civil war, burdened by his aging, less adaptable parents, and yet hopeful that the Bolshevik era would be a mere interlude, that soon everyone would go home and resume the lives from which they had been cast so brutally. At the time he still cultivated his ambition to paint, but circumstances had compelled him to take a number of jobs, some of them eccentric: he had been, briefly, a guard in a museum and a movie extra, as well as an illustrator, a set designer, and an art director, which, of course, were the more lucrative occupations that had allowed him to support his parents. His gregariousness and his charm, and perhaps also his talent (on which I cannot pass judgment; legend had it that he was a great painter who had been stifled early on by the need to earn money), had brought him into contact, and sometimes into collaboration, with the major figures of the emigration — Diaghilev, Stravinsky, Bunin, Alexei Tolstoy, Kerensky, Miliukov, and so on — and also with some of the Montparnasse crowd of the twenties, Picasso, Léger, and Cocteau. I imagine he would have shunned the Surrealist wing, because of their communist rhetoric, but through Picasso or Léger he may have met Gerald and Sara Murphy and the expatriate American and English writers. Even I, who had known Kuratkin less than a year, discounting the last pathetic portion of his life, was aware that he had once met Proust; that he had had at least one conversation with Ezra Pound, during which he discovered that the poet had not read Pushkin; *und so weiter, und so weiter.* There was the ethically interesting question of the paintings Kuratkin had bought at interesting prices from Jewish refugees fleeing Germany in the thirties. (Irina had once presented this episode to me in a cynical, accusatory light, and then later reversed herself and described it as a charitable gesture from which he had derived no profit.) And finally, somewhere here in the south of France lay a spot where Kuratkin, years later, had dropped from the sky under a billowing silk parachute, in the middle of the night; after being collected by the local Resistance men he was driven to his appointment with their chief, who introduced himself as Colonel Berger but whose oddly familiar features, agitated by numerous tics and twitches, soon registered on Kuratkin's excellent memory as those of André Malraux, opposite whom he had been seated, fifteen years before, at a luncheon at the house of Louise de Vilmorin.

Michael had come expecting to spend a year or so among these alluring ghosts. He must have imagined that as he went around with his tape recorder and his notebooks, visiting sites and interviewing survivors, he would find himself, through a kind of osmosis, not just learning about his grandfather's past but coming to possess it as his own. He planned to write more than a biography of Kuratkin; he would write Kuratkin's memoirs. The knowledge he would assemble in his research, and the work he would perform on that knowledge, as he reflected on it and transmuted it into scenes and narrative, was to bring alive in him memories that would be no less real for not being his own. He seemed to feel entitled to them; to feel that they ought to have been passed on to him with the shape of his nose and his money — which he had almost completely finished spending, less than four months after receiving it.

He would not have settled for less. He was not a scholar who had decided to exploit his intimate knowledge of a subject in order to produce an interesting book. He was, instead, a victim of inspiration, a midnight pacer pouring vodka and lighting each cigarette from the stub of the previous one, with the record player going full blast in the background while the scenes of his life of Kuratkin played themselves out in his head. His own memories were all shame and humiliation. At such times he was able to replace them with stylized versions of his grandfather's; and in writing them down and making a book of them, he would overcome his failure.

Such illusions are difficult to maintain in daylight, without the vodka and the record player. They evaporate as soon as you have to sit down at a desk and try to make sense. That is the kind of lesson most people learn in their twenties, but Michael had been absent all that time — drunk, or cocooned in his heroin, or zinging from cocaine. His hours of sobriety had been spent railing against the circumstances — chiefly lack of money, which his absent father had ceased to provide when he reached twenty-one, and which his mother had cut off shortly after, because he spent it on drugs — that prevented him from leading the inspired life he had imagined for himself. The small inheritance from Kuratkin had at last freed him; but on one hand he found it had come too late, on the other, he knew it wouldn't last long.

His months in Paris must have been lonely ones. Some old schoolmates of ours lived there, but he hadn't seen any of them in years, and probably most of them had jobs and families by now and little time for him. He would have had neither a plan nor the energy to embark on his research in a systematic way. His attempts to do so would have been disappointing, compared with what his imagination had promised. He soon distracted himself from these problems by turning back to drink and drugs, re-entering a familiar life that presented other problems, to be sure, but problems that were so acute they absolved him of having to take care of anything else. And having done that, as he had so many times already in the past ten years, he had come to see that he would never get away from the person he had made of himself: a collection of addictions, impotent dreams, and idleness. Some impulse, some convulsion, had led him down here to find his father, seeking either a reunion that he thought might save him, or one of those confrontations with members of his family that he seemed to relish. As always, he had found his father gone.

He had just finished telling me that he didn't plan to live much longer. Since I didn't know what to answer, and not wanting to argue with him over such trivial matters, I asked whether we could light a fire. "It's bloody freezing in here," I said.

"We'd have to get wood from outside," he said.

He seemed not to feel the cold. I still hadn't taken off my leather jacket, and I had a sweater underneath, but Michael took off his tailcoat as soon as we got outside. We walked around to the back of the house and returned with armfuls of the logs Laugier had been poking at with his lead pipe an hour earlier.

"Let's get some more and just pile it up inside," I said. It seemed a good therapeutic activity, linking us in common work, and giving us something to do while I awaited the next development. Once Irina arrived we would make a decision about Michael, and in the meantime I wanted to keep us both busy. We made a second trip to the woodpile, and then stacked the logs next to the fireplace in the living room. There was also a large ceramic stove there, its tiles decorated with the same pastoral scenes as the oilcloth on the kitchen table, only blue instead of brown. The room was so big and its ceiling so high that I doubted it could be heated effectively.

After the second trip for the wood Michael abandoned me.

"Come on, just one more load and you'll be set for days," I said.

"No, I'm too tired, and I'm not dressed for it. You keep at it; I'll clean up in here."

Before returning to the woodpile, I explored the other side of the house. Beyond the French windows at the back of the big room, all of which were shuttered at the moment, lay a bare flagstone terrace bordered by laurel hedges, its eastern extremity sheltered under a pergola where clusters of grapes were rotting on the vine. There was a plaster nude against the wall of the building between two of the shuttered French windows, and another of stone, this one actually female, half hidden in the laurel. The small cherry orchard sloped down to the left; then came the oak forest, beneath which I could see the lowest houses of the village of Augères, and below that the valley floor with its poplar-lined road. Across the way, on the southern slope, someone was burning dead leaves. The wind carried the smoke away from me, up the mountain, atop which stood another stone village that grew straight out of the woods.

The third wing of the house was an unusual structure, part storage barn, part studio. One of the shutters was loose, and I was able to peer inside through a dusty windowpane into equally dusty columns of light falling from a skylight. Hanging from the rafters were large racks containing Jack Albers' stacked canvases, beneath which stood several trestle tables made from old doors, spattered with paint and ink, and some white wicker furniture that must have stood on the terrace in the summer. On the far wall were rows of bolted metal bookshelves. The roof of the studio jutted out beyond its wall, forming an open but sheltered area adjacent to an unexpected swimming pool, also surrounded by laurel hedges, whose existence couldn't be guessed from the road or even from any other part of the house. It was not covered yet, merely untended — only half full, the water green and opaque, its surface littered with sodden oak leaves and dead ants. I crouched down beside it and for a moment contemplated the activities of strange insects — they had dark oval bodies a quarter-inch long and two long jointed appendages they used as oars — that were cruising about near the surface but dived deep down into the murk when I stamped my foot on the pool's cement lip. As I stood there, the bright sunlight was suddenly snuffed from the air and replaced by a humid shade. The leading billows of a bank of rainclouds had just slipped under the sun. It was heading southward, still far away but moving steadily and swiftly.

I was going to ask Michael to tell me about his father. We would need topics of conversation, and I had always wondered about the man. Irina had almost no memories of him, but Michael, who was five years older than she, probably remembered him well. The taboo surrounding him was so strict that I had never seen even a photograph. The only object connected with him that was not on the index was the landscape hanging in Irina's bedroom; the pictures stored in Fincham had survived probably only by neglect. I had known that those Midwestern Alberses were rich, but if he could live like this on a black sheep's share, with a place in Paris and another in Morocco, the scale was far beyond what I had imagined.

When I returned with the last load of logs balanced in my arms, managing the handle of the front door with my elbow and backing up the step and into the house, Michael was huddled sideways on the couch, his back against the armrest and his knees drawn up. He had put on the tailcoat again. He had also wrapped a plaid blanket about his shoulders and was hugging himself gently. His eyes were half closed, and twice while I watched him his head fell forward onto his chest and then snapped back. A green velvet sleeve with gold frogging appeared from under the plaid blanket, and one hand scratched his neck and then the back of his other hand. It was at that moment that I understood he was taking heroin again, that it wasn't just a question of alcohol and cocaine. To be truthful, this was reassuring to me, because it meant there would be moments of calm, that we wouldn't have to resort to Irina's tranquilizers to make him docile. (She would have had trouble parting with them anyway, even for a good cause; especially in moments of crisis, she derived a strong sense of security from having a nice rattling little bottle of the things.) He had his own.

I was to learn that he had brought with him from Paris a generous supply of drugs. By the time I arrived, about two weeks later, he had evolved a fairly stable routine. He would come to in his father's lavender sheets at some point around noon, often hung over. A little heroin would ease the discomfort; a little cocaine would rouse him enough to get him up and puttering — cleaning up the mess he had left on collapsing into bed (like his mother and sister he was by nature very neat), or maybe even contemplating getting to work on his notes. Once in a while he went down to the village to buy cigarettes or some food in his father's Range Rover. He had smashed one of its windows and hot-wired the car, because Laugier had pretended he didn't have the keys. (So far, he had put only a few scrapes and dents on the machine. Michael was such a talented wrecker of cars that his license had been revoked long ago, and he had once had a terrible crash that kept him in a Boston hospital for three months with a broken back.) He would force himself to eat something. Then, a few hours later, he would start on the cocaine in earnest, fetch a couple of bottles of wine from the cellar, and spend the rest of the day in internal travels, starting letters, starting on his notes, changing the record on the turntable every time he wanted to hear something new.

Eventually he would get too worked up: he would listen only to the opening bars of each aria — his father's records were almost all opera — or play the same one over and over, and the intervals between the lines of cocaine would become shorter and shorter, and each one seemed to make him less euphoric and more jittery than the last. Then he would douse the fire in his head with heroin and simply nod in its warmth, and wander about the house and listen to more music until his body told him to take it back to bed. But once in a while things would go wrong, the chemical balance would fail, and it was then that Michael would call New York and threaten suicide, or go on a rampage like the one that had destroyed the upstairs room. My arrival, in disrupting his routine, was also bound to make trouble. He suspected that I had come to dislodge him from the house. He knew very well that a strait-laced fellow like me would be shocked by his state and start imagining that he needed doctors and hospitals and God knew what other nonsense.

I started stacking the new logs on top of the others.

"Good thinking," Michael said, as though this were the first load I had carried in.

"Are there any newspapers anywhere?" I asked.

"Haven't been following the news," he said. A few seconds later, he said, "Try the basket where the kindling is."

There was indeed a two-month-old issue of *Le Monde* in the wicker basket by the fireplace. While Michael nodded and dozed, occasionally smiling to himself, I built a fire and lit it, but the room immediately began to fill with smoke; the flue was closed. Before the flames could grow to their full height I managed to locate the lever inside the chimney and give it a good tug. It worked immediately, drawing the flames upward as I heard a hollow rush of air above me, and I got my arm out just in time; the sleeve of my leather jacket was hot to the touch.

"You're not doing yourself any good, staying here all alone," I said, waving my arm like a windmill to cool it off. "Why don't you go back to Paris? It's just going to get colder and nastier and lonelier here."

"Is that what Irina is going to try to convince me to do? Has she got some sort of detox center lined up for me there?"

"No. I don't know what she'll want you to do. But the detox center isn't a bad idea."

"Not interested," Michael said, hugging himself again. "I've been there." He went through some complicated manipulations to light a cigarette trying to do this without letting the plaid blanket slip from his shoulders. He then dropped the match, still burning, onto the rope carpeting beside the couch. He reached out from inside his cocoon and tamped out the flame with his fingers.

"I keep changing my mind," he said. "It's interesting. One moment I think I'll go to a nice white hospital and let them take care of me for a while. Then I think: Why? I like it here in the fag palace. The problem is, I'm going to have to go back to Paris anyway, because I'm running out of dope. I wouldn't know where to get any around here. The main problem with dope is you have to find it. Nothing in life is simple," he added sadly. "There are never any ashtrays where you need them."

I brought him an ashtray from the rack beside the kitchen sink and returned to tending the fire. It was burning well; the tepee of oak logs that I had built was beginning to catch, with tender blue shoots of flame curling around the bottom of the logs. I had always been proud of my ability to build a good fire. It was the same kind of satisfaction I derived from doing a good job of carving a chicken or a turkey. They were both family skills, head-of-the-table skills. That was it: I was in training to have a family.

"Once," Michael said after a long drag on his cigarette, "I was staying in Fincham, alone. This was a long time ago. It was winter. It was incredibly cold. You've never seen cold like that; it was like Siberia. I'd slipped on the ice and hurt my head. Irina came to fetch me with the little men in white coats and the butterfly net. It was a good thing, too. I had frostbite on my toes and I hadn't noticed it. They didn't have white coats, really. They were all wrapped up against the cold and they had these earflaps on their hats that made them look exactly like dogs. Poor Irina, it was in the middle of final exams or something like that. But you know, if she pulls that one on me again, if that's what you two are planning, it's a very bad idea. They'd have to register me with the police, and there'd be hell to pay. The damnedest thing has happened to me . . ."

"Your ash," I said. He had smoked the whole cigarette without tapping the ash off, despite my having gotten an ashtray for him. Now he was holding it up between thumb and forefinger, waiting for it to burn itself out on the filter.

"That's how my grandfather smoked," Michael said. "Except he had this ebony or cherry-wood cigarette holder, with the Dunhill dot on it. He trained Irina and me to remind him of his ash. He taught us the Russian word for it — *pepiel*. It was the first word of Russian I ever learned."

I had already heard this story from Irina. When she first told it to me I had been jealous of her family's rituals and secret words; mine had had almost none.

"The worst thing they could do to you," I said, "is expel you as an undesirable alien."

"No, no, that's the whole point," Michael said. "The damnedest thing. When I first flew into Paris, coming from New York, they stopped me at passport control and told me I couldn't come into the country. Well, they said I could come in if I wanted to, but they'd have to arrest me immediately. It turns out I'm a French citizen through my mother and I never showed up for military service at eighteen. I had absolutely no idea. I'm what they call *insoumis*. They checked on me at the airport for some other reason — I think they can sniff junkies themselves; they don't need dogs — and my name came up on the computer."

He had deposited the burned cigarette in the ashtray and was holding another, unlit, cupped in his hand.

"I'm not supposed to be in this country at all," he said. "I had to fly on to Geneva and then I snuck across the border."

"You did what?" I said.

"Yes, near Divonne, and then I took a train to Paris. Listen, brother of mine," he said, "what I really feel like is a glass of wine to go with my smoke here. Could I convince you to join me? It's just a little trip down to the cellar, and you were so efficient with all that wood."

"Yes, I'll have a glass too," I said, but I was reluctant to leave my fire. I was roasting happily inside my jacket now, and my hands and face were almost burning. There was going to be a problem in a minute: the logs had begun to pop, showering sparks, and the grate was too low to stop them all. Perhaps Michael had relied on the stove because he knew he couldn't manage the fireplace.

"You get down to the cellar through the door that's right next to the staircase in the entrance," he said.

I tore myself from the fire and paused for a moment in the doorway, hoping to hear Laugier's motorcycle.

"A bottle of Graves," Michael said. "They're in the first rack on the left."

Down in the vaulted cellar one wall was lined with a honeycomb of wooden racks. The place was lit by a single bare bulb, but hanging from the low vault was a crystal chandelier I had to step around — probably acquired on a whim and stored there because it would have looked out of place upstairs. My jacket still retained the warmth of the fire, but down here the air was cool on my head and hands, a delicious contrast. That was all Michael was doing upstairs, alternating physical sensations and states of mind for the sake of the change, to make time pass. I had assumed that his fear of the police was a delusion brought on by the drugs and booze and loneliness, but if he had indeed been AWOL for a dozen years and had entered the country illegally, it wasn't surprising that he didn't want to draw attention. The whole thing was typical of the Alberses. It was typical of Michael, who even as a boy had found the most extraordinary ways of getting into trouble — not content to smoke cigarettes or go over the wall after curfew but borrowing teachers' cars without their knowledge, or, once, seducing the stepmother of another pupil. And it was typical of Mrs. Albers that she should have neglected to clarify the question of her children's citizenship, so that Michael could discover, at thirty, that he was French. Typical not just of her vagueness but also of the way she always stressed her own and her children's Russian parentage, which allowed her to ignore the existence of her ex-husband and to shunt her Jewish mother out of the picture. Mrs. Albers was perfectly capable of referring to a neighbor at Central Park West, as I had heard her do, as "the Jewish gentleman upstairs," and of stressing the fact of Isaac Behr's Jewishness in a manner meant to convey an absence of prejudice. And it was typical of Michael, finally, to stroll blithely into a country where he knew there were warrants out for his arrest, to stroll in with his hands in his pockets, whistling a tune, so to speak — and then, on reflection, become terrified of what he had done.

He had misled me about the emplacement of the Graves. I pulled bottle after bottle from the lozenge-shaped slots and found none. I abandoned the search and climbed back upstairs with a Beaujolais. Outside it had started to rain. Michael was asleep, still propped up on the couch. He had hoovered up a bit of heroin from the glass table — I saw the traces of it, it was like pink talcum powder. My presence was disturbing him, perhaps, and he had felt the need to boost the previous dose.

I put down the bottle and disconnected the telephone by the couch. Then I went to the kitchen and closed the door behind me. I lifted the receiver off the wall phone and called Central Park West to get news of Irina's progress.

"Where are you?" was the first thing Mrs. Albers asked.

"I'm with Michael," I said.

"Is he all right?"

"He's taking a lot of drugs," I said.

"Oh, my God," Mrs. Albers said.

"Irina isn't here yet," I said.

"Irina isn't going there," Mrs. Albers said. "Irina is in Fincham."

"She what?" I said.

"She tried and tried to get a ticket," Mrs. Albers said. "Then she gave up. She went straight to Fincham from the airport; she didn't even come back here. She had her bag with her, you see, since she thought —"

"Mrs. Albers," I said, "I'm going to call you back in a few minutes."

"Wait," she said. "What are we going to do?"

"I don't know," I said. "I'll call you back."

"It's no use trying to talk to her. She —" Mrs. Albers started.

"I'll call you back," I said.

I hung up and got my address book out and called Fincham. I had to try several times, because I kept getting muddled.

The phone was picked up after the first ring.

"You bitch," I said.

"Who is this?" a male voice said.

I let this sink in for a moment. Maybe I had a wrong number.

"Is Irina there," I said.

"Is this Michael? *Eta tii, Misha?*" the man said.

It was, unmistakably, Isaac Behr.

"May I speak with Irina, please," I said.

"*Ekh,*" Isaac said. "Perhaps I can tell Irina who it is before you start calling her bitch."

I had several wild impulses, all simultaneous: to hang up, to start shouting, to identify myself as Jack Albers.

"What's going on, Isaac?" I said. "Are you her secretary, suddenly? It's Patrick; I'm with her brother. Let me talk to her, for God's sake."

He put the phone down. I heard him say my name.

"I can't talk to him. I can't," I heard Irina say.

Then Isaac covered the mouthpiece. Almost a minute went by.

"Are you there?" he said. "Irina will call you later. She can't talk on the phone right now."

"Oh, Christ," I said. "Look, I won't say anything bad to her. But I've got to talk to her. It's a crisis here."

"*Ekh*," he said again, sadly. "Is a crisis here, too."

Finally Irina took the phone.

"Yes, I'm here, I'm here," she said.

"I think he's going to die," I said.

"Have you called an ambulance?" she said urgently.

"I don't mean now," I said. "I mean tomorrow or next week. For one thing, he's driving your father's car around, stoned, without a license. He's also trashed half the house. Right now he's happily nodding off with heroin on the couch. How could you do this?"

"Listen to me," she said, her voice strangled. "You can't help him. Believe me, I've been through this half a dozen times in the last ten years. I know. Just leave. I'm sorry my mother asked you to go there. I never would have asked you, you know I wouldn't have. Just leave him."

"You don't understand," I said. "He's going to get himself arrested sooner or later, and he has this problem with French citizenship and military service —"

"I don't want to hear," she said. "Don't pay any attention to what he says; it's paranoid babble."

"It's not paranoid babble. He's wanted because he never showed up for military service. It turns out that he and probably you too are French citizens, through your mother. Sooner or later something's going to happen — he'll crash the car, or he'll get busted for the drugs, and then they'll throw the book at him."

There was a silence while Irina took this in.

"It doesn't change anything," she said. "You mustn't think you can help him. You can't. If you're afraid of what might happen if you leave, then call an ambulance and have them collect him. But don't stick around and take responsibility for him; it's no use."

She began to gulp for air.

"I don't understand," I said. "You did ask me to come. You said you were coming."

"I'm not asking you to understand. You couldn't understand unless you'd been through what you're going through a hundred times before. There's nothing anyone can do for him. It's for your sake I'm telling you to leave him; it's for you I'm doing this. Do you think it's easy?"

We were both in tears now, and on the last words her voice rose to a wail. In the background I heard Isaac Behr repeating her name, rolling the *r* in the middle. "Calm down," he was saying. "Calm down."

"I never could trust you," I said. "I stuck by you through a lot, and you never did shit for me. Tell Isaac what you just told me to do," I said. "Tell Doctor Scheinbaum to go fuck himself," I said. "You're going to fry in hell for this," I said.

After hanging up I went outside and jumped across two puddles and got in my car and closed the door. It was raining hard now. The windshield was a shimmering sheet of water covered in small explosions. I turned my head and tried to look into the house — from where the car was parked I could have seen through the living room window to the couch — but everything was hidden by the rain. I could easily do what Irina had told me to. I had my jacket on; my bag lay unopened in the back seat; the key was in the ignition. I could turn that key and drive away and never have to see or speak to any of these people ever again. It wouldn't be difficult to lose Irina in New York — I had spent all summer trying to bump into her and I hadn't seen her once. As I reached for the key I remembered there was that fire going in the living room, with showers of sparks swirling up every time a log tumbled, and the grate that was too low, and the rope carpets. I got out of the car and jumped over the puddles again and let myself in to break it up.

Michael was standing in the kitchen, wearing the Pushkin

jacket. He was holding the bottle of wine by the neck, which gave him an even more anachronistic look. In his other hand was a corkscrew. He thrust both objects at me.

"Could you deal with this, please?" he said. "I can't seem to manage."

I opened the bottle for him while he chose two glasses from the cupboard. He did this carefully, changing his mind several times, and finally settling on a pair of ordinary wineglasses. The corkscrew was of the type with the semaphore arms that you press together to extract the cork, and it hurt my cold hands to use it. I poured a modest amount into each glass, afraid that Michael might spill his, and not wanting to impair my already skimpy driving skills.

"To your health," Michael said.

"To yours," I said.

"Ah, that tastes so good," he said.

I took my glass to the living room, where I crouched before the fire and scattered the logs with the poker. Michael watched me with interest, sipping his wine. I felt like his prisoner now.

"I'm going to drive into town to buy some cigarettes," I said. "Yours are too strong for me."

"Could you bring me back a few things?" he asked. "Could you get me three packs of Gitanes and a couple of cartons of milk? And some meat, some prosciutto or something. They call it jambon de Parme here. And anything you want to eat for dinner. I should get some food in the house if Irina's coming."

It was the kind of thing his mother always said, that use of "in the house." I tried to get myself to tell him about Irina, but I couldn't.

"Let me give you some money," he said. He grasped the frogged front of his jacket with his left hand and reached inside its satin lining, producing from an unexpected pocket a thick wad of bank notes. He flipped through them, trying to find something smaller than a hundred-franc bill. There wasn't any.

"You're doing all right," I said.

"Well, what you see is all I've got left. When this is gone I'll be a pauper again." He flipped the bills off his thumb like the pages of a book, looking at them. "I should have gotten my teeth fixed," he said.

"Don't lose that," I said. "I'll be right back."

"The road gets washed out when it rains like this," he told me. "There's a dip right in the middle of the forest and it becomes a real swamp. You can see it coming, though. You've got to get your wheels all the way onto the embankment on the uphill side."

"Okay," I said. "Thanks."

"Leave a message for Irina at the café; tell her to call us when she arrives so we can go fetch her. We don't want her on Quasimodo's bike in the rain. Besides, I can't stand the sight of him anymore. He keeps coming around to snoop."

"Right," I said, heading out.

I had an urge to look at him as I shut the door, thinking it might be the last time I would see him. It was one thing to think that way when I had gone to visit my wasting father in the hospital near Geneva; as for Kuratkin, his decline had been so gradual and I had seen him so often that I never really believed he would die before I returned to the apartment. But Michael, although thin and right now unsteady of hand and vague of mind, was thirty years old and not sick; he wasn't injecting himself with the drugs and ran little risk of an overdose; Laugier had surreptitiously removed the gun from the house. That left a rope or a razor blade or a deliberate overdose — he'd have to swallow the drugs, perhaps washing them down with alcohol — or the Range Rover, if he could seal up the garage or find some tubing with which to reroute the exhaust back into the car. None of this seemed very likely. I had no doubt things would end badly for Michael, but I didn't think they would end quite yet. He would live to see more trouble.

Yet I did hope I was taking with me my last image of him — gaunt and unshaven, uncombed, wearing blue jeans that were yellow at the knees and a wild green velvet tailcoat with gold frogging down the front and on the sleeves; sitting cross-legged before the fire I had just destroyed, his small square hand cupped around his wineglass.

XVIII

BEFORE TURNING the engine on, I made sure I had all my gear with me. I hadn't taken anything from my pockets while in the house except my address book, which my groping fingers now located in its home berth inside my jacket. Its first pages were scrawled with two years' worth of telephone numbers for Irina and Michael — Central Park West, *Glee,* Fincham, Boston, Augères, the Chelsea printmaker with whom Michael stayed in New York — all of them useless now. I would buy a new book and start over again, skipping straight from Adamson to Amarante. My bag still lay on the back seat, unopened. I checked my other pockets to make sure nothing had fallen out while I carried the logs or crouched by the fireplace or the wine racks in the cellar.

I started the engine and hunted down the switch for the windshield wipers. I drove a tight circle on the wet gravel around the fountain and then headed up between the walls of cypresses to the oak forest. The road in there was soft but still manageable. It was sheltered from the wind, and the rain fell in fat drops collected in the trees, thudding on the roof of the car. It was beginning to grow dark and I turned on the headlights, creating a bubble of yellow light that I followed through the woods. I drove down through Augères without stopping, past the café and the phone booth in the square, both bright with neon, and stopped at the bottom of the hill and peered carefully between the black trunks of the poplars to make sure the main road was clear of oncoming cars. By accident I shifted into third gear instead of first, stalled the car, and cursed myself yet again for my bad driving while I calculated how long it was going to take me to get to Avignon.

I was too tired and upset to try to make it over the mountains to Caziers in this rain, packets of which swept across the road in the wind. I planned to spend the night at the same hotel in Avignon and then start all over again tomorrow morning, as though this day hadn't happened at all. The last time I had driven in bad weather was on our return from Fincham last spring, with Irina and her mother giving me contradictory directions all the way. I would have to stop remembering such things now, especially in circumstances like these, when absent-mindedness could be fatal. "*Une seconde d'inattention . . .*" as the French said. They also had a good expression for this kind of dangerous dusk: *entre chien et loup*. It was too dark for me to see the road clearly, not yet dark enough for the headlights to make a difference. I might not get all the way to Avignon that night; perhaps it would be better to stop and find a room somewhere in Apt. But that would mean a grim, idle evening with only my conscience for company. By now Michael would already be waiting for his cigarettes.

I began to feel worse and worse about it. When I failed to return, he would think at first that I had run into Irina and that we were sitting together in the café in Augères, conspiring against him. Then he'd probably think I'd had an accident. Even after he realized I wasn't coming back he would continue to wait for Irina. He might very well be making efforts now to go easy on the drugs and the wine, since he was expecting her. He would be struggling with himself, pacing about that vast room with the plaid blanket thrown over his gold epaulettes, with the craving for cigarettes added to all the others. It wouldn't become clear to him until midnight that he had been abandoned.

I pulled over onto the shoulder and let the car coast to a stop. I stayed there for some time, thinking about Michael intermittently. I rolled the window down a crack and rested my head against the cold glass. Rain flew into my hair. I too was craving cigarettes, from thinking about them too much. I turned my mind to other things. Tomorrow I would go to Caziers; I would stay there a week, writing the Giffern article and gathering information for the other. After Caziers, I could go to Paris for my week of vacation, or I could drive down into Italy or Spain, just drive south until I freed myself of the oncoming winter, and find a small village by the sea and rest there before going back to New York and putting on my wretched harness once again. But the thought of New York was actually not unpleasant. It would be getting toward Christmas when I returned; the streets would be crowded with shoppers; there would be buds of light on all the trees. I thought of riding down Park Avenue in a taxi after dark, snug in the bright night, the tires hissing in the slush, a gilded tower glowing in floodlights at the end of the avenue, and a woman in furs and her husband with a camel-hair coat over his tuxedo waiting in the light under the awning of an apartment building. Another French saying: "*Il faut voyager loin en aimant sa maison"* — a platitude fit for a fortune cookie, but at that moment an appealing one. This was what I was going to do: I was going to set myself up as a travel writer. I could do it just as well as the hacks I had employed for that purpose for the last two years. No more office, no more subway; I would wander to interesting places . . . in fact, I had already begun. I started to get excited about it. I knew exactly what to do. I would quit *Glee,* sublet the apartment for a year, call every magazine I knew and collect assignments . . .

I rolled the window down all the way and peered around me in the rain. A few cars had rushed by in the last minutes but now the road was clear. I put the engine in gear, swerved over to the other side of the road, backed up until I faced away from Avignon, and started back to Augères. I was going to bring Michael his cigarettes and his food. I would look him in the eye and tell him that I had spoken to Irina that afternoon and that she wasn't coming. I would suggest firmly that he get out of France and go home and get treatment. Then I would shake his hand and wish him well and drive away with a clear conscience.

I drove fast for once; I felt invulnerable. I saw everything clearly. That Afghanistan business, for instance, that longing to get into trouble — it had been no more than restlessness, the fear of getting tied down to Irina and having children and being forced to stick it out at *Glee* or some other magazine for the rest of my life. I didn't really need to go to Afghanistan, I wasn't that kind of person at all. Such things could be left to Steyer and Hélène. Irina had been right about that. She had been sound on a lot of things, I thought generously from the high ground of my new life. And who was I to pass judgment on her treatment of Michael? After a few hours with him I had tried to slink away without saying goodbye.

The shops would be closed for the night by the time I got to Augères. While there was still time I stopped in another village on the way and bought Michael his cigarettes, his milk, and the other things he had asked for.

I shot through the sloping curl of Augères and wound up into the woods. Everything was sopping wet now and the black tree trunks and the bare dripping branches sparkled in the headlights. The car kept drifting this way and that through the dead leaves and the muck, the engine whining as the wheels spun helplessly; every few moments one of them dropped into a pothole and threw a spray of muddy water over the side of the car.

Then, as I came around a bend in the forest, I had to swing the wheel sharply to the right and slam on the brakes. The nose of the car skidded up the embankment and bumped over the roots of an oak. The engine stalled. A late acorn, left behind by its brothers, pinged gratefully on the roof. On the other side of the road, half wedged into the yellowed leaves of a bush, was a figure on a piebald horse. Although the rider was hooded under a black poncho, I could tell, I'm not sure how, that it was a woman. She had heard me coming, with my engine complaining in the mud, and had stopped there, as far to the side of the road as she could. She kept the reins very tight, her gloved hands high on the animal's neck, while its front hooves kept leaving the sodden ground together for a half second at a time, as though it couldn't decide whether to panic. It tossed its head and tried to back up farther into the bush, rolling its eyes back, so that the rider had to spur it on while simultaneously tugging on the reins. She leaned forward and looked right into my windshield and said something I didn't hear through the closed window. I assumed she was asking me to turn off my lights, which I did. I rolled my window down and said, *"Pardon?"* but she didn't answer, still struggling with the beast. Finally she forced it back onto the road, where it sank up to its knees in muddy water. It sloshed by my open window in the darkness, tossing its head, walking half sideways; the woman, speaking soothing words to the horse and patting its neck, glanced at me furiously from under her hood. I let her go by without greeting her, though I was grateful. This was the place Michael had warned me about, where the road got washed away in the rain, and had she not stood guard there I would have driven straight into it and gotten stuck.

I waited until she had disappeared around the bend and then started the engine again and turned on the lights. With both my front wheels already on the embankment, I skidded successfully through the mire, although twice the engine started to race, accompanied by my heart.

As I came out of the woods and headed down the slope toward the house, my beams illuminated another poncho-clad figure walking ahead of me, leaning away from the weight of a heavy object hanging from its right arm. The figure entered the courtyard and started to make for the door, but then paused at the fountain, hoisting the heavy object onto its rim, and stood there as I drove down, apparently waiting to see whether I was coming to the house or just driving by. It was Michael, in a poncho identical with the one the rider had worn, only olive green instead of black. Looped over his shoulder was a thick coil of steel wire. His other hand rested atop the rim of the fountain on a compact blue metal contraption with a long lever.

"I didn't think it was you," he said as I got out. He looked sober and grim. "I heard a car stall up there, and I got the winch and started on my way up. It's not the first time it's happened."

"There was this woman on a horse —" I said.

"Ah, yes, Death," Michael said. "She comes by every night. She rides only after dark, because of the hunters."

We were entering the house. Michael put the winch down and pulled his poncho over his head.

"I've talked to that woman a bit; she knows my father and seems to hate him," he said. "Probably thinks he lowers the tone of the neighborhood," he added.

I put the food and the packs of cigarettes on the kitchen table. There was the same bottle of Beaujolais there, still almost full, and our two glasses.

"Thank you," Michael said. "I just spent an hour talking to Irina on the telephone. She called from Fincham, it must be the middle of the night there. She told me about your conversation. I didn't think you'd be coming back."

"I came to bring you this stuff and say goodbye. I'm off to Caziers. I've got that article to do."

"You're more than welcome to stay the night," Michael said. "It's getting late."

"I don't know," I said.

"I'm stone sober, if that's what you're worried about. Or else the house gives you the creeps. God knows it gives me the creeps. I didn't tell Irina about it. Did you?"

I sat down at the table and poured wine into a glass. I didn't remember which glass was whose and for a moment I had a senseless reluctance to risk drinking out of Michael's, as though his problems were contagious.

"What else did Irina have to say?" I asked.

"She said I had to go back to the States and go back into rehab."

"Well," I said.

Tears came into his eyes. He pulled a chair out, sat down across from me with his elbows on the table, and covered his face with his hands. He didn't sob; he just cringed every few seconds, and then gasped. I had never before seen a grown man cry, except in movies or on television. Through some horrible nervous short-circuit it made me want to laugh. God knew I didn't find it funny, though. I too covered my face with my hands. I pinched my nose. Then, in desperation, I busied myself with one of the packs of Gitanes. I peeled off the wrap and pushed up the bottom of the box and pulled out a cigarette and walked over to the stove and lit it. It was so strong that my throat locked on the smoke.

It was interesting that Irina had changed her mind yet again. I knew why, too: it was because I had told her that Michael was going to wind up in jail. She had been willing to let him die, if that was going to be the outcome. She had made herself ready for that. Michael would be out of his misery; she would eventually recover from hers. But she couldn't stand the possibility of his being arrested and imprisoned. That was much more complicated and would involve continued suffering for everyone. Irina could manage only clean breaks. That night she had been unable to sleep, despite Dr. Scheinbaum's drugs and Isaac's arms.

"Look," I said, regaining control of myself. "Tomorrow, if you want, I'll drive you to Avignon and put you on the train to Paris. You'll be in New York within twenty-four hours. You can call Irina or your mother and someone will come and pick you up at the airport."

"It's too late," Michael said, and he cringed again in that terrible way. He wiped his face and got up and walked over to the sink, meeting his reflection in the black window. He took the dishrag from the rack and wiped his face and hands with it. He leaned against the sink, his hands gripping the edge.

"I've already been through all this," he said. His voice was thickened with tears and mucus. "I've already done all this, several times. It's just never going to end."

"Look," I said again. I felt dizzy and nauseated from the cigarette, but it seemed to have stifled my nightmare giggles. "Quitting anything often doesn't work the first time, or the second, or even the third. The important thing is to keep trying. What other options do you have? You can't just stay here. Your father's going to come back eventually. You don't want him to see you like this. And you said yourself you're going to run out of money. What'll you do then?"

"I can't leave from Paris," he said. "They'd catch me at passport control."

"Then leave from Switzerland. How did you get into France in the first place?" I asked, suddenly doubting that he'd told me the truth.

"I walked over the border," he said.

"Then walk again," I said.

"It's too complicated," he said, shaking his head in resignation. "I'm not up to it. I'd have to get to Lyon, hitchhike to Divonne, hump up the mountain with my suitcase . . . I'm just not up to that anymore."

"I'll drive you there," I said. "Shit!" I said a second later. "Shit! I'll put you on the damned plane in Geneva myself. Okay? Is there anything else I can do for you? And for your family? Is there anything else?"

He didn't answer. Our eyes met in the mirror of the black window. Then I looked at myself and rearranged my face into something human.

"Look, I'll drive you," I said, calmly.

"Too much hassle," he said.

"No, I'll do it," I said. "Where did you cross the border?"

"Above Divonne," he said. "Through the forest, every single road has a border post. It's steep, I don't think I can do it."

"We can worry about that when we get there." I said. "I'll do it if you're willing to leave very early tomorrow morning. We can finish this bottle of wine, but you have to eat some food. No coke. We're going to bed early. You can take your heroin tonight, but tomorrow you stick to the absolute minimum."

"I'll think about it," he said.

"No. You get up now and fetch your whole stash of coke and bring it to me."

He looked at me through red-rimmed eyes. His face was blotched in the same pattern as Irina's when she cried.

"This really sounds like fun," he said.

"Well, for me too," I answered.

He pushed himself away from the sink, as slow as an old man, and walked by me into the living room. Even if he was going to fetch the cocaine, I knew very well he would bring me only part of it, keeping a safe amount in reserve.

He returned two minutes later with a handful of small waxed-paper envelopes and put them on the table. They were of the same type used in America — snow seals, we called them. Even in my druggier college years I had never been good at estimating amounts of cocaine, and this stuff may have had a different degree of purity, but it looked like a lot of drugs. Given that he probably had more of it hidden away somewhere else, and that both stashes together amounted only to the remains of what he had brought from Paris, he must have bought an enormous weight of it there.

"Jesus, Michael," I said, "you could live for months on this money."

"Sell it, then," he said. "You deserve some compensation."

From one of the rear pockets of his jeans he pulled a folded map. Printed on the cover was "Carte nationale de la Suisse" and below that "St. Cergue," the name of a town in the Jura Mountains, which, for a hundred and fifty miles north of Geneva, form the border between France and Switzerland. I moved the bottle and the glasses aside and Michael unfolded the map on the table. The scale was large enough so that in the villages you could see individual buildings, represented by small black rectangles.

"This is where I crossed," he said, his index finger hovering for a moment over the pale blue crescent of Lake Léman and then landing in the mountains. "You just have to get me to Divonne."

It seemed a logical route. It crossed the dotted line of the border high on the mountainside, in a forest, and yet there was no great distance, nor, apparently, difficult terrain between the nearest towns on the French and Swiss sides. The forest trail that would take him up the mountain was, as he had said, quite steep — you could tell by how often it switched back — probably steeper than the one on the Swiss side of the mountain, which he had climbed when he was in much better shape and spirits.

"I left from here — this little place — and walked up, and then down the other side to Divonne," he said.

"How long did it take you?"

"I can't remember," he said. "A couple of hours."

"I can drive you beyond Divonne, look. To this place, Les Mouilles. You're right at the edge of the forest there; it'll shorten your walk."

"I don't know," he said. "I'm not sure that's much of a road."

It was already night outside. The kitchen clock said ten minutes to seven. I tried to remember at what time it began to get dark. It had happened just as I left the house on my attempted escape, but I hadn't bothered to look at my watch then and didn't know how long it had been.

"If we can make Divonne by two-thirty or three you'll be sure to have enough light to make it across. That means we'll have to leave here around seven in the morning."

"I've got a good flashlight, anyway," he said.

There was also the problem of the weather, though I didn't bring it up. It was still pouring. If the rain was this heavy in the Jura tomorrow, the crossing would be hell. Even if it had been like that today the ground would still be so wet that Michael's stroll in the forest would be a muddy horror.

I pocketed the cocaine envelopes.

"Is there a TV in the house?" I asked.

"Is that how we're going to spend the evening, like a cozy little family?" Michael said.

"I'd like to watch the news, if you don't mind," I said.

Michael's father kept the television concealed in the upper cabinet of the sideboard that also housed the record player and the tape deck. Michael and I sat side by side on the rope carpet, smoking, with an ashtray and the bottle of wine between us. Outside the valley of the Lubéron, the world continued to spin. I had read the *Herald Tribune* a little more than twenty-four hours earlier, and yet I was almost surprised to find some of the same stories unfolding in the news, as if I had been here with Michael not for an afternoon but for several weeks. In Paris, the president and the prime minister were in opposition over the military budget; in an unrelated development, students were protesting obligatory conscription, which drew a bitter laugh from Michael. In both England and Italy the trade unions were acting up, with the British government taking a firm stand against them while its Italian counterpart panicked and quarreled with itself; in West Germany there were demonstrations demanding the withdrawal of American troops; in Washington the president reaffirmed his commitment to NATO, stressing the Soviet Union's continued desire for the expansion of communism, as demonstrated not only "in our own back yard" in Central America, but also in Afghanistan, where the rebel forces appeared to have the capital locked in a kind of episodic siege that clamped down at night and relaxed during the day. None of this interested me in the least. I wanted to know whether it would rain tomorrow in the Jura.

At last we came to the weather. The maps and display systems were quaintly primitive compared with their American counterparts, but the cheerful manner of the weather wizard was the same, if a little more formal. The rain that had fallen on the eastern and southern portions of the country that day was represented by slanted streaks underneath a stylized stratocumulus that was made to appear on a screen while the weatherman, like a teacher at a blackboard, pointed at it with a long stick. For tomorrow a different symbol appeared, wherein half a sun was wedged into the upper part of the same stratocumulus, indicating, he explained, *temps variable,* with possible sprinklings of *pluie.* We then continued through the rest of the country, or the *hexagone,* as the wizard called it. In any case, there was no question of postponing the trip. We would do it tomorrow or not at all. Followed by my suspicious eyes, Michael stalked off to the kitchen, where he shrugged himself back into his tailcoat. By the time I switched off the television, after watching some commercials that impressed me both by their inventiveness and their erotic appeal, he had cleared the map off the table, set two places, and arranged the food I had brought back — some ham, some shrimp salad, and some cucumber salad with dill — on platters in the center, augmented by the half-eaten roast chicken I had seen earlier in the refrigerator.

We ate mostly in silence, like a couple who have nothing to say that isn't potentially explosive, or like wary strangers thrown together by circumstance; we were a bit of both. I seemed to have acquired the same bossy tone of voice with which Irina often addressed Michael, poisoned by an undercurrent of rage; it startled me, but Michael, who was perhaps accustomed to it, hardly reacted.

"So how does this work?" I said. "How long ago did you last have a hit of heroin?"

"A few hours ago," he said, chewing.

"And then you're going to take some more after dinner."

"Yup," he said. "Why, do you want some?"

"No, I was just thinking that you might try to get packed and organized beforehand."

"It's okay. I've packed a few suitcases in my life. Do you imagine it turns me into a gibbering maniac or something?"

"To me you don't look like you're in great shape."

It was shocking to realize that I had signed on for another day of his company and volunteered to drive him three hundred miles. Then I'd have to drive back. Really, I hated him; I hated the silly jacket he was wearing; I hated that oily, porous skin of his; I loathed his complicated American manipulations of knife and fork — his American father had still been around at the time Michael was learning table manners, but Irina had been trained solely by her French mother.

I washed the dishes while Michael went upstairs to pack. The dishes had the same pastoral scenes on them as the oilcloth on the table and the ceramic tiles of the living room stove, and the name of the pattern, toile de Jouy, which had been teasing me all afternoon, came percolating up through my fatigue just seconds after the big platter that had held the chicken leaped from my soapy grasp and broke in two in the sink. For all I knew it may have been an antique worth a month of *Glee* salary, but what with the disaster upstairs it didn't seem to matter. It felt almost funny to be washing dishes and tidying up, as though Michael and I had been house sitters or renters here. But I had nothing else to do. There was a whole evening to kill, and even though I was by now exhausted, I knew I was going to have trouble falling asleep, as I always do when I have to wake early for a Big Day.

When I was through with the dishes I went out in the rain to get my bag from the car, and carried it into the house. Michael's flippant offer of a taste of heroin, which I had never tried, became tempting. It would dispose of the next few hours, clear my depression, and help me sleep; it might even prove a useful form of bonding with Michael, relieving me of the role of policeman, and perhaps making him more malleable tomorrow. I was also curious. But I had decided some years ago that I was through with drugs, and the disaster of my single relapse, with Michael at Big Tam's some months earlier, had only affirmed the wisdom of that decision.

In the third wing of the house were two guest bedrooms and a bathroom, sober and undecorated. I heaved my bag onto one of the beds, extracted my alarm clock, and checked it against my watch. In the bathroom I let the shower run for several minutes, but it remained achingly cold; this part of the house probably had a separate boiler that had not been fired. I put my shaving kit and some clean clothes under my arm and grabbed a couple of towels from the linen closet on the landing and made my way over and up to the loft to take a shower there. Michael had righted one of the chairs in the wrecked library and was sitting on it, immobile, in the midst of the devastation, with the tails of the Pushkin jacket folded over his knees. His face was expressionless, uninhabited, his eyelids drooping slightly and his lips parted. The Priapus still lay on its side among the shards of mirror and glass on the carpet, which was stained a deep brown from the wine. The books were still strewn all over the couch and the floor; many of them had opened in flight and landed face down, with bunches of pages folded over. The mauve curtains still hung crazily from their broken rod. One thing I hadn't noticed during my previous viewing of this exhibit was a painting that had been smashed on the arm of the sofa and remained stuck there, with the corner of the arm protruding through the back of the canvas. Michael roused himself enough to give me a weak smile.

"Would you see any point in my trying to fix this place up?" he asked.

"There's not a whole lot you can do about it now," I said.

"I could write the man a note," he suggested.

"There's probably not a whole lot you could say," I said.

"I appreciate all this," he said. "Don't think I don't appreciate it, but I'm not sure I'll be leaving with you tomorrow." As he spoke he flapped the satin-lined tails of his jacket on his thighs, first the right, then the left, then the right again.

"I'm leaving at seven," I said. "You're free to come if you want."

"The bathroom's through that door, if that's what you're looking for," he said, lifting his right tail and pointing with it.

In the bedroom, a large leather suitcase of the same manufacture as Irina's traveling bag lay open on the bed. It was packed carefully, Albers-style, just as the bed was carefully made.

"Did you carry this suitcase with you over the border?" I called out.

"No," he said from the next room. "A friend drove it in his car from Geneva to Paris." I thought I heard him laugh then, perhaps at the idea of traipsing through the woods with such a heavy load.

Next to the suitcase on the bed were three objects, neatly lined up in a row, which he had no doubt bought in Geneva for his first crossing: the map we had looked at earlier, a professional-looking compass encased in matte black plastic, and a Swiss Army flashlight, which I picked up and turned over in my hands, fascinated. I had owned several of these, successively, in childhood, and had quite forgotten about them, the archetypal flashlight having become, in my mind, the tubelike American kind. While I stood over Michael's suitcase and Jack Albers' wide bed in Provence, beneath the gaze of a winged stucco cherub hanging from a corner of the ceiling, the sight and feel of this flashlight broke open in me a flood of memory far more powerful than any I had experienced in Switzerland the week before. It was a boxlike object of olive-colored metal, approximately the size of two packs of cigarettes. Its round lens was covered by a hood that could be raised by means of a hinge. There was something peculiarly anthropomorphic about this hood, which, when lowered, bore an abstract resemblance to a military helmet; moreover it also had an architectonic affinity with the hood covering William Tell's head on Swiss five-franc coins, an association reinforced by the embossed outline, located centrally beneath the lens, of a crossbow, a symbol meaning "Made in Switzerland" and also a deliberate reference to Tell, for it is that weapon, and not the standard bow, that he used to shoot the apple off his son's head; and the idea of Tell unveiled a visual imprint stored somewhere deep in an attic of my mind, the picture my child's imagination had formed of a particular episode in Tell's legend: his steering a small boat through a violent storm on Lake Lucerne, wearing the hooded cape of the five-franc pieces, rock-solid at the helm among monstrous waves. This train of trivial associations, all of them abstract, brought my whole childhood back to me, the whole feeling, the essence, the very taste of it, more completely and more powerfully than any of the sights and smells I had so recently searched, my nose up in the Alpine air. I could not recall a single childhood event involving such a flashlight, let alone one that may have marked me; it was just that these associations, repeated thousands of times, over thousands of days, had bored through my mind a gorge deeper and wider than any powerful emotion could have done.

One is rooted most deeply and most solidly in what one has forgotten. I put the flashlight down tenderly. The world appeared to me an infinitely rich and mysterious place; opiates, alcohol, anything that interfered with one's grasp of it were best avoided. I took off my clothes in the bathroom and stood under a strong jet of hot water. It was a luxurious white room, with enormous framed mirrors, tarnished at the edges, and a deep lion-footed bathtub as well as the frosted-glass shower stall, inside which a magnifying shaving mirror was affixed to the tile. I used it, after reaching out from the stall and groping blindly inside my shaving kit, which I had left on the edge of the marble sink. Michael and Irina's father must have been a tall man, because I had to stand on tiptoe and tilt my face upward to see myself.

When I came out, Michael was tidying the wrecked room. He was going about it very slowly. He had pulled the curtain down and folded it on the floor beneath the windows, and removed the broken curtain rod. Wearing a pair of gardening gloves, he was picking up all the broken glass — the remains of the mirror and the wine bottle, a lamp and the glass top that had covered the rattan chest — and dropping them in a large plastic garbage bag.

XIX

AT TWO O'CLOCK in the morning I was awakened by the banging of a loose shutter. It had stopped raining, but the wind had risen again to whistle and boom about the house. I had been dreaming insistently of my old headmaster firing a starter's pistol for a hundred-yard dash; the blocks kept slipping back as I tried to launch myself forward, and we would have to begin again. My room was freezing and completely dark except for the faint green circle of my clock's dial on the nightstand. I had not made the bed before going to sleep but merely wrapped myself in a sheet and two blankets, without removing my underwear and my socks, and every time I turned over I felt the slick material of the bare mattress under me.

A whole hour passed before I stopped trying to go back to sleep and got up to search for the maddening shutter. Probably Michael had let it bang every night, not caring or not waking. I held one of the blankets around me and crept down the stairs, my ankles cracking and the coldness of the stone steps going right through my socks. I couldn't remember the location of the light switch in the entrance and had to grope about the walls with my free hand, and when I found it, the bulb in the ceiling lamp flashed and blew out with a pinging sound, leaving me blinded. I made my way across, or rather around, the entrance, running my hand over the cold front door and then along the wall until I encountered a void that was the doorway to the kitchen, and reached inside and groped again until I found another light switch. Then I went from room to room, turning on all the lights as I went, because it was a scary night. The country outside seemed noisy and wild, and it felt as though this house, with its naked boys and Venetian mirrors, did not belong in it and was not a shelter but, on the contrary, a kind of target. Similarly, Michael's presence in the other wing was not a reassuring one, because I imagined that he attracted bad luck, that such a mess of a man was a lightning rod for trouble.

The shutter was still banging somewhere. It made a ticking noise as it began to swing on its hinges, and then an accelerating groan, and then fell silent a second before it slammed against the house. Even though I had ample warning, I jumped every time. Alone in the night, my eyes hurting and my rib cage shaking from sleeplessness, I kept expecting to hear someone pounding on the front door — the police, neighbors Michael had angered, some drug connection who had tracked him down, professional kidnappers from Marseille . . . I couldn't find the shutter anywhere.

I double-locked the door and fastened a window in the main room that had been left open behind the shutters and then forced myself to turn the lights off as I made my way back up to the guest bedroom, where I lay down again, rolling the blanket around me and raising my feet to tuck its end under them, and tried again and again to make my mind blank and fall asleep. The shutter began to sound like a man in despair, moaning and then banging his fist on a table. I tried to convince myself that soon all this would be over, that the night would come to an end, and so would the next day, and I would never have to think about Michael or Irina again. At last I noticed that I could see the window from my bed, and from then on I waited as a gray light seeped gradually into its panes, and the hands on my clock, which I couldn't read without holding it against my face, crawled into vertical alignment at six o'clock.

Michael came to quite easily and without protest. It was probably the first time in weeks he had not drunk a great deal nor taken cocaine the night before, though he had fallen asleep fully dressed again. He sat up and swung his legs out of the bed, holding the covers across his middle. Half his hair was flattened against his head, and the rest stood up in spikes. Staring at his feet, he brought his fist to his mouth and cleared his windpipe with rolling coughs and hacking, and then made for the bathroom, where he spat and hacked and spat again, then lifted the toilet seat and unzipped his jeans.

"What time is it?" he asked, over the noisy burbling in the toilet.

"Six-fifteen. I want to get going by seven. You can get some more sleep in the car," I said. "I'm going downstairs to make coffee."

Ten minutes later I climbed up to the loft to make sure he hadn't gone back to bed. He had stripped the mattress and was carefully folding a lavender sheet, its borders wedged under his chin. After being shaved for the first time in days, his cheeks were shiny and smooth, and he looked remarkably healthy.

"We don't have time for that," I said. "Just leave it."

"I have to close up the house," he said.

"There's no time. We'll leave the keys and a note for Laugier at the café and let him do it."

He finished folding the sheet and lay it at the foot of the mattress. He glanced around the bathroom to see whether he was leaving anything behind. I watched him, wondering what it felt like to be embarking on a long trip, at the end of which one would be put under lock and key, not for the first time, at a treatment center. The night before, I had deliberately avoided making suggestions about calling airlines and reserving a seat on a Geneva–New York flight, knowing that any obstacle we encountered would make him change his mind and decide to stay. The way I saw it, my first and only task was to get him out of the house and carry him to the Swiss border; after that he was on his own. He put on the tailcoat and zipped his suitcase shut and carried it down the stairs behind me. In the kitchen he pulled from the inner pocket of the jacket an envelope with his father's name on it, Mr. John Albers, and placed it in the center of the table, and then stared at it while he sipped a steaming mug of coffee. Moments later, as we were loading the bags into the back of the car, he dashed back into the house and emerged with the envelope in his hand, only to turn around again and leave it a second time. I don't know what explanations, apologies, or reproaches it contained.

My eyes ached with fatigue, and I dreaded the long drive ahead and another day of Michael's company, though so far this morning he had been docile and nearly silent; yet I was happy to get under way and leave that house behind. In the oak forest the gale had dried the trees overhead, but the road was still a slippery mess, littered with a new crop of sodden leaves.

"It's coming up around the next bend; you've got to stick to the right," Michael said.

"I know, I know," I said, but still I almost managed to get

stuck, the front wheels spinning madly for a moment, the right one sending up a geyser of muddy water, while Michael buried his face in his hands.

"I'm going to need another cup of coffee when we stop in the village," he said after I got us out.

"You're not going into the café in that ridiculous coat," I said.

"No," he said mildly. He peered down its frogged front. "I've become attached to the thing," he said. "I remember it from when I was very small. My grandfather had it made for a fashion shoot for the magazine, and he wore it to the dinner table one night as a joke. I must have been six or seven years old."

We were coming down into the village. I was low on gas and tried to remember where I had passed a filling station the day before. I had to drive especially carefully and avoid an accident, because both of us were carrying drugs. I had disposed of most of Michael's cocaine last night by flushing it down the toilet in the guest bathroom — not a simple task, because it turned out that the little envelopes floated, and I had to open each one and shake the powder out — but I had kept one envelope containing about a gram, I guessed, which was now in my shirt pocket under my sweater. I was convinced that Michael had another stash somewhere about him, but I wasn't taking any chances and thought that if it became necessary I could use it as a goad or a bargaining tool.

"Do you remember a few months ago I came to the magazine to take a look at old issues?" Michael asked.

"Yes, I remember."

"Well, I saw this jacket in one of them. It was on a guy in the background of a photograph, just a background detail, but it jumped out at me and I remembered that dinner when my grandfather wore it. And then I found it in my father's closet; God knows how it wound up there. I guess I'm stealing it. I feel kind of bad about it. Also I left him that stupid letter. I think I want to retrieve it. Can we go back?"

"No, we don't have time."

"I really trashed that room," Michael said.

"Can't be undone," I said. "Just forget you were ever there. Tomorrow at this time you'll be on a plane to New York, and Irina will come down from Fincham to meet you. You're going to be just fine."

I parked the car in the square.

"You know," Michael said as I opened my door and started to get out, "a couple of months ago I turned thirty. I couldn't help myself, I kept thinking, There's got to be some kind of way around this. It was amazing."

I waited for him to continue, but he didn't. He just stared out the windshield. Nor did he seem to expect a response. I got out. He got out too, shaking himself out of the tailcoat and throwing it in the back seat.

"Shit," he said.

"What," I said.

"Nothing. Just an unpleasant memory," he said.

The café had opened moments before. Only the boss, the boxer, was there. He was taking the chairs off the tables and wiping down the tables with a wet rag. Michael and I each ordered a coffee at the counter. I tried to buy the two ham sandwiches that were under the plastic dome with the croissants.

"You don't want those," the boxer said. "They're from yesterday; I keep them for my dogs. Some fresh ones will be here any minute with the van."

"Surprisingly solicitous," Michael said in English. "I'm not very popular here, usually." Without the tailcoat he was cold, and he hugged himself.

"I wouldn't mind another coffee when you have a minute," he called to the boxer, who had left us to finish taking the chairs down from the tables. Then he patted his pockets. "And a pack of Gitanes, please," he said.

"You're going to have to eat something, okay?" I said. "That's a long trek you have ahead of you."

"Not hungry yet," Michael said.

"May we leave the keys of the house with you for Monsieur Laugier?" I said when the boxer got back behind the counter. "We're leaving today; we're on our way now."

"Very well," he said. "The demoiselle is no longer expected?"

"No, she's not coming after all," I said.

"I'll give them back to Laugier," the boxer said. Michael dropped them on his outstretched hand, and he turned to hang them on a nail next to the telephone.

"Please thank him for me," Michael said.

"I'll do that," the boxer said.

He pushed Michael's new cup at him across the counter and turned his attention to the cash register, banging the drawer open and starting to count the money inside. From Michael's need for coffee I deduced that he hadn't started on his secret stash of cocaine before leaving the house. I was interested, in a detached sort of way, to see when he would start. The important thing was to get some food in him beforehand. It was going to be the old problem, not encountered since college, of snorting drugs in a moving car — finding a flat surface, a cassette box or the back of a book, on which to lay the lines, balancing it on one's knees, ducking under the level of the window if there were other cars around. Of course it had been a long time since Michael had seen this hour of the day except from the wrong side of sleep, and probably his body wouldn't start making demands until later. For a moment I envied him: his desires and ambitions were so far beyond his grasp that he was absolved of making any effort in their direction. He had, in fact, no ambitions — only fantasies, which don't require you to get up in the morning. I was astonished at what a single night's sleep and a shave had done for his appearance. He no longer looked ravaged. In fact, now that he had lost all that weight, one would have thought him younger than he was.

"Let's go," I said.

We both shook hands with the boxer across the counter.

"The van from the bakery will be here in five minutes if you want to wait," he said.

"No, thank you, we've got a long way to go," I said.

"I'll give the keys to Laugier," he said, and he wished us a good trip.

Out in the square the wind had begun to blow again, again from the north, where I could see blue sky above the mountain and an armada of tall fair-weather clouds sailing our way, the eastern ones still pink-bellied. Across the street a man in a cap was opening the shutters of what proved to be the butcher shop, muttering to himself through a dangling cigarette. A long-legged dog whose pelt looked remarkably like a hyena's came galloping down a side street into the square, where it stuck its nose to the ground and scuttled by us in zigzags, pretending to investigate a scent but in fact aiming right for the butcher, who gave it a friendly kick. Undeterred, the hyena followed him into the store for its breakfast of blood sausage or scraps.

Before getting into the car Michael opened the hatchback and unzipped his suitcase and extracted from it a tattered gray sweater, which he put on instead of the Pushkin jacket.

"Put your seat belt on," I said as I turned the key in the ignition.

"Look," Michael said. "Enough with that tone of voice, okay? I'm grateful for your driving me, I'm grateful you came, I'm fucking grateful for everything. But you don't have to talk to me like that."

"Keep an eye out for a gas station," I said.

By the time we reached Apt, I had already grown afraid of my driving. I wasn't afraid I'd fall asleep; it was just that I felt a little muddled, as though neurons were misfiring in my brain, and I didn't trust my judgment should I get into trouble. I had decided that no matter how tired I got, I wouldn't let my licenseless and accident-prone companion take the wheel. He had already begun to complain about how slowly we were going, and when we stopped for gas and sandwiches he offered to take over, but now I slowed down even more. It was past eight o'clock and there were more cars on the road. As we neared Avignon about an hour later, an old Peugeot began to tailgate me, flashing its lights. We were on a relatively straight stretch of road and I put my right blinker on to let it go by, but it didn't accept the offer and remained glued to my bumper, giving up on the lights and now honking its horn. Michael turned around in his seat and looked.

"Shit," he said. "It's Quasimodo and Tiny from the café. Don't stop."

"What do they want?" I asked.

"The hell if I know, but don't stop."

"Maybe Irina came after all," I said, checking again in the rearview mirror.

"No, that's not it," Michael said, glancing at me for a moment and realizing, at the same time I did, that I was crazy. He was turned around, with the back of the seat in his armpit. As far as I could tell from the rearview mirror there were only two people in the car. The boxer was at the wheel, with his flat head and his big ears. He swerved out into the other lane, but just then a truck appeared around a bend up ahead and he had to swerve back.

"Step on it," Michael said. "Step on it, they'll overtake us and block us."

"For Christ's sake," I said as the truck roared past. "Maybe we just forgot something at the house. Are those keys we gave him the right keys?"

"For Christ's sake!" Michael echoed, much louder. "Move it!"

I took my foot off the gas, put the right blinker on again, and coasted onto the shoulder.

"Oh, no," Michael said. "You're hopeless. You're just hopeless. Keep the engine running, keep it in gear. Keep it in gear," he insisted; "use the clutch."

I compromised by letting the engine idle in neutral, my foot on the clutch and my hand on the stick. The Peugeot came to a sharp stop thirty yards ahead of us, its tires squealing, and then backed up until its rear bumper almost touched our front.

"Oh, no," Michael said again. "Now you know it's trouble. Put it in reverse. Put the fucking thing in reverse and keep it like that."

This time I did as he said. Michael opened his door and got out, keeping one foot inside the car and placing the door as a barrier between himself and the two men approaching from the Peugeot. The boxer looked twice as large as he had inside his café, and Laugier was swinging his game leg in a particularly energetic way.

"There is a lot of damage to the house, upstairs," Laugier said when he reached the door. He put his hand on top of it.

"Yes, unfortunately I broke a mirror," Michael said.

"Not counting the window downstairs and the state of the car," Laugier said.

I could only hear this conversation; I couldn't see any of the faces, which were hidden by the ceiling of the car. There was a small gap between the edge of Michael's door and the steel barrier at the shoulder of the road. The boxer turned sideways to squeeze through and came to stand directly behind Michael, towering over him. I felt him lean his elbow on the roof — the car sagged to the right — and he put his fist on his hip and crossed his ankles. I sensed that my left leg, which was keeping the clutch to the floor, was going to start trembling in a minute.

"And it is not a question of a mirror or a window," the caretaker continued. "The upstairs room was ransacked." He used the word *saccagé*. "I am responsible for that house in Monsieur Albers' absence."

"Not while I'm there. Not while his son is in residence," Michael said calmly. "Do you mean you pursued us all the way from Augères —"

"Monsieur Albers never mentioned anything about his son," Laugier said, in his rapid Provençal accent. "We are going to the police in Apt, young man, to make a deposition. Given that you are his son, I'm not going to press charges. But I want it in black on white that these damages were caused while you were in the house."

"What police?" Michael said. "Leave the police alone. I left a note for my father explaining everything."

"I saw an envelope in the kitchen, but for all I know it could contain a lot of wind," the caretaker said. Then he banged his hand on the roof of the car for emphasis. "It has to be black on white, young man."

"It'll take half an hour, Michael," I said from inside the car. "Let's just get it over with."

Michael bent over; his face dropped into the opening of the door and stared at me. He was white. I had never seen him scared. It had seemed almost an impossibility. It gave me an extremely brief moment of satisfaction, after which it proved contagious.

"It'll take a whole day; we'll have to go back to the house with the cops," Michael said, "while they assess the damage, while they check my papers, while they sniff around for dope. Then it'll take five years at hard labor, for desertion, just for starters."

"Okay," I said. "Shit."

"Shit is right," Michael said. He stared at me a moment longer. "Do me a favor and shut up," he said. He straightened up, leaving me alone in the car again.

"*Écoutez,* Monsieur Laugier," he said. "Let's be reasonable. As I say, I left a note for my father explaining the unfortunate circumstances. Of course it was stupid of me not to discuss this with you before leaving. But my friend and I are very much in a hurry. I happen to be a diabetic," he said, "and I've run out of medicine and I must get to my doctor in Paris before this evening" — this was a good touch, I thought, since we were headed for Switzerland — "or I am in danger of death. Let me leave with you on account a sum of money that will cover the damages, and then you can arrange yourself with my father."

There was a moment of silence while the caretaker considered this proposition. My foot had indeed begun to shake on the clutch, and it was going to slip at any moment, making the car jump backward and stall, probably knocking down Michael and the boxer in the process. I shifted into neutral, put both my feet on the floor and my hands in my lap, and waited.

"We are speaking of a strong sum," the caretaker said.

"I think a thousand francs would cover the damage," Michael said.

"*Non, monsieur,*" Laugier said. "I would say twice that amount, if not more. If I recall, the carpet will have to be replaced and the walls repainted . . . I happen to be in the trade, you see."

"In that case, you know more about it than I do," Michael said. "Let's say that I give you two thousand francs, and if anything is left over you arrange yourself with my father."

He folded the passenger seat forward, reached into the back seat of the car, and dug into the tailcoat. Upstairs, the boxer had taken to drumming his fingers on the roof. Hunched over inside the car, Michael pulled his wad of bills from the lining of the tailcoat, peeled off a number of them, and hurriedly folded the coat over the rest.

"*Voilà,*" he said, straightening up and handing the money through the open car window. The boxer had taken a step forward and was presumably peering over Michael's shoulder to better admire the transaction. Laugier's hand took the bills and counted them with a broad thumb. Then he put them in his pocket. I still couldn't see his face; it might be wearing a satisfied smile, or he might be honoring the farce with a solemn expression, or his eyes might have been narrowed in contempt.

"*Eh bien,*" he said, "I'm glad we've been able to settle this matter without involving the authorities. Once one starts with the authorities, one never knows where it will end, isn't that the case," he added. "Messieurs, I wish you a good trip."

Michael sank into his seat and slammed the door. I backed the car away from the Peugeot as the two men got in, both from the passenger side, because cars were whipping by continuously on our left. I found a gap and got out into the first lane, overtaking the Peugeot just as the boxer put his blinker on and started waiting for his chance.

"That just cost me five hundred bucks," Michael said. "Five hundred bucks! We could have lost them in Avignon if you hadn't stopped."

"Yeah. Well," I said.

He was lighting a cigarette.

"Give me one of those," I said.

"Make a right. Can't you read the fucking signs?" he said.

I made the right.

"Well, at least we have the satisfaction of knowing that they're now arguing over how to split it up, how they're going to make the repairs, and what they'll tell my father. I hope they shoot each other over it," Michael said. "Stop at that Agip station up ahead; I've got to pee," he said.

When he returned he had had his first hits of the day: the heroin to calm him down and blanket the world, the coke to keep him alert. He was now in a settled, quiet mood. But as I drove on, bypassing Avignon and getting onto the main highway going north, I began to get the creeps. I was trying to make myself tell Michael something that had occurred to me while he was off taking his drugs in the stall of the gas station bathroom, and it was such bad news that I kept stopping before I got started. The fact was that when Michael had so casually walked across the border from Switzerland into France, three months before, both countries had been at peace; now Switzerland was, for our specific purposes, at war. The army was on alert everywhere, executing complicated maneuvers and fighting mock battles all over the country, with the red team and the blue team staring at each other through binoculars and infrared scopes day and night in every forest and every valley. The army, of course, was on the lookout for other armies, not for lone heroin addicts in green velvet tailcoats; but in Switzerland everyone minds everyone else's business, everyone is a policeman. I wondered whether he could possibly make it across without being intercepted. Whether that section of the border was held and guarded by either team was impossible to know. If he was caught and handed over to the French border guards, he would again be facing prison. That it was not I but Michael who was in danger seemed to make no difference. I was slowly being overcome by dread, and my inability to speak about it was making it worse. My hands were locked on the wheel in a death grip.

"*Why* are you driving so slowly," Michael asked, for the third time that morning.

These innocent words, spoken without impatience, loosed in me an appalling terror. It came swimming up through my body like nausea. I was suffocating. I was dizzy. There was a strange roaring in my ears. I wanted to pull over and stop, but I was in the center lane, with cars all around me, in front, behind, and on either side; all of us had been traveling at approximately the same speed, but now I couldn't move my foot on the pedal at all, either to accelerate or slow down. I couldn't turn the wheel. I couldn't look into the rear-view mirror because my eyes were locked on the road that was being swallowed by the maw of the car. The edges of my vision began to blur and darken, and the roaring in my ears grew louder. I was going deaf and blind while driving at sixty miles an hour on a crowded high-way.

"Jesus Christ!" I heard Michael say from very far away. "What's going on!"

That was exactly my question, but I didn't answer it, being entirely involved in trying not to kill us.

"Are you all right?"

"No," I said, "I'm frightened."

"Of what?"

"I don't know," I said.

"Pull over," Michael said.

"I can't. I can hardly see," I said.

"Of course you can see," Michael said.

"I think . . ." I said, but I couldn't remember what I thought.

I could sense that Michael was moving in his seat. His left hand rose out of his lap and began to approach the wheel.

"Get away!" I said.

The part of me that could still think was reflecting on the following problem: how I could get Michael to signal to the other cars that I couldn't be counted on to drive normally, that what looked like a Renault containing two people driving north in the center lane was in fact a shell that had no control over its trajectory or speed.

"When I tell you to, you're going to turn the wheel gently to the right. Gently," Michael said.

"Okay, okay," I said.

"Just a bit, now," Michael said.

"I can't," I said.

"Okay," Michael said. "I'm going to reach over and take the wheel."

"No."

"Don't worry about it," Michael said. "I'm just going to take over; you won't have to do a thing."

"Okay," I said.

He looked over his shoulder again and then put his hand on the wheel. It seemed to calm me down a bit to have his hand there, and I was able to follow his instructions. We did it in stages, first switching over to the right lane, then slowing down, then getting onto the shoulder, and gradually coming to a stop. I turned the engine off. I could breathe again, I could see, but I wasn't any better. My clothes were drenched.

"What's wrong," Michael said.

"I'm having a panic attack," I said. "I've read about them. I've never had one before."

Michael smiled at me.

"It's all right," he said. "We're going to switch seats."

"No," I said. "You can't drive."

"Do you want me to give you a little dope?" Michael said. "You'll feel a bit nauseated and wobbly at first, but then you'll be just fine."

"No!" I said.

"You won't get addicted from taking it once," Michael said. "That's not how it works."

"No!" I said.

It was making me feel worse, this calm and reasonable voice of his. Now I wasn't frightened by nothing; I was frightened by everything, including Michael. I needed to get away from him for a moment, to get out of the car and be alone, but that too was a terrifying thought.

"Do you want a tranquilizer? I have a few. It's not half as fast, but it might help."

"Yes," I said.

Michael pushed his door open until it touched the steel barrier and squeezed himself out and walked to the rear of the car. He opened the hatchback. I felt a little better for not having him in the car with me. I heard him unzip his suitcase and then open a smaller zipper. I was trying to control my fear by telling myself that there was real trouble in the world, that I could have been in a legitimately frightening situation. Nothing helped.

Through the opening of the door Michael handed me a Valium and a silver flask. The flask contained whiskey. I took a good pull from it.

"Thank you," I said. "Can you just stay out of the car for a minute, just for a minute? I need to be alone."

"Sure," Michael said.

I put the flask down in my lap and gripped the wheel with both hands and waited. Leaving the door open, Michael went to sit on the steel barrier at the edge of the road. I watched his curved miniature form in the rearview mirror. He lit a cigarette and removed a speck of tobacco from his tongue. He pulled a long drag from the cigarette and crossed his arms on his chest as he exhaled, the cigarette sticking out of his elbow. He looked around him. He looked up at the white cap of Mont Ventoux, squinting. He seemed perfectly at ease in the world. When he finished the cigarette, he dropped it ɔn the asphalt and ground it out with his foot.

"Better?" he asked, leaning in.

"Get in, it's all right," I said. "I'm really sorry. I don't know what happened. I couldn't sleep all last night, I've been

traveling for three days, and I hate driving. I think my nerves
are shot.''

"It's all right, it happens," Michael said. "You're just a
stay-at-home. Are you sure you can drive?''

"I'm fine," I said.

About half an hour later I dozed off and came to just as
Michael shouted something and grabbed the wheel. The side
of the car scraped the divider — it was the nastiest sound I
had ever heard — and drifted back into the lane. All four of
our hands were on the wheel.

"Are you awake? Are you awake?" Michael said.

"I've got it. You can let go; I've got it," I said.

"Pull over," Michael said.

"Right."

For the third time that morning I stopped on the shoulder.
It was hard work getting the car there. Eighty miles back,
when we had stopped to buy sandwiches, I had been so intent
on getting Michael to eat that I had neglected to do so myself,
tearing a single bite out of my sandwich and then wrapping
the rest for later. The Valium and the whiskey, multiplying
the aftereffects of the sleepless night and the panic attack, had
done the rest.

"That does it. I'm driving," Michael said.

"You don't have a license, we're not insured unless I drive,
and you have car crashes all the time," I said. I could hear
myself slurring the words. "I need to take a little nap here,
and then I'll be fine.''

"I'd rather take the goddamned train," Michael said. "I
don't want to die.''

Several sarcastic comments occurred to me, but I left them
unsaid.

"Look, you're in far worse shape than I am," Michael said.
"I'm driving. We've already lost a lot of time. I'll drive, you
take a nap, and then we'll switch again.''

"All right," I said.

"Watch it when you get out. Watch it."

Cars were shooting by on my side. I waited for an opening.

"Now," Michael said. "Hurry!"

Our paths crossed at the nose of the car. My legs felt like boiled noodles. I got in and strapped myself into the passenger seat, already falling asleep. I remember Michael bending over as he searched for the lever that released the driver's seat so that he could push it back to accommodate his long legs.

I woke several times in the next few hours. "Are you all right?" Michael would ask. I would shift in the uncomfortable seat and drop off again. Once I awoke to find us not on the highway but on a small country road, parked next to a high wall of reeds, with the snow-dusted Alps in the windshield. Using a small brass tube, Michael was snorting his drugs off the slick plastic cover of a pocket notebook. It was hot in the car, and I unclamped my seat belt and wriggled out of my jacket and tossed it into the back seat. When I rolled the window down I heard birds in the trees on my side, and the rustling of the wind in the reeds, and the rush of the highway on the embankment behind us.

"Where are we?" I asked.

"About twenty miles from Lyon. We'll get to Divonne with just enough light to spare if we step on it, but I'm afraid of breaking the speed limit. It would be just too dumb."

He wiped the surface of the notebook with his index finger and rubbed the remaining powder on his gums. He sniffed violently, laying his head back against the headrest, and closed his eyes. He arched his body out of the seat while his right hand blindly put the notebook and the brass tube in the pocket of his trousers.

"Can I have a cigarette?" I asked.

"They're on the dashboard. Don't fall asleep again and burn us up."

I smoked in silence for a while, keeping my arm out the window. Then Michael opened his eyes and smiled at me.

"Everything okay?" he said.

"Yes."

"Let's go, then. This'll soon be all over for you."

We drove along the reeds, and then turned away from them and drove through a modern village of gas stations and low cement houses and cruised onto the on-ramp of the highway, picking up speed. Michael glanced over his shoulder a couple of times, looking for oncoming cars as he shifted gears.

"You're going to have to do something more for me," he said.

"What?"

"After you drop me off at Divonne, you'll have to drive my suitcase to Geneva and meet me there to give it to me. I can't carry it over."

"Where should we meet?" he said.

"I don't know. In the parking lot of the Richmond?"

"I may be a while. I have to get all the way back to Geneva by taxi. Do you know the café on the main square of the old city?"

"The Carnivore?"

"No, that's the restaurant. Just across from it, on the corner."

"Yes," I said. It had been a common meeting place for the pupils of our school when we traveled down to Geneva on weekends. It was there that, a few weeks ago, I had placed my imaginary meeting with Dr. Halik, my former algebra teacher.

I asked him for that large-scale map of his and unfolded it on my knees.

"So how do you get to Geneva?" I asked.

"When I come out on the Swiss side, I walk down to a little village. I can't remember the name," he said.

"La Rippe?"

"Right. There's a café there. I'll call a taxi up from Nyon and have it drive me to Geneva."

"That's too complicated," I said, examining the route. "Why don't I just meet you at the café in La Rippe?"

"That would be great," Michael said.

"It won't take you much longer on foot than it'll take me by car."

"Great," Michael said.

"There's just one thing. I'm not taking any drugs across the border, in case they open the suitcases."

"No, I've got everything on me."

"I wouldn't advise you to wear that tailcoat."

"I guess not."

"Are you sure you can manage the climb?"

"Don't worry about me. I'll be fine," he said.

"There's another thing," I said. "You know those war games the army has every couple of years? When the colonel would leave the school and everything would go to hell?"

"Yes."

"They're in full swing now. There are troops crawling all over the place. They're probably sitting on all the borders, too."

Michael didn't say anything. We were just bypassing Lyon on the autoroute and he was concentrating on following the signs for Geneva. We had to follow that route for a while and then strike north off the highway before we came to the frontier and head for the town of Bellegarde. Michael unfolded my larger Michelin map on his own knees.

"I've got to be incredibly careful from Bellegarde on," he said, "because the border snakes around that area in a kind of unpredictable way. One wrong turn and we'll hit a customs barrier before we know it. You're going to have to navigate. Look out for little blue flags on the road on the map; that's what we have to avoid . . . Wait, we have to figure this out," he said.

We pulled into the next gas station and parked off to the side. After my long sleep I was recovered and alert. Although Michael's driving had been perfectly adequate, and although his manner was mild and normal, I could tell that he was all drugged up because he kept getting confused as we traced the route on the map. It was maddening: for a moment or two he would have it right, and then his finger would wander off along precisely the wrong road. When I'd point out his mistake he'd catch himself and say, "Right — of course — sorry," and repeat it once again. Finally we got it straight. The crucial thing was to take not the main road from Gex to Divonne but a smaller country lane to the north of it, and then turn off and start climbing the mountain.

"Do you remember what I told you about the army maneuvers?" I asked when we got under way again.

"They won't bother me, an innocent mushroom picker," Michael said. "In fact I should take a satchel and pick some as I go along. I'm a mushroom expert, you know. I bet you I'll meet you in that café with a bag full of chanterelles and cèpes. What's the name of that village?"

"La Rippe."

"Right," he said. "When we were kids we used to go up to Fincham on weekends especially for mushroom-hunting expeditions. All Russians are mushroom fanatics. Regular mycological maniacs."

"You won't look like an innocent mushroom person with a map and a compass," I said.

"I don't need those; it's a simple walk and I've done it once before. As long as I keep the uphill slope on my right, I'm headed east, and then I'll run into the trail on the Swiss side and just follow it down."

"You have to keep the uphill slope on your left, not your right," I said.

"Right," he said. "I mean, right, on the left. No, what am I saying?"

"You're all confused," I said.

"Just direct me, just direct me, we'll do just fine," he said. "What was the name of the town on the Swiss side, where we meet in the café? Wait, wait, we're coming up on Bellegarde now. Where do I go?"

I led him through a sad little city, most of it modern, and over the bridge crossing the Rhône, whose valley we had followed since Avignon. We came to a hill atop which stood a grim, looming nineteenth-century fort; we passed underneath it through a tunnel and turned straight north. We had now left the Alps. On our left rose the first rampart of the tired old mountains of the Jura, through which Michael would make his crossing. On our right, crammed with villages that already bore Swiss-sounding names, like Pougny, which made me nervous, was the narrow plain, which, after squeezing between the Jura and Lake Geneva, eventually widens into the rich flatlands of northern Switzerland. It was already past three o'clock. For a mile or two the road ran exactly parallel to the border, with a stretch of no man's land on our right. We stopped in the village of Saint Denis to buy another sandwich — Michael wouldn't eat, but I forced him to drink some milk. He complained about the taste like a child, claiming it had been squeezed straight from an udder into the carton. Then we struck north again, deeper into safe France, along four miles of straight uphill road, bordered with chestnut trees and plane trees, to Gex. Many of the cars we passed had Swiss plates.

We drove around Gex several times. I was getting nervous again. Despite the signs, despite my instructions, Michael kept exiting the town on the main road to Divonne, which was just what we wanted to avoid; so we would return to the main square, and, orienting ourselves by the high white mass of the Mont Blanc, try again. Finally Michael agreed to switch and let me drive. I got us out on the right road, and five minutes later we came to the hamlet of Vesancy, immediately after which I swung to the left and began the climb. It was a steep narrow forest road, with room for only one car. Yesterday's rain had knocked the last chestnuts from the trees, and their green husks littered the road like small mines, bursting under our tires. Michael closed his eyes, his hand on the lever of the open window, taking the air. Gradually the chestnuts gave way to birches; here the woods looked a lot like those around Fincham; you could guess at gnarled oaks and beeches deeper inside. As we continued the steep climb, there was nothing left but dark pines and spruce. The road was no longer paved and I had to go very slowly, dreading an encounter with a tractor or another car. Once in a while the path was cut by a logging trail that shot straight down through the trees. Smaller trails branched off the main one. We stuck to the right at every intersection and finally reached the first big switchback, the point, according to our map, nearest the Swiss border. It coincided with the end of the path. There was no place to pull over. I stopped the car in the tracks, pulled up the handbrake, and turned off the engine. For a moment we sat in silence.

"Okay," Michael said. "Time for a little hit, and then I'm off."

Out came the waxed-paper envelope, the brass tube, and the glossy notebook.

"You're not going to dope yourself and go staggering through the woods like that, are you?" I said.

"No, this is a bit of coke I saved from yesterday's holocaust," he said.

"I wondered how much of it you'd kept," I said.

"Just enough to keep me human until I get to New York. I can't do without the dope anymore, and this stuff keeps the nods away."

"If you were stopped — you won't be, but just imagine

that it happened — you wouldn't want to have anything on you, anything at all. I'd keep it all handy and be ready to dump it if you think you see trouble."

"Good idea," he said, folding over in his seat and applying the tube to the notebook. After vacuuming the lines up his nose, he put all the gear back in his pocket. Then, sniffing, he got out and walked to the back of the car, opened the hatchback, and unzipped his bag, from which he extracted a faded blue windbreaker. He reached over the top of the back seat and grabbed the tailcoat and went through its inner pockets. I had gotten out of the car too, and I was leaning against it with my arms crossed on the roof, stretching my legs. I needed another nap. Not far away there was a rustle in the woods, followed by the flapping rise of a chough.

"Shhh," I said. "Listen."

"It's just a deer, or a skunk, or a badger, or a little squirrel," Michael said. "The question is, do I need a passport for an illegal crossing?"

"No. If you were stopped, and claimed you were out picking mushrooms, you wouldn't want a passport on you."

"Yeah, but who's going to stop me?" he said.

"There's probably a whole division hidden in these woods," I said. "Headed by the colonel himself."

"Thanks," he said, handing me his passport over the roof. "If I never come out the other side, you can have Irina paint it," he said.

"You don't want any French money on you either," I said.

"I guess not," he said after reflection. He passed his wad of bills over the roof.

"But if by any chance we fail to hook up on the other side, you're screwed," I said. "Here, take some Swiss money, just in case." I still had some small bills I hadn't converted into French francs.

"We meet at the café in La Rippe in an hour at the latest," he said.

"If anything goes wrong, we meet at ten P.M. at the café in the old square in Geneva," I said.

"Stop worrying," Michael said. "It's a straight line, a little climb, a little descent, and then I'll run into the trail on the Swiss side."

He thrust his hands in the pockets of his windbreaker. The collar was askew, half of it folded inside out, and I had to resist the urge to straighten it out for him. He smiled at me, sniffed one last time, and stepped off into the trees. A fallen branch cracked under his foot, I heard a rustle or two, and then a disturbed chough, perhaps the same one as a moment before, came swimming out over my head and then went back in on the other side of the road.

I felt like staying there, leaning on the roof of the car, my head in my arms, in the damp stillness of the forest. But I had to make a plan. First, shed Michael as soon as we reached Geneva. Drive him to the airport, shake his hand, wish him good luck, and leave; return to Geneva, find a hotel room, have a bath, call Hélène, and if possible take her out to dinner. No doubt we would talk only about Eric Steyer, but that was all right too. Tomorrow, drive the car back down to Provence, taking my time, and install myself at Caziers and begin my work. I would have to find a way to justify charging all this mileage and the hotel room to *Glee*. I couldn't afford it myself. I had also put a gouge in the side of the car when I fell asleep on the highway, and I wondered how much that would cost the magazine. Unlike most of my colleagues, I had always been reluctant, even Swiss, about spending *Glee*'s money on myself. But after all, these expenses had been not for my own pleasure, far from it, but for the salvation of the grandson of the founder of the magazine — though that was not the explanation I would give Nancy Eberstadt.

I walked around to the passenger side of the car and opened the door. From the glove compartment I took the window-cleaning shammy and moistened it in the grass and used it to wipe down the passenger seat and the top of the dashboard. I removed the rubber mat from the footwell, shook it, and slammed it against the side of the car several times. Having a guilty conscience, I knew that I was going to be checked thoroughly at customs. My name wasn't on any computer, but my status as an accessory to Michael's illegal activities, I was sure, was plainly written on my features. I was glad that Michael wasn't around to see me taking all these fussy precautions. I went to search his suitcase in the rear to make sure he hadn't stashed any drugs in it.

In order to give myself some room I lifted my own bag and dropped it over the backrest into the rear seat. Then I unzipped the leather suitcase with Kuratkin's initials on it and raised the cover and began to remove Michael's clothes. They smelled of stale tobacco smoke. I ran my hand through the pouches on the sides and came up with two ballpoint pens, an eraser, spent airline tickets — New York–Paris and Paris–Geneva — and the stub of a New York or Boston movie-theater ticket that had somehow come to rest there. One by one I removed the shirts, sweaters, trousers, socks, and underwear, all folded and packed with Albers neatness, piling them up in roughly the same order on the polyester carpeting next to the suitcase and running my hand through their folds while trying not to muss them. I went through the toilet kit carefully; the only drugs were French effervescent aspirin and a bottle of Dr. Scheinbaum's Valium, prescribed to Irina, with only two pills left in it; he had probably pinched it from her months ago.

At the very bottom of the suitcase were several manila folders lined up side by side. Each was labeled "Kuratkin's Memoirs" in block letters. I picked up and opened the thickest one, and found only some blank rag paper of that European format, slightly too long and too narrow, that looks somehow all wrong to American eyes.

The second folder contained half a dozen sheets of it, covered with Michael's handwriting, in ink, with a few hesitations and corrections.

"Chapter One," I read. "My earliest memory is of being carried to a window to see the Northern Lights. I remember the sensation of being lifted by my armpits. The hands lifting me were those of my English nurse, Miss Pelham. She smelled of starch and of Pear's glycerin soap. My breath condensed on the glass. I thought the 'lights' Miss Pelham was talking about were those in the windows across the street, all but one of which were heavily curtained against the Petersburg winter. The lighted room was all white and contained no furniture. I stared into the empty room across the way while above me Miss Pelham uttered cries of admiration and delight. Gradually our combined breaths fogged up the window. Miss Pelham took my hand by the index finger and traced the letter N in the condensation. 'N is for Nicholas,' she said, 'and for naughty.' "

Michael had really meant to go all the way in imagining his grandfather's memoirs, down to details such as these. I put the folder aside and looked at the third one. It contained a yellowed typescript, its edges brittle, the ink fading. It had been banged out on an old typewriter whose commas and periods pierced the paper. "*Premier souvenir: ma nounou anglaise, Miss Pelham, me soulève a la fenêtre pour admirer l'aurore boréale,* 'the Northern Lights,' *me dit-elle . . .*"

It was the missing manuscript of Kuratkin's memoirs, which Mrs. Albers and Irina had searched for both in New York and Fincham. Michael had found it first and removed it for his own purposes.

Leaving the jaws of the hatchback still yawning around Michael's open suitcase and the belongings piled next to it, I placed the folder on the roof of the car and skimmed through to the end of the manuscript, turning the fragile pages carefully and pinning them down one by one with my elbow. It had seemed to me a very quiet and still afternoon, but now that I was handling sheets of paper I noticed the interference of a breeze. For an account of Kuratkin's life, it wasn't much. It never got beyond his childhood. I kept turning the pages, waiting for the inevitable appearance of the din of demonstrations in the streets beneath the window, for the clamor for bread, the steel rasp of Cossack swords unsheathed, for the scenes from *Doctor Zhivago,* but Kuratkin remained serenely in the kingdom of the nursery, near Miss Pelham's modest bosom. Later, a French tutor entered the picture; there were about ten pages of pastoral idyll at the country estate; there were trips to the south of France, with the change of railway gauge at the Russian frontier, to escape the perpetual darkness of the Baltic winter. There was Kuratkin's father's leather library (which I pictured, of course, as identical with Kuratkin's study at Central Park West), his mother's neat feminine studio, the somewhat frightening transformation — the fierce concentration that seized her dear features — every time she picked up her brushes. There were the famous visitors and the famous sitters, the former including Stanislavsky, the latter Princess Yussupov, "*la plus grande beauté de Saint Pétersbourg*" . . . I had known about that. But mostly Kuratkin dwelled on the particular details of life that every child knows and then forgets: as a boy he had judged people's character by the way they held their pens; he had also been a primitive physiognomist, classifying all men as dog faces or monkey faces and all women as bird faces or cat faces . . .

That little breeze was picking up, the trees were rustling above me, and the shaggy paw of a fir tree began to nod over the road. A sheet of Kuratkin's memoirs tried to sail away from me as I read about the family joke of calling the Croisette in Cannes the Noisette. I bundled up the typescript, banged its lower edge on the roof of the car to align its pages, slipped it back into the folder, and repacked Michael's suitcase. He would probably reach the café in La Rippe before me now, especially as I anticipated, once again, with a small knot in my stomach, a delay at the customs booth, with the képi'd Swiss officials looking me over carefully.

I had to go down a hundred yards in reverse before I found a gap in the trees that gave me room enough to turn around. In the middle of the maneuver, while struggling with the stiff steering, I remembered with alarm that I still had the reserve envelope of Michael's cocaine in my shirt pocket. Before setting off again, the engine idling and my foot on the brake, I extracted it, opened it, and — what the hell, I was already smoking cigarettes again, and I needed courage — helped myself to a healthy snort, tearing a corner off one of the maps and using it as a spoon. I scattered the remaining cocaine to the breeze, and crumpled the waxed paper into a little ball and tossed it into the woods. Then I wiped my nose, checked its appearance in the rearview mirror, and proceeded down to the main road, where I turned left and headed, at a slow pace, toward the border.

I had decided to cross not at Divonne but at a place called Borex, a couple of miles farther along, closer to where I was to meet Michael. I therefore made my way through the center of Divonne, passing first a golf course, then a cakelike palace in a well-tended park, which I thought was the casino, and then, in a fountained square, took the Nyon road. Five minutes later I reached the border. The French customs booth was untended, its gate up; I drove through, coincidentally, behind another car with French rental plates. A hundred yards farther on, the Swiss customs man merely checked the driver's passport and then waved him through, but, just as I had expected, he showed more interest in me. I was, however, in

an extremely good mood, thanks to the self-medication of
ten minutes before; I even had to restrain myself from com-
plimenting the man on the beauty and cleanliness of his country, which also happened, by heritage, to be mine, despite
my American passport, and so on. It was with a dignified but
friendly readiness that I answered his questions: how long I
would be staying, the purpose of my visit, whether I had
anything to declare. He then took my passport into his office;
I had to make an effort not to turn around to peer nervously
through the window.

During this time several cars came to a stop behind mine,
and another customs official emerged from the office to take
care of them; my own man, when he returned, told me to
drive my car out of the way and into the small parking lot
next to the building. He directed me into a slot, walking
backward and signaling, as though we were on the deck of
an aircraft carrier.

"Please get out of the car," he said.

He had me open the hatchback. He pointed to Michael's
suitcase.

"Please open it," he said.

While I struggled with the zipper, which had suddenly become recalcitrant, he picked up the green tailcoat, shook it
open, and admired it before placing it back next to the suitcase. He reached into the open suitcase and parted the piles
of clothes, without any great thoroughness, and then told me
I could shut it. Leafing through my passport once again, he
told me that I had already visited Switzerland once this year.
Had my purpose also been tourism? No, I said, I had been
writing an article for an American magazine. Which magazine? *Glee,* I said, *"un journal de mode."* *"Gli,"* he repeated,
with amazement. Where would I be staying? In Geneva, I
said. At a hotel? Yes, I said, the Richmond.

I knew there had not yet been time enough for Michael to

be captured, tortured, and forced to confess that he had an accomplice who would soon be arriving in a blue rented Renault. Other cars, however, continued to stream through unmolested. It was time to ask this man why he was keeping me.

"What is your date of birth?" he said, before I could start.

I told him.

"What is your name?"

"Patrick Scheffler," I said patiently.

"Why do you have a passport in the name of Mika-el Albers?" he asked.

With a convulsive motion I dived into the inner pocket of my jacket and extracted my own, which I thrust at him.

"Ah, yes," he said, after opening it. "The resemblance is greater."

"I'm terribly sorry," I said. "That's the passport of a friend I was staying with in France. I must have picked it up by mistake."

"And where is your friend?" he asked.

"He's probably in Paris," I said. "He was flying back to America. He must think he's lost his passport. *Aïe, aïe, aïe,*" I said, meaning every word of it.

The customs man closed my passport. He looked at its cover and compared it with Michael's. He pointed at my bag.

"Could you open that one, please," he said.

He looked through it very carefully, taking out each article of clothing separately, ignoring only — or else he was leaving it for last — the plastic bag that contained my dirty laundry. He found an open envelope and peered at its contents — all the receipts from the Gasthaus Oehrli and my credit card. I was dying for a cigarette, but I feared that lighting up would show a lack of respect. In Michael's suitcase there were airline tickets in his name, and now that the customs man was being so thorough I was sure he would ask me to open it again. I tried to think up a likely story that would explain why I had Michael's suitcase as well as his passport, but nothing plausible came to mind. My heart, which had been banging pleasantly from the drug a minute before, was now getting out of control.

"What do you think I should do?" I said. "He's probably stuck at the Paris airport without his passport."

"I would contact the American consulate in Geneva," he said. He reached for the zipper of Michael's suitcase. "I would tell them to get in touch with the consulate in Paris, because that is where your friend will go." He carefully zipped Michael's suitcase shut. He handed me both passports. "I wish you both good luck," he said.

"Thank you," I said.

He tipped his képi, and, once I was back in the car, he guided me to the barrier with more hand signals, a look of great concentration on his face.

I fired up a cigarette as I headed for La Rippe. I wasn't even going to tell Michael what had happened. Had I made the same mistake at the French border post, where Michael was on the computer, I would have ruined both our lives.

I had lost another ten minutes. Michael had probably been waiting and worrying at the café in La Rippe for some time now.

XX

SINCE THAT DAY, in my wanderings as a travel writer, I have often faced problems of bureaucracy and transportation, some of them far more absurd and more alarming than those I encountered while trying to get Michael Albers out of France. I have endured traveling companions who, though sober and sane, were far more difficult to put up with. I have crossed several borders I was not supposed to. I have accumulated a large hoard of tales and anecdotes, some of which I have written down, of course, for that is how I earn my living; others, for various reasons, do not belong in articles or books, or have not yet found their way there, and I tell them merely for amusement, my own and, I hope, others'. There is none, however, that I relish more than the story of the day I had to transport a drug-crazed fugitive, who happened to be my ex-girlfriend's brother, from France to Switzerland. Of course I have on occasion embellished the tale — adding, for instance, while describing our roadside dealings with Quasimodo the caretaker and the giant café owner, that the people of that part of Provence have a long-standing reputation for violence and crime, something I have learned since but did not know at the time. Whenever I tell it I find myself thinking of Kuratkin, for several reasons: first, because Kuratkin, that day, was on my mind; second, because it is the kind of story that he used to tell — or, rather, I try to make it that way, and sometimes discover that my hands are waving the way his used to, and that my face is wearing the expression of retrospective astonishment that would appear on his as he brought out the more outrageous elements of the tale; and third, because the first time I told the story, at a table in a Tribeca restaurant (to an audience that included Jamie Schwartz, who, knowing both Michael and me, found it very funny), was after leaving the opening of a group show in a SoHo gallery, one whole wall of which had been covered with Irina's trompe l'oeil documents.

Two years had passed since the events I have described in this book; life goes on, as idiots like to say; and although I had not seen Irina nor Michael in all that time, I had been pleased to receive, while staying in New York between trips, an invitation to the opening — though there was no personal inscription added to it and I assume, as I assumed then, that it was sent not on Irina's initiative but the gallery's, for I had visited it several times in my *Glee* and Irina days, and occasionally found outdated invitations to its shows in the rubber-banded stacks of bills and junk mail that greeted me on my return from trips. I made sure that Jamie would be there (so that I would have an excuse for showing up), and arrived at the appointed hour, curious and somewhat jumpy, with much the same stage fright I would have felt on going to a party where I knew I would be among strangers. Irina had her back to me when I came in, and as she turned away from the couple she was talking to and caught sight of me, we both tried to hide our surprise. She had not expected to see me, and I had not expected to see her hugely pregnant; but I saw right through her affectionate greeting to the discomfort underneath, and I don't doubt that I was just as transparent to her.

Guided in her research by Isaac Behr, Irina had reconstructed more than two dozen documents that would have concerned or belonged to her grandfather during his lifetime, beginning with a page of an 1899 ledger in which some sad Gogolian clerk would have recorded, in Cyrillic script, the date and particulars of his birth; continuing with a report card from the Tenishev School in Tsarkoe Selo (its remarks invented by Irina and translated into Russian by Isaac); his White Army papers, which — a vulgar touch, if you ask me — she had stained with fake blood; his Nansen passport, various French *permits de résidence,* the American naturalization document, which Jamie Schwartz, himself the son of immigrants, bought that very evening (insisting on placing the little red dot beside the frame himself and then crossing the room to point it out to Irina and hug her), and so on. As I say, there were about two dozen of them, covering a whole wall; an unintended effect was that it resembled the wall of a crazed doctor's office, with all his diplomas up for sale.

Isaac Behr had, that year, been awarded one of the "genius grants" from the MacArthur Foundation. I had seen it announced in the *Times* a few months earlier. When I congratulated him, on that and on his impending fatherhood, he whinnied and blushed and shifted his weight from hoof to hoof, and said, "Yes, I am trying to be brave about it." The person who was really trying to be brave about things was Mrs. Albers, who, when I also congratulated her, responded immediately, in French, "And after all, one tells oneself, who wants to get married these days? Catholic priests want to get married, that's who" — a quip I had heard, word for word, from Kuratkin's mouth.

Michael wasn't there, but Irina told me he had called recently, from a treatment center for alcoholics and addicts in Canada where he had spent the last four months, with another two to go. It was either the second or third time — I couldn't quite figure it out from Irina's comments — that he had had himself locked up since our trip. While talking to the girl who had come with Jamie, leaning against one of the columns, I almost embarked on the story of my travels with Michael, because it too had involved document problems and questions of nationality and identity. Being in the same room as Michael's mother and Irina, however, I became self-conscious and found something else to talk about. The image that flickered on my inner screen, during that moment of hesitation, was of the closed café at La Rippe, where I had driven to meet Michael, still sweating and jumpy after my documental accident at the border post.

I had expected to find Michael already there, seated at a table of varnished wood with a cup of coffee and a restorative shot glass of kirsch next to it, of which I too would have partaken gladly; but the curtains behind the café windows were drawn, and between the curtain and the glass pane of the door was a handwritten sign saying "Closed for cause of death." Michael was nowhere in sight.

I stood there for a moment or two, peering around me, uncertain as to what to do next. I left the car parked in front of the café and walked once around the center of the village; it formed a rectangle that must once have been a single farm around a central courtyard. I passed two old ladies in overcoats and knitted caps who were returning from a shopping trip to a Migros supermarket somewhere, both of them hobbling on bowed legs and breathing heavily, with fat plastic shopping bags dangling from each hand. A mechanic in blue overalls hurried by with a wrench, cursing to himself, and a moment later I walked by his untended workshop, a smell of rubber and motor oil emanating from its open door, through which I saw incomprehensible machines of wheels and belts. A farm boy puttered by on a moped, with a pal on a bicycle hanging on to his shoulder. Ahead of me a throbbing tractor was approaching, pulling a long flat cart loaded with a mixture of manure and hay, with a prune-faced old farmer vibrating atop the metal saddle. There was no Michael, but I was reassured to see that there were also no signs of military activity. I didn't think I could have missed him on my way up from the border post. His own crossing must also have taken longer than we had expected.

I got back in the car and slowly drove another mile up the road, the first hundred yards bordered on the left by depressing new villas that probably belonged to people who worked in Geneva or Nyon, on the right by newly ploughed fields that filled the cold air with a smell of earth. The edge of the forest coincided with the abrupt rise of the mountain. Michael could come from no other direction. I climbed on slowly in the damp shadows until the road began the first of its loops, which led away from France. There I stopped and wedged the car in as far to one side as I could, leaving just room enough for another vehicle to pass. I left it unlocked but took the keys from the ignition and trudged on upward, listening for Michael but hearing only the breath of the wind high in the trees and, somewhere, a trickle of water accompanied by the repetitious monologues of toads. I had looked at the map so closely and so often in the last few hours that I carried in my head a clear image of the point at which Michael was going to emerge onto the road, just after the next switchback, where it met what I assumed was a coal burner's trail.

I found the trail where I expected it, but discovered that it died out in the underbrush after just a few yards. Moreover, as I explored further, it became clear that the map, detailed as it had seemed, was misleading. What had looked on paper like a smooth forested slope was in fact a gnarled brown network of small ravines, ten feet deep or more, hidden in the trees. Some of them were rocky and carried streams of water down to an unseen river. The underbrush, though mostly November-bare, was thick enough to force detours. I wandered in a little farther, hoping it would become sparser, and knowing that if I missed Michael he would find the car lower down and wait for me there. Every few yards I stopped and listened.

The third ravine I encountered was a good twenty feet deep, and as I scrambled up its farther bank, pulling myself up with the help of the occasional sapling, I began to take note of various landmarks, so as to be sure I would find my way back, and decided to turn around once I checked out the other side. Nevertheless I experienced a queasy moment of disorientation when, four steps later, having suddenly half tripped and half slipped down into an actual rift in the mountain, almost falling into the rocky stream at the bottom, I realized, first, that it wouldn't be easy to make my way back out, and, second, that the slope here ran counter to that of the rest of the mountainside; because the trees above me at the edge of the gorge masked the mountain and the sky, I had to keep in mind that what appeared to be downhill was, in the larger scheme of things, its opposite. I had to turn back immediately, because I could see that Michael could easily have gotten lost in here and there was no sense in imitating him. This couldn't possibly be the route he had taken into France three months earlier; somehow he had gotten confused.

The immediate problem facing me was how to get out of the gorge. The side I had just come down proved, after a few attempts, to be too slippery and too steep. Looking for an easier spot, I followed the stream upward, one foot on the bank and the other on treacherous little rocks in its bed, several of which, inevitably, overturned under my weight and dunked my ankle into icy water. Just when I thought I had found the right place to clamber out — there was a solid-looking bush growing out of the slope, which I could hoist myself up with and then use as a step, and above it a rocky outcropping I could grasp in order to execute a scrambling chin-up — I heard something other than myself working its way through the bushes atop the embankment. It could have been Michael; it could also have been anything else — deer, boar, hunter, or forester — and trapped as I was in my hole, I froze uncomfortably and let it pass, thinking I would investigate it once I got out. Unfortunately, that solid-looking bush I had planned to use proved to be bare not because of the season but because it was dead, and it came apart in my grasp with an awful cracking of branches, one of which scratched my cheek badly, barely missing my right eye. The creature above me on the embankment, as startled as I was, crashed away through the bushes at a vastly accelerated pace.

The front of my leather jacket was now covered with mud and dead leaves. I peeled off the leaves, mentally said good-bye to the jacket, and continued to pick my way along the bed of the stream. The gorge widened as I went, its slope decreasing, and eventually I was able to clamber over the top — only to see that I would immediately have to go down into another one. I wiped the grit off my hands anyway, against the paperlike bark of a birch. My feet were soaked, and my loafers ruined too.

On the other side of the gorge, thirty feet above me, Michael stepped out from behind a tree.

"Was that you?" he said. "You gave me a hell of a scare, you sounded like a herd of elephants tearing down trees."

"Is this where you crossed the last time?" I asked.

"I don't know," he said. He was out of breath. "I've been wandering around in here for days. I can't find the damned exit."

"It's over this way," I said. "Get over here. Go down there, across the stream. Try not to fall in."

He picked his way down carefully and jumped across the stream. I pulled him up the last step on the other side, hanging on to the birch with my other hand for support. His clothes were immaculate, but his hair was matted with sweat and he was breathing hard. His face had strange patches of purple on it, like bruises. He leaned against the birch with one hand and placed the other on my shoulder. He hung his head, breathing.

"The car's over this way," I said.

"I've just come from that direction; there's a goddamned precipice," Michael said.

"Just follow me," I said. "Ready?"

"Ready," he said.

We were higher on the mountain than where I had started out. We climbed still a little more, and then, just as I had expected, the earth became much smoother. What had been ravines and canyons lower down were just depressions here. It seemed to me that we had been walking for a long time and should have reached the road by now, but I remembered how the road looped back and forth and realized that we were probably walking parallel to it. At last I began to see more light between the trees, and, abruptly, we happened onto the road.

"Thank God," Michael said. "It's going to start getting dark any minute."

"I left the car a little farther down," I said.

"I've got to rest for five minutes," he said.

He unzipped his windbreaker and sat down at the edge of

the road. I sat down next to him. He took a pack of cigarettes from his pocket and we both lit up.

"This used to be my favorite jacket," I said, peering down the front of it. "And I think these shoes are ruined too."

"Christ, I haven't been that lost in years," Michael said. "Since the colonel used to send us on those goddamned forced marches."

"You can't have crossed here, the last time," I said. "Where do you think it was?"

"I crossed in a car," he said. "I hitchhiked."

"You hitchhiked?"

"Yes. I was planning to cross on foot. I bought myself the map and a compass . . . I was going to carry my suitcase on my head. I took the train to Nyon and hitched from there. The first guy who picked me up happened to be a Frenchman who lived across the border and drove through every day to work in Nyon. I figured I could just go with him — the border guards saw him go through twice a day, and I thought they wouldn't bother to stop us, which they didn't."

"That was a stupid risk," I said.

"Not really. Even if they did stop us, which they weren't going to, and even if they checked my name on the computer, which they probably wouldn't have, chances are they'd just turn me back, the way they did at the Paris airport. *Then* I would have walked across."

"Why didn't you want to risk it this time?" I asked.

"Because this time I was coming from France. I'd clearly been on French soil. It wasn't the same situation."

"Yes, but I mean" — this was really what I'd meant to ask — "why did you *tell* me that you'd walked across, that it was the easiest thing in the world to do?"

"Just so you wouldn't worry," Michael said. "You would have gotten completely paranoid."

"Thanks," I said.

I meant to be sarcastic, but Michael didn't get it.

"It's nothing," he said.

This was offensive. It was more offensive because it was true: I had indeed been paranoid about that crossing, going so far as to search his bag beforehand. It was most offensive because those precautions had turned out to be justified. But I couldn't tell him about the incident at the Swiss border post without revealing what an ass I'd been.

"Well, I took it for granted that you were lying to me in some way," I said. "I went through your things to make sure you weren't making me carry your drugs in. I found your grandfather's manuscript. Irina and your mother were wondering what had happened to it. They didn't know you'd stolen it in order to plagiarize it."

"Those are a couple of nasty words," Michael said. "It's also not nice to go snooping through people's underwear."

"I was just protecting myself," I said. "It's a good idea to be careful around people who are known to steal and lie."

Michael ground his cigarette out under his shoe. "Look," he said, "I wouldn't have had you carry anything through like that. You know perfectly well I wouldn't. As for my grandfather's manuscript, you didn't have to look at it. And if you looked at it, you could at least have looked a little more closely before accusing people of being plagiarists. There are about fifty pages, and the story stops when he's about twelve years old. I'm just going to use that as a springboard. All the rest will be mine. You see, when he sat down to write his memoirs, he got bogged down in his childhood, and once he was through with that he lost interest and stopped. It's a pity. He had a fascinating life, he knew everybody, he did everything, and in the end the only thing that mattered to him was the little details of when he was five."

After a second of silence, he said: "I'm going to give it back to my mother when I'm through. I just don't want her meddling in my projects. There's no reason why Irina should know about it, either."

"Let's go," I said. "It's getting dark. The car's just down the road."

We started to walk. Michael had cooled off and he pulled himself into his windbreaker again. We walked in silence for a while. I was going to put Michael out of the car with his bag as soon as we got to Geneva.

"Here's your passport," I said, taking it from my jacket. "And your money."

"Thanks," he said. "If I had been planning to have you smuggle drugs into the country, do you think I would have planted my passport on you and given you all my money?"

"I guess not," I said.

"Listen," he said. "Don't tell Irina about the manuscript. Let me tell her."

"I don't think I'm going to be seeing Irina for a while," I said.

I was feeling increasingly uncomfortable. We had been walking down the road in the gathering gloom for a while now, and we should have found the car. Since Michael already considered me a poltroon, I didn't mention it.

"In the spring of 1944," he said as we walked, "my grandfather walked from France into Switzerland, with a Resistance man whose network had been broken and who was about to be rounded up. I don't know where he crossed, but the route I've just taken is the simplest and most straightforward — probably the one they chose."

I was about to tell him to shut up, but just then I realized there was something familiar about this particular bend. It struck Michael at exactly the same time. We both looked down and saw the tire tracks in the grass.

"Shit," Michael said. "We're back in France."

★

When I tell this story, I don't bother to mention anything about Kuratkin's memoirs. The story I tell is about getting Michael across the border in the woods in the dark, with his stopping every ten minutes to take more drugs, with both of us crashing around in the bushes, tripping over stones, and falling into streams. I present all this, of course, in a comical light. But I leave out the things that are important to me.

Yes, I got frightened in the forest that night. Yes, I disliked Michael Albers, at that moment, as much as I have ever disliked anyone. But the memory I have of those nightmare hours we spent together, covered in mud, exhausted, in woods that seemed to change and shift perversely as we tried to find our way out, without the compass, without the flashlight, without the map — all these things were safely in the car we couldn't find — is one I recall only with pleasure. The mystery is this: it has the quality, the vividness, the importance, of a childhood memory. It is as though some small dying ember of my childhood had flared up that night and burned brightly for a few last hours. I had always known that I would spend my life on perilous missions with my friends, crossing borders under the cover of darkness.

Life makes sense not when reason tells you that everything is as it should be. Life makes sense when some imponderable and apparently random event confirms your most irrational prejudices about the world. When at night, in a dream, I find myself in a jam, held prisoner in some monstrous place, and my father arrives, knowing just what to do and how to speak to the terrible people who are holding me, and then sees me out of my cell, his hand on my head, slightly amused by my terror — although I am aware even in my sleep that none of this is real, not the jail, not the jailers, neither my father nor myself — when I wake, I feel at peace. At the most frightening moment the years fall away and vanish, and I find that nothing has changed, that everything is still as I know it really to be.